CW00469831

LOVE'S LONG ROAD

GD Harper is a past winner of a Wishing Shelf Red Ribbon for adult fiction, and has been shortlisted for the Lightship Prize for first-time authors and longlisted for the UK Novel Writing Award.

Also by GD Harper:
Silent Money
A Friend in Deed

LOVE'S LONG ROAD

GD HARPER

Copyright © 2016 GD Harper
Cover Design © 2016 Spiffing Covers

Reprinted June 2016; October 2017; April 2019; September 2019;
November 2019; March 2020

'It's Alright Ma (I'm Only Bleeding)' Words and Music by Bob Dylan © 1965.
Reproduced by permission of Special Rider Music/ Sony/ATV Music Publishing Ltd,
London W1F 9LD.

'Visions of Johanna' Words and Music by Bob Dylan © 1966.
Reproduced by permission of Special Rider Music/ Sony/ATV Music Publishing Ltd,
London W1F 9LD.

The moral right of the author has been asserted.

Apart from any fair dealing for the purposes of research or private study,
or criticism or review, as permitted under the Copyright, Designs and Patents
Act 1988, this publication may only be reproduced, stored or transmitted, in
any form or by any means, with the prior permission in writing of the
publishers, or in the case of reprographic reproduction in accordance with
the terms of licences issued by the Copyright Licensing Agency. Enquiries
concerning reproduction outside those terms should be sent to the publishers.

Glasgow, June 1975

chapter one

Should you be at someone's funeral, if they died because of you?

That was the question on everyone's lips, on their minds. I knew it. Joe was dead and it was because of me. Nice, kind, butter-wouldn't-melt-in-my-mouth Bobbie Sinclair. I'd always tried to think of other people, to care about their feelings. I was the sort of person my friends liked to introduce to their parents, because I was the sort of person that parents approved of.

But then I killed someone. Someone who loved me.

Two years I'd known Joe; two kids who met at a student disco and fell in love. Two years of being the couple everyone said were made for each other. And the last six months of realising no, he was a nice enough guy, but he wasn't the one for me. And just as the class of '75 was about to step out into the big wide world with our whole lives ahead of us, Joe was dead.

It shouldn't have been like that. I'd planned it so well, or so I thought. I said nothing, gave not an inkling of my decision, until after his final exam. I didn't want to do anything that would affect his grades. Then the pain of telling him. The quizzical look in his eyes as I started. The long, deep breath I took before I told him it was over. I said everything the *Cosmopolitan* article on breakups told me to. I delivered my lines perfectly. Should have, of course, I'd practised them endlessly the day before. I believed I'd left nothing to chance, we'd break up in a mature and adult way. Get on with our lives, no hard feelings.

But that outburst, when he had said life wasn't worth living without me. Should I have taken his words seriously? I'd read somewhere that people who talk about suicide never actually do it. It was obviously a ploy, he knew me too well. Just a ploy to win me back.

I'd sounded so cold-hearted, but I honestly thought being tough was the fairest way. Any hint of indecision would have been seized upon, holding out hope of reconciliation, a change of heart. And that would have been cruel. I didn't want to prolong the pain. My words had been blunt, final and uncompromising. How they must have hurt. 'I need to find myself.' 'I can't simply make myself love you.' 'I need something more.' Horrible.

I had done one last sweep of my flat to make sure I was rid of his stuff. I'd found his Rubik's Cube and was deliberating whether to chuck it or not when the phone rang. Joe's uncle. It was weird him calling me, I'd only met him once and it took me a second to recall what he looked like. And his voice. Very serious. Very formal. He told me he was calling on behalf of Mr and Mrs Dawson, Joe's parents. The sickening dread as I realised something bad was coming. Told me to prepare myself. I knew then Joe was dead.

The hard, cruel truth. Suicide. The note. To me. 'I told you so.'

Should I be at his funeral, I asked myself again. I saw

the furtive glances, everyone looking away quickly as I caught their eye. The only people my age were three of Joe's friends, huddled at the street corner, having one last cigarette before going into church. If ever I needed Duncan to be around, it was then. I was aching to have someone to talk to, but I had to deal with it without my best friend to help me. He was travelling somewhere around Europe; there had been no way to get in touch with him. My other friends were cast to the four winds following the exams. It gave them an excuse, I suppose, but for most of them it was a cop-out. And of course, my dad had found an excuse for him and Mum not to be there. Typical of him.

I went over to the huddle.

'Aye, Bobbie. Terrible, terrible, isn't it? Who'd have thought?' Fergus said.

'I'm still in shock,' I replied. 'It doesn't seem real somehow, I keep expecting him to appear any second. I can't believe I'm never going to see him again.' My voice seemed to be coming from somebody else. I felt another wave of sobbing rise up inside me.

'Aye, aye, terrible, isn't it? Who'd have thought?' Eloquence was not Fergus's strong suit.

'Yeah, it's a drag,' said Kenny. He and Joe used to go to Partick Thistle matches together, a masochistic pursuit I'd managed to avoid. At the very least, I owed Kenny a debt of gratitude for that. So I agreed with him. Joe's death was, indeed, a drag.

We agreed the weather could not have been better, and that East Kilbride was a bummer to get to from Glasgow's West End. I stole a glance at the third member of the group, Ian. He was the only one who looked angry at me for being there, shifting from foot to foot as he tried to disguise his hostility. I wanted to tell him to be patient. The minute the service was over I'd be gone, but I came to pay my respects. If Joe's parents were magnanimous enough to say I could be there, so should he.

Instead we nodded awkwardly to each other.

'So are you still doing that play about Virginia Woolf?'

Kenny's question snapped me out of my thoughts. He knew about my ambitions to be an actress. With my exams out of the way, I was going after whatever parts were up for grabs in Glasgow's burgeoning theatre scene.

The question threw me. I hadn't thought about it to be honest. 'Yes, I think so,' I said. 'And it's not about Virginia Woolf. It's just called *Who's Afraid of Virginia Woolf?* a sort of joke by the writer.'

'Who's Virginia Woolf anyhow?' Ian obviously felt he had to say something.

'It disnae matter, Ian, it's no' about her,' said Fergus.

'Oh. Right then. Nae bother.'

I can't go through with this, I thought. I walked away.

I stood on my own, a lonely island of despair in a sea of condemnation, convinced that every whisper, every murmur around me was full of censure and blame. I felt so isolated, so forlorn. It was a mistake to have come. Would it be even worse now to leave? I wished again Duncan could have been there. Or someone, anyone who would understand what I was going through.

'You're... Bobbie, aren't you?' An unfamiliar voice broke into my thoughts. 'This must be awful.'

A stranger. Middle-aged, like pretty much everyone else there.

'Thanks. I mean, not thanks, but... well, yes. It's awful. So sad. Joe... What, what can I say?' It was not the most coherent reply.

'Yes, the Dawsons told me about it. I can't imagine what they're going through. And you. It's good you came today. You're very brave. I'm Felix by the way. How are you feeling?'

He knew. But 'how are you feeling?' His question was too direct, too personal. I felt my face redden, my neck tingle. I took a deep breath to compose myself. Who was he, anyway? And Felix, what sort of a name was that?

'I'm fine, thank you. Very sad, of course. I'll miss Joe. I'm so fond of him. Was so fond of him, I mean.' I could hear myself talking mechanically, my words stilted and cold.

I walked into the graveyard; it fitted my mood. It was only a short time until the service began. As I came back I saw Felix again. Maybe it was me that was rude, walking away like that. I gave him a half-smile of apology.

'I'm sorry, I didn't mean to intrude,' he said. 'It's just that you're here, everyone knows the tragic circumstances, and you're being left on your own. I can't begin to imagine the horror you're facing. Your friends over there don't seem to be helping much, if you don't mind me saying so. Do you want to talk about it?'

There was something soothing in his voice, comforting, reassuring. He was looking at me, straight in the eye. None of the furtive censure I could sense all around me. I could feel the pain welling up inside me again. But he was right. I did want to talk, to confide, to confess. He smiled. The first real smile I'd seen in days.

'I feel as if every pair of eyes here are following me. Accusing me, judging me.' My voice trembled as I spoke.

I stared down at the ground, embarrassed by what I'd blurted out. But then I heard myself talking about blaming myself, how the rancid poison of my last words to Joe were eating away at me. Once I started I couldn't stop, it was like a cascade of self-reproach. Felix nodded and gently led me away from the other mourners.

'I don't think you did anything wrong.' He was speaking very quietly now, like he was sharing a confidence with me. 'Could you have foreseen this happening? Of course not. Could you have handled the breakup differently? Maybe, but we all do things that make us feel guilty later on when we find out the consequences of our actions.'

I nodded, not lifting my eyes. Instead, I looked at his shoes. They were shiny and polished. I wondered how he kept the mud off them.

He leant forward. 'The key is to accept you're only human. Don't blame yourself because you should have acted differently or should have been an ideal person. You're not, and neither am I. That's how people are.'

I liked this. I liked him. Someone able to put my feelings into words, not just offer the usual platitudes. We must have been talking for another five minutes when he said, 'I think we should head inside. I can see funny glances coming our way. Maybe a thirty-five-year-old man shouldn't be chatting so long to a beautiful young woman at a funeral. Particularly you, at this funeral.'

I'd forgotten he was old. I nodded in agreement, but pursed my lips so hard I could feel the blood being pushed out of them. I was aching to keep talking. I didn't want him to go, but maybe it was best he did. I caught him also having a quick glance around, giving a nod of recognition to one of the other men in the crowd. The man stared at me. It felt uncomfortable so I moved away.

Joe's father arrived. I hardly recognised him. His face was drawn and haggard, as sombre as a mask. He walked as if the life force had been sucked out of him, like an old caged circus animal. He glanced over at me. I held his gaze for a second, scrutinising it for a sign of reproach or anger. Nothing. Then Joe's mother, being helped by two friends, her grief disabling in its intensity.

I didn't want her to see me. I hurried away to sit at the back of the church, in the corner. I had the row to myself. I stared at the coffin. It had a photo of Joe on top of it.

The minister started talking about Joe. Stories about Partick Thistle to try to make us smile. Carefully chosen words to describe his personality. No mention he had killed himself, that in the eyes of the church he had incurred God's disapproval. But the stilted innuendo was suffocating in its insincerity. There must have been some sort of negotiation to get a church funeral and this was the result. The minister summarised Joe's life but there was no mention of our last two years together. He must have known I was in the congregation. Did he think I was desecrating the service with my presence? Probably. When everyone stood up to sing 'All Things Bright and Beautiful', I slid along the pew and slipped out of the church.

Once outside, I sagged against the church wall, felt a hollow exhaustion. I should go home now, what else was there to do? Or maybe a walk, some fresh air would do me good. I felt paralysed by the emptiness I was feeling inside.

'Bobbie? Are you okay?'

I turned and there was Felix. The church doors were still closed, everyone was still inside. He must have left before the end as well. I blinked in confusion. What was he doing here?

'I heard a noise and saw you were leaving,' he said. 'I wanted to check you were all right, whether you would like to talk some more. Would you like that?'

I was tempted. Talking to him had made me feel a little better. And it would good to hear what someone his age had to say to me. Someone who could maybe give me some answers. But I didn't know him, how could I ask a stranger to help me like that?

'No, it's okay. Thanks, Felix. I'm going home now. I'll be fine.' Even as I said the words I knew they weren't true. I wanted to talk. I looked at his eyes. There seemed so much wisdom in them.

'You don't look fine. Come on, there's a Wimpy Bar a few streets away. We can talk as long as you want.'

I hated Wimpys but that didn't matter. I wasn't there to enjoy myself. We sat down and the waitress came over. I said I would like a coffee. 'Two coffees,' Felix said. 'Do you want anything else, Bobbie?'

I said no.

'Why did you leave the service?' I asked.

'Because you left. And I promised to help you. You're young, unhappy and alone. And needlessly blaming yourself for what happened. Your trouble, Bobbie, is that you have an overactive conscience. You feel terrible about the whole saga, but no one's blaming you. You're accusing yourself, to the point where you're starting to believe things about yourself that aren't really true.'

'I wish you were right,' I replied. 'But the truth is, Joe died because of me. Every time I fall asleep I have a nightmare, where I'm holding his hand as he hangs off a cliff and then I let him go. Or another one, where my father is lecturing me in front of everyone, telling me it's my fault Joe killed himself. I wake up, and for a few seconds I realise it was a dream, that the horror isn't real. Then I remember it is and cry myself back to sleep.'

'The dreams will go away, over time. What you're going through is only natural. Soon your subconscious will let you forgive yourself. And don't be afraid to tell yourself it was right that you broke up with him, if he wasn't the one for you.'

It felt like I had a real-life agony aunt sitting across from me. I told him more about Joe, about how I'd arrived at the conclusion we weren't right for each other.

'It sounds terribly shallow, but his looks were the main thing that really attracted me to him,' I confessed. 'When you're experiencing freedom for the first time, having a boyfriend with Cat Stevens eyes, Mick Jagger lips and who fills a pair of jeans like Robert Plant is very important.'

I'd never told anyone that before. I felt ashamed for being disloyal. And a little embarrassed by my Robert Plant comment. But Felix laughed, didn't seem to mind.

'Joe's beautiful, deep-brown eyes,' I said, lost in my memories again. 'He had a lovely faraway expression, which at first I thought was a sign of some profound philosophy he was contemplating. It was only later I found out his only deep and meaningful thoughts were whether Alan Rough would still be Partick Thistle's goalkeeper next season.'

I smiled at the fond memory of Joe's wee obsession. Then, stupidly, I started crying. Of course Joe had deep thoughts. Deep melancholic thoughts. How could I not have known he was like that? Was I too wrapped up in thinking about my future to spot them? That question again. Was it my fault?

I looked at Felix in despair, begging him to give me an explanation, some understanding. I needed, wanted him to judge me, to tell me whether it was true I'd committed an unspeakable wrong. I took a deep breath and shook my head. 'Sorry,' I mumbled, as I stared at the floor.

He looked around, as if suddenly realising the intensity of our conversation. 'A Wimpy Bar isn't the right place for this conversation. We need to find somewhere more discreet. Do you like Italian food? I bet you haven't eaten all day. There's a nice Italian restaurant five minutes from here. Luigi's. Good food and everyone minds their own business. Let's go there.'

It seemed such a natural thing to do. Somehow it seemed right this stranger was leading me out of the abyss of self-loathing I had been feeling the last few days. Somehow it felt preordained that he was here to help me. Whatever it was, I never for a moment thought about saying no. We got up and left.

We walked briskly to the restaurant, both of us wanted to get back to our conversation. He opened the door of the restaurant to let me in, put his hand on my shoulder as I entered. The warmth of his touch seemed to release some of the agonies inside me. I smiled my appreciation.

The restaurant had just opened. They offered us a table by the window but Felix gestured to a table by the far wall. It was broad daylight outside, but they still lit a candle for our table. I munched on a breadstick in a basket in front of me. It made me realise how hungry I was.

The conversation should have been awkward, two people who knew nothing about each other, but it wasn't. I found myself telling him everything; my dreams of being an actress, how nothing I did ever seemed good enough for my father, my relief my exams were over and my struggle to be enthusiastic about starting a career. He was a good listener. I kept gulping down wine as I talked. Felix kept topping up my glass.

We hardly mentioned Joe again until it was time to leave.

'Well, you're looking a lot happier now than when we first met,' said Felix. 'I think you're finally coming to terms with the fact that it's not your fault what happened. You've done nothing to be ashamed about.'

I didn't want to be forgiven that easily. It wasn't shame I felt, or guilt, but something stronger: remorse. A pain more complicated, more primeval, more unforgiving.

'That's easy for you to say,' I replied. 'You didn't kill someone.'

My reaction took him aback. I saw the shock in his eyes and felt terrible about what I'd just said. He'd spent all this time trying to help me and now I was behaving like a spoilt ungrateful brat. 'Oh, Felix, I'm sorry,' I said. 'I didn't mean that. Please forgive me.' I leant over and took his hand.

'It's exhausting to watch you martyr yourself,' he said. I felt relief to see him smiling as he said that. 'Sometimes to escape the clamour of haunting memories, you need someone to help erase the sound and fill you with a sense of peace, even if it's temporary.'

I nodded, not quite sure what he was talking about.

My hand was still over his. He squeezed it. 'You shouldn't be alone on a day like this. Come on, I'm taking you to my place. What you need right now is comfort and love.'

I looked up and stared at him in confusion. Comfort? Love? Did he mean… no, he couldn't. But he was a man after all. He may have been thirty-five but he was still a man.

'Bobbie? That's okay isn't it?' He didn't wait for a reply. 'Let's go.' He stood up and I found myself standing up as well. I felt numb. He helped me put on my coat. Very gallant, a gentleman.

I knew what was about to happen but it didn't seem wrong. I was aching for a hug, to feel some tenderness. I looked at him again, with new eyes. He held my hand again as we crossed the street. It felt nice, like he really cared for me.

We walked over to his car. A Rover. Leather seats, still smelt new. I'd never been in a car with real leather seats before. It was like a cocoon, a place of warmth, of security. We glided effortlessly to his house, a big place in the Glasgow suburbs, with only sporadic small talk to break the silence.

We walked up the stairs to his front door and went inside. He took my coat, hung it up carefully. Everything was in slow motion. I went to say thank you again. But instead, he kissed me.

It was a long, slow, tender kiss. For the first time, I forgot the horrors of the last few days. He very gently took my hand and led me to the bedroom.

'Get into bed, I'll be there in a minute.' It felt like an order but his voice was soft and gentle. He went into the bathroom. I heard the loo flushing, then the sound of the shower.

I did as I was told.

It was wonderful. So, so different. Okay, there had only been Joe for the last two years, so I didn't have much to go on. Yes, he seduced me. Yes, I was vulnerable and naive. But every bad thought, every demon, left my head. The hurt finally stopped. One minute it felt relaxing, like soaking in a hot bath, a world where my pain was melted away by his butterfly kisses all over my body. The next it was frenetic and exhilarating, where nothing else in the world seemed to exist.

I didn't stay the night. Felix wanted me to and I must admit there was something very inviting about the thought of falling asleep in his arms, feeling a warm body next to me. But I needed to have some space, to get things clear in my head. I certainly felt good; for the first time in days I felt relaxed, almost happy. Did I have a right to feel like that? I know it sounds silly, but I imagined Joe looking down on me. Was he angry, upset? Or pleased I was already moving on?

Felix wanted to call a taxi, but I didn't fancy an awkward hanging around waiting period. He looked horrified when I said I would get a bus and made quite a scene. He said he would drive me to my flat but I said no.

Like every student with any semblance of a social life,

I had an encyclopaedic knowledge of the Glasgow night bus routes. Of course, Felix had no clue about timetables, but being about four miles from the city centre there would be one in the next fifteen minutes or so. It was not a joined-up service, the buses went out and came back to George Square at the same time and there was a raucous twenty-minute period as people drunkenly staggered from one bus to another to head out to their final destination.

'No, Felix, you don't have to walk me to the bus stop. I'll be fine, honest.'

Gosh, he was insistent. The sexual glow was receding and he was becoming a bit uncool. I wasn't sure I'd been that smart; maybe sleeping with someone to get over a funeral wasn't such a good idea after all. I needed to get away from him, at least for the moment. I scribbled my telephone number on a piece of paper as he insisted, the price of my escape. I could decide later if I wanted to see him again.

I was right about the bus, I only waited ten minutes for it to arrive. I took off my black jacket to try to look a little less funereal, helped a lot by my hair being a mess after the evening's activities. Didn't think I'd need a comb so much when I set off for the funeral that afternoon. I thought about Joe again and realised it had been hours since my awful final words to him had rattled around in my head. I remembered instead our good times, like the day we took the train to Largs and ate a huge knickerbocker glory at Nardini's, feeding each other ice cream with long spoons.

I was smiling as I stared out of the window, lost in my memories. I was thinking of Joe and smiling, and it felt good.

chapter two

I hadn't done the changeover in George Square on my own for ages. Around me was the usual pandemonium. Good-time girls trying to look invisible on the ride of shame after their post-disco nookie; gangs of lager louts egging each other on to see who could chant and swear the loudest; a few old men, their sad and lonely eyes betraying a hint of the vacuum of their existence. And just my luck to attract the attention of three skinheads who were trying one last roll of the dice to get a conquest for the night.

'C'mon, darling, how about a real man instead of these fairies you hang out with? Peace and love, what do you say?'

I walked away, but they were persistent.

'Hey, hippy chick, where are you going?' the second one yelled after me.

'Leave her, Scuzzie, she's not worth it,' the third Neanderthal said. They turned their attention to an emaciated-looking girl sitting on a window-sill away from the crowds. 'Hey, skinny, you look like you want to have a good time.'

The girl was out of it. Not just a bit high, but spaced out completely. She gazed blankly at them as they surrounded her and then her head slumped forward.

'Oh dear, I think you've maybe taken one pill too many,' the leader of the group said. 'You need someone to take care of you, don't you? C'mon, little darling, I'm going to take you for a walk to get you sobered up.' He put his arm under her elbow and lifted her up.

I walked over and pulled the girl away from him. 'Janice,' I said to her, 'our bus is coming in.'

The girl looked at me, her puzzled brows not helping my attempt at her rescue. I thought for one horrible moment she was going to mumble her name wasn't Janice, but she vacantly shook her head.

'Hey, hippy cock-teaser, your junkie friend needs help. We're trying to be nice, that's all.'

'Be nice to someone else,' I said. 'C'mon, Janice, let's get on the bus.'

I bought her a ticket for my bus to get her away from them and sat next to her trying to get her to make sense. I established that she lived about half an hour from me, but on a different bus route. She was getting it together now, but I didn't want to leave her at the mercy of the packs of wolves on the streets.

I looked out of the bus window, the skinheads were nowhere to be seen. It was still another five minutes until the time when the buses left George Square. We got off my bus, jumped onto hers. She still didn't look in a fit enough state to get home safely, so I bought another two tickets to make sure she was okay. It was turning into an expensive journey home.

She was just about functioning as I walked her to her flat, and kept saying, 'Sorry, sorry, thank you, thank you,' like a stuck record. She was a bit of a drag, to be honest.

We arrived at her flat, I rang her doorbell and scarpered. I didn't want to get involved any more. Never did find out her real name.

After all the drama it was two o'clock in the morning before I got home. Sally wasn't there, another post-exam holiday that had been booked long before the funeral. I was glad actually. I wasn't in the mood to explain where I'd been.

The flat looked so studenty after the comfortable middle-class, middle-aged house I'd been in. The fridge was empty except for the TV dinner I'd planned to eat that night, the larder stocked with Sally's pulses and lentils. Blu-tacked *Lord of the Rings* posters were on one wall, Che Guevara on another. Chianti bottles with red candles shoved in them on the coffee table, my favourite Snoopy doll face down on the sideboard. Sally's astrology star charts were on the desk in her corner of the living room, a few glossy brochures promoting the delights of a career working for American multinationals were on mine, application forms partially filled in. The script of *Who's Afraid of Virginia Woolf?* I'd been rehearsing to myself that morning was lying open at the page I'd left it. Van Morrison's new LP, *A Period of Transition*, was sitting on the turntable.

That was me at that moment, in a period of transition. Two years in a relationship, then sleeping with someone I just met. The innocence and naivety of student life coming face to face with the harsh realities of adulthood and careers. Having to decide whether to become a graduate trainee for some big company or pursue my dreams of acting. I needed to make sense of it all.

I drifted off to sleep, into the world of dreams. No nightmares.

The phone call came at two o'clock the next afternoon. Two o'clock exactly; it must have been a milestone for him, a calculation of how long to wait not to seem pushy, but not too late I would be annoyed he took so long.

'Hi Bobbie, it's Felix here.'

'Oh hello, Felix.' It was strange to hear his voice again, like a dream that had come back to life.

'That was a wonderful time last night, I'm just calling to check you got home okay. How are you?'

'Fine, very good, Felix. You were very good for me, Felix, thank you.'

I could hear the relief in his voice. 'It was you who was very good. And very bad as well. I preferred the very bad.' He laughed at his own joke. 'Would you like to meet for dinner tonight? That is, if you're not doing anything else.'

'Well, Felix.' I started to speak before I made my decision. I decided to let my voice surprise me. 'Well, Felix, yes, that would be lovely. Where would you suggest?' It was a bit prim and proper, but even after last night's intimacy, it felt as if I was talking to a stranger on the phone.

'The Buttery. You know it? Best restaurant in Glasgow. How about seven o'clock?'

Yes, of course I knew it. On another planet as far as a student was concerned. A good choice. No chance of being spotted.

'That would be wonderful,' I said. 'See you then.' That was it. The deed was done.

The phone rang again. Mum this time. 'Hello, dear, I've been trying to reach you but your phone was engaged. I just want to check everything's okay.'

'Thanks, Mum. That was one of my friends, asking how the funeral went.' Why did I say that? There was no need to invent any lies. Nothing suspicious about being on the phone. 'I'm fine, Mum, really I am.'

Luckily Mum wasn't interested in who called. 'That's nice. Did you know a lot of people at the funeral?'

'Not really. Everyone had disappeared after sitting their finals. Bad timing.'

I cringed inwardly at my crass remark.

'Shame we didn't go, but your father was against it. I'd have liked to have talked to Mrs Dawson. Poor woman, I can't imagine what she's going through. Even though you and Joe were together for so long we never saw his parents that much. I kept saying to your father we should have them over for dinner but it never seemed to work out.'

I knew why. Dad never approved of Joe, always said I was too young to be in a serious relationship. And he definitely didn't approve when he found out to his horror Joe stayed at my flat most nights. 'I didn't raise a daughter of mine to get shacked up with the first boy who asks her', was his response when he twigged what was going on. After that, Mum was the only one who received my confidences. I'd even been known to hang up when he answered the phone, although I did feel a bit ashamed about that.

'I didn't talk to the Dawsons at the funeral. I wouldn't even have gone if Joe's uncle hadn't told me they said it was okay. But it felt wrong for me to be there so I left early.'

'Well, I think it was right you went. And I don't care what you say, I'm sure a few more of your friends could have been there too. That took courage, Bobbie, for you to go. I'm proud of you. And your father is too, of course.'

'Thanks, Mum. Tell Dad thanks too.' Yeah right.

'I'm worried about you,' she said, getting to the point of the call. 'Don't you want to come home for a few days?'

'No, I'm fine. I've got job applications to fill out, and I'm going for an interview tomorrow, an art gallery in the city centre. And I need to get rehearsing my play if we're going to be ready for opening night.'

'Okay. Keeping yourself busy, that's good.' I could hear Dad's voice in the background. 'Oh, your father is telling you to get the job applications finished before you get too caught up in rehearsing. Be quiet, Nigel. Bobbie can take care of herself these days.'

That was my dad. He never missed an opportunity to let me know what he thought of my acting ambitions. He didn't come to the phone, but I didn't ask to speak to him either.

As I got ready for the evening, I kept asking myself why I was doing this. Felix was from a different world. Was it about sex? Or Joe? Or having a fancy dinner? Was I drifting into a new relationship? I didn't have the answers. When I looked around the flat, the ephemera of my student days didn't seem me all of a sudden. Ephemera. I'd started using words like that in my final year at university. It seemed the sort of vocabulary an English graduate should use. What was the point of reading all these books if you didn't use the new words you came across? It had annoyed Joe, who thought I was being pretentious, that it was me showing off. Just one of the things that told me committing to one guy didn't work for me, at least not while I was still growing, still trying to find myself as a person. I was moving on, and somehow Felix was a part of that. I didn't know if I needed a mentor, a sponsor or a distractor. All I did know was, I didn't need another long-term lover.

Felix was waiting for me at the restaurant. He didn't look as old as he had in his dark suit and funeral tie from the day before, his jaunty cravat a valiant attempt at middle-aged trendiness. The restaurant was a fascinating jumble of windows, doors, railings, panelling and light fixtures salvaged from the beautiful traditional Glasgow homes that were being mowed down by a city council obsessed with urban renewal. I'd never been to a restaurant where the waiters fussed over you as much, brushing the crumbs off the tablecloth between courses, constantly topping up your wine glass. It made me feel special. Felix held my hand as we talked.

'I've thought a lot about what we discussed yesterday, about how you feel about Joe,' he said. 'And I think last night was the start of you putting it behind you. It was a crazy thing to have happened but I think it was right for both of us.'

'I slept better than I have for a long time,' I replied. 'You were the distraction I needed, Felix, getting me to move on.'

I meant it as a compliment, as a thank you, but I could see I'd annoyed him. 'I hope I can be more than a distraction, Bobbie,' he said. 'I think we can be good for each other. You need someone solid and reliable at this time in your life. I can be that for you.'

That sounded very convincing, very reasonable. But I knew the price I'd have to pay. The price would be me entering into a world where I didn't belong. Maybe even falling in love. The thought of that responsibility, these obligations again, filled me with dread. And when I grew a little more, and it moved us away from each other, there would be the heartache and hurt of another break-up. And it was inevitable, the break-up. If ever a relationship was for a specific moment in time, it was that one.

He was going on about things we could do together. A city break to Paris in a few weeks, did I want to go shopping next weekend? It was cute seeing him, as excited and eager to please as a puppy, completely transfixed by little old me. I played the game, sounded enthusiastic, but gave away nothing, just enjoyed the food and drank the wine.

All I was really thinking about was how long it would be until we had sex again. I shocked myself with that thought and I didn't recognise myself when we got into bed. I took control, it was me who chose what to do next. I was shouting out commands, using the smuttiest, filthiest words I could find.

Around eleven o'clock I slid off the bed. 'I have to go,' I murmured.

'No. Stay,' was the predictable reply. 'And next time bring some things with you to change into in the morning, if you like.'

It was time to tell him my decision. 'Felix, don't take

this the wrong way, but I don't want anything serious to develop between us. After what I've been through, I'm sure you can see why. I think this is the last time we should see each other.'

'Bobbie you're not serious, are you?' he replied. 'Didn't what I said earlier tonight sound good to you? Is the problem the age gap? Because that doesn't matter, it's all in the mind. It's how old you feel that matters. Don't say it's over. Please don't.'

I could feel my conscience fighting back, telling me I was behaving badly. But I pushed these thoughts out of my mind. I still hadn't fully worked out my new philosophy, but I knew that sex would be what I was going to use to banish the guilt I felt for Joe. Staying with Felix might have been a safer, more normal way to get over grief, if I'd thought about it for a moment. But I didn't.

'I've got breakfast for you,' he said. 'Told them I will be late into work tomorrow morning.'

For a moment, I wavered, wondering if I was being too abrupt. After all, he helped me through the worst day of my life. Didn't I owe it to him to not end it so suddenly?

But no. 'I'm sorry, Felix.' I said. 'But I do really have to go. I've loved our time together.'

The doorbell rang. Felix jumped up with a start. 'Who the hell is that?' he said, looking at me with a worried expression on his face.

I glanced at the clock. Eleven thirty exactly. 'My taxi, I think.'

'Taxi? You always planned to leave now?'

I did think it was a little shabby having the taxi booked

all along, but it seemed the smart way to avoid another tortuous night-bus journey. I gave him a chaste peck on the cheek by way of an apology.

'I'm sorry, Felix. Goodbye. You were a great lover, but let's face it, this is never going to work out. In our heart of hearts, I think we both know it.'

I smiled to try to soften my words. 'You've been so good to me. Thank you, Felix.'

And with that, I was off, leaving behind my older, wiser, two-day lover bemused and confused. I was high on my audacity. I was shocked by my behaviour, but boy did it feel good.

When I got back to my flat I lay in bed, thinking of Joe, cherishing another little memory of him before I fell asleep. And in return Joe let me have the sweetest of dreams.

chapter three

The next morning the radio beside the bed burst into life. I woke up halfway through 'Bye, Bye Baby,' the Bay City Rollers. The worst possible start to the day. No, it could be worse, I could have woken up to the beginning of a Bay City Rollers' song. I smiled at my joke. Not bad for seven thirty in the morning.

I was in a good mood. Not embarrassed by my performance last night, not shocked by my transformation into the sex monster from Maryhill, not even guilty for treating Felix so shabbily. Something as simple as having sex had put me on the right path again. I even found myself singing along to the last chorus of 'Bye Bye Baby' as I climbed out of bed. Bye bye, Felix. Maybe I was being unfair on the Bay City Rollers. After last night, 'Bye Bye Baby' was the perfect song to wake up to.

There was another reason why I was excited. I had a job interview to go to. And not just any job interview, a meeting with Tom McGrath, one of the great polymaths of the Scottish arts scene. He was thirty-four, and already had been part of the London underground movement and a big player in CND, before he'd come back to Glasgow to go to uni and become a mature English and drama student. Here I was being organised and disciplined about weighing up my career options, methodically researching and selecting the best companies to work for, all the while hoping my big acting break would come along before I had to make the decision. He went out and made things happen.

And now he was opening an alternative art gallery in Sauchiehall Street, The Third Eye Centre, and I had a chance of a job there. That could get me into the inner circle of the avant-garde arts scene and, who knows, he might even be open to me juggling the job with any drama parts that came along. That was about the limit of my self-sacrifice to keep my dreams alive. I couldn't bring myself to do what he had done, risk everything to be a success. I wanted the job, whatever it was.

I say whatever it was, because it sounded a bit vague. I'd heard about it from one of my fellow drama students who hung about in his circles and I'd sent him a letter with my CV, telling him of my love of drama and the arts. I couldn't believe it when he replied, and now I was off to find out what The Third Eye Centre was about.

Tom McGrath was a pretty cool guy, but a rubbish interviewer. Brevity was not his strong point, shall we say. He talked about working in London, setting up the counter-cultural magazine the *International Times*. Just going to London would have been enough for me, to be where it was happening for once. He described the *International Times* as having the fervour of a revolutionary movement and the mystique of Zen. I'd no idea what that meant, but it sounded wonderful.

In between his soliloquies, I managed to find out something about the job. It was a receptionist basically, and it just about paid enough to keep my head above water. It looked a bit flaky, opening a gallery in the biggest shopping street in Glasgow, sandwiched between Marks and Spencer's and What Every Woman Wants, showing stuff that, let's face it, was not to everyone's taste. Still, they had John Byrne for the opening show and he was sure to attract the students at the very least.

Tom finally got around to asking me an interview question, why I wanted to work there, so I told him of my plan to combine the job with trying to get my acting career off the ground. Honesty is the best policy, I thought to myself. No point in pretending that it was only because of my love of contemporary art.

'Wonderful idea,' he replied. 'The Third Eye Centre is going to revolutionise the Scottish arts scene, and who knows, maybe society itself. We're not a business with employees and bosses, we're a movement. We support each other and if that means taking time out to fight the system, or help striking workers, or to achieve personal goals that fit with The Third Eye Centre philosophy, then that's exactly the ethos of what we are all about. Theatre is a key part of pursuing a radical agenda, to get our message across, and I want to give grassroots drama and actors every chance to succeed.'

Gosh. I'd better point out I was not trying to be an actress to smash the system.

'Our drama group focuses on the experimental rather than the radical,' I replied. 'You've got The 7:84 Theatre Company to do that. We do stuff like Arthur Miller, Bertolt Brecht and the like. Our next production is *Who's Afraid of Virginia Woolf?* the Edward Albee play.' Not totally dedicated to the overthrow of capitalism and all it stands for, but hopefully it met with his approval.

'Excellent play,' he replied. 'A merciless dissection of the intellectual's disease of ennui and gamesmanship, wrapped up in domestic torment.'

Does he think this stuff up on the spot, I wondered.

I got the job. Not sure exactly why, but Tom told me to turn up a week on Monday once the fit-out was completed to help get everything ready for the public opening a week later. I walked out on to the street and felt like I was floating on air.

The rehearsal that afternoon brought me down to earth. We were The People's Theatre, a drama group with a loyal but selective following from the middle-class intelligentsia types who lived in Glasgow's West End; arty students and lecturers from the uni; and, if I'm honest, a few gawkers for the flashes of nudity that always featured in every production. All essential to the plot of course.

Who's Afraid of Virginia Woolf? was a great play, lots of meaty dialogue and I had the lead role of Martha. Over the hill, drunk and foul-mouthed, a real challenge. Even more of a challenge with Jason as the director.

'Inner thoughts, Deirdre? Inner thoughts?' It was the third time Jason stopped the scene we were rehearsing because of Deirdre's performance. Deirdre was playing the part of Honey, 'a mousy little type without hips or anything,' as the play described her. Deirdre was mousy all right, and okay, she wasn't the greatest actress in the world, but Jason needed to back off.

'Inner thoughts' was one of his favourite techniques.

Jason had been to drama school and done a course on directing and liked to remind us of that at every rehearsal, using at least one of the workshop techniques he had learned there. When he shouted 'inner thoughts' the actor had to stop performing and spontaneously reveal what the character would be thinking. I thought it phoney myself, but it made Jason happy.

'I'm nervous, anxious, feeling very insecure,' Deirdre replied. 'I'm... scared of what lies ahead and don't know the right decision to make.' It was the point in the play when her character was about to confront the demonic couple of Martha and George so that sounded right. Although I wasn't sure whether it was Deirdre speaking or her character.

'Good, good. Let's see more of that in the performance. We need to feel the uncertainty, not just hear you saying the words. Okay, Bobbie, from your last line.'

Jason slumped back in his director chair. It didn't have 'Jason' written on the back of it, but he was probably working on that.

We did the scene again. Deirdre laid on the insecurity mannerisms as requested. It wasn't difficult, the poor girl was almost in tears. The second the scene was over, she was off to fish out a Peter Stuyvesant Menthol from her army bag. She took a deep draw and exhaled and sighed simultaneously.

'It's no use, Bobbie, I'm not up to this,' she said to me. 'Jason's always picking on me and I know why. I'm worthless in this part, that's obvious to everyone. I know you all hate me for bringing the play down.'

'Deirdre, it's not you. Jason's a tough director, he's so

31

obsessive. I find him just as scary as you do. But his heart's in the right place, he wants the show to be a success. And he knows you'll give a great performance. That's why he keeps pushing you.'

Sounds convincing, I thought.

I saw Jason walking over to us, and I managed to catch his eye and give a quick shake of my head to ward him off. He noticed, thank goodness, and took a step back and headed away to cajole someone else.

'Really?' said Deirdre. 'When I see you doing the confrontation scene, it's so powerful, it seems so effortless. I know I'll never act like that. I'll settle for not getting booed off stage.'

'Nobody's going to boo you,' I replied.

Jason clapped his hands together. 'Act One kitchen scene everyone.'

That was my first big scene in the play and I walked over to my mark. 'She'll be fine, back off,' I hissed as I passed him.

It was a long monologue and Martha's words were laced with venom. Great stuff, something you could really get your teeth into. She's not the most likeable of characters, in fact she's an alcoholic catastrophe. She swears like a trooper and it would be so easy to go over the top in crassness, but I wanted to play the part where her inner soul is revealed. I'd decided the real reason why Martha was so spiteful to everyone is that deep inside her she had so much love to express. I didn't want the audience to hate her. I wanted her behaviour to break their hearts.

I sat down on the chair in what would be her messy,

chaotic kitchen and lit a cigarette. I decided to try out a deep, throaty, cigarettes-and-bourbon voice as she and her husband George raged at each other.

'Fix me another drink… lover,' I slurred. The tiniest of smiles as I said the word 'lover'. I wanted to show real feeling beneath the irony.

'My God, you can swill it down, can't you?'

'Well, I'm thirsty.' Defensive. I gave George a look of pleading rather than defiance.

'Oh Jesus,' he replied.

That was enough of the pathos. It was time for the she-devil again. 'Look, sweetheart, I can drink you under any goddam table you want, so don't worry about me.'

'I gave you the prize years ago, Martha. There isn't an abomination award going that you haven't won.' George rose to the challenge.

'I swear to God, George, if you even existed I'd divorce you.'

There was so much emotion in that scene it was enthralling. I could feel myself breaking down like the character I was playing. I loved my Martha, because deep, deep down, she also wanted to be loved.

I decided. Working at The Third Eye Centre would give me the time to make a real go of trying to be an actress, and if I hyped the job up to my parents it would keep Dad and his 'Is this what we spent our money putting you through university for?' speech off my back for a while.

We wrapped up the rehearsal for the day. There was a pep talk from Jason about how wonderful we were. I caught his eye and nodded towards Deirdre, which he was smart enough to respond to by singling her out for praise. I don't think anyone noticed my prompting.

I walked with Deirdre to the bus stop. She'd perked up now, Jason's words had done the trick. 'It's coming together, isn't it?' she said, trying to convince herself. I told her again she was great for the part. She invited me to a party on Saturday night as a thank you and I said yes.

When I arrived at my flat the smell of a lentil bake in the oven told me Sally was back from her travels and we spent a few minutes catching up on the funeral. But only a few minutes. Sally was caught in a 1960s time warp and her groovy-chick-speak was not what I wanted to hear when talking about Joe. I agreed that his death was a real downer and then said I had to rehearse the play.

'Cool. I can dig that,' Sally replied. 'We can hang later when the lentils are ready. But chill, Bobbie, no need to be uptight about this acting gig. You're one power actress freak.'

Sally lived in her little peace-and-love fantasy land, where the Beatles had never split up and Jim Morrison was still living incognito in Paris. She'd returned from hanging out with some 'cats with a lot of bread', she explained, who ran a hippy commune in a district in west London, Notting Hill she said it was called. Bit of a dodgy area apparently, lots of racial problems, but great houses for group living, cheap by London standards.

'This chick's old man bought her a big semi-detached house in Ladbroke Grove,' she said, 'The street that was in a Van Morrison song. It was pretty far-out, man.'

There had been an open invite for every pothead and freeloader to hang out there. Sally came back early because they were busted by the fuzz, some of them getting fined for possession of grass. Nothing serious, in fact it was becoming a badge of honour to have a drugs conviction.

As we ate her lentil bake that evening and I listened to her stories of the people she had hung out with, the life they led, I couldn't help but feel a chapter in my life closing. Don't get me wrong, I loved the stuff I did in my student days, but it was starting to feel juvenile and self-indulgent. There was a grown-up world out there I was about to enter, that clearly Sally wasn't ready for yet. I could sense our lives were about to drift apart.

★ ★ ★

That Saturday, nine o'clock, I met up with Deirdre in George Square to head off to the party, being thrown by some friends she had on the South Side. Even though I say so myself, I was looking very classy in my kohl eye makeup and black polo neck, with my Afghan coat betraying the last vestiges of my inner hippy. I brought a bottle of Blue Nun to be polite, didn't want to feel like a gatecrasher.

'You look very glamourous,' Deirdre said when she saw me. 'I feel frumpy in comparison. I'm going to get invited to a lot more parties if I turn up with someone looking like you every time. Expect a lot of attention, and don't say I didn't warn you.'

'Don't be silly, you look lovely, Deirdre. I thought I'd make an effort. I need to put Joe's funeral behind me.'

Deirdre gave a start. 'Oh Bobbie, here's me, wrapped up in my own wee world and not asking about you. Was it really… suicide?' She said the last word in a whisper.

The drama group knew of Joe's death but I hadn't told them about the note. 'Yes it was suicide,' I replied, shaking my head. 'The funeral was very tough but I met someone who tried to give me the strength to put it behind me and move on. I don't think I ever will though, put it behind me. Not completely.'

'No one would expect you to. But whoever told you to move on was saying the right thing. Something like that can take over your life if you're not careful.'

'It was a stranger actually. I hardly knew anyone there. He told me I had an overactive conscience and I should stop blaming myself.'

'Sounds like good advice. And moving on, that's definitely right too. I can see why you're dolled up for the party now. Good for you, Bobbie.'

The bus pulled up at the stop and Deirdre gave me a hug before we got on. 'You are such a strong woman,' she said once we sat down. 'How you can focus on the play at a time like this is incredible. I'd be a basket case if something horrible happened to a boyfriend of mine.'

'He wasn't my boyfriend any more,' I said. 'But it doesn't make it any less tough. I still think of Joe all the time, but it's getting easier, a little less painful. I'm ready to start meeting new people again.'

'That's good. Although I don't think you'll meet Mr Right at this party. The guy who invited me is okay, a bit on the posh side, but some of his friends, well let's say they were born with a silver spoon in their mouths and don't appreciate it.'

'Don't worry, I'm not on the prowl for a husband just yet.' I looked around to check no one was listening. 'I was thinking more along the lines of a fling tonight. If I want to start living again there might be someone at the party who'll help me do it.'

'Gosh, that is moving on,' said Deirdre. 'But you've been through a lot, so if that's your plan, good luck to you. I'm sure you'll find plenty of takers. I hope you've come prepared, that's all.'

'Prepared? You said you liked the look,' I replied. 'And I've brought some wine to help things along.'

'That's not what I mean and you know it. Contraception. You'll need to have protection, you can't rely on boys to be responsible.'

'All sorted. Never came off the pill when I split with Joe, so all systems go.' I gave Deirdre a conspiratorial wink.

'But, you should think about, you know, other reasons,' Deirdre said, lowering her voice. 'You can't be too careful.'

'Oh really, Deirdre, you mean a johnny? No way, tried it once with Joe on our first time together, it was a disaster. I am fussy, you know. I'm not going to go with the sort of guy who could give me something.'

She didn't seem too convinced so I dropped the subject. The number 59 bus was a bit too crowded to continue that sort of conversation.

We got off at the stop at the end of the street where the party was. No trouble in finding it, it was clear from the noise where it was happening. I heard the strains of *Razamanaz*, the new Nazareth album, from the house as we approached. Good sign. Dan McCafferty was belting out 'Bad, Bad, Boy'; it greeted us as we let ourselves in.

Bad, bad, girl was going to be more appropriate.

It took me twenty minutes before I headed upstairs to the bedroom. Greg, his name was. He latched on to me straight away, seconds after I'd come back down the stairs from throwing my Afghan on the pile of coats in the small back bedroom. Full marks for initiative. 'Love your patchouli oil' was his opening gambit. I'd heard worse.

He was one of those guys who considered themselves God's gift to women, and wanted everyone to know it. He had a slightly annoying Scottish public schoolboy accent which sounded like a gay Scottish duck doing an impersonation of Prince Charles. He was an entrepreneur, he told me, and was looking to set up a chain of record stores. Big plans. I tried to look impressed.

It was funny how he had this whole seduction scene going which was geared to luring an unsuspecting conquest into a bedroom with promises of restraint and hints of gentle caressing, only for the poor victim to be pounced on when the door was closed. Trust me, Greg, I thought about telling him, it wasn't necessary.

It was straight into the action the minute we got into the bedroom. Greg was obviously not used to full co-operation from the off, but he soon got the message that no battling was required. There was another couple on the bed, they were into their thing, and we soon got into ours. He started to get heated up, and there was no sign our neighbours were about to leave.

'Let's go next door,' I whispered.

We were about to finish when there was a knock

on the door. A guy came in without waiting, mumbled, 'Sorry, coat,' grabbed his coat and ran out. It was quite funny, to freeze in mid-bonk. Good for Greg, he was back to business before the door closed.

It hadn't been the greatest shag in the world, but it served its purpose. Felix was well and truly confined to the past. And Greg would be even easier to get over.

We thought we'd better vacate before the coat collection rush hour began, so we got dressed and went back downstairs in post-coital bliss. Lots of little kisses and handholding, very lovey-dovey. The number of partygoers petered out until there were just couples left downstairs and dope fiends upstairs. Off went the lights and we settled down for some serious snogging, the incense sticks, red light bulbs and *The Dark Side of the Moon* on the turntable making it very atmospheric.

Greg managed an encore of his performance before the end of the evening, and then turned into a bit of a pain, making little attempt to disguise from me that he was going around his mates telling them he'd shagged the easiest lay he'd had in months. I got my own back by showing my boredom of his company for all to see. Not my most restrained performance, lots of yawns and glances at my watch while he was in mid-sentence. He was so up himself he didn't seem to notice, but everyone else could clearly see I was not a helpless maiden smitten by his wonderfulness.

He announced he was leaving to get the bus home. Turned out the whole 'entrepreneur, looking to make it on his own' story was a load of bollocks. Still lived with his mum and dad and got fired from any job they found for him within weeks for being an idle tosser, his friends gleefully told me when he left. And he had to leave, he was on a strict curfew after some recent trouble which no one wanted to talk about. He asked me to write down my number in his entrepreneur's diary. Didn't look very full. I wrote down 041 1234567. It didn't seem to occur to him I might just have made that up.

I stayed on after he left. Deirdre was embarrassed I'd ended up with such a tosser, blamed herself for some reason. I tried to explain to her that what he was like didn't matter, I still enjoyed my romp with him. She looked at me like I was a complete trollop. The night was still young and there was another guy starting to make moves, but I could see shocked glances from Deirdre so I brushed him off.

Pity really, it would have been good to have measured up Greg's performance. Felix had experience, Greg had enthusiasm. I was already wondering what the next one would be like.

chapter four

It was how I felt the next morning that convinced me these last two flings had definitely not been a mistake. When I thought about the party, two things I was sure about. Firstly, Greg was a prat, and secondly, that didn't matter in the slightest.

I was surprised by how relaxed I felt about my own behaviour. But why not? I'd had a big buzz, all the exciting stuff you got from a man, without the hassles, the responsibility, the commitment. Who said a girl couldn't have that if she was careful? Who needed to know?

The only bugbear was, a thought had been creeping into my mind about Joe. That I was being disrespectful, unfaithful even. After all, Kenny at the funeral even questioned whether I should be acting in the play right now.

As I tidied up the flat, thoughts about sex, love and morality kept going over and over in my head. Okay, no one was going to kill themselves over me again, that's for sure, but why should I take on the responsibility for some guy's feelings? What was wrong with taking all the caramels and leaving the coffee creams? So what if guys like Greg thought I was a slut, an easy lay? That was their language, not mine. If I could look myself in the mirror and say it was okay, then it was up to me how I behaved.

I picked up my *Cosmopolitan's Survival Guide*. 'Everything You Need To Be a Total Success', it promised. I opened it up at the 'You and Your Relationships' chapter. 'Live for the Moment' was the *Cosmo* philosophy. They said it was okay for girls to want to have sex, you didn't have to pretend to fight off a guy to show you were a good girl, but they didn't say I should go out and screw around. It was still about getting a man and keeping him. I put the well-thumbed paperback down. Not for me, *Cosmo*. I was going to get drunk on sex and never have a hangover.

Rules. Not having them was where girls went wrong. I needed to know how I was going to win and survive. Rule number one was discretion. I needed to be careful about rumours spreading. Deirdre was already in the know, and I'd tell Duncan when he got back. But that was it. If I was to keep it up there would have to be the maximum possible distance between my two lives. And heaven forbid if my father ever got a whiff of my behaviour. I'd have to play the nice respectable girl to perfection to stop him getting any suspicions.

And rule number two, distance. Don't let anyone get too close, or stay around too long. Responsibility for others was a burden, so no one would get to hang around.

And decorum. Rule number three. Never look slutty, in fact just the opposite. I needed clothes to make me appear classy and sophisticated. Every man had to think he'd got me into bed because he was special. Based on a sample of two, that didn't look as if it was going to be difficult.

Discretion, distance and decorum. The three Ds: the secret of dating success.

I decided to head off to the city centre for some action. The Muscular Arms was ideal. It was an über-trendy pub at the corner of West George Street and West Nile Street in the city centre, too self-consciously trendy for the people I usually hung out with.

I called Deirdre and persuaded her to come along on Monday, hoping she'd be cool with what was going to happen. I wanted one last time with someone, to give me the confidence to go it alone in future. And she could keep a secret.

★ ★ ★

It was time for the wardrobe transformation. Monday morning I headed off to Buchanan Street where there were boutiques that catered for career-girl types. I had saved up two hundred pounds from my Saturday job. But two hundred pounds on clothes? I don't think I'd ever spent that amount in a year, never mind a day.

I headed straight for Smythe's where I chose a glamorous halter-neck jumpsuit in bright green for disco nights, and a canary yellow trouser suit with the most amazing bell bottoms. That would be perfect for The Muscular Arms. Knee-high laced-up boots with a gypsy top and maxi skirt for when I wanted to look like the girl in the Smirnoff adverts for somewhere more bohemian, white polo neck jumper and black flares for when I wanted to be a demure ice maiden. The shop assistants looked sniffy at a scruffy hippy chick walking in, but they soon got I was having a makeover. So funny they thought I was going respectable, when the opposite was the case.

Sally was home when I got back to the flat. 'Fab vibe, Bobbie, Duncan called,' she said as I struggled through the front door with my shopping bags. 'From a call box in Dover. He found out all about the heavy Joe shit when he called his mum to tell her he was back in the country and said he'll be here to see you pronto like. He's trucking up from London on the train tomorrow and I said he can come round and hang out with you about four o'clock, if you can dig it. I'm going to...' She stopped mid-sentence as she noticed the bags. 'What's with these threads, Bobbie? You been shipping some bread in Smythes? They're for squares, aren't they?'

'Image makeover. Now I'm not a student. But come on, Sally, what else did Duncan say? Did he sound okay? How was his trip?'

'Yeah, he's cool. Sounds like it's been far-out, bumming around Europe for the last four weeks, he was pretty stoked. But we didn't talk much, the pips went. Anyway, you guys can hang, I'll crash somewhere else. And hey, who knows, the two of you might even get it on. That would be cool.'

'Nice thought, Sally, but I don't think so. Duncan's been a friend for so long neither of us wants to ruin it. Stay around if you like, no problem.'

'No, I'm going to split. You guys dig your rap.'

Four o'clock, tomorrow, perfect. My best friend Duncan, back from his travels. We had so much to talk about.

★ ★ ★

The Muscular Arms was an amazing place. It was run by disco king Danny Lynch who got some Glasgow School of Art students to design a Pop Art masterpiece. Superman, Batman and Captain Marvel leapt at you from the walls, a Desperate Dan plastic statue talked to his girlfriend. A 1936 Chrysler was embedded in one wall, Carmen Miranda and a three foot banana was on another. Fred and Ginger danced down a staircase. The place was nuts.

Deirdre and I arrived to find it heaving. I looked around, happy to see the yellow trouser suit fitted right in. Maybe I'd laid on the kohl a bit heavy, but Deirdre was suitably awed by my new look.

And so was Lennie. He hit on me the minute I walked in. Nice suit, but there was something a little rough around the edges about him, like he'd been hewn out of granite by a none-too-skilled sculptor.

'Hello ladies,' he said. 'That was quite an entrance the two of you made. Love your outfit, darling. Can my friend and I buy you two a drink?'

'No, thank you,' replied Deirdre, a bit too fast for my liking.

I smiled and gave a shrug as Deirdre tried to catch the bartender's eye. Deirdre didn't exactly have what you would call bar presence and I could see it was a hopeless task. I joined in the futile attempt to attract the barman's attention with some seriously uncool arm waving, all the time feeling granite man's eyes boring into the back of my neck, no doubt finding the whole scene hilarious. I felt my face burning with embarrassment.

'Here, let me,' he said eventually. 'Bartender,' he boomed, and sure enough the bartender came over. Volume rather than arm waving was the secret around here. And it helped he was a big lad. 'Two gin and tonics,' he said, a bit too smugly. He turned to us. 'So, ladies, what's it going to be?'

'Piña colada,' I said. I'd never had one before but it sounded the sort of drink a girl dressed like me would order in a place looking like this. Deirdre ordered a half pint of heavy, just to be contrary.

The two of them were a well-polished double act. His pal turned his attentions to Deirdre, slipping in between us with his back to me so they could divide and conquer, and I got all of granite man's charm. He introduced himself as Lennie, but I didn't tell him my name yet. Now I'd got a good look at him, he wasn't particularly attractive. Not that he was ugly, but there was something a little strange-looking about him, the way he was both coarse and sophisticated at the same time. He might have been the foreman of a bunch of construction workers perhaps, or the manager of a coal mine, a foundry, something like that. And he was a bit on the old side again, in his mid-thirties, maybe older. It was difficult to tell in the light.

'So what do you do then?' he asked.

Deirdre leant over to interrupt. I could see she wanted to escape the attentions of Lennie's weedy mate.

'We're actresses, actually,' she replied for me.

She'd decided to show off. I'd have preferred to have given them a little less ammunition.

'Actresses?' said Lennie. 'Very impressive, but I should

have guessed. What movies have you been in?' I detected a hint of sarcasm.

'I don't do movies, only theatre,' I said. 'And it's just part-time for the two of us. But who knows, maybe one day I'll be famous. We'll see.'

'And then I can tell everyone I bought you a piña colada in The Muscular Arms. But I'd need to know your name for that, wouldn't I?' Lennie took a sip of his gin and tonic and looked at me expectantly.

'Bobbie. And this is Deirdre.'

He saw he was making progress and boy, did he look like the cat that had got the cream. 'And what do you do, Lennie?' I looked him up and down. 'You look like you keep in shape to me.'

A grin showed Lennie was quickly realising it was his lucky night.

Deirdre's conversation wasn't flowing so freely, and she gave me a look over weedy guy's shoulder that showed she thought I was moving too fast. I downed the rest of the piña colada. It was a bit sweet for my taste, but not bad.

'I knock down buildings,' Lennie replied. 'Clearing away the slums so the city fathers can come in and build nice new shiny tower blocks. Ever seen a building getting blown up?'

I shook my head.

'It's something special I can tell you. Bartender, another piña colada,' he said without asking. 'And does your friend want anything?'

'No, her friend's fine, thank you,' said Deirdre. She was clearly getting hacked off now. 'Come on, Bobbie, let's find a seat.'

'It looks like there are no seats anywhere,' I replied. 'And I've got another drink on the way.' I gave Lennie my best grateful look.

Deirdre looked exasperated. Lennie gave weedy guy a nod and the hint of a thumbs up.

'Suit yourself.' Deirdre turned away from me and continued to endure the attentions of Lennie's friend.

The second piña colada tasted better than the first. And the strange thing was, I was feeling very sexy. It couldn't have been Lennie, I didn't really fancy him. It must have been the drink. I was desperate to jump into bed with someone. I looked at the bartender. Hunk. That's who I wanted. Or a combination of the best bits of Felix and Greg. Or both of them at once.

I started to giggle.

'What's so funny?'

'I was thinking of someone else.'

Oops, that annoyed him.

'I'm not interesting enough, am I?'

I laid on the apologetic look. 'No, very interesting. And so masterful at getting drinks. You've got the bartender at your beck and call.' I drunk some more of my piña colada. That was the trouble with these things, it was like drinking Irn-Bru.

'That's not who I want at my… beck and call.' He leant over and touched my shoulder to make the point. I didn't back away.

Deirdre was getting fed up being ignored and having to fend off the weed. 'Look, Bobbie, I think I'm surplus to requirements here. I'm going to split. See you at the big rehearsal on Wednesday. And take care.'

'My friend's getting mad,' I said to Lennie, as Deirdre picked up her bag and left.

'And you're getting smashed,' he said. 'I think I'd better get you home before you get into trouble.'

That was pretty smooth. Pretending that taking me home was only for my safety. His friend disappeared into the crowd.

'Let's keep you out of trouble.' Lennie raised an eyebrow.

I finished my drink, staring at him as I sucked provocatively on my straw, making a slurping noise in the empty glass. 'You're so nice,' I said innocently. 'Keeping me out of trouble.'

'That's right,' he said, smiling. 'I'm a regular saint. We don't want to see you getting into trouble now, do we?'

★ ★ ★

Sally's away, Sally's away, the mice will play, I chanted inside my head as I fumbled for the keys outside the flat. Lennie took them from me and opened the door. The light was on, as I'd left it when I headed off, a hundred years ago. I gave him a woozy smile.

'Thank you for taking me home, keeping me out of trouble, Lennie. Lennie the Lion. *Graarr!*' I found that hilarious.

He closed the door and took me in his arms. He smelt of aftershave, a bit off-putting. We kissed in the hallway for a long time. I backed away from him, towards my bedroom. He smiled and there was a glint of victory in his eyes. I sat on the edge of the bed, kicked off my shoes and turned out the light. In the darkness I could see him taking off his jacket, his tie and his trousers, neatly folding them over the back of my chair. I was not so careful, I was naked before he got into bed.

'You've been so nice,' I giggled again. 'Maybe I should be nice to you for a change.'

He climbed on top of me. He was a lot bigger than the other guys, and not in as good shape as I'd imagined. His suit disguised his paunch pretty well. I didn't care he felt really heavy. I didn't care he was a nobody, that I didn't like him. He was in my bed and we were having sex. That was all that mattered.

As soon as it was over, I wanted him to leave. Couldn't face the prospect of seeing him in the morning light, having a friendly cup of coffee together, that sort of stuff.

'You have to go,' I said.

'What for?'

'It's almost morning.'

'So?'

I needed a reason. 'I don't think my boyfriend will be very pleased to find you here.'

'Boyfriend? You never mentioned him before.'

'You never asked.'

He muttered something under his breath and jumped out of bed to get dressed. I lay huddled under the blankets, pretending to be asleep. I surfaced to kiss him goodbye. I didn't want him to see me naked any more so I wrapped a blanket around me as we exchanged a final, awkward embrace. The buzz from the alcohol was wearing off and I was starting to feel a bit grotty. I left him to walk down the hall and when I heard the front door close I went into the kitchen and glugged down a big glass of water, then another.

I stumbled into the living room, put a John Martyn LP on the turntable and went back to bed, leaving the door open so I could lie there and listen to the mesmeric singing and guitar playing, letting it seep into my soul, replacing the momentary emptiness.

I needed to work on goodbyes, I decided. Had to be more stylish.

chapter five

I opened my eyes and quickly closed them as the midday light hit me. Ouch. I scrambled to look at the time on the clock radio. Twelve thirty. Duncan would be arriving in three and a half hours. Mad panic to get ready.

Duncan and I were at primary school when we became friends. He was already skinny and gawky, absolutely useless at football, and teased for his unruly mop of fiery red hair. In high school, we made an odd couple, although we never dated. In fact when puberty kicked in, I'm ashamed to say I backed off him a little.

He sprouted into this tall, gangly explosion of energy, jumping about like an oversized grasshopper. When Joe and I started going out together, Duncan stayed part of my circle of friends. I had my boyfriend, Duncan had his girlfriends and our friendship co-existed alongside them.

Getting the flat ready and trying to look presentable was the easy part. I'd decided that as he'd been travelling for four weeks around Europe, what Duncan needed was some home cooking. That's why I was in a panic. I was going to make him a full roast dinner as a surprise; roast beef, Yorkshire puddings, the whole shebang. It would have been stressful at the best of times. I'm not the world's best cook, and the clock was ticking.

I dug out the Fanny Cradock cookbook my mum had given me when I moved into my first digs, hiding in shame at the bottom of Sally's pile of veggie cookery books. Her books were well-thumbed and food splattered; mine was in pristine condition. I didn't have time to nip to the shops, so I had to use wholemeal flour for the Yorkshire puddings and rub the joint with cumin powder rather than ginger. How could Sally have every herb and spice known to man and not have ginger? But other than that, everything was under control.

Meat in the oven, I went back to my room to get ready. Unless I imagined it, there was still a dent in the mattress. I made the bed and hung up my yellow trouser suit. By three thirty the place was looking tidy, food was sizzling away.

Ten past four the doorbell rang, and I have to say my heart leapt a little. There was Duncan, new haircut, but the same patched denim waistcoat with all the badges on it. He had a copy of the new David Bowie album, *Young Americans*, under his arm. Bowie's new look was a testing time for Duncan. He was in shock that David had gone all soul and disco and killed off Ziggy Stardust.

'Hope you don't mind but I bought this on the way and thought we could listen to it. Only heard the title track on the radio, desperate to find out what it's all about. Bowie's singing about Richard Nixon now, instead of the Jean Genie. Do you think I should be worried?'

'Put down that album and give me a hug, you silly sod,' I replied. The longest, the tightest of hugs. I gave a whoop as he spun me around.

Duncan. Always full of energy, a hyperactive beanpole exploding with crazy ideas. Nothing ever happened with them, he was a dreamer through and through, but he made me laugh. Told more tall tales than a drunken sailor. I'd missed him.

'What the hell is that smell?' he asked. 'Has someone thrown up in the kitchen or something?'

'Bloody cheek, you ungrateful sod. I've been slaving over a hot stove all afternoon to have some traditional home cooking ready for you.'

Duncan feigned a look of sheer horror. 'You're kidding, right? I still wake up at nights in a cold sweat thinking of your Pineapple Chicken. Do you remember?'

'Vaguely. Look, if all you're going to do is moan, you can buzz off right now.' I laughed and stepped back to look at him. 'Duncan, it's great to see you. What's with the new haircut? Is it a feather cut or something?'

'Like it? I think I look like Bowie on the cover of *Pin Ups* in the right light. Greta did it. My Swedish hairdresser girlfriend.'

'Girlfriend? Is that how you've spent your time on your grand tour? I hope she was the only one.'

'Not exactly. I think it's safe to say I've now got a broader understanding of European cultural differences.' He went serious for a moment. 'But more to the point, Bobbie, I'm so sorry to hear about Joe. I dropped the phone when Mum told me. What happened?'

I shook my head. 'You knew I was having doubts about him before you left. I thought if I was going to end it I should do it…' I tried to think of the right word. 'Firmly. Not let things drag on and be painful for both of us. So I was harsh when I told him we were splitting up. A bit too harsh, as it turned out.' I could feel my voice wavering.

'You could never have known, Bobbie. I'm sorry it's taken me so long to get back, missing the funeral and everything. Did it go okay?'

'As well as these things can, I suppose. Fergus, Ian and Kenny were the only ones to make it. Everyone else was away. It made it even sadder his friends weren't there to see him off.'

We sat and talked about Joe for a while. Laughed about his Partick Thistle obsession, went over all the times the three of us spent together. Good times. I'd got so worked up by Joe's lack of intellectual curiosity, how he was completely uninterested in art, books, new ideas, the things that drove me away from him, I'd forgotten how much fun we'd had together.

'Oh gosh, the roast!' I yelled, as the smell of burning meat interrupted our reminiscing.

Sure enough, it was done to a frazzle. The Yorkshire puddings were like lead weights and the less said about the gravy the better. Duncan made a valiant effort to enjoy it. Oh well, at least I tried.

'So tell me about the trip. And what's the story about Greta, the Swedish snipper, and your new haircut?'

Duncan produced some photo booth pictures of him and Greta, sticking their tongues in each other's ears.

'Very classy, Duncan. And is the lovely Greta going to turn up with her suitcase any time soon?'

'Ah, no. She's not the settling down type. A bit of an eye opener, I have to say.'

'Spare me the gory details. And job? Career? Any thoughts on that while you've been away?'

'All under control. My folks kept yesterday's *Evening Standard* with the jobs section. I'm going to work through them alphabetically. Sending off my application to be an abattoir assistant tomorrow. If that doesn't work I'll try being an accountant.'

That was the trouble with Duncan, you never knew when he was joking.

'You should try journalism, you know. Or something else that involves writing. That's what's you're good at.'

'We'll see. And what about you? How's this play you're starring in? You must be excited.'

I told him about the play. He said of course he'd be there for the opening night. I wasn't sure how I felt about him seeing my nude moment when I would let my dress slip to go topless in my big seduction scene with George, but Duncan found it a hoot.

'I'll be in the front row. With binoculars,' he said with gleeful relish.

'As you can see, you'll need them,' I retorted.

It was great to have him back.

I offered him my job search folders, my research on careers with Procter and Gamble, the Civil Service and the like, as I wouldn't be needing them, at least for the moment. He took them but I could see his heart wasn't in it. That was Duncan, always the dreamer, never the doer.

I told him about my plans to move out of the flat, live on my own. First time I'd said it out loud; even Sally didn't know. She was stuck in the past. I was scared I would find out Duncan was too, but no, there was still a strong bond and he had enough excitement about life to make up for his procrastinating tendencies.

We settled down to listen to the Bowie album and Duncan produced a big chunk of weed, top of the range from the Amsterdam cafés apparently. It was pretty spectacular, although not so sure about the album. Might take a bit of time to get used to. Duncan was in raptures about the last song on side two, 'Fame, Fame, Fame', I think it was called.

The music finished and we let the silence fill the room. We were more than a little stoned.

'You're in good spirits tonight,' said Duncan, after he stopped staring at the album cover for clues about its meaning. 'After what you've been through, you're looking great.'

I smiled enigmatically, wondering when to tell him the secret. He took it the wrong way.

'I don't mean you stopped caring about Joe, no, of course not. Of course you're not great. Sorry.'

'Don't be shocked, Duncan, but I've started… dating again.' Dating. What a very polite word.

His eyebrows shot up in surprise.

'I suppose it's a rebound thing,' I went on. 'Met a guy at a party Deirdre took me to.'

'Are you still seeing him?'

'No, it was a one-night stand.'

There, I said it. I waited for his reaction.

'I'm pleased for you. That's the way to deal with it. No point moping about, blaming yourself. Best thing really.'

Hhhmm. Okay, here goes.

'There's more to it than that, Duncan. I don't want the pain of commitment again. Having a guy without a relationship gave me a buzz. So I went out last night to The Muscular Arms, just to pick someone up.'

'And?'

'And, yes. Are you shocked?'

'No, of course not, this is 1975 after all. Bobbie, if you think that works for you, who am I to judge?' He took a long draw on the joint. I could see he was going to add something else. 'Getting it on with someone is cool in the short term, but if you're screwed up about Joe it won't help deal with your hang-ups. At some point you'll need to work your problems out, not run away from them. Might be tough to begin with, but it'll get you to a better place in the end.'

We were too stoned to keep the discussion going. Pity really, it was the one time I let my guard down and was receptive to some sound advice from someone who cared about me. The moment passed. And we didn't have sex either, just crawled into bed when the dope made us too sleepy to keep talking. Fell asleep, fully clothed.

Amsterdam weed was pretty strong when you're not used to it, so we never had that conversation about working problems out instead of running away from them. Things might have turned out differently if we'd smoked some milder stuff that night.

chapter six

I woke about nine and made two mugs of coffee. Duncan was just waking up as I got back into bed. We sat up in bed together, drinking our coffee. It felt nice. Weird, but nice.

As we talked, Duncan would lean forward and touch me on the shoulder, on the arm. He nodded when I nodded, almost mirroring my movements. I put down my coffee and shifted closer to him. Our eyes met, we seemed glued together. I had slipped out of bed during the night and changed into my pyjamas. Now I could feel myself naked underneath them.

But then, unexpectedly, I was hit by a panic attack. I could feel the electricity in the air. If I stayed there much longer my new lifestyle would be over. My smart philosophising about how to have a fulfilling life without commitment would be in tatters. I'd be back in a full-time relationship and a pretty intense one at that. In terms of what I was trying to avoid, Duncan would be the worst possible lover. I jumped out of bed, a little too abruptly. Duncan moaned that I'd made him spill his coffee.

We said our goodbyes clumsily but affectionately. I hoped he didn't take my sudden leap out of bed the wrong way, that it didn't spoil the moment. They say unfulfilled love is the most romantic of all loves, that as long as something is never started, you don't have to worry about it ending. And I never wanted Duncan to end.

There was only one thing for it. Another sex partner to help me move on from the doubts and draw me back into my new libertine world. I found Sally's old student handbook, the magazine the university gave to all new students to introduce them to Glasgow. I flicked through it, looking for ideas.

Page seventy-one, West End Pubs. Perfect. No-nonsense drinking dens like The Halt in Woodlands Road, selling 80/- beer and spirits in quarter gills, where the main attractions were an automatic glass washer and a colour TV. Not the sort of place a respectable young girl went on her own, but if I sat down in the corner and got engrossed in a good pulpy book, eventually I'd attract the attention of my next conquest.

I headed straight there after the rehearsal. At first I thought it wasn't going to work, I stuck out so much from the rest of the clientele. A bunch of lads took it in turns to come over with pretty crass chat-up lines, as much to show off to their mates as to try to win me over. I was about to leave when I heard a voice behind me.

'I dinnae like to see a bird on her tod in a place like this. Where's your fella? If I were you, I'd give him the toe o' my boot for standing you up.'

I turned around. His face was different from how I imagined based on his voice. It was his dreamy eyes that excited me the most. Eyes that seemed to be a gateway into a world of poetry and beauty.

Bingo.

'I don't have a fella,' I replied. 'I came here to sample the ambience.'

'Ambyance? What the fuck's that? A new fucking lager?'

Maybe they weren't the dreamy eyes of a poet.

'Something like that,' I replied. 'Nice pub. You a regular here?'

He saw he was in with a chance and didn't muck about. In a flash he picked up his drink and plonked himself down next to me. 'Yeah, that's me, hen,' he said. 'A regular. A regular sort of guy. What's that you're reading?' He took my paperback from me and flicked through it.

'Sidney Sheldon. *The Other Side of Midnight*. Have you read it?'

'Naw. Me and books dinnae get on.' He looked inside the front cover. 'Bobbie Sinclair, is that your name?'

I nodded as I took the book back from him.

'Well, Bibbi-Bobbi-boo, has this dive got enough... "ambyance" for you? If no', dinnae worry. I can give you all the fucking "ambyance" you can handle.'

And with that, he kept up a non-stop repartee of compliments, jokes and innuendo. It was quite a turn on, to see some beefcake with lumpish vocabulary trying to be gracious and charming as he attempted to bed me.

He didn't need to worry. He was perfect. A strong guy, obviously did heavy physical work for a living. A miner, steelworker, brickie or the like, every muscle bulging with power and energy. Someone who would want simple, uncomplicated sex and lots of it. Gosh, he was hot. A body I couldn't wait to get my hands on.

We went to his place, all the way out to Shettleston. Students never ventured into the East End and I didn't know where we were. It was a basement flat. Messy. Typical guy's place, but the bed was clean at least. And that energy he had at the bar was there in other places too. Boy, was he well-endowed, and boy, did he know what to do with his blessings. It was non-stop. It was frenetic. It was great.

I hadn't scrutinised his place too closely when we arrived, I had other things on my mind. So I was a little freaked out to see a flick knife beside his bed. These things were illegal and, anyway, why would he have one?

'What's this?' I said, picking it up gingerly.

'You like it, little Bibbi-Bobbi-Boo?' he replied, taking it off me.

I felt scared and looked around the flat, calculating how I could get out in a hurry if I had to. 'No, I don't actually. What's it for?'

'What's it for? It's something I like having around, Bibbi… Bobbi…'

Click. The blade shot out.

'Boo!'

My heart almost leapt out of my throat. 'Put it away. Put it away now,' I said, trying to keep my voice calm and controlled.

'Dinnae fuss yourself. It's just a blast from the fucking past. There were a few heidbangers round here that didnae take no for an answer. It's helped me out of a few wee scrapes in its time. Now it's for… sentimental reasons.' He folded back the blade and threw the knife under the bed. 'There, it's gone. You can take it and hide it, if you like.' He gave me a big disarming smile.

Maybe I was overreacting. No one with eyes like his would use a thing like that. But, yes, just to be sure, I slipped it in a drawer when he left the room.

In fact, I stayed the night. I know I said I wouldn't do that. Rule number two, 'distance', a slippery slope to making it more than sex and so on, but I couldn't pass up on the opportunity to get more of him in the morning. And it worked. My wobble with Duncan was forgotten.

I didn't have any breakfast, said my goodbyes nice and cool and friendly. I was slightly put out he didn't ask for my number, or say he wanted to see me again, but I guess we both knew what the score was. He had just wanted sex and so had I, so we left it at that.

★ ★ ★

I was still feeling a delicious ache in my body as I walked up the stairs to see Granny Campbell. Her tenement flat was on the way back to my place and I hadn't been to see her since the funeral. My other grandparents lived in England and I didn't see them much, so she was the only real family I spent any time with. I thought about last night as I walked up the stairs, the hard muscular body I'd been entwined with for hours on end. Not the image to have in my mind when talking to my lovely grandmother.

I always loved visiting Granny. I could never understand why so many of my friends found visiting their elderly relatives a chore. For me it was a gateway into another time, another world. She talked slower, thought slower and moved slower, but that was not a source of frustration, it was a source of pleasure. Conversations took on a Zen-like calm, became more meaningful.

'So how are you, dear?' she asked. 'Are you all right after that… business? I'll make some tea.' She bustled off to the kitchen.

'Fine, Granny.' She was of a generation who didn't like to talk about these things openly and I caught myself from going into detail.

She came back with a tray and I recognised the fine china tea set. Her way of showing sympathy for my ordeal. Two garibaldi biscuits sat on a plate next to the cups. Two garibaldi biscuits appeared with every visit and neither of us ever touched them. It was part of our ritual.

'Tonight is your dress rehearsal, isn't it?' Granny leant over and gave my leg an affectionate squeeze. 'You're a real trouper to be able to keep going after all this kerfuffle. And you still find time to come round for a wee blether with your auld granny with everything you've got going on today. Bless you, dear.'

'Wouldn't have missed coming round to see you for the world, Granny. Yes, I'm excited. The play opens tomorrow and the man from the *Glasgow Herald* will be there. You should be able to read a review next week.' I wasn't sure if I should have told her that, just in case they mentioned my nude scene. But I was sure there would be others in years to come.

'*Glasgow Herald*. Who'd have thought it? And are your mum and dad coming to see you?'

'Mum wants to, but Dad said no,' I replied with a bitter smile. '"It's only encouraging her," he said. He sees it as a waste of my time, and more importantly a waste of the money he spent putting me through university.'

'That man. I told your mother about him.' Granny caught herself from saying any more. 'I should be there for you, Bobbie, and I would be except for my leg. Still giving me gyp, you know.'

'I don't think it's your cup of tea, Granny. Lots of swearing. But it's okay, I don't mind about Dad. I've got used to his ways.'

I was right about that. Nothing I did was good enough for him. Everything I said was contradicted. At first it used to hurt, but over the years I'd developed a carapace of cool detachment, insulating my heart from pain. And now, I was beginning to realise, that was the coping mechanism I was adopting to get over my guilt and shame over Joe. Finally, there was something Dad had given me.

We chatted for about half an hour, mainly about the trials and tribulations of her gammy leg, and then I had to be off. Jason wanted one last troubleshooting workshop, to iron out the final kinks before the dress rehearsal. Not sure it was strictly necessary, but as long as he didn't freak out poor Deirdre, I supposed there was no harm in it.

★ ★ ★

The next day I went over my lines one last time so I didn't have time to dwell on the big night ahead. But once I arrived at the theatre the nerves kicked in big time. Deirdre and I were alone in our dressing room. I put on my wig and the vampy middle-aged costume. One of the helpers had studied stage makeup at drama school and helped me put on the greasepaint. The effect was amazing, a middle-aged woman stared back at me in the mirror. Me when I'm forty. Scary thought. That would be almost the twenty-first century, when we'd probably be flying about in spaceships.

I started the mental transformation. I thought like Martha, I spoke like Martha, I became Martha. The final call came. Deirdre gave me one last big hug and I went off to stand in the wings, waiting for the house lights to go down.

I walked on stage until I felt the heat of the stage lights above me warm up my face and eyes, alerting me I was standing where the light was strongest. I remember the first ripple of appreciation from the audience when I finished my big monologue. And the disconcerting murmur of conversation that followed when I let my dress slip to reveal my breasts in my drunken attempt to seduce Nick. But I sailed through the performance. Deirdre was fantastic and as we took our bow at the end she looked straight ahead, saying, 'Thank you, thank you, thank you, Bobbie', over and over again.

It was a great night.

Both Duncan and Sally were at the after show party, along with a couple of my art student friends who had drifted back to Glasgow after the holidays. It was great to see friendly familiar faces after the gut-wrenching emotions of being on stage. Duncan was the first to give me a congratulatory hug. The next few minutes were a whirlwind of praise as everyone fought to be next to tell me it was wonderful.

Most people melted away after about an hour, but I didn't want the party to stop. I had all that adrenaline to burn off and was proud of myself for resisting the advances and propositions I'd received. There was a certain type of stud who loved to bed a leading lady on opening night and I attracted the attention of more than a few of Glasgow's resident celebs. Not tonight, I decided.

Soon it was just Duncan and me, sitting in a corner, drinking cheap wine. 'So you liked it?' I asked him. 'The critics have gone now. You can tell me the truth.'

'No, it was great. Weird seeing you as a middle-aged brazen hussy, but great all the same. And of course I averted my gaze for your nude scene, you'll be pleased to hear. But was it cold up on stage or something?' He laughed.

'Very funny. I was trying not to think about you and your binoculars as I got ready to drop my top. Almost spoiled the scene with an inappropriate grin.'

'I don't know, I think that would have added something. Anyway, you didn't need to worry. Nobody was looking at your face.'

I punched him on the arm. 'How's the job hunting going? Got to B yet?'

'Ah, that strategy's been abandoned. I'd have to try to be an actor after failing as an accountant and that looks like too much stress for my liking. No, seriously, you'll be proud of me, Bobbie. I've taken your advice and been very busy the last few days. Enrolled in an evening class to be a journalist, learning to take shorthand, that sort of thing.'

'Journalist? So you're going to use your writing after all? Excellent. What brought this on?'

'I sent a review of a Led Zeppelin concert I went to in Stockholm to *Sounds*. It was such a great gig I wanted to share it with someone. Believe it or not, they want to publish it and gave me a call saying they'd like more of the same. Being a music journalist, that's my career plan now.'

'I'm impressed. A life of free records, backstage passes and all the groupies you can handle? Sounds right up your street. You'll be hanging out with Bowie next.'

'That's the plan. Talking of groupies, how's the mad bonking strategy working? I'm surprised you're still here, thought you'd have headed off by now with one of the city celebs that turned up after the show.'

'I'm not a complete harlot,' I replied. 'Granny Campbell thinks you and I should be settling down together. I could do a lot worse apparently.'

'Too right you could. But you've missed your chance, Bobbie, I must have been taking handsome pills while I was away. I'm stepping out with the lovely Kathleen as of last night. Life in the fast lane, eh?'

I decided not to tell him about my Shettleston adventure. Funny how there were different standards for men and women.

chapter seven

Monday morning was my first day working at The Third Eye Centre. I arrived to the sound of drilling as the painstaking process of hanging the John Byrne paintings began. Tom was laying them on the floor, semi-organising them into thematic groups – moonlit woods, the streets of 1950s Paisley, the teddy boys and the portraits. And of course the guitars. John Byrne's guitar paintings were my favourites, with their curved necks and vibrant colours, contorting themselves into ever more fantastical shapes, creating a symbol of psychedelia from the very thing that made the music happen.

'Ah, Bobbie,' said Tom. 'Welcome aboard. Bit of a madhouse today, trying to work out what goes where. Do me a favour and start unwrapping the rest of the paintings, will you? Then I'll need your help to bump them in.'

'Bumping them in' turned out to be show-speak for setting up an exhibition, so I got bumping. It was thrilling, trying to work out what paintings worked together, making sure the best pieces got prime position and organising the others around them. And straight away my opinions were taken seriously. When I suggested the woodland paintings could be organised like chapters in a story, Tom was impressed. 'A narrative flow of dynamic puzzles,' he described it as. If you say so, Tom.

Most of the afternoon was spent with me up a ladder, pencil in hand to mark the spot where Tom decided the arrangement on the wall was pleasing to the eye, harmonious and even. We got about half done when we stopped around five and called it a day. I felt proud I'd played a part in turning the stark bare walls of the gallery into a kaleidoscope of colour, seething with movement and energy.

Wednesday's papers had the play reviews and they were fantastic. The *Glasgow Herald* had a photo of me in their review, *The Scotsman* said I was a 'new shining talent on the Scottish stage'. I must have re-read that line a hundred times, I couldn't believe it was little old me they were talking about. The only criticism I saw of my performance was that I was too young and good-looking to be completely believable in the part. I'll take criticism like that. Even better, they didn't mention the nudity, so Dad wouldn't find out and go apoplectic. And it meant I was able to take the reviews around to Granny Campbell. She was very impressed. She was less impressed when she found my parents still hadn't been to the play.

'I'll have a word with your mother. The way Nigel behaves towards your acting is shocking,' she said. 'You're only young once and you'll never get another chance to try your luck. An old biddy like me doesn't want to see a play like that, my granddaughter playing the part of a scarlet woman, but your mum and dad should be there to cheer you on.'

Sure enough, a few days later a congratulations card

turned up at the flat, signed Mum and Dad. It was in Mum's handwriting of course. Dad conceding in writing I'd done well was obviously a bridge too far.

Poor Jason was the only one to get criticised in the reviews. 'Jason Donaldson's overbearing direction can't detract from the dazzling display of new talent on show,' went one review. Water off a duck's back though. Proud as Punch he was, festooned the back of house with the newspapers. Even ordered fresh flowers for the dressing room to make us feel like stars. Boy, did I pack a punch at that night's performance. When the time came for me to snog my stage husband George, he didn't know what hit him. Consummate professional that he was though, he took it in his stride.

The trouble was, with a full-time job during the day and straight into makeup after work, there was no outlet for the adrenaline building up after every show. On the second week of the run I got laid by a guy I met at the bus stop on my way home. Our courtship lasted six stops before I got off at his place, the foreplay was even shorter. Tacky I know, but when you're burning the candle at both ends, you don't have time for niceties. At least that's what I told myself.

* * *

The publicity about the play led to a phone call from Frank Fontane, the Scottish film director. There was a thriving film industry springing up in Scotland, making more whimsical slice-of-life movies than the hard-boiled kitchen-sink dramas being made down south. 'Would you like to come along for a casting session for my new movie?' he asked. Just when I thought things couldn't get any better.

It was time for a lesson in the harsh realities of acting. Yes, he'd seen me in the play, and yes, I was asked to read some lines from the screenplay of the movie he was working on. But the real reason for the audition was pretty clear after a few minutes.

'That was sensational, Bobbie baby,' he said when I finished my monologue. But there was something in the tone of his voice that stopped me whooping with glee. 'All you've got to do now is be nice to me and the part is yours.' He put his hand on my knee.

'Don't, Frank,' I said. Maybe my excitement at meeting him had been misinterpreted. I felt embarrassed I'd led him on, and put him in an awkward position. I tried to think about how to extricate myself. He didn't seem in a hurry to take his hand away.

'Look, I'm sorry if I gave you the wrong impression, but I want to keep our relationship professional,' I said, more forcibly. 'I don't get personally involved with the people I work with. It's not you, it's just my rule.'

He shrugged. I thought he was going to be cool, but he grabbed me by the shoulders and started kissing me. He knew I didn't want to but that didn't seem to matter. He slipped his hand under my blouse.

'Please stop, Frank. I have a boyfriend. No, please no.' I pulled myself free and couldn't get away fast enough. I was all for having impersonal, anonymous sex with someone I met at a bus stop, but no one got to demand it of me.

I lay in bed that night, in the twilight moment before the start of dreams. In my drifting thoughts I saw Joe again. He sometimes came to me at that time of night, like a guardian angel guiding me though life. He nodded that I'd done the right thing to walk away. Things might not happen so fast now in the Scottish film scene, but there were some prices not worth paying.

I'd had a chat with Tom McGrath a few days before, about Joe's death, the whole thing about atonement, whether I should be doing a penance to wash away my sins, living an ascetic existence out of deference to his memory. I asked him because I wanted to hear him say no, but as usual with Tom, what you hoped for was not what you got.

'Yogi Hindus believe in *tapas*,' he told me, 'Deep meditation, solitude to achieve self-realisation. In the yogic tradition it's the fire that burns within that is needed for the *sanyasis*, the yogi warriors, to achieve the goal of enlightenment, to be mindful of their sins and to atone for them. Acts of penance like fasting, lying on rocks heated by the sun, feeling physical pain, they can all help drive out mental pain. We forgive ourselves too easily in the west, whether it's a few Hail Marys after confession or slipping a fiver in a collection box to assuage your guilt.'

'You've got a point, Tom,' I said. 'But I guess I'll never make it as a *sanyasi*. Too much of a coward.'

If I was suffering any consequences for my new life, it was the alienation it was causing between me and my old friends. Sally and my university girlfriends were planning to move into a ramshackle old mansion in Gaylord Street, which was going to become an outpost of Women's Lib in

Cathcart. It was not for me. I was moving in a different direction and being part of a commune definitely didn't fit with my no-obligations-to-anyone strategy. I needed independence, anonymity and no scrutiny, to live the life I wanted to lead. And they were stuck in the past. It was time to move into the future. Life was about chasing your dreams, always moving forward, that's what I told myself.

So I was feeling a little vulnerable when, out of the blue, Dad turned up at The Third Eye Centre. I'm sure he had the best intentions, maybe even felt embarrassed he'd cold-shouldered me over the play. There was definitely an attempt at a fatherly smile when he walked in.

But it was horrible. Straight away, my sitting at the till at the souvenir shop at the entrance gave away the fact that an assistant manager was, in fact, a glorified shop assistant. He was singularly unimpressed by the current exhibition, a lot of framed vertical brush strokes of paint by a German artist. He made no bones about his belief they could have been done by a six-year-old.

'Is this how you spend your day, Bobbie?' he said, looking around. 'Does anyone care about this…"art" as you call it?'

'Some people do. It's not commercial but it leads to new ideas. People used to say the same things about the early impressionists.'

'Oh, I know I'm a philistine when it comes to these things. And I'm sure there's always going to be someone with more money than sense to buy this stuff. But it seems a waste of the money your mother and I spent supporting you through university, if you ask me.'

I'm not asking you, I wanted to say.

'It's a very important gallery. Tom McGrath has big plans to use it to shake up the Scottish art establishment,' I replied defensively.

'McGrath? He's a communist, Bobbie, did you know that? Nothing but a trouble-maker.'

When he criticised me I was immune, but slagging off Tom got me riled. 'Tom is a genius, an inspiration to work for,' I snapped back. 'And I'm here as part of trying to be an actress, to pay the bills, to get noticed on the scene.'

'Why can't you get yourself a real job, a real career? By all means have this arty stuff as a hobby, but you need to start making your way in the world. Your mother's worried sick about what must be going on so you can "get noticed", as you put it.'

'There's nothing that goes on in the acting world that isn't strictly professional,' I replied, trying not to think of my casting-couch experience the other day. 'And if you think there's any man out there that can take advantage of me, you're wrong, Dad.'

It was blowing up to be a full-scale argument but at that point a couple of students wandered in from the street.

I had a chance of one last retort before they came into earshot. 'I'm sorry if I'm a disappointment, Dad. But I live my life on my terms now. If you can't handle that, maybe it's best to leave me alone.'

'You're right, Bobbie. Maybe best for both of us. You don't need me any more, do you?' And with that he stormed off.

I was still upset when I met Duncan that evening. 'I know I should be grateful for everything my parents have done for me,' I said, 'but since I left university my dad and I can't talk to each other for two minutes without arguing.'

'He wants the best for you, Bobbie. He worries.'

I wasn't convinced. 'It's about career, money, success with him. And not getting pregnant until I meet Mr Perfect, no doubt. He's got no idea who I am, what's important to me.'

'He grew up in a different generation,' Duncan replied. 'After the war, everything was tough. He feels he's achieved something, starting with nothing, now owning a nice house, going on a foreign holiday every year, and, yes, even having his daughter be the first in the family to go to university. You've a different agenda and I think he resents you for it.'

'I don't think he came into the gallery to pick a fight,' I said. 'Maybe he was going to say well done or something about the play and when he saw me he sort of freaked out. He's not a bad man, I suppose.'

'Can't you work on that, try to talk to him?' Duncan tried to be conciliatory. 'I mean, you both want things to work out, don't you?'

'Difficult,' I replied. 'When he's at home, it's like he isn't even present half the time. Sits reading the newspaper, lost in watching the telly. I've tried talking to him but it's impossible getting him to respond.'

'Then maybe you're right, you should keep out of his way for now. Just make sure you stay close to your mum and granny so you'll see the right time for things to work out between the two of you.'

★ ★ ★

Duncan could drive, so he became my 'man and a van' to help me move flat the next week. Not a word of complaint at the junk I was moving, that he would have to help me lug up two flights of stairs to my new bedsit. It was in a grotty section of Maryhill, but it was cheap. I liked it was a bit run down. I didn't want to stamp my identity on anything. I wanted to live anonymously, give no clues about the real me to anyone I brought back there.

Duncan tried not to look shocked as he entered the cell-like room with its couple of pieces of cheap Formica furniture left behind by the previous tenant. 'Well, it's... compact, it'll be easy to keep clean,' he said. 'Not much of a kitchen, but knowing your penchant for cooking, that won't be a problem. A few licks of paint and it'll be great.'

I shrugged. 'It's all that I need at the moment.'

I'd promised him a few glasses of Blue Nun in return for helping me with the move and we were well through the bottle before we got to the latest saga with his girlfriend, the lovely Kathleen. Rubbish taste in music, apparently. According to her, the Carpenters were at the cutting edge of the American music scene. Only David Bowie song she liked was 'The Laughing Gnome', said it was cute. And when Duncan had told her he might consider moving south to make it in the music business, she had responded by saying it would be like moving to Mars. I tried to say nice things about her, to show I was supportive of him having a relationship, but frankly, I struggled.

Kathleen was a typical Duncan situation. Drifted into his life a few weeks ago and he was too disorganised to get her to drift out again. She was attractive enough, but she was going to hold him back. It was difficult to get Duncan to make progress on anything at the best of times and having Miss Prudence around wasn't going to help matters. I'm sure that was why Duncan did his best to keep me and his girlfriends apart. Only the most paranoid ones thought we were shagging each other, but they knew he listened to what I said about them.

Our talking had eaten into the Saturday evening. 'Leave the boxes, Duncan,' I said. 'You've done enough already. I'll do the unpacking and you head off to see Kathleen. Go out and enjoy yourself. I've got plenty to keep me occupied here.'

He didn't protest too much. He was already in trouble for spending the day with me. I gave him a big thank-you hug and, as I heard the van pull away, I contemplated whether to start unpacking and organising my new digs or go out and enjoy myself. I looked around at the chaos in my flat. Unpacking and organising was the sensible, responsible thing to do.

I decided to go out and enjoy myself. The decision that would change my life.

chapter eight

City-centre discos with their jacket-and-tie dress code had always been a no-no for the cheesecloth-shirt-and-love-beads brigade I hung about with. The biggest disco in town was Tiffany's in Sauchiehall Street. Plastic palm trees and plaster Roman pillars. Medallion men and big hair floozies from Glasgow's South Side.

The halter-neck green jumpsuit got me past the bouncers at the door, no problem. Inside, a different world from the student union disco. Faux-sophisticated. The guys in high-waist velour trousers, competing to see who had the widest flares. Satin shirts over the collar of their jackets, giant kipper ties. Girls in Lycra and Spandex, clingy and shiny under the disco lights. A big spinning glitter ball cast a million stars around the room like Christmas.

And so many guys. It would be like hooking a plastic duck at the fair.

I quickly checked out how it worked. At first glance you would have thought the action was on the dance floor, but where it was really happening was on a walkway running all the way around it. Just the place to bump into someone for a chance encounter.

I watched one girl doing the rounds. Chatted up six

times on one circuit. The place was like a conveyor belt of pick-ups.

I set off, the carpet sticky with beer spilt by the jostling punters. The men were a succession of Bryan Ferry quiffs, Jason King perms and David Soul moustaches. Some of them seriously overdosed on the Hai Karate or Brut. Tonight I was going to be selective. I wouldn't hook the first duck I saw. I was going to find the one with the jackpot number.

I was enjoying myself with my cool brush offs to all and sundry. Some guys took it as a personal affront that I dared to resist their charms, but most entered into the spirit of the game. Seconds after declaring undying love and admiration and telling me I was the most beautiful girl they'd ever seen, they'd have the next drunken lassie in their sights.

Then I saw him. Up in the corner in a red velvet booth, red rope in front, the VIP area. The entrance guarded by a big guy with no neck. And him, the centre of the attention. Very dapper. I was no expert, but that suit looked expensive. Everyone around him was laughing a bit too heartily. But not him. Very controlled. Made no effort. He called the shots. The master and his sycophants.

I walked up to the red rope, I was only a few feet away but he still hadn't seen me. I stood in a pool of light to get noticed, half turned to look at the dance floor. KC and the Sunshine Band's, 'That's the Way I Like It' was finishing. Then the O'Jays were singing 'Love Train'. I bet 'Hi Ho Silver Lining' and 'Brown Sugar' never got a look in here. I concentrated on trying to look cool, resisting the temptation to give him another glance until the song was over.

When I did, I caught his eye. Held his gaze a little too long. I felt his eyes assessing me with a calm, self-assured authority that was thrillingly unnerving. I looked away first, laughed at a pretend internal joke and right on cue was helped out by a handlebar-moustache-and-bad-perm guy delivering his chat-up line.

I brushed him off with my effortless femme fatale, feeling a buzz of victory that the moment played perfectly into the image I wanted the VIP guy to have of me. Although my back was to him, I could feel him looking at me.

The grooving masses on the dance floor were shimmering to 'Love to Love You Baby', Donna Summer. The sinuous sensuality of the music made my skin prickle. In its natural environment disco music was bloody good. Maybe Bowie was on to something after all.

'Excuse me, Miss, Mr Mitchell is asking if you would like to join his group.' The gorilla in the dinner jacket guarding the VIP booth had slid up behind me, achieving the impressive feat of whispering in my ear and being heard over the noise of the crowd and the beat of the music.

Not a hint of friendliness. I looked over to his boss. He raised his glass with a smile. I hesitated for a second, using my acting skills to portray a studied nonchalance about my decision. Let him see I wasn't the sort of girl who would come running at his command.

The red rope was unclipped to let me through and I felt a strange feeling of trepidation, that it was a moment in time that would come to define me forever. I pushed the thought from my mind and sat next to him.

His friends were well blessed in the chest hair department. From what I could see under the satin shirts there was enough to stuff a sofa for sure. But he was dressed conservatively. Dark cashmere lounge suit, crisp white cotton shirt, understated silk tie. Very different from the rest. His slicked-back dark hair accentuated his high cheekbones, an incongruously feminine feature, given his hard, muscular body. It gave him a powerful, leonine presence. His skin glowed from an expensive tan, softening the crinkles around his preternaturally grey eyes. He looked mature, not old. Experienced, but still in his prime.

'Hello, pretty girl, I'm Michael. I haven't seen you here before. Your first time? I'm sure I would've remembered you.'

'Yes, first time. I'm Bobbie.'

'Bobbie. That's an unusual name for a girl.'

'Short for Roberta. I think my dad was disappointed I wasn't a boy.'

'Well, I'm not,' he said. 'Pleased to meet you, Roberta.'

'I prefer Bobbie.'

'But I prefer Roberta.'

I was shocked at his cheek. And a little impressed by his audacity. I decided to ignore the affront. 'Is this your club?' I asked.

'Oh no,' he laughed. 'Far too exciting a business for me. I run an estate agents and have a travel agency. Boring stuff.'

That was the first time someone had tried to downplay themselves to me in that scene. 'So, are you a leader of industry? Should I have heard of you?'

'I hope not,' he replied. That got a gale of laughter from the men around him. 'As I say, just a boring businessman. But sometimes I get lucky with a big deal, and that's why I'm here tonight. Celebrating a very successful business transaction.' He took out a cigarette from a silver cigarette case, held the cigarette to his side as he looked at me. Someone jumped forward to light it.

'Smoke?' he said.

I shook my head. 'Just finished one, thanks.'

'Then care for champagne, lovely lady? I never touch the stuff and I hate to see it go to waste. You have to buy it to get this booth. The management is so unreasonable.'

I said yes. I wanted to see what the fuss was about with champagne and I wanted to find out if the self-effacing charade he was playing would continue. I wanted to see him try to impress me with some great tale of derring-do. I wanted to see him desire me.

Nothing. There was something fascinating about someone who gave nothing away after the bravado I'd seen on the walkway.

I wanted him. My plastic duck for the night. When it came time to leave, I was quivering with excitement. Would he ask me to come with him? But he never asked, just got up to leave and took me with him, like we'd known each other for years. His car was waiting outside, engine running. He had a driver. A driver! Not just a taxi either. His own driver, a uniform and everything. He opened the door for us, doffed his cap as I stepped in. I smiled magnanimously.

The back of the car was huge, a screen separated us from the driver. Michael took an eight-track cassette from a holder next to him and put it in the player. The sound of opera filled the air.

'Very nice, I said. 'What is it?'

'Wagner. *Lohengrin*. Have you seen it?'

I shook my head, smiling to acknowledge the ridiculousness of the idea.

'Then I'll take you to Bayreuth in Germany, to the Wagner Festival. It's the only place to hear Wagner's music in all its glory.' For a moment his eyes were in a far-away dream as he lost himself in the music. *'Lohengrin.* It's an opera about someone who has a secret. Secrets make people more interesting. Do you have one?'

'I do. A secret as to why I was at the disco, on my own, waiting to be swept off my feet by a handsome prince. But if I told you what it was, it wouldn't be a secret.'

'One day we will know each other's secrets,' he replied. 'And then we will belong to each other.'

And with that he kissed me.

The kissing was passionate, uninhibited, arousing. I could feel his hands effortlessly loosening my jumpsuit. The lights from the streetlamps swept across the car, each one revealing me in more and more a state of undress. I put my hand on his crotch and zipped down his fly. He took me there and then, the intensity was overwhelming. I thought I'd feel embarrassed as the car stopped at traffic lights, as I heard people's voices outside. But no. The daring, the recklessness, the irresponsibility of what we were doing made it all the more exciting.

The car stopped, the engine was switched off. We were here, although I had no idea where 'here' was. I straightened my clothes and the driver came round to open the door. He stared straight ahead, his face expressionless. He must have known what had been going on, but he didn't display a flicker of judgement. I stepped out demurely. Michael gave the driver a curt nod and we headed inside.

His house was a mansion. Michael opened the door and I saw the lights were on, turned down low. We went upstairs, walked down a long corridor, strip lights over the paintings on the wall the only illumination. Portraits of Elizabethan nobility and Victorian generals, their eyes seemed to follow me as we passed them by. Somewhere in the house I heard dogs barking. I squeezed Michael's hand.

'Here,' he said, the first time he spoke since entering the house. He pushed on a large door and we entered his bedroom. A fire had been lit and the warm glow of the flames was welcoming after the stygian gloom. His bed was a big circular affair, with black satin sheets. An Allen Jones modern art painting was on the wall, a naked woman with pneumatic breasts, orange and black PVC knee length boots and bodice. A room that oozed sensuality.

I sat on the edge of the bed. It moved. A waterbed. Gosh.

'Are you thirsty?' he asked.

I nodded. He had read my mind. My mouth was

parched by delicious apprehension. He opened a bedside cabinet and I saw it was a little fridge.

'Then more champagne,' he said, untwisting the wire cage of a bottle. I wondered how the bottle and glasses happened to be in his bedroom and who lit the logs in the fireplace. But as the cork came off and white foam tipped the top of the bottle that thought flew away. He poured me a glass, almost to the brim. I never knew champagne could be pink, a beautiful gentle colour.

'For you,' he said, holding the glass delicately with his three fingers at the bottom of a stem as thin as a spring flower. He passed the glass to me. 'Please. Drink.'

I tipped back my glass, the cold drink tingling my tongue. I realised I'd drunk it in one gulp. Michael filled my glass again. I took a smaller sip and placed the glass on the bedside table.

'Finally we're alone. I like that. Now I can look at you all night long.' He smiled, the corner of his eyes crinkling where a light web of wrinkles touched his skin. 'You are beautiful.'

There were candles around the room, large and tall, some half burned with thick wax streams slipping down their sides. Michael struck a long match and very slowly started lighting each one in turn. The candles' soft flickering light gave the place a magical allure, as if I'd walked into a fairy tale.

Michael moved with a lithe, feline grace, like he was circling me, choosing his moment. When we kissed it was slower than before, so I could taste him for the first time, as sweet as summer rain.

I felt his hands on my neck. He unzipped my jumpsuit

and it slipped down on the floor. I wanted to take off my shoes but he stopped me.

'Keep them,' he said, and stepped back, staring at me. I trembled under his intense gaze, heat rushing to my face. 'You are so beautiful,' he whispered again, his voice hoarse.

He stepped back, unbuttoning his shirt, not taking his eyes from me. I went to help him undress but he pushed me gently away. When his shirt was off I bit my lip not to gasp. His body was golden in the candlelight, his stomach flat with a relief of muscles, like a young man. He was fantastical, like a Greek statue come to life. I reached for my glass and drained the rest of the champagne.

We started kissing again, the tiniest increment of intensity. I could smell his sandalwood scent, mixed with the earthy fragrance of his body. His skin felt uncannily smooth; my fingers slid over his back.

He reverentially removed the rest of my clothes, piece by piece. His eyes held a greedy hunger as he savoured every inch of me. I'd never noticed how large his hands were, they were leading his eyes around my body as he took in my every detail with a connoisseur's delight.

I thought that any second he would be on top of me, but instead he moved away. I felt a pang of anxiety that I wasn't pleasing enough for him. He saw the confusion in my eyes and his lips twitched with pleasure. He lifted me as if I was weightless and carried me to the bed.

He slipped off my shoes. 'You have the most beautiful feet,' he said, stroking the pad of each toe in turn as I lay down on the satin sheets. But I remained silent. I wanted to remember every second. I wanted it to stay with me forever. His hands traced a line right up my body. He stopped at my mouth, and stroked the little groove under my nose.

'And this, your philtrum,' he said. '*Le philtre d'amour* is the scent of love. When you are ready for love, it becomes an erogenous zone, sending out a secret aphrodisiac. Let me see,' he said, touching it with the very tip of his tongue. He looked at me and smiled. 'Almost.'

Almost? I was burning with desire.

He slipped his face down to my breasts, kissing the space between them and then each nipple. I felt a tingling in my throat, in my stomach.

'Beautiful. Modest. Dignified,' he said with each kiss.

His voice was croaking now, passion tightening his larynx. He struggled to disguise it but it was there. He was coming under my power.

Then his head was resting on my pelvis. 'That's the most beautiful clitoris I've ever seen,' he said in wonderment, stroking it tenderly.

I blushed like a schoolgirl.

He stared at it as if he had never seen a clitoris in his life. 'Like a little rosebud, waiting to flower.' He smelt it, filling his lungs. He licked it softly, as if he was thirsty, in search of drops of dew from between the petals. He sucked it. Hard. I gasped.

He grabbed my hips, pulled them onto his and thrust into me. It felt like there was no space in my body for breath, I was going to suffocate with desire. An orgasm racked through my body. I think I fainted for a split second. We drove our bodies together with a feral intensity and I could feel myself coming again, just as strong, but different. Not so concentrated. Fuller, rounder.

We were making love and he was silent now, only his heavy breath making any sound. I was uttering faint whimpers of pleasure. I could feel his body tighten with determination as he fought to keep himself under control. He stopped, withdrew for a few seconds and I saw his body trembling with desire. Drops of sweat were rolling down his chest, gathering in his muscular torso. I bit my lip in pleasure watching him suffer. I pulled him back. Back inside me.

He was gentler, slower. He was trying everything not to finish. I saw that, so I squeezed my legs together, dug my nails into him, held him with all my strength. He let out an involuntary strangled groan and I felt a delicious warmth spread within me. I'd conquered him. I'd defeated him. All that power, all that self-control. And he couldn't stop himself.

Our breathing synchronised, slowing down in tandem. He went to move off me, but I squeezed him tight to keep him inside me a few seconds longer. He kissed me on the forehead and slid to my side. I lay next to him, staring at that beautiful but still unfamiliar face. I kissed him on his collarbone, licking the little hollow on his shoulder. I had a deep feeling of satisfaction, but also an aching, a longing for more. My moment of victory was short-lived.

I had stepped over the red rope into another world. I was going to stay for a while.

chapter nine

In the morning I was introduced to Lucifer and Satan. The two enormous Doberman Pinschers I'd heard barking last night.

'They're big dogs,' I said, trying to sound enthusiastic.

'The best. Loyal, intelligent, alert. But don't worry, one word from me and they'll shoot straight off to their baskets. Lucifer, Satan, meet Roberta.'

'Nice doggies.' I patted their heads. They eyed me warily. I eyed them warily back.

We walked down the staircase; ceremonial swords and pistols lined the walls. The house looked huge, but it was difficult to tell how big. The door to every room was closed.

'To fend off burglars?' I said, gesturing to the swords. What with demon dogs and walls full of weapons, the house was making a bit of a statement.

'Decoration only,' Michael laughed. 'Can't cut through butter, any of them. But it's the artistry and provenance I love. Look at the engraving on this one. It was awarded to a lieutenant in the Household Cavalry after the Boer war. Over seventy years old.'

He could see me looking a little freaked out. 'Come on,' he said. 'In here.' He opened the door and we went into the kitchen.

A vase with a single white flower in the centre was on the kitchen table, the Sunday newspaper neatly folded, the business section lying on the top. Two plates with a croissant and roll on each, glasses of orange juice on the side. The smell of freshly baked croissants lingered in the air, although there was no one to be seen.

I sat down and he poured coffee. Lucifer and Satan sat a few feet away, looking attentively at Michael, waiting for his command. I was ignored.

'Nice coffee,' I said.

'I like Costa Rican in the morning, something mellow to get me into the day, a dark roast Ethiopian in the evening when I want something stronger. And you, what coffee do you drink?'

'Fine Fare Own Label. Do you have any?'

'Sadly, I think we just ran out,' he replied. 'I'll remember for next time.'

I felt a little thrill. I wanted to see him again, and not just once either. As I sipped my coffee, I fantasised about the world I was seeing a glimpse of. I wanted to discover more, to see what was behind every one of these closed doors, to see the secrets Michael had alluded to. And I wanted plenty more of the sex we'd had last night.

He courteously but firmly ushered me out of the house after breakfast. His car was in the drive, chauffeur waiting. I slipped my hand under his robe as we kissed goodbye, to feel his skin once last time and I buried my head in his chest to breathe in his scent. I didn't want to leave but he wanted me to go. I gave the driver my address and Michael stood in the doorway to see me off. As the car headed down the lane I turned for one last look at him. He was already gone.

It took me about ten minutes in the car to collect my thoughts. I saw from the street signs we were leaving Rutherglen, but I realised I didn't know exactly where Michael lived. I slid open the screen that separated me from the driver. 'Can you let me know the address we've just left?' I asked.

'I'm sorry, Miss, I just drive for Mr Mitchell. I'm not allowed to give out any personal information.'

I could see his eyes scrutinising me from the rear-view mirror. He turned on the music. Conversation was closed.

I realised I had no way of getting in touch with Michael. No phone number, no address. We hadn't actually talked much after we got back to his place but what conversations we'd had were intimate and intense. But he had given away nothing about himself. An estate agent who liked Wagner and had good taste in coffee. Second name Mitchell. That was it. Lohengrin had kept his secrets.

★ ★ ★

Unpacking took all day. Two o'clock came and went, that was the time when Felix had called to ask to see me again. He had been so besotted, couldn't wait to get back together. But with Michael… nothing. Was I not good enough for him? Too inexperienced? I could imagine the women he must sleep with, maybe I wasn't in their league. Maybe I wasn't smart enough, not knowing about Wagner and Costa Rican coffee. Maybe I wasn't nice enough to his bloody dogs. Too many maybes.

At five o'clock the doorbell rang. My heart leapt with excitement. Michael, turning up unannounced. How romantic. How could I have been so silly as to think he didn't want me again, after the night we'd had?

I opened the door. A bloke with a bouquet of flowers. 'Roberta Sinclair?' he asked. I nodded, feeling a crush of disappointment, took the flowers and went inside.

Red roses. Twenty-two of them.

'One for every year the world has been more beautiful because of you,' said the card.

I read the note, thanking me for a great time, saying he'd be in touch after he returned from a business trip. He never mentioned a business trip. Signed with kisses, but not the word 'love'.

I stared at the card for ages, trying to read hidden meanings into every word. This is ridiculous, pull yourself together, I ordered myself. But he'd ordered and had the flowers delivered on a Sunday. How had he managed that? I stared at the card again. Not the slightest hint about when the 'business trip' would be over. Damn.

Silence for five days. Then on the Friday a single red rose turned up. No message. What was I supposed to read into that? A goodbye symbol? Or a precursor to getting back in touch? If he was on a business trip he could have still called me. That must mean it was over, but why didn't he say so in his note? He was driving me nuts.

There was only one thing for it. Tomorrow was Saturday, so back to Tiffany's. If he was there, I'd find out once and for all where I stood. And I wouldn't run up to him. Oh no, I'd let him come to me, ideally while I was being fêted by a multitude of admirers. I'd make him sweat before I said yes. That would show him.

I put on my canary-yellow trouser suit and headed off. The VIP booth was empty, looking a little forlorn. I found one of the managers, asked him if he knew about the guy who was there the Saturday before. Completely unhelpful. Patronising even.

I flushed with embarrassment and anger. Another conquest, that was what I needed. That'll teach him. I stood on the sticky red carpet, waiting for the Don Juans to make their move. And make their moves they did, one after another. Every one of them banal, every chat-up line predictable. I cursed Michael for messing with me. I was nothing but a peanut to him and I hated him for it.

I got my coat and started to walk to the underground station when I saw the familiar car, parked on the road just ahead. As I walked up he wound down the window.

'Roberta, how nice to see you. Where are you going?'

'Michael, you bastard, where have you been? Why didn't you call me?'

He stepped out of the car. He looked surprised, bemused, the slightest of smiles dancing in his eyes. 'What on earth do you mean?' he replied. 'Didn't you get my note saying I was away and that I would meet you at Tiffany's tonight?'

'I got your flower today, but there wasn't any note.' I felt petulant, embarrassed by my outburst.

Michael shook his head in exasperation. 'I'll have a quiet word with my florist. That's disgraceful he forgot to attach the note. But here you are anyway. Are you leaving? The night has just begun.'

I was confused. Could it have been a misunderstanding? Should I say sorry? After all, he had turned up here to see me. Or had he? I shook my head. I didn't know what to think.

'Maybe next time you want to meet me you should try calling, rather than relying on someone to give me a note.'

I wanted to show him who's boss. And it worked, he was grovelingly apologetic. 'You're quite right, Roberta, I've behaved abominably. Things are a little... complicated at the moment and I've not been as attentive to you as I should have been. Let me make it up to you. You look cold standing there. And you shouldn't be getting on the underground dressed like that. Who knows what sort of undesirable attention you would attract, looking so beautiful on an empty train late at night. Come on, let me give you a lift at least.'

He opened the door of the car. I stepped inside, giving him a haughty look to let him know it was on my terms. As the door closed behind him, the memories of our last car journey came back. I couldn't wait to have him again.

The sound of a French tenor filled the car. 'Wagner again?' I asked.

'No, Charles Gounoud. It's his opera *Faust*, the story of someone who sells their soul to the devil for unlimited power and worldly pleasures. A good deal, don't you think?'

I couldn't think of a suitably witty riposte so I didn't give him the satisfaction of a reply. I gave him satisfaction of a different sort. His driver must be getting used to me by now, I grinned to myself when I finished. Perfect timing. I heard the crunch of the gravel driveway just as I leant back in my seat.

We went inside, Lucifer and Satan ran to greet us. I was honoured with a cursory sniff.

'Let me show you a bit more of me.' He opened a door leading into a long corridor and turned to the dogs. 'Go,' he commanded. Off they went, through the door.

He took me into a room off to the left at the bottom of the stairs. Quite a contrast from what I'd seen so far, decked out in shades of white. In the centre was a huge cream cage with brightly coloured birds flying about inside.

'Finches,' he said, bending down to tap the side of the cage. I could see real affection in his eyes. 'Look, these are Zebra finches.' He pointed to the ones with the orange beaks. 'Lively little fellows, always bustling about. And the brown ones, Society finches. Not so colourful, but the male has a beautiful song.' He picked up a tiny pewter watering can and poured a few splashes of water into a tray inside the cage. 'These are my favourite,' he said, pointing to the most multi-coloured birds. 'Gouldian finches, exotically beautiful, but shy. Very peaceful and gentle. I keep an eye on them to make sure they're not getting bullied by the other birds.'

'Stunning. But should birds be kept in a cage? Seeing a bird in flight, soaring above us in the skies, that's freedom. To confine a bird to a cage where it can barely fly, isn't that kind of... cruel?'

It was the first time I saw that flash of anger in his eyes that appeared for a split second when someone contradicted him, when things were not to his liking.

'Not really, Roberta,' he said, very quietly, very firmly. 'They never need to worry about food, about predators. They give me pleasure, they amuse me, and in return I look after them and care for them. They have a great life.'

That gave me goose bumps. I didn't feel scared exactly, more a frisson of excitement that shuddered through my body. I gave him a knowing smile, to let him realise I got what he was talking about and it wasn't intimidating me in the slightest.

'Let me show you something else,' he said.

We went into another room, a library. That was where the dogs had gone; they were lying in two big wicker baskets in the corner. They raised their heads as we came in, instantly alert, but one gesture from Michael and they lay down again. There was a big mahogany desk in the centre, pen and paper laid out with geometric precision. A grandfather clock in the corner, the gentle tick exuding a sense of sanctuary, of calm. The rest of the room was lined, floor to ceiling, with leather-bound books.

'Another of my hobbies. First editions.' He walked over and lifted a battered-looking book from the shelf. '*Beyond Good and Evil*, Friedrich Nietzsche, original first edition in German, published in 1886. Have you heard of Nietzsche?'

He was obviously expecting a no, so I felt chuffed I knew who he was. 'I did General Philosophy in my first year at uni. But Nietzsche was an option course. I did the easier stuff, Descartes and the like.'

'A missed opportunity, Roberta, there's a lot he can teach us, even today. But come on, I'm boring you. Last room of the tour next. There's something there you might like.'

Into the living room. Like every room in the house, it was immaculate. I don't know who his housekeeper was, but there was not a single thing out of place anywhere. And above the fireplace a big painting of three men in bowler hats with expressionless faces.

'Wow, a Magritte,' I exclaimed. 'But not a real one, surely?'

'It is, actually. But don't tell anyone, will you? Keep it our secret.' He gave me a wink, to let me know I was being invited into his world, that he trusted me to be discreet.

Okay, another reassessment of what Michael's worth. Nobody, but nobody, had an original René Magritte hanging in their living room in Glasgow.

'Your travel agency and estate agents must do awfully well for you to afford all this. Your place is seriously cool.'

I meant it. I thought my new lifestyle could be a passport to meeting some unusual guys, but this was way beyond my expectations.

'Oh, that was a very satisfactory outcome from someone's misfortune,' he said nonchalantly, pointing to the Magritte. 'I'm in the process of setting up an art gallery, selling exclusive, upmarket stuff to the well-heeled Scottish gentry. And one of my prospective clients fell on hard times and needed someone to take it off his hands in a hurry. I got it at a knock-down price.'

'Art gallery? What a coincidence. I'm the assistant manager at The Third Eye Centre when I'm not acting.'

I saw Michael's eyes narrowing as he processed this piece of information. 'Interesting. Tom McGrath's place?

So you'd be a credible manager for my gallery? Might be something to talk about one day.'

I wasn't sure what he meant by 'credible manager', but I nodded anyway. Didn't want to burn any bridges.

We lay in bed afterwards, the waterbed still gently swaying after our exertions.

'Michael, did you really send me a note with the rose yesterday?' I asked. 'And were you really parked outside Tiffany's because you said to meet you there? It wasn't that one of the managers called you to tell you I was asking after you, was it?'

'Hush, hush, what a lot of questions,' he replied. 'What you've got to ask yourself, Roberta, is are you glad you're here now? I know I am, and I promise it won't be so long until we see each other again. It was silly of me not to give you my phone number before. Let me give it to you right now so we won't have any more misunderstandings.'

We spent the weekend making love. John the driver took me back to my flat early Monday morning so I could get changed in time for work. I walked into my little hovel and smiled to myself. Talk about a clash of two worlds. A Magritte would look good on the wall here, maybe even a Picasso. Good for hiding the damp stain if nothing else.

It had only been forty minutes since I'd said goodbye to Michael but I already wanted to see him again. What was going on? It didn't count as a relationship, I reasoned to myself. It was the same as a one-night stand, except it was a one-night stand over and again with the same person. There was no danger of having any responsibilities for love. I could see why the Magritte painting was in pride of place in his house. The dapper, immaculate businessman without a flicker of emotion inside. That was him exactly. Cool, aloof, but fascinating. I loved him all right, the same way as a moth loves a flame.

Radio silence again. Three days in a row and not a peep out of him. No way was I calling him so early in the relationship, that broke the *Cosmo* rules. I started to get angry and then the red rose turned up again. This time with a note.

'Pack for the weekend,' it said, 'we are going to the country.' Now I could teach him. I couldn't drop everything just to be with him. Duncan had landed a major assignment for one of the music papers and we'd arranged to meet for a curry lunch to celebrate, a rare encounter between me and the gormless Kathleen. She was still hanging around, so I figured I might need to try to develop a rapport with her. And as the genius who had nudged Duncan in the direction of a career in journalism, I wanted to be there to toast his success.

I phoned Michael to tell him no-can-do and maybe if he communicated with me more we could avoid this sort of thing happening in future. I sensed our first row was in the offing. I dialled his number. A man answered the phone, very cagily. Deep gravelly voice, clipped delivery. That was the first evidence I had that there was ever anyone else in the house other than the mysterious provider of breakfasts.

After a short pause Michael came to the phone. 'Roberta, so nice to hear from you. Did you get my message this time?'

And another thing. A little small talk would be nice to start a conversation. 'Yes, I did, Michael. It sounds lovely but I've already made other plans for lunch on Saturday. Maybe we could meet in Glasgow instead?'

'Ah, not really. I'm meeting with some important business associates at Turnberry in Ayrshire. The big five-star hotel and golf course where they hold the Open Golf Championship, you might have heard of it. They're bringing their girlfriends and I thought it would be nice if you came too. Such a shame you can't make it. Another time perhaps.'

He didn't seem bothered at all. In fact, it was me that was bothered. It sounded pretty cool, what I'd be missing. But I was determined not to show it.

'Anyway, I'd be a liability, Michael,' I replied. 'Crazy Golf at the seaside is about the limit of my abilities.'

He laughed. I liked it when he laughed. It was like I'd achieved a victory; I'd painted a comic smile on one of the Magritte businessmen.

'I'm not a golfer either,' he replied. 'The plan was to meet the others for dinner on Friday night and stay in the Ailsa Craig suite all day on the Saturday, the best room in the hotel, while the others play golf. Then a little business discussion before dinner and John would take you back to Glasgow on Sunday afternoon.'

'You're not coming back too?'

'No, another business trip, I'm afraid. Flying off to Switzerland Sunday afternoon, I'll be gone all week. Oh well.'

I so wanted to see him. The thought of being pampered all weekend in five-star luxury was very appealing. A round of golf takes ages and I imagined what we could get up to in that time. Delicious.

And another thing. I had got nothing out of him about what his business actually was. No way could he live that lifestyle on the back of a travel agency and two estate agents. And why does a guy running Glasgow shops have to go off to Switzerland all week for a business meeting? Seeing him in action could give me some answers.

He sensed my hesitation. 'Such a shame you made other plans. Are you sure you can't move what you've got on?'

Duncan would understand. It was only a curry. But I wasn't going to give in so easily.

'Okay, Michael, I'll see what I can do. But you can't do this again, you hear? You can't not talk to me all week and then expect me to drop everything for you at short notice. Just so we're clear.'

Duncan was more put out at me cancelling our lunch than I'd anticipated. Apparently it had been a big deal getting Kathleen to agree to me coming along to share in his success, but I managed to mollify him eventually. A mid-week curry with me picking up the bill was agreed to be suitable penance for my bad behaviour. I decided to splash out on Michael as well. I bought the flimsiest, sexiest negligée I could find for my first ever dirty weekend.

We arrived at Turnberry and I finally met people from Michael's world. Ron, his operations director, was the sort of person who, when he walked into a room, it felt five degrees colder. It was his voice I'd heard on the phone. Hair plastered with so much Brylcreem I bet he left an oil slick behind every time he had a bath. There was someone who Michael called his compliance manager, whatever that was, who went by the distinctly unbusinesslike name of 'Big Jockie' and who also dealt with, ahem, company security issues. He was more than a little disconcerting, his elephantine bulk filling the room. And then there was the finance guy, only ever referred to as Mr Jenkins, who had a bulging lever arch file of ledgers under his arm he never let go off for even a second. The odd man of the bunch, he looked as if he would be more at home pottering in his garden shed than mixing with that cabal of characters.

They had a brief huddle out of earshot from me before Michael and I were shown to our room. I'd never seen such opulence; it made Michael's place in Rutherglen look like a Barratt starter home. Velvet flock wallpaper, deep pile carpets, even a blooming chandelier, and it had its own living room and study as well as bedroom and bathroom. And what a bathroom. Floor to ceiling mirrors, a sunken bath for two with jets on the side that squirted water at you. Jacuzzi, I think Michael called it. Gosh.

The two businessmen Michael was meeting were cold fish in the extreme. Eddie from London, as skinny as an anorexic ferret, and Dick, a Brit who'd moved to Spain a few years ago, mahogany tan and dripping in gold chains. Steady Eddie and Dick Dastardly I called them. 'Taciturn' was probably the best way to describe their inter-personal skills. I could see why their girls had been brought along, to lighten the atmosphere. Groomed to within an inch of their lives, they looked as if they could take an eye out with their nails and had beehive hairstyles as rigid as candyfloss, hair piled so high they probably had to duck to come into a room. Two perfect Barbie Dolls, sharing a brain cell between them, gossiping away in breathy baby voices like a pair of cockney Marylyn Monroes.

It was tough competition, but Michael was the alpha male in the room. I felt a curious pride that I had the man with the power, the one everyone respected. And I loved how Michael played with that aura, dominating the dinner with his charisma and then pretending to be submissive with me when we had sex afterwards, making his task to pleasure me, to be my slave. And to finish he would turn the tables on me and make me beg for sex, to worship him. Yes, it was some trip.

And telegrams arrived every day from him while he was in Switzerland. He'd learnt his lesson. Silly little jokes, sly references to our weekend, hints on what he was planning for me next. Goodness knows what the postman must have thought. Actually, I loved it that the postie knew, it made it feel even more decadent.

★ ★ ★

We had been going out together for just over four weeks when I told Michael about the casting couch incident with Frank Fontane over dinner one night. I thought he'd enjoy the story, a risqué anecdote that showed I didn't put out for just anybody. Instead there was that look in his eyes again.

'Nobody should be allowed to behave like that to you, Roberta. I'll have a quiet word with him, give him a ticking-off and ask him to apologise. His behaviour was very… inappropriate.'

I was horrified. 'Oh no, Michael, please don't. That's the way it works in my business. I don't want to upset someone like Frank Fontane. It would do my career no end of harm. Please, Michael, don't say anything.'

I didn't ask him how he could just call up Frank Fontane 'to have a quiet word'. Probably best not to know.

'Don't you worry, I won't upset him if you don't want me to.' He gave me a big smile to reassure me. I wished he wouldn't do that, it made me think of Shere Khan talking to Mowgli in the *Jungle Book* movie. 'And to lighten the mood, I've got something for you. To celebrate our one-month anniversary.'

He produced a diamond necklace with a big ruby as its centrepiece. I gasped in disbelief. 'You are joking, aren't you?' I said. 'I mean, get me a new Snoopy doll if you want to give me a present. I can't take something like this.'

'Relax. It's just something left over from a business deal. One of my business partners had a little liquidity problem and gave me this to settle some debts. It would have been too… problematic to dispose of it and I think it will look good on you. Please keep it.'

'It's not me, Michael. And whoever it belonged to before will have hated to have parted with it. It doesn't seem right to wear something with a sad history.'

'Look out the window, Roberta.' We were in a penthouse restaurant overlooking the city centre. 'All of these dots of lights out there are people, in their houses, in their cars. Do they mean anything to you?' He pointed out the window. 'Would you give this necklace to that dot of light there if you knew it would help their problems? Or even give them the cost of this meal? Of course not.

Morals and scruples are all very well, but they never put food on the table. And we've got expensive tastes.'

He raised his glass in a kind of toast. I knew in that moment he was the absolute opposite of everything I stood for. That's when I should have ended it. But I didn't.

Because two days later Frank Fontane called. Yes, personally. 'I've got good news, Bobbie,' he said. 'I've decided to reconsider you for that part in my movie. Principal photography starts in January and if you can still make it, the part is yours. And, I promise you, no strings attached.'

It was not a coincidence of course. Yes, I was excited to get the part but I was also appalled by what Michael must have said or done to have made it happen. I blurted out a yes, I think, but my mind was in turmoil. I needed Duncan.

Somewhat unbelievably, he found the whole thing thrilling. 'Wow. I mean, this is something straight out of *The Godfather*. This Michael guy is a gangster and he gets you a part in a movie? Hats off to you, Bobbie, you said you want to explore the dark side but this is something else.'

We were in a noisy pub, but I still lowered my voice to keep from being overheard. 'I don't understand you, Duncan. This guy is a criminal, I'm sure of it. And if I go along with him, that makes me a criminal too. How can you say that's okay?'

'Look, what have you done? Slept with a guy and he's tried to help you out. How do you know he's a criminal? He could have offered to finance part of the movie. I mean, have you any proof that Michael's done anything illegal?'

'Not really, I suppose. At first I thought he was just a bit weird, someone who belonged to secret societies with funny handshakes who sacrifice goats, that sort of thing. But over the last few weeks I've started to notice the people he hangs out with. There's this guy, Big Jockie, they call him. Built like a barn and follows Michael everywhere. He's obviously a bodyguard and I'm sure I've seen a bulge under his jacket. Why would someone who runs a travel agents need a bodyguard, tell me that?' Big Jockie is always talking to Michael about 'smurfs' and I don't think he's the sort of guy who spends his time reading obscure Belgian comics.'

'There's only one thing for it. You either tell Lex Luther thanks and goodbye or you get him to sit down and tell you the truth about what he does and see if you believe him. But in the meantime, don't look a gift horse in the mouth. Here's to your first movie role.' He lifted his pint in a toast. 'First of many, Bobbie. Well done.'

I called Michael the next day. 'I've got good news, Michael, and I think you know what it is,' I said. 'I can't thank you enough.'

'I've no idea what you're talking about, Roberta. But if you've had good news, I'm happy for you.'

'You know fine well what it is. Fontane called and offered me the part in the movie. Can I come over tomorrow to see you? I'm in a good mood and I'd like to show you how good a mood.'

'How can I resist? Come over at eight, I'll cook us supper. You can tell me all about it.'

That was the part of Michael I was attracted to, I thought, as he bustled about the kitchen making us an Omelette Arnold Bennett. He loved to cook, he told me, said it relaxed him. Ninety per cent of the time he was a cold, detached stuffed-shirt, whose values and outlook on life were anathema to me. But occasionally I saw another side of him, like when we took the dogs for a walk and he would laugh at their antics, or when he sat in a trance listening to his opera in the evening. Then I saw a Michael that was warm and human. Maybe it was my challenge to thaw him out, and when I did and saw glimpses of the other Michael, I felt I was getting a sneak peek of someone he struggled to keep secret.

He popped the omelette under the grill to toast the cheese and poured me a glass of wine. Not for him, of course, just a sparkling water as usual. 'You got the part in the movie, Roberta? Congratulations. Well deserved.'

'It might be well deserved, Michael, but you and I both know I didn't get it off my own bat. They'd already cast someone else for the part and it was a bit suspicious Fontane changed his mind after I told you about him. I need to know, Michael, what did you say to him?'

He took the omelette out from under the grill and left it to settle. 'I can make inconvenient things happen to people who bother me, Roberta. Fontane was out of order in his behaviour and he needed someone to point that out to him.'

I went to ask him who he was really, what did he do, just as Duncan told me to. But something held me back. I was living in a fantasy world and didn't want it to end. It can wait for another day, I decided. In the end, I chatted about safer things, the big show opening tomorrow at The Third Eye Centre, my plans for Granny Campbell's birthday party at the end of the month.

Anything, everything, other than the world I was being drawn into.

chapter ten

It was unusually bright the next morning. I turned groggily to squint at the alarm clock by Michael's bed. It had been a marathon sex session last night and I'd not got much sleep. To my horror, I saw it was eight thirty. I was supposed to be at The Third Eye Centre at eight and it would take about an hour to get there.

'Michael, the alarm hasn't gone off!' I cried. 'Shit, Tom will kill me. I had to be in early for the show today. What happened to the alarm? Shit, shit, shit.'

Michael sat up. I was already out of bed, gathering up my clothes strewn around the floor, hopping on one leg as I tried to get my tights on. 'Oh no, Roberta, how could that've happened? You saw me set the alarm for six for you to get to work early. Are you in trouble?'

'Big trouble. Can you get John to give me a lift straight away? I'm really late. And can I call Tom to let him know? Oh God, he's going to be furious.'

Tom McGrath was not impressed. Of all the days for the alarm not to go off it had to be the one when I was most needed for a show. I ran down the stairs. Michael was already on the phone to his driver, calm and assured as usual. By the time I was at the front door the car was there waiting for me.

There was a frosty atmosphere at work all day. It was a side to Tom I'd not seen before; he didn't seem very forgiving about a mistake that could have happened to anyone. It probably didn't help he saw me turning up in the limo, John jumping out to open the door for me. The reason I was late was that I'd been in bed with a rich running dog of capitalism, which was probably as heinous a crime in his book as having to hold up the show opening for two hours.

For the first time since I started working for him, I was glad to see the back of Tom as we closed for the night. I tried apologising again, but it was obvious I was not forgiven. I knew I was in the wrong but there was no need for him to keep sulking about it.

Michael agreed with me. I told him about it when we met again, two days later. Unprofessional behaviour, he described it as. Probably due to the fact that McGrath was under a lot of pressure at the moment, he said. The word on the street was that The Third Eye Centre was struggling.

'I've not heard that,' I replied. 'In fact, we seem to be getting busier all the time. Are you sure?'

'I can only tell you what I've heard. Actually, now is as good a time as any to tell you about my latest business venture. Have I mentioned my new art gallery, the Avalon?

'You mentioned something about it when we first met. What is it?'

'A high-quality art gallery selling top-end nineteenth-century Scottish art. The Glasgow Boys, Henry Raeburn, that sort of thing. London has traditional galleries like this in Mayfair and Old Bond Street, but we've got nothing like it in Scotland. What do you think?'

'Gosh. A bit different from The Third Eye Centre. Very adventurous, Michael.'

'I'd like you to be the gallery manager. What do you say?'

'Oh, Michael, I couldn't do that,' I blurted out. 'I'm not qualified.'

But he knows that, I thought. Something was not right.

'Nonsense. You're an assistant manager at the moment. I've had someone choose the six paintings we open with, and he'll help you choose any new ones we buy. I'm talking about you running the most prestigious art gallery in Scotland. Only showing the best of the best. A big step up from working at The Third Eye Centre, but a natural progression.' I could see him warming to his theme. 'No worries about working for a struggling gallery. Not having to deal with a moody boss. A salary increase, enough for you to start living comfortably at last. Your parents proud of you. Especially your dad.'

He was right about that. Even my dad couldn't say the Glasgow Boys were a load of old rubbish.

'But I only took the job at The Third Eye Centre so I'd have time for acting. That's what I really want to do, Michael, that's why I work there.'

'You'll have all the time you need for your acting career, you can even close the gallery for the day for an audition or to go to rehearsals. And think of the contacts you can make at exhibition openings and the like.'

I took a deep breath. 'Michael, don't take this the wrong way.' I plucked up the courage to ask the question that had been haunting me since the first moment we met. 'Is your business completely legit?'

'What a question,' he laughed. 'I don't know what you've been imagining but you don't need to worry. I want you to run my art gallery, that's all. Organise the hangings, chat to whoever comes in to have a look. Be a real curator, make the artistic decisions. You'll be a legitimate employee, pay your taxes. The books will show the business being a bit more successful than it is in reality, that's the only thing, because it's tax efficient to divert part of my overall income stream through a start-up company. But that's normal practice. What do you say?'

'I'm not sure. The job sounds too good to be true. And I'm worried about this "income stream" thing you mentioned.'

'Well, you shouldn't be. Do you think the girls at the travel agency are criminals? Or the receptionist at the estate agents? Of course not.'

He caught the look in my eye that showed I was tempted. There was a little smile of victory.

He delivered his final *coup de grâce*. 'And when the acting becomes full time, you can help me find your replacement and, puff, off you go. To be a star. Just think about it.' He took a sip of his mineral water and raised his glass, as if to acknowledge I'd said yes. He already knew he'd won.

I promised to think about it. I went back to my flat and as I lay in bed that night, I kept staring at the ceiling, thinking to myself, over and over again, even if Michael is a crook, would running his art gallery make me a criminal too? There was definitely something dodgy about him and the story about the gallery making more money than it actually was, that sounded too slick and suspicious.

But it was perfect for my acting. And it would seriously impress my dad.

In the night I heard a dog barking. It set off a bunch of others roaming the streets, the price you had to pay for living in a down-at-heel part of Glasgow. They kept me awake; I couldn't stop thinking about what I was going to do. I would only be doing what any actress would surely do to make it in the business, in order to get the breaks that would start a career. I was sure they all had done something in their past they were not proud of, whether it was telling a few white lies about their experience, or stabbing a fellow actress in the back, or, yes, being more than a little accommodating to a casting director, But that didn't make it any easier.

I knew saying yes was wrong, but I also knew that was exactly what I was going to do.

That's what I told Duncan anyway, when I shared my concerns the next day. That although the art gallery was a completely legit business it might be connected to Michael's shady dealings. 'But even if it is,' I said, with as much conviction as I could muster, 'it's nothing to do with me.'

'As you say, it ticks all the boxes as far as what you're looking for at the moment,' he replied. 'But I'm not sure this is completely a smart move. It's one thing to be a gangster's moll for a wee while, but it's another to go on the flipping payroll. I'd make it absolutely clear to him you don't want to be caught up in any funny business. I suppose if all you're doing is running a shop, you can't get into trouble. But if you do, I promise I'll come and visit every week. You'll look good in stripes.'

'You're not taking this seriously,' I said, shaking my

head. It was true. Normally I loved Duncan's humour, but it was a time to be sensible 'I think I should do it. Michael's as slippery as a Teflon snake, I can't imagine him coming to any harm. And there are more noises from all sorts of directors about other acting opportunities I could be considered for after the movie shoot is over. That's all down to him as well, I'm sure. But if I say no, I think it'll work the other way. He'll make sure nobody in the arts scene touches me with a barge pole.'

'I still can't believe you're making a movie,' said Duncan. 'That's seriously cool. The highlight of my day is passing a shorthand test. This journalism gig isn't as glamorous as I thought it would be. All I've got that's permanent is my weekly column on what's happening in the Falkirk music scene for the *East Stirlingshire Gazette*. It takes a bit of imagination to fill it, let me tell you.'

'We've all got to start somewhere. And remember, my super-glamorous movie part is hanging around a film set in East Kilbride for a week to say about twenty lines.'

I tried to downplay my fascination with Michael, but Duncan saw through that straight away. 'The devil has the best tunes, Bobbie,' he said. 'But hey, maybe I'm the one being too cautious. Taking a walk on the wild side sounds pretty good to me. And besides, I'm looking forward to hearing the juicy gossip.'

I told Tom I was quitting a few days later. I felt more than a bit shabby about it, after all the help he'd given me, but he was pretty relaxed about me going. 'The place won't collapse without you, Bobbie, despite what you might think,' he said. But he was more concerned when I told him I was leaving to run the Avalon Gallery.

'I've heard about that place,' he said to me. 'I'm not sure it's going to be a success, Bobbie. They're going to stock a lot of stuff people in Scotland can't afford to buy. But if anyone can make a success of it, you can. I'll be watching out for you.'

I thanked him for that. Still felt a bit of a heel, though.

Michael took me to see the gallery the week before it opened. A small basement in Bath Street, but very tastefully decorated. The walls painted in strong dark colours to show off the paintings to their full glory. Six stunning pieces of Scottish art, a spotlight on each one making them leap out at you in the subdued lighting. A solid antique desk and leather chair against one wall, for me, the gallery manager. My own little empire. Thrilling.

The day before the opening I went shopping. Michael had decided I needed to look the part of a glam gallery owner and had given me a clothing allowance with the instruction it was only to be spent in the upmarket boutiques in town. A Jackie Kennedy wardrobe was the brief, Yves St Laurent, Chanel, that sort of stuff. It was horrifically expensive, but if someone else was paying, who was I to complain? A couple of outfits later, I headed back to the flat to get ready to meet him. I put on the Coco Chanel outfit to surprise him.

It was me that was surprised. Shocked would be a better word.

'Who's Duncan Jones?' he said. Very direct, no pleasantries and with not a single word about my outfit.

'Duncan? He's a friend.' I replied. 'How do you know him?'

He placed some photos on the table. Duncan and me, from our coffee yesterday. Just yesterday and he had photos already. 'You seem to be very close. Quite an intense conversation you were having.'

'What is this, Michael? Are you spying on me?'

'Please be calm, Roberta. There's one thing which is very important to me, and which I put a lot of effort into getting right, and that's security. Glasgow can be a mean city. Robbery, kidnapping, that sort of thing. Now you're starting working for me I've had someone keep an eye on you for your own protection.'

I backed away from him. 'This is too heavy, Michael. You're scaring me.'

'I'm sorry if these pictures startled you. One of my business associates is being a little... troublesome at the moment and I'm probably being more thorough in my surveillance than normal. I hope you'll forgive me. You look beautiful in that dress, by the way.'

'Michael, who exactly are your customers? Are we talking about murderers and armed robbers here?'

'Of course not. You've met Edward and Dick, the guys I'm talking to about expanding my businesses. They might look like a couple of rough diamonds, but that's just their way. They're not criminals by any stretch of the imagination. So, if you don't mind me asking, who is Duncan and what does he do?'

'I've known him since school. My best friend. And only my friend.'

He smiled. 'Good. I'm pleased to hear that. I'm so glad we've sorted out this misunderstanding. I've got no problem with you seeing Duncan, or any of your friends.

But I care about you, Roberta, and I want to make sure no one takes advantage of you.'

'Michael, I'm sorry, but I mean it. I don't want the job any more.'

Those steel eyes of his bored into me. 'Please don't overreact, Roberta. I think you know by now I like my world to be organised, maybe a little too organised perhaps. I'm the first to admit I probably overdo my security. Let's call it my foible.'

'So can I leave?'

'If you want to, of course.' There was no smile now. 'But McGrath's hired someone to take your place at The Third Eye Centre, hasn't he? Everything's ready for our opening tomorrow, you've got these wonderful clothes, I think I'd need to ask you to work your notice period at least. And those Scottish Arts people who are coming to the opening night party, do you want to tell them you're quitting on your first day? But of course, it's up to you.'

I bit my lip. 'I'm not sure, really I'm not, Michael.'

'Look, are we going to let one stupid little incident spoil everything we have together? Roberta, if I thought there was the slightest problem with you taking the job, I wouldn't want you to do it. If I say once more I'm sorry about the Duncan incident, will you at least consider staying on?'

I shouldn't have done it, but I said yes. Just until I make it as an actress, I promised myself. But one good thing about that little scare, it definitely stopped me from falling in love with Michael. I was in the relationship for thrills, for experiences, for the opportunities it opened up to me. And as long as I realised that, I wasn't being exploited; my heart would never be broken.

I was pleased I'd realised that when I lay talking in bed with Michael one night. We'd had some very tender lovemaking and Michael was doing a silky interrogation about my hopes and dreams, my life, my loves. I'd told him about Joe, the secret I'd mentioned the first night we met. 'He thought I loved him,' I said. 'But I think I'll never be in love, now that I've seen what the consequences can be.'

I could see he agreed. 'Love? Being in love is such an over-rated concept, all that opening up your heart to let someone come in and mess with it. And then your life isn't your own any more. No, if I want unconditional love, I've got Satan and Lucifer. And for anything else, I've got you.'

'So I'm just one of your little finches, am I? Tell me, is there anyone else in the gilded cage with me?'

He laughed. 'Touché, Roberta. I like that mind of yours behind your innocent face. Since you ask, some of my finches look beautiful, some sing beautifully and some have charming personalities. Which one I like most at any moment in time depends on the mood I'm in. Does that answer your question?'

'Just tell me I can fly away one day, Michael. If the cage gets too crowded or I want my freedom again. Until that day, I'll enjoy being your little finch. Your little Faustian finch.' I was pleased with my response. I bet he was expecting me to be angry and moody and ask him to tell me he loved me. If he wants to play it cool, then I can too.

The nights were now a master class in sex. We were working through the *Joy of Sex* from A to Z. Handcuffs,

119

blindfolds, whips, you name it. It was so funny when his business associates arrived at his place in the morning for meetings. He looked so straight-laced and businesslike when he met them. I always had a grin when I thought of what we'd been up to half an hour before.

The only thing I wasn't into with Michael was the pornography he made me watch with him, pretty hard-core stuff from Scandinavia. He had a home movie set up where we watched the films on a Super 8 projector. It was so tacky, and the acting was appalling. But I don't think the actors were recruited for their thespian abilities.

Apart from that, it was exciting, the dark, decadent new world I was finding myself in. Where sex wasn't just exciting, spontaneous fun, but was altogether more debauched and depraved. And to be that dark, it took planning and knowledge. Michael was leading me into a new world, a dissolute world, where the pursuit of sexual pleasure was taken to extremes. And I was adjusting fast, what would have shocked at first was almost normal a few weeks later. Duncan didn't get to hear about the details. There were some things that should stay private.

I had a different sort of shock after the first month of working in the gallery. It's surprising how busy you can be, working in an art gallery that doesn't actually sell any paintings. The chatting to whoever comes in, changing the paintings around, doing marketing and promotion and so on. It hadn't dawned on me none of it was making any sense. It was time for a rude awakening.

Mr Jenkins, the accountant came by on the last day of the month, clutching his briefcase like it contained the crown jewels. 'Nice to see you, Miss Sinclair,' he said. 'Would you mind putting the "gallery closed" sign up while we go through the month-end accounts?'

'Not at all. Shouldn't take long.' I'd been told to keep receipts for anything I'd bought for the gallery and I had them in my desk drawer. The princely sum of £22.46. I was not a leader of industry yet.

'Good. I've prepared the invoices for this month's transactions, I need your signature on them as the gallery manager. Just there, under the total amount.' He produced a sheaf of six invoices for paintings, each one of them for between two to three thousand pounds.

'What? We've not sold any paintings.' I looked at the invoices. 'I don't even know what these paintings are. I'm sorry, Mr Jenkins, I can't sign these.'

He looked flustered. 'This is most irregular, Miss Sinclair. Mr Mitchell assured me when you took the job he explained we would have an expanded cash flow through the business to mitigate his overall tax position and you said you were happy to go along with that. I need this paperwork to tie in with the accounts. It's a formality, but I do need you to sign them.'

I felt a wave of panic come over me. 'I need to speak to Michael about this. I'm sorry, but I'm not signing anything. I've got my receipts for you, £22.46. That's all I can sign for.'

'Oh dear. This is most unexpected.' Mr Jenkins took off his glasses, gave them a wipe and put them back on. 'I'll need to ask you to sort this out straight away. Mr Mitchell is very insistent the accounts are always completed in full and on time every month. I'll need to tell him it's you holding things up, I'm afraid. He will not be pleased, let me tell you.'

Michael came by an hour later, a determined look on his face. 'Roberta, Jenkins tells me you have a problem with the paperwork. Can we have a quiet word?'

I closed the shop. 'It's not a problem with paperwork, Michael. He wants me to lie on a tax return. Say I've sold paintings I've not even seen. I can't do that, Michael, that's not what I agreed to.'

'Yes it is, Roberta. I was very clear when I explained the job to you we would be accounting for additional revenue. You do remember us having that conversation, don't you?'

'Yes, I do, but I didn't realise you needed me to get this involved. You never explained that to me, Michael. Can't someone else sign the invoices?'

'It has to be you, Roberta. You are the gallery manager, it would be expected you would be the person to sign. But don't worry, all the paperwork ties together, that's what Jenkins is good at. If it makes you feel any better, I can tell you they were sales done directly with the purchasers away from the gallery. That's why you didn't see them.'

'I don't want to, Michael.'

'Then the gallery closes until we find another manager. I'm sorry, Roberta, but that's the harsh reality. Is that what you want? To tell your parents you were fired after a month? Lose all the contacts you made with Scottish Arts? Disappoint me? It's no problem, Roberta, I wouldn't ask you to do anything risky. Could you possibly imagine I'd ask that of you, of all people?'

'Are you sure I won't get into trouble?'

'Trust me, Roberta. Jenkins has given me the invoices. Just sign here.'

I signed. Michael wasn't leaving until I did and I needed to keep in his good books, at least until the movie shoot.

'There you are, Michael,' I said, handing them to him. 'But I'm really, really not happy about this.'

'I can tell. I'm sorry if it's upset you, Roberta, I should have made it clearer when I explained the job to you. But I'll make it up to you this weekend. Have you ever been deer stalking?'

'What? No, of course not.'

'Then let's go away for the weekend. I want you to put this unpleasant moment behind us. Let's have a very nice weekend, another experience for you to enjoy. It's the least I can do to make it up to you.'

'I'm not sure I'll be good company at the moment. I'm still in shock about these invoices.'

'Next weekend then. Look, close the gallery for the day, let's do something more low-key. Take the dogs for a walk, go for a meal afterwards. What do you say?'

He was so attentive to me that weekend. No expensive gifts, no elaborate entertainment, just enjoying each other. He conjured away my worries. I was a lot more calm and happy when I went to work on Monday, my bad feelings had gone away. After all, if the price I had to pay for all this was to sign a few dodgy invoices from time to time, that wasn't too bad, was it? Surely I couldn't get in that much trouble?

chapter eleven

The estate road to Glensporret House was like an obstacle course of potholes and even the inscrutable John the driver was becoming frustrated about how long it was taking to complete the last mile of our one-hundred-mile drive to the Speyside hunting lodge. We turned a corner and saw the building in front of us. I stepped out of the car, gave a big stretch and yawn, and looked at the surrounding countryside. Stunning. The lights from the lodge looked inviting as the afternoon gloom started drifting into the darkness of a long winter night.

The lodge was like stepping back to another time. The walls were festooned with stags' heads, their multi-pointed antlers testament to their long-deceased magnificence. Craggy gillies in weathered tweed jackets and plus-fours were purposefully organising the next day's stalk. Corpulent English businessmen smoked fat cigars, aquiline Scottish gentry sipped rare single malts. Fresh-faced Highland lassies in virginally-white long dresses served the meals. I'd never seen anything like it.

But the thing I remember most from the weekend was the moment of the kill. We tracked the deer for an hour, its quiet dignity as it walked across the heather making me more and more apprehensive. I was willing the poor animal to make a run for it, even at one point kicking over a rock to try to alert him, to the glares of Michael and the gillie.

Michael and I lay next to each other, face down on a large rocky knoll, less than a hundred yards from where the stag was standing, alert. It gave a twitch of nervousness from an ancient, primeval instinct that it was in danger.

Michael pulled me over to look down the barrel. 'Line up the two sights,' he whispered. 'And put your finger on the trigger to steady the gun.'

I went to protest that I couldn't kill something so beautiful but I stayed silent as the drama of the moment overwhelmed me. The deer was in target for a second, then it drifted out again. I could hardly breathe.

'Keep steady, don't move,' Michael said, even more softly. 'Say when you have it between the sights.' He slid his finger over mine on the trigger.

'Now,' I said, as I saw the brown mass of the deer move into target.

Michael squeezed down on my finger. There was a loud *crack* sound. The rifle pushed back into me.

For an instant I felt a flood of relief that I'd missed; in a split second the stag would burst into action and escape over the distant horizon. But then I saw its legs buckle, and the beautiful, innocent animal crumpled on to its side. We walked over, stood about ten feet away. Blood-specked saliva frothed from its mouth, its eyes bulged with fear and panic. A second shot from the gillie and it was dead.

Dead because of me. The phrase from Joe's funeral came back to haunt me once more. But this time I'd had my finger on the trigger.

That was the moment I died a moral death. That was the moment Michael knew he had conquered me. I felt like I'd passed a devilish initiation rite and was now immersed in his world.

I needed once and for all to know what that world was.

'Let's not eat in the dining room,' I said when we got back to the lodge. 'Have something in our room instead. I don't feel like facing people this evening.'

After the room-service waiter left, I took a big sip of my wine. 'Michael, if we're to continue seeing each other, I need to know what you do for a living. Really do, I mean.'

I steeled myself for his reaction.

'I was wondering why it took you so long,' he smiled. Shere Khan again. 'Come on, let's enjoy our supper and I'll tell you all about me.'

We sat down at the dining table. I didn't touch my food.

'The first thing you need to know is I'm not a criminal,' said Michael. 'I don't rob anyone, I don't harm anyone. All I do is provide financial services to some people who, for whatever reason, have activities that operate outside of the normal banking systems.'

'I don't understand. What sort of services?'

'I take someone's money, money that perhaps they've made a little... creatively, shall we say, and make it disappear for a while. And when it comes back, it is nice and respectable. Stocks and bonds, Treasury bills, certificates of deposit and the like, which my clients are free to spend as they like.' He gave a nonchalant shrug, as if what he was describing was the most reasonable thing in the world.

I frowned. 'But that's money laundering, isn't it? It's against the law.'

Another shrug. 'Technically it might be, I suppose. But whatever my clients do to make their money is no concern of mine. And it would still carry on if I wasn't there. I just provide a service. I don't get mixed up in any unpleasant business.'

I shook my head. 'I'm sorry, Michael, that sounds too smooth. How does this make you any less of a criminal than the thugs who do the dirty work to get the money?'

He leaned forward and looked me in the eye. Confident, self-assured, he had complete belief that what he was doing could be justified to me.

'I think you're missing the point. All I do is run a financial process that I sell to clients. Just like any other service business does. Is that so bad?'

I took another large sip of wine to steady my nerves. 'But it's illegal,' I persisted. 'If you get caught, you go to jail. And so do the people around you. Me, for example.'

'You're not eating the meal you ordered, Roberta.'

'Sorry,' I replied, dutifully taking a mouthful.

'Let me tell you a few of life's realities,' he said. 'They passed a law in America a few years ago. The Bank Secrecy Act, making banks responsible for reporting large cash transactions, to keep records to show the authorities. Do you know what law we have like that here? No? Because we have nothing like that.' He shook his head in disbelief. 'You can walk into a bank with a suitcase full of cash, and they'll be delighted for your business, no questions asked.

And you know why? It's the establishment protecting itself. Politicians and coppers getting kickbacks. Businessmen not paying their taxes. Everyone's at it, Roberta. I'm just better at it than most people.'

I ate a few mouthfuls while I thought about that. 'But if it's that easy, that commonplace, why doesn't everyone else do it?' I eventually said. 'How can you afford all this, doing something that simple?'

'Because it's only simple when it's small potatoes. Take the suitcase of cash I mentioned. That only works when it's not very often, or not very much. So, yes, a petty criminal can pay his ill-gotten gains into a secret bank account and hope he'll get away with it. But when the police come looking, he'll stand out like a sore thumb.'

'How do you do it?'

A flicker of the Shere Khan smile again. 'A three-stage process. Placement, layering and integration. Placement is where I take the cash and split it into smaller, more discreet amounts, and I have people to pay it into bank accounts in dribs and drabs to avoid suspicion. I call them "smurfs". Then layering, when I send the money abroad, consolidate it into Swiss bank accounts, making sure it becomes unconnected to the smurf money. Then integration, when the money comes back to my clients. It's now inside the banking system, clean as a whistle, and can be paid into any bank account my client asks for.' He leant back in his chair and held his hands out, like an open book.

I felt my skin prickle. 'Michael, why are you telling me this? Aren't you afraid I'll tell someone and you'll be found out?'

128

As soon as I said that I panicked, but he was calm, relaxed, as if he didn't have a care in the world.

'That would be unfortunate if you did, Roberta, very unfortunate. Do you remember the first time we met, I said telling each other our secrets would bind us together? You told me your secrets a long time ago, and now I'm telling you mine. Because after today, when you let me help you to pull the trigger to kill that animal, I knew I would never have to worry about you betraying me. I know I can trust you.' That smile again, to show just how ridiculous the thought was I would betray him. Then the smile vanished.

'Now let me tell you the last piece of information you need to know about my business. It's growing, and growing fast. And smurfing is very labour intensive, and a lot of trouble when some of the smurfs misbehave. That's why I have Big Jockie around. He has a quiet word with any smurfs he finds have been shooting their mouths off, or if we find they've "misplaced" some of the money they've been given.'

I took a nervous gulp of wine. He topped up my glass and went on. 'That's why I've got the travel agent, estate agent and art gallery businesses. People like to pay for holidays, pay their rent and buy art with cash. Especially expensive works of art, funnily enough. Another way for the less scrupulous members of society to use their extra income. Over the next twelve to eighteen months, all the placement stage is going to be through these businesses and some more I'm setting up with Edward and Dick, the guys you met at Turnberry. My clients' money will be blended in with the real takings. But in order for it to work they have to act like real, credible businesses.'

'And that's what the money was, the invoices I signed?'

'Yes, it was. But it's not something you ever need to worry about. As far as the outside world is concerned, you bring experience and glamour to Scotland's top independent art gallery. You'll never see or be involved in any other aspect of my business.'

'Will you let me get out of this, Michael, as you promised? When I make it as an actress I can quit as your money launderer? Or even if I don't, I can still get out?'

'Of course. As we discussed before, our objectives at this moment are happily coinciding. The day you want to stop, when you don't need any more help in becoming an actress, when you feel you want to go it alone in the world, then of course you can go.'

It was what I wanted him to say, but also it wasn't. I didn't want to hear our relationship described as a cynical partnership of mutual self-interest. I realised for the first time I wanted him to love me. My biggest fear was not the world I'd been drawn into, it was that one day he would tire of me and move on to his next conquest.

It was a few days later I realised I was being silly. Michael did want me but being Michael he always had to dress it up in business-speak rather than show his true feelings. 'I'm concerned about your flat, Roberta,' he said. 'My driver tells me it's in a rough part of Maryhill and I worry about you living there on your own. By a piece of good fortune I seemed to have acquired a little flat in Kelvinside, ended up with it as part of a barter arrangement in a property deal I was involved in, another of my accountant's brainwaves. It's empty, and it seems silly you're paying rent for somewhere else. Would you do me a favour and at least have a look at it, see if you'd like to stay there, until we can get it off the books? I'm sure you'll like it.'

Like it? It was wonderful. First floor of a traditional tenement building, but there was nothing traditional about the inside. The lounge, blood-red fitted carpets and the most amazing psychedelic wallpaper. The bedroom feminine rather than sexy, contrasting Laura Ashley wallpaper and fabrics. A stunning avocado bathroom suite, very stylish.

Michael sorted things out with my landlord. I was supposed to give him three months' notice but Michael spoke to him and he said it was okay for me to move out immediately. Another of his 'quiet words', I suppose.

I moved in two weeks later, just before Christmas. My first visitor was, of course, Duncan. No need for him to hump boxes up and down stairs, Michael paid for a removal van so I had everything unpacked before he arrived. I hadn't told him what to expect. I was looking forward to seeing the look on his face when he walked in.

He was surprised all right, but not in a good way. 'Bobbie, I think you need to put a check on this Michael stuff,' he said, after a long pause. 'First a job, then the clothes and now this place. It doesn't smell right, no one's that generous. This was fun for you at first, but you seem to be getting sucked into a world that isn't you. I think maybe it's time to take a step back.'

That hurt. 'I'm surprised at you, Duncan. Wasn't it you who told me to take a walk on the wild side? I'm still the same Bobbie, nice to animals and small children. Only now I've got a generous boyfriend.'

'What happened to the "bonk a different guy every day of the week to avoid commitment" strategy? That seems to have gone out of the window.'

'No, nothing has changed. It might not look it, but this isn't a love affair. Michael isn't capable of love, as you and I know it. All I'm doing is going along for the ride and using him and his connections to establish myself as an actress before he gets tired of me and moves on to the next dolly bird. As long as I'm going into it with my eyes open, he's not taking advantage of me.' I was trying to convince myself as much as Duncan.

'If you say so, Bobbie, but watch yourself. And just so I know, are you actually working for a living with this job he's given you?'

'Yes, sort of. I re-arrange the paintings every couple of days, do a bit of marketing and pitch the art to anybody who comes in. Everything apart from actually selling anything. Actually, I almost sold one on Tuesday, still waiting to hear if the guy wants to buy it. So yes, I am working for a living.'

'And no dodgy stuff?'

'No, not at all. The only two guys from Michael's company I see are Mr Jenkins, a weedy accountant who comes around to do the books. Nervous bloke, fiddles with his glasses a lot, had a charisma bypass as a child. And Charlie, who I think was one of Michael's gophers. He used to come round every day, to check up on me for Michael, I presumed. With so few customers, his visit was the highlight of the day. We used to close up shop and nip out for a coffee together. He was actually quite dishy. But he's stopped coming, unfortunately.'

'Why's that?'

'He quit. Saw him on the Tuesday and then Wednesday, poof, he was gone. All very sudden, but I suppose job security's non-existent in Michael's line of business. So now I've got Mr Jenkins popping in more often instead, which is a bit of a bummer. And can't get a dickey-bird out of him as to how I can get in touch with Charlie to wish him well. Although it was rude of him, not telling me he was quitting.'

'Well, be careful. Make sure you don't get drawn in too deep.'

Of course I agreed with him, but the truth was I was getting more and more involved. The Saturday before Christmas, we went to Scottish Theatre's Gala Ball, black tie and posh frock, where Michael was fêted by one and all because of his track record of generous donations. I lost count of how many people who promised me great parts in just about every play being performed north of the border.

And working in the gallery was a doddle. Most of my days were spent reading, chatting to any friends who popped by and putting the 'Gallery Closed' sign up any time I needed to disappear for an acting audition. Mum and Dad came to visit and left very impressed. I secretly punched the air as Dad said it wasn't the career he would have chosen for me but it seemed I was making a go of it.

It was a great Christmas. I swapped presents with Michael on Christmas Eve. He got me a new Snoopy doll, served me right for being so sanctimonious when he bought me the necklace. I bought him a hardback book for his library, Mario Puzo, *The Godfather*. Michael claimed never to have read it, claimed it was too violent for his tastes. The only downer was that he declined my offer of Christmas lunch, said he had other plans. Maybe just as well, I wasn't really ready to introduce him to my folks. I even managed to get through the whole day without one word of criticism from Dad. It helped I looked a million dollars, wearing the pink Chanel dress and Michael's necklace. 'Found it in Paddy's Market,' I told Mum. She was very impressed, said you almost couldn't tell it from the real thing.

After I'd done the washing up I sneaked out and called Michael from the phone box to wish him Merry Christmas. We chatted till the pips went.

I spent New Year's Eve with Michael, just the two of us. A quiet night in, lying in bed, drinking Krug and eating steak pie and black bun, watching Andy Stewart on TV present the *White Heather Hogmanay Show* with Kenneth McKellar and Sydney Devine, giggling at the kitsch entertainment.

We kissed each other at the bells, welcoming in 1976. I felt full of excitement, full of optimism. It was going to be the best year of my life. I would finally achieve my dreams.

1976

chapter twelve

The movie *Emmanuelle* was showing again at the Glasgow Odeon and Michael and I went to see it. It was good to be watching something with a semblance of a plot and less explicit than the Super 8 porn. Michael liked Emmanuelle's adventures. In fact, he suggested one a few days later.

'Remember the scene where Mario talks the Thai boxers into fighting each other for the right to have sex with Emmanuelle while he watches? I'd like you to let me watch you doing that, screwing another guy.' Like all of Michael's suggestions, it was more command than request.

I played along with his fantasy. 'Oh yeah? Who do you have in mind? There are a couple of cute guys on your staff who I wouldn't say no to. Just as long as I'm not going to get crushed under Big Jockie.'

'No one we know. Definitely no one who works for me. They'd see it as a weakness, not an adventure. It would have to be a stranger.'

'So you're pimping me out now, Michael,' I teased.

'No, I want a performance. You say you're an actress. This would be the ultimate challenge. I would choose someone who's a complete nobody, someone who would never be in your league, and watch you seduce him.' He paused for a second, as a thought struck him. 'No, even better. I won't watch. I'll keep away so you have to tell me every little detail afterwards. Then you and I go to bed, so I can wipe his memory from your mind.'

Our game had suddenly turned serious. He meant it for real.

'Oh, no, no, no, Michael. You've taken me to some dark places recently, but I only go there with you. I'm not a whore who'll screw anyone you want.'

He realised he'd gone too far. 'You're quite right, Roberta,' he said. 'There are some things you shouldn't do if they make you feel uncomfortable. Let's keep it as our fantasy, okay?'

It was then things started to change. Suddenly Michael was 'oh so busy'. A week went by, no invites to meet up. He wasn't available all weekend, no explanation. I thought it must be business, but when it went into the second week I started to worry. With his libido the world would need to be falling down around him to go this long without sex. When I was eventually summoned to his flat it was such a relief, but summoned was the right way to describe it. A phone call at the gallery just before closing time, telling me to come round that evening. Curt, brusque even. None of Michael's usual charm.

Sex was different too. Mechanical, unimaginative, selfish. When we finished I turned away from him. I felt like crying. I willed myself to ask him what was wrong, to find out what was on his mind, to see if I could help. Instead, he spoke first as he got out of bed and started to dress.

'Glad you could make it at such short notice, Roberta. I have gallery business to discuss with you and thought it best to do so face-to-face. I hear congratulations are in order, that you've finally sold a painting.'

I looked at him carefully for any sign of sarcasm, any sign he was annoyed with me for taking so long to sell something. Whether that was why he was being so horrible to me. But that couldn't be the reason. We both knew the gallery was not about actually selling paintings.

'I'm sorry, boss, it won't happen again,' I said. He nodded in an offhand way. 'That's a joke, Michael,' I said more seriously. 'And it was no easy feat to sell a major painting like that. I hope you're proud of me.'

'Of course I am. The more we sell the better.' He smiled. Reassuring or patronising? I couldn't tell.

He walked towards the bedroom door. 'The painting we're going to replace it with is in the bird room. Come on, put your clothes on and have a look.'

'But, Michael, you said I could choose the new paintings. Or at least have a say. There's a Sotheby's auction in Edinburgh next week. I was hoping to go to it.'

'Hush, hush, I'm sure you'll like what I've chosen.'

It was dreadful. A pretentious piece of ugly abstract daubing by someone I'd never heard of. 'Are you sure, Michael?' was all I could say. 'Who's Judy Allen? I've never heard of her.'

'A future star on the Scottish art firmament. Still in her twenties but very talented. And she's so grateful for a chance to be shown in your gallery.'

'You know her? You've never mentioned her before.'

Michael turned to the birdcage, his sudden move

startling the finches. 'Will you listen to that, Roberta? My little Society finches with their beautiful song. My favourite finch at the moment. Lovely, isn't it?'

He was trying to hurt me, to get a reaction. I was determined to be strong. 'If it's your choice, Michael, of course I'm happy to show it. Is that enough business for tonight?'

'Yes, of course. Thanks for indulging me. I'll call John to take you home.' He saw the shocked look on my face. 'I'm sorry, Roberta, I've got a lot on my plate at the moment, need to catch up on my sleep. You don't mind heading home, do you?'

I lay in bed that night, unable to sleep. Michael was drifting away from me and I hated him for how much it hurt me. Now he'd conquered me, I no longer interested him. I cursed myself for feeling like this. I had become dependent on him emotionally, financially, sexually. I didn't want it to end, to fade away. I had to find a way to win him back.

So when Michael mentioned his fantasy again, about choosing someone for me to sleep with, it was like a test, an opportunity. To show I would do anything for him, that there was nothing he could ask me that I wouldn't do willingly. Maybe he needed further proof he could depend on me. Maybe the secret of winning him back was not to challenge him or wait for him, but to pretend to be totally submissive to his schemes and desires. I told myself it was no different from my random guy pick-ups. It wouldn't mean anything.

'Okay,' I said. 'I'll do it, Michael.' I tried to sound enthusiastic. 'Where do we go to find the lucky guy?'

'I won't be involved. Go with Ron, he'll choose.'

'Where do you want me to do the deed? A hotel?'

'No, your flat. Then I'll come round after and savour every detail.'

As an aspiring professional actress, I took my role very seriously. I was going to be a sex goddess for the evening, Barbarella and Emmanuelle rolled into one. I borrowed a few sex toys from Michael's collection. Mr Lucky wasn't going to know what hit him.

I met up with Ron a few days later. I'd put on my sexiest underwear, but otherwise dressed as scruffily as I could. Ron found the whole thing intensely amusing, greeted me with a laugh as he smoothed back his dirty blond hair, his hands thin with pianist fingers, delicate and bony. But there was no laughter in his eyes. They were cold and calculating, a merciless, piercing blue. Without a word, he opened the car door and I got in. We drove to a pub, well away from our usual haunts, the silence a malign presence between us.

Some choice. The lounge bar of a dive in a little-known backstreet, full of middle-aged men. Cigarette smoke hung in the air like a blue fug, the colour of missed chances and broken dreams. No need to worry about ever coming back here again. Ron looked around, I tried to guess who his choice would be. The reality of what I'd agreed to was beginning to sink in, but it was too late to back out now. He nodded towards a guy sitting alone at the bar. Short back and sides haircut, polyester suit. Face like a crumpled newspaper.

'Enjoy,' Ron whispered, and then he was gone.

I plonked myself down at the table next to my prey.

My request for a light from him resulted in just that, a light, no conversation. But my question about what beer he'd recommend moved us on. His name was Norman. I told him mine was Lizzie and I was waiting for my date. My performance five minutes later when I went to the phone and came back angry and disappointed I'd been stood up was one of my finest.

Believable improvisation. The test of a good actor.

Getting me on the rebound. It began to dawn on him that it was a possibility. He tightened his tie and I noticed when he came back from the loo he'd combed his hair. I asked him what his star sign was and gushed about how I was a Taurus, which made us so compatible. I played with my hair as I talked to him, laughed at his pathetic jokes. And when I reached over to touch his arm as I shared a confidence with him, he definitely began to realise that it was his lucky night, that he was the answer to this maiden's prayer. Gosh, men can be gullible.

He suggested we go somewhere quieter and was in a hurry to get me out before we were noticed together. He was wearing a ring. Married, obviously. Wanted me to be his little secret.

We got into his Ford Cortina and he didn't waste any time. Straight into a pounce, it couldn't have been any more uncomfortable. He suggested driving out to the country but I was having none of it. Back to my place.

I deserved an Oscar. And the striptease was like Liza Minnelli in *Cabaret*. His jaw dropped when he saw what I had on under my nondescript clothes. I meowed like a cat, asked him to bark like a dog. He was a good sport, but you could see he was well outside his comfort zone. The you-are-a-naughty boy scene with the whip felt more like *Carry On Teacher* than *Kama Sutra*. But I kept from laughing even with the look of horror on the poor sod's face. He just wanted an easy shag and he had to put up with all this nonsense.

I was lost in my performance for about twenty minutes when the spell was broken. I glanced across at the mirror at the bottom of the bed. I didn't see an erotic, *Emmanuelle*-style love scene. I saw a fat, middle-aged bloke grinding away monotonously on top of me. It wasn't me, it wasn't the world I wanted to inhabit. In that second I realised what attracted me to Michael was finding my boundaries, the limits to where I would go. This was well past them.

Norman looked like he was going to take hours so I rolled us over and started to give him head, the fastest way to get it over. Obviously a new experience for him, and he tried to force himself down the back of my throat. I started to retch, it was so bad. He finally came, more and more until I was sure I'd be sick. Just when I thought I couldn't take any more, he stopped.

I buried my face in the sheets, I couldn't bring myself to look at him. I felt ashamed and disgusted with myself. I leant over to the bedside cabinet to light a joint to cushion the pain. He took a few puffs to be polite. I saw him sneaking a look at his watch. Well past his bedtime, Mrs Norman was going to be waiting for him. I steeled myself to hold it together for a few minutes more. I gave him the 123 4567 telephone number, and saw the flash of anger in his eyes. But there was another look, suspicious, even a little frightened. Had he guessed it was a game? Maybe. I tried to leave him with the fantasy that he was a great seducer catching me at a vulnerable moment, but I was struggling to keep up the façade.

He looked anxiously around the room, grabbed his coat and was off.

I staggered into the bathroom, brushed my teeth so hard my gums bled. I got in the shower to try to wash away the night's memories. The whole sordid incident was an awakening for me. I'd wanted to be tested on my devotion to Michael and when it came to it, it had snapped me out of the spell he had placed over me.

It was time to get my life back.

chapter thirteen

Michael got his description of events but I couldn't bring myself to dwell on the salacious details. I did try, to see if something good could be salvaged from the disgust I felt with myself, but my heart wasn't in it. Goes to show how much it meant to him; my monotone recital of the bare facts got him more animated and excited than I'd seen in a long time. He especially loved the cat and dog noises and was fascinated by us smoking dope at the end. But I'd woken up to the horror of what I'd become. I was not his plaything to mould into what he wanted until I was a glorified prostitute. Last night was a serious wake-up call.

Michael acted as if I'd passed a final test that proved I was his to command. 'I can see you hated it, Roberta,' he said. 'I'll never ask you to do something like that again. No more sleazy stuff from now on, I promise.'

A big bunch of flowers turned up at my flat. It should have felt romantic, made me feel special, but it didn't. It felt tacky, that I was being used, like it was my payday for my night with Norman. I looked around the flat. The décor, every poster on the wall, every single ornament was chosen by Michael. I rummaged through a clothes drawer and found an old pair of patched denims I used to wear at uni and my favourite red-striped cheesecloth shirt. I changed into them and spent the night listening to my old Joni Mitchell LPs, trying to fill my soul with beauty again. Trying to find the person I used to be.

★ ★ ★

It was three days later when I saw the *Daily Record* headline. Happened to glance at the newspaper stand on my way home from work. 'Top Cop Death Riddle,' it screamed, next to a photo of Norman. DCI Norman McDonald, one of Glasgow's most senior detectives, found dead from gunshot wounds in his car in a wood near Barrhead on the outskirts of Glasgow. I stared at the photo in disbelief. It was him all right, no doubt about it.

I couldn't breathe, I looked around, expecting to be shot, arrested, kidnapped, whatever. The air crackled with danger. I fumbled through my purse, found some change. Bought the *Glasgow Herald*, *The Scotsman*, *Scottish Daily Express*, the papers that carried the story. I ran over to a nearby café and frantically read the articles, trying to piece together what had happened. Norman was a cop. He specialised in investigating organised crime and had been found shot dead in his car. But there was something strange in the way the papers reported it. 'Suspicious circumstances' was the phrase they used. What did that mean? Surely it was murder? Gangland retribution? Why didn't they just say so? One thing was for sure, it was not a coincidence.

I called Duncan, said we had to talk and rushed over to his flat, grabbing a copy of the *Evening Standard* on the way. The story was still on the front page.

Duncan answered the door as soon as I knocked. 'What the hell is going on, Bobbie? A Glasgow cop gets killed and you were involved? I couldn't understand a word of what you told me on the phone. Calm down, tell me what's happened. How on earth do you know this guy?'

'I'm not sure where to start. You know my great plan, to use men for fun and excitement and avoid the sort of commitment that caused the pain with Joe? Well, it's backfired on me big time.'

'Bobbie, what the fuck is going on?'

It was painful seeing the levels of understanding Duncan had to go through as I told my story. Especially the seduction game. That devastated him.

'I can't imagine that side of you, Bobbie. Sometimes I think I don't know you any more. The rest I can cope with. Enjoy sex, why not? But this sordid game, for God's sake, why? Do you really need to get these sorts of kicks? You've let yourself down, Bobbie. You're better than this.'

He was right, of course.

'I got carried away, I suppose,' I tried to explain. 'I had this anxiety attack that Michael was going to dump me and I needed to prove my devotion to him. Sounds pathetic when I say it now. I've no excuses, no justifications. I'm sorry, Duncan.'

I could hear the hurt in his voice. 'To give yourself away so cheaply, I don't know what that's about. And "proving your devotion"? Is that really you? I don't think so.'

'What should I do, Duncan, what should I do? It must have something to do with Michael. I know it. Should I go to the cops, turn Michael in?'

'I don't think you've got any choice. Take his side and

147

you'll be in big trouble. But what I can't understand is how you sleeping with this guy led to him getting shot three days later.'

'It has to be blackmail. It's so stupid when I think about it now, Ron took me to a specific bar, miles from here and chose a specific guy for me to sleep with. McDonald wasn't random. It wasn't just a kinky sex game or sick test of my loyalty. It must have been part of a plan to get rid of McDonald.'

'That would fit with what the evening paper said.' Duncan pointed to the second paragraph of the story. '"Links to organised crime", it says here. "Photos were found at the scene of the crime that meant suicide couldn't be ruled out." Do you think they mean photos of you together?'

'Then why haven't they published them? And why would Michael make me go through with having sex with the guy? Once they got the photos of us in the pub, they had what they wanted. Maybe they photographed us going back to my place. But that still wouldn't explain why Michael would insist on me having sex with him.'

'Well they won't be able to publish them if they're part of a criminal investigation, I guess. And you're right, photos of the two of you chatting in a pub is a pretty lame blackmail threat. It doesn't make sense.'

I took a deep breath. 'Think what I would tell the police. I'm sleeping with a gangster. I work in a shop that's a front for money laundering. They find out I got a movie part because someone leaned on the director. I live in a flat that's paid for by Michael. Play a sex game where I shag a random stranger. And that random stranger turns out to be a detective.'

Saying these words brought home to me how deeply I had sunk into Michael's world. There was no kidding myself, it was going to be catastrophic. My ambition to be an actress had blinded me to the monstrous world I'd become part of. If I went to the police I was going to suffer. I shook my head in disgust. It was no more than I deserved.

'Shit, Duncan.'

He nodded. 'Shit, indeed. And how do you know Michael isn't coming after you anyway? I don't want to scare you, but if you're in this so deep, does he want you hanging around?'

'Bloody hell.' I sunk my head in my hands. 'I'm screwed, Duncan, screwed whatever way I go.'

Duncan came over and gave me a hug. 'Sorry, that was tactless. But if I can be blunt again, you're still around, aren't you? If Michael wanted you gone, you'd be gone by now. It might be this is just a coincidence and you're not involved.'

I so wanted to believe that. One big coincidence. Ignore it and it would go away. I could easily have not seen the papers and then I'd know nothing about it. As far as DCI McDonald was concerned, my behaviour had been shocking but I hadn't broken any law. I had been used as a patsy. I might have been stupid, but I wasn't a criminal.

'Maybe you're right, Duncan. Maybe we should cool it for the moment. If McDonald was investigating Michael they'd have been on to him by now. And if Michael was involved he wouldn't wait for me to read about it in the papers.'

'You're right. As I said, if he wanted you out of the way, he'd have done it by now.'

'Maybe, maybe not. It's no secret we hang out together, think of that big Christmas ball we went to. He can't do anything to me, not right away. He'd know that if I disappeared they'd link it to him. But what it comes down to is that I've got no proof he's involved in any of this.'

'Good point. So maybe we shouldn't rush things. I still don't understand why the police have been so vague about what they found. If we knew the answer to that we'd know for sure if you were involved.'

I so wanted Duncan to convince me to stay quiet. 'I hate to say it, but I think the smart thing is to go back to my flat, call Michael as if I've just read the news and see what he has to say for himself. Act confused, ask him what to do. And make a decision then.'

I took an hour to compose myself to make the call. As I heard the phone ringing, ringing, I could feel my insides quivering, my heart racing. After four rings, Michael picked up the phone.

'Michael, it's me,' I said, gripping the phone so hard my hand hurt. 'Have you seen the newspapers today?'

'Of course,' said Michael. 'The first Concorde flight to New York. Wonderful, isn't it?'

'That's not what I mean. DCI McDonald, the detective being found dead. That's what I'm calling about.'

'What a strange thing to call me about, Roberta. Yes, I saw that as well. A few of my clients won't shed any tears, I'm afraid. He'd been rather successful over the years in putting more than a few undesirables behind bars. I hope they find out what's happened. He might not have been good for business, but it's always a sad moment when someone dies before their time. But why are you calling me about it?'

'Because he's the guy Ron chose for me to sleep with as part of your sex game. And now he's dead. What's going on, Michael?'

'Good Lord! Are you sure? I told Ron to take you off the beaten track. How did you manage to end up with him?'

'Because Ron chose him for me. Please, Michael. No games. What's going on?'

'I can assure you this is a complete shock. You're not suggesting I had anything to do with his death, are you Roberta? You know I hate any sort of violence. I could never do anything as dreadful as that.'

'Michael, please. This is too much of a coincidence. Tell me what's going on.'

'Look, Roberta. I don't know McDonald. I've heard of him, but that's because of his reputation for bringing down Glasgow hard men. That's what he did. Went after razor-wielding thugs, murderers. It's a dangerous line of work. But that's not my business, and you know that.'

I thought back to how Michael justified his business to me. A financial service. No one gets hurt. Everyone's at it. I so wanted to believe him.

'But I met him three days ago and now he's dead,' I insisted. 'That's too much of a coincidence.'

'Look, we shouldn't talk about this over the phone. I'll talk to Ron and see if he has any clue as to who the guy was he picked for you, see if that sheds any light on this. But don't do anything rash, Roberta. If you think you can help the police, then by all means talk to them.' He paused for a second to see if I'd respond. 'But think about the shame with your family, the scandal affecting your acting career. Being under suspicion for a crime you didn't commit, all because of a dreadful coincidence. Let me look into it and get back to you.'

I put the phone down. I wanted the whole sordid business to go away. I lay on my bed, listening to the saddest music I could find. Lou Reed's *Berlin* fitted my mood perfectly. I stared at the ceiling, going over the same thoughts, over and over again. Should I tell the police? What would I tell them? Or wait for them to find me first, plead ignorance about knowing about the murder? One thing was for sure, whatever happened, I needed to finish with Michael

I dragged myself into the gallery the next morning. I needed to keep things looking as normal as possible. Called Duncan on the way, told him what Michael said, agreed it would be best for him to keep away from me for the time being. We went through the maze of possibilities again, a fruitless attempt to come to a decision.

There was no knock on the door from the police during the day. Michael called, said Ron had no idea who he'd chosen and asked me to come over that night to talk through my concerns. I said I needed time on my own. He said of course that was okay.

No police. No threats from Michael, just the opposite. I couldn't go to the police with this uncertainty in my mind. I hated myself for thinking that, but I couldn't.

I lay in bed again that night and went over the events

of the last twenty-four hours for the hundredth time. I still couldn't see how me having sex with McDonald fitted with his death three days later. But it was too great a coincidence. There had to be a connection.

Then, a dawning horror, I realised what it must be. Someone saw us here, in the bedroom. Maybe even photographed us. How? I frantically looked out the window. No, not there, the curtains would have been drawn. I looked under the bed. Nothing. In the wardrobe, the bedside table. Behind the posters. Nothing.

I sank down on the bed in relief and stared at myself in the mirror on the wall opposite. The mirror that had these funny black lines that always bugged me when I was trying to see how I looked when I got dressed.

The mirror. I felt I was going to faint.

I rummaged around in the kitchen and found a screwdriver and started to unscrew it from the wall. My hands were shaking as I undid each of the four corner screws. I could feel my blood pumping through the veins in my head. I put the fourth screw on the floor and used the screwdriver to prise the glass off the wall.

It came off easily, too easily. There it was. Behind the glass a little room, with a door leading to the outside hallway. A grungy mattress leaning against the far wall, porn mags and Mars Bars wrappers on the floor.

I rushed out to the hallway. There was the door into the room. It must have been an old common toilet bricked up when the tenement was renovated and every flat got their own loo. I'd walked past it every day without giving it a second thought. Someone must have been waiting there when I came back from the pub with McDonald. They could have photographed everything. I ran back inside to be sick, the acidic bile burning my throat.

But I needed to keep a clear head. Carefully I screwed the mirror back on, concentrating like mad to get it looking exactly as I found it. Waves of disgust flowed over me. I felt defiled, debased, debauched. A seething fury towards Michael and even more with myself that I'd allowed myself to be taken in by his persuasive, seductive words.

I couldn't spend another minute in the flat. I looked at my watch. Nine o'clock. Late, but not too late to get round to Duncan's.

I was paranoid about being followed as I headed off to the underground and ran down the stairs. The earthy odour of the tunnels felt stale and suffocating. The dilapidated Victorian train headed off in the opposite direction to Duncan's flat. At the next station I got out, crossed the platform. A train pulled in almost immediately going back the way the way I'd just come. I got on, looked behind me. No one followed.

I got off the train at Hillhead station, ran to Duncan's flat and rang the doorbell again and again, willing him to be in. I was flooded with relief when I heard his voice. 'Hold your horses, I'm coming, I'm coming,' I heard him complaining from behind the door. 'Who the hell is it anyway?'

'Duncan, it's Bobbie. Let me in quick.' There was a look of consternation as I rushed past him in the hall. 'Close the door, lock it. We need to talk.'

I told him about the hidden room. 'That clinches it, doesn't it?' I said, shaking my head. 'It was a blackmail attempt to get McDonald to back off from investigating Michael. McDonald said no and then either Michael killed him or he topped himself to avoid the shame, it doesn't matter. I'm in this, and in this deep. Michael used me.'

'What can you do? It doesn't look good for you, Bobbie. Now that you've waited before going to the cops, I'm not sure whether you'd come out of it okay.'

I thought back to the photos Michael had of Duncan and me. The longer I hung around, the more Duncan was in danger. Michael would know I would confide in him. 'There's only one thing for it, I have to disappear. Go somewhere Michael will never find me.'

'Easier said than done. This is 1976, Bobbie, you can't just disappear these days. What about money? Your parents? You can't vanish and not tell them. They'd be worried sick.'

'I know. But I don't think I've got a choice. I could head to London, start a new life there. Get a few acting jobs to pay the rent. There's so much theatre down there and I'd be well away from Michael.'

Duncan shook his head. 'That would never work. Michael will be watching you like a hawk. And he knows you love acting, the theatre's the first place he'd look for you. And it isn't exactly a profession where you can keep a low profile. If you're serious about this you'd have to make a complete break. New career, new identity, new everything. And no contact with anyone here. Do you think you could do that?'

He was right. It was a huge decision, bigger than I even realised. 'I'm still not sure I'd get away with it anyway,' I said. 'If he catches me, I'm done for. And if I do disappear, you'll be the first person he'll go after. I can't do that to you, Duncan, I don't think you realise how much danger there is here.'

'Oh, I realise all right. Don't think I haven't thought of that. I'm also scared shitless. I'm a loose end too, I see that. He'll suspect we've been talking and after he's decided what he wants to do about you, I have no doubts I'll be next on his list. We've got to think it through. We're in this together now.'

I squeezed his hand as I bit my lip. I tried to give him a smile of encouragement. 'I'm so, so sorry, Duncan. What can I say?'

'Don't worry, you owe me for this, big time. Look, are you really serious about disappearing?'

I nodded furiously.

'Here's what you need to do. Firstly, if you are going to do anything, it has to be now, before you make the movie. You can't stage a disappearing act and be a movie star at the same time. You'll have to give up on being an actress. That's over if you do this. Do you see that?'

I heard a voice screaming inside my head. *No! No! No!* Just as I was about to realise my dreams, they were to be snatched away from me. It was so unfair. Then I felt ashamed. Someone had died; Duncan was putting himself in danger to help me, and all I could think about was myself.

'You're right, Duncan. I hadn't thought of that.'

He paused and gave me a long look of sympathy. 'Michael knows how much the movie part means to you. He's going to figure you won't do anything until after the shoot. That gives us time. You've got to cover your tracks. Call up some estate agents in Edinburgh tomorrow, ask them to send you particulars of properties for rent there. When Michael finds out, that will be where he starts looking. Tell your family you've landed a big acting role in London, all very sudden, you're quitting your job and heading off there next week but don't yet have an address where you're staying.'

I'd never seen Duncan like that, fired up and decisive. It wasn't Duncan the dreamer, unable to plan his way out of a paper bag. 'How are you able to come up with this stuff?' I said in awe.

'I'm a journalist. I'm paid to make things up for a living.'

I smiled at his wee joke. He went on with his plan.

'This also gets me off the hook. When Michael comes to ask me how to find you in Edinburgh, I tell him you've gone to London. I'll act pissed off, say I don't know why, that you wouldn't tell me an address. If he gets that confirmed by your parents it'll look as if I'm not trying to cover up.'

'But how can I get there? He'll be watching me.'

'That's tricky. I think we have to take a risk. Act normal tomorrow. Do nothing to raise his suspicions you've found the hidden room. And put something on the door of your flat, a tiny piece of Sellotape or something, to see if it's checked on while you're at work. Pop back at lunchtime and let me know if you're in the clear. When you go back to the gallery, I'll drop off my two big suitcases.'

'No, that's too dangerous,' I protested.

'It will be okay,' Duncan replied. 'If they're following

anyone it will be you. When you get home, pack, just the essentials, nothing to connect you to your life here. Don't leave any photos behind, either destroy them or leave them for me to pick up. I'll come back the next day when you're at work and collect the suitcases. Then that night, do the underground station dodge again and meet me at the bus station in time to catch the night bus to London. I'll give you the suitcases and you're off.'

I could feel my muscles jumping under my skin. 'I can't go back to the flat, I just can't,' I said. 'I can never sleep in that bed again, knowing someone could be watching me.' I shuddered at the thought.

'You need to go back, Bobbie. The secret to this working is you behaving normally. And I can't pack your stuff for you. You've got to go back one last time.'

I took a huge sigh. 'I know. You're right. And I'll need to get a new name, a new identity when I get to London,' I said, sighing at the enormity of what lay ahead of me. 'I suppose I could call myself Bertie, which will fit with Roberta being on my records. A new haircut. Money won't be a problem, thanks to Michael's… generosity.' I spat out the last word, then tried to look brave. 'Duncan, this might work.'

Duncan smiled reassuringly. 'It has to. And once Michael doesn't find you, if he's sensible about it, he'll realise it's a win-win for him. If he wants you out of the way and you disappear, he's got what he wants. Okay, he's a control freak and he'll try to track you down because he won't like you getting one over him, but I think he'll back off eventually.'

'I'm not so sure. He isn't somebody who forgets a grudge easily. But I can hope.'

We talked some more about the details. I would pay all my bills before I left, so no one else was looking for me. Once I'd been in London for a week or so I'd call my parents and tell them I'd be moving around, so it was best if I called them to keep in touch. Mum would worry, but I could deal with that. I would need to figure how I'd get a job down there, and somewhere to live, but one step at a time.

'You've got a plan now, Bobbie. The question is, are you going to do it?'

I pressed my lips together, took a deep breath before replying. 'I don't know,' I said finally. 'How do you make a decision of this magnitude? Should I wait to see if Michael will let me go? Maybe we should see if we can come up with another plan before rushing into this one? Or would it be smarter to go now, before he gets his claws into me any more? I don't know what to do, Duncan, I just don't know.'

★ ★ ★

I couldn't wait to get out of the flat in the morning. I stuck the tiniest piece of Sellotape onto my front door and another on the door to the spying room. Then off to the gallery, playing the part of someone without a worry in the world. I told my family about the big acting opportunity in the morning, visited Granny Campbell during my lunch break. She was so excited for me, it broke my heart to see her so overjoyed, hearing myself invent all sorts of lies about what I'd be doing. I promised to write, send her the reviews, tell her how it was going. I made a quick trip back to the flat, the Sellotape was in place so I called Duncan to drop off the suitcases. Then round to my parents straight after work. Dad predictably hostile, couldn't understand why I was throwing away a permanent job. Mum in the background, silently supportive.

The suitcases were there when I got back and I spent the evening packing, agonising about what to take. I decided to take the designer clothes Michael had bought me. And the necklace, of course. Part of me wanted to rid myself of everything to do with him, but the sensible part of me said they'd be useful. And I liked the irony it was helping my escape.

I finished the packing with two hours to spare before I had to leave for the bus. I couldn't resist one last look at the spying room, to see if there was anything I'd missed the last time. I unscrewed the mirror and peered inside. No sign that anything had changed. I thought of someone being there, watching me, probably masturbating at the same time. I shuddered. It had been a bad idea to take a second look. I lifted the mirror up and put it back on the wall. My hands were trembling.

I gave the last screw one final quarter turn to make sure it was on the wall tightly. Suddenly there was a loud snap and a black crack shot across from the screw hole to the other side of the mirror. I looked at it in horror. Now Michael would know for sure I'd found him out.

I couldn't believe my stupidity. I let out an anguished scream, so great was my torment. I stared at the crack in horror, willing myself to believe it would be all right, that no one would notice. But I knew I was deluding myself. I called Duncan to tell him it was too dangerous for him to come to the flat. If anyone went into the flat once I left they'd know immediately I'd found out what Michael had been up to. His phone rang and rang, he must have been already on his way over.

I had no choice but to leave. That would make it safer for Duncan at least. If someone was watching me they'd follow me away from the flat so he could get the suitcases without being spotted. I stared at the mirror again. The crack was like a maniacal grin running from one side to another. Cursing myself one last time, I rushed out.

Posting the letter to Fontane was the hardest part for me. I wrote that I had some personal problems, I was pulling out of the movie, sorry and all that. It was two days before filming started, and I'd had my wardrobe fittings and everything. He'd be furious. My name would be mud, I'd never get another opportunity like this again. I stood holding the letter in the slot of the post box for an eternity. Couldn't bring myself to let it go. Silly really, I was already past the point of no return. I stared at the letter one last time. Then I dropped it though the slot and pictured it falling to the bottom, along with my dreams.

I hung around my old haunts for about half an hour, a last poignant reminder of the life I was leaving behind. I tried to imagine how terrified Duncan would be, picking up my suitcases, seeing the cracked mirror. The flat felt like a time bomb waiting to go off. I did the one-two on the subway to be confident I wasn't being followed. To be on the safe side, I did another platform switch again, five minutes later.

I arrived at the bus station twenty minutes before

departure time. Duncan was already waiting with the suitcases. Before I could say anything he told me his news.

'There were lots of rumours flying about amongst the journalists at my paper today,' he said, his gaze bouncing around the bus station. 'Lots of deliberate leaking from the powers that be. The police are still undecided about McDonald's shooting. Apparently they've had a tip-off that he was dodgy. Their theories are it is either a retribution killing or he got mixed up in something that spun out of control, or maybe even it was suicide, all got too much for him.' His face reddened. 'There's talk of incriminating photos I'm sorry to say, but with the girl's face blacked out so she can't be identified. And too red-hot to publish in a family newspaper. Anyway, the word from on high is we've been asked to play down the story until they get a better handle on what's going on. Everyone's sensitive about police corruption at the moment, what with the Operation Countryman investigation going on.'

I told him about cracking the mirror. He tried not to look at me like I was a moron, but I could see what he was thinking.

'Did you notice it?' I asked tentatively.

He gave me a look of mild incredulity. 'I'm afraid I did,' he said, with as much tact he could manage. It was not a time for recriminations. 'Don't worry, Bobbie, these things happen.'

'What have I done, Duncan? Will I ever be able to live a normal life again?' I gave him a hug and held him tighter. Then, tighter still. Eventually I had to let go; the bus was about to leave. We said our last goodbye and I kissed him on the lips, the first time ever.

As I got on the bus, the radio was on. *Sounds of the 70s* on Radio 1. Whispering Bob Harris's dulcet tones introduced the next record. 'He not busy being born is busy dying,' sang Bob Dylan, as I stepped on board.

I was going to be busy being born again, to have a new life.

Better than being busy dying.

London, late January 1976

chapter fourteen

I'd only been to London once before, when I had come to take part in an anti-apartheid demonstration in Hyde Park, one of Duncan's pet causes. Joe hadn't come along. He said there was no point. Nelson Mandela would never be released and South Africa was too rich a country to bow to sanctions.

I'd not seen much of the city on that trip, so despite the anxiety gnawing away at me, I couldn't help but be thrilled at my first sight of Big Ben, Westminster Abbey and the signs to places I'd only ever heard of: Battersea, Fulham, Mayfair. The bus terminated at Victoria Bus Station. I dragged my two suitcases on to the pavement. Everyone headed purposefully off, until it was just me standing there.

I carried my suitcases over to a nearby bench and tried to think of a plan. Nothing. I closed my eyes and started rocking backwards and forwards, annoyed with myself. I'd had two days and four hundred miles to think of that moment and yet there I was, still clueless about what to do next.

Okay, pull yourself together, I thought. The first thing was to stash these two monsters while I looked around. I spied a left luggage office and headed over. A pound a day to drop off my bags. Extortionate, but I didn't have a choice.

The luggage guy heaved the first suitcase up on to the counter. 'Okay, open it up, love, I need to take a look.'

I was surprised. And more than a little embarrassed at the stupid things he would see in my suitcase. 'Oh, it's just clothes and stuff,' I said. 'And I'm not sure I'll get the cases shut if I open them. They're jam packed.'

'Sorry, love, them's the rules,' he replied. 'IRA, you know. Can't be too careful these days.'

I hadn't thought of that. The IRA had been setting off bombs on tube stations for months. London stopped feeling new and fascinating and started to feel scary and dangerous. I would need to use the tube to get about. I felt my insides quiver.

I opened the first suitcase and the guy gave a cursory flick through my clothes. 'Thanks, love, now the other one.'

That was it? That was his search for bombs? I wasn't sure if I felt better or worse. I looked at the pile of bags stacked on the shelves behind him. I was sure I could hear ticking. I bounced on my toes, wanting to make a quick getaway. His second check was even more perfunctory than the first.

'Blimey, staying here for a while, are you? You'd need to be Geoff Capes to lug these around.' He cleared a space on the floor section and slid the cases in.

'I've just moved here from Glasgow. Fresh start and all that. You don't know somewhere I could stay around here, do you? Cheap and clean, doesn't have to be too fancy.'

He handed me two tickets for my suitcases. 'Earl's Court is where you want to go, darlin'. Nothing cheap 'round this manor that ain't dodgy. Tube's over there, Circle and District line. And you watch out, won't you? Lots of young things like you come a cropper moving down here.'

I'd heard of Earl's Court, but only because a bomb had gone off there in March, at the Ideal Homes Exhibition. People lost arms and legs. Still, if it was the advice from a local, I figured I'd better take it. I found Earl's Court on the massive tube map, figured out how to buy a ticket and looked for the platform.

Escalators, sleek modern trains, the tube was very impressive. But so crowded. If a bomb did go off, it would be carnage. I stepped out of the station with a sigh of relief and saw the massive Earl's Court Arena in front of me. That must have been where the bomb went off. It was silly, but I quickened my pace as I headed straight for the back streets.

There was certainly no shortage of choices. Earl's Court was an endless maze of Edwardian terraces, full of faded grandeur, every second house converted into a hotel or guest house. I followed a sign to South Kensington but that wasn't for me, far too posh. I set off in a different direction and I found myself at the corner of Old Brompton Road and Seagrove Road, wondering which to try first.

'Looking for somewhere?' said a voice behind me. I turned to see a scruffy-looking guy, standing just a bit too close. He glanced left and right. 'Or is it some shit you're after? I've got great shit, if that's your scene.'

169

I stepped back. 'No thanks,' I said and turned on my heel and walked up the steps of the guest house immediately in front of me.

'No, man, you don't want to stay there. Rip off artists, the place is a dive. There's great digs in Pembroke Road.' He gave an exaggerated intake of breath as if inspiration had struck. 'Hey, I'm walking that way myself, let me take you.'

I don't know why I agreed. Still a bit overwhelmed, I guess. With the left-luggage guy being helpful, maybe southerners weren't as unfriendly as I thought they would be. Within a minute I knew I'd made a mistake. He tried to be super friendly, did I want to know where to find a job, find out where were the happening places? 'Sleekit', Granny Campbell would have called him.

He danced around me, waving his arms, like a marionette controlled by a frenzied puppeteer. 'So, that accent. You're Scottish, aren't you?'

I gave a pained smile of acknowledgement.

He looked very proud of himself. 'See? You can't get anything past Davey. I spotted that as soon as you spoke. I know a guy from Scotland. Bill McGregor. You know him? Comes from Dundee. Or Dunfermline, somewhere like that. Has a tattoo.'

'No, I don't think so. It's a big place.'

'Well, if you meet him, watch out. He's a bit of a prick.' He nodded vigorously in agreement with himself. Then he looked around, a paranoid stare in his eyes. 'But don't tell him I said so, okay? That's between you and me.'

'Okay,' I replied, trying to be polite. 'Look, you really don't have to help me find a place. I'm sure I'll manage.'

He circled around me, a whirling dervish of inane prattle. I sped up. He almost had to run now to keep up with me. 'Hey, pretty woman, walk with meeeee...' he sang. He jumped in front of me, blocking the way. 'Tell me, pretty woman, are all Scottish birds as gorgeous as you? Maybe I should get myself up there. What do you think?'

I put my head down, willing him to leave me alone. He stuck next to me, taking my arm as we crossed the street. I pulled my arm away and glared at him. 'Go away, would you? Please.'

'Look, Pembroke Road,' he replied, smiling smugly, as if he'd pulled a rabbit out of the hat. 'Go in here, gorgeous. Tell them Davey sent you, you'll get a great deal.'

I hurried up the steps. The smell of damp cabbage greeted me. A stout matronly woman was sitting behind the desk.

'Um, how much is a room here?' I asked.

No matter what she said I wasn't staying. I had decided the instant I walked in, but I needed to kill a few minutes to let the pest go away.

'Five quid, love. That's for a room of your own, mind, shared facilities. Do you want to take a gander?'

I glanced outside. No sign of Davey. 'No, thanks,' I said. 'It's not what I'm looking for. Thanks anyway.'

I smiled and turned to leave when I noticed my handbag was unzipped. Sure enough, my purse was gone and the two hundred pounds that was in it. 'My purse, it's gone. That bastard's stolen it,' I cried. I got up and ran out the door and looked frantically up and down the street. He was nowhere to be seen.

I stepped back inside. My body was wracked with heavy sobs, dense tears rolled down my cheeks. I'd been in London an hour and I'd been robbed, was in a disgusting hellhole of a hotel and had no one to turn to. All my great plans and I'd barely survived one hour. I slumped on the moth-eaten sofa in the lobby.

'Cor, darling, that's terrible. How much did he nick off you?'

I turned to look at the woman, full of hatred and despair. Was she in on it too? 'Two hundred pounds,' I said between sobs. 'All the money I had to see me through my first month here.'

'Blimey. Two ton. You need to tell the fuzz. Do me a fave, love, keep me out of this, would you? I've got enough on me plate without having the cops on me case.'

I couldn't take it any more. 'Sod you and your bloody hotel. He led me here. Bet you're in on it too.' I took deep breaths, trying to get myself under control. 'It's not fair, it's not fair.' I sunk my head in my hands.

'Hush, hush,' she said. 'For what it's worth, love, I don't know nothing about who nicked your money. Believe me or don't believe me, I don't care. Was it all the money you had? Don't you have luggage?

'Mind your own business,' I snapped.

She laughed. It transformed her and for a brief second I saw a different person behind those world-weary eyes. 'Good, good, don't trust anyone as far as you can throw them and you'll do all right. Shame you've had to learn the hard way, but that's life, I guess. There's nothing I can do for you here, darlin', we're not a charity. Two streets away is the Pankhurst Hostel, a women-only hotel for strays like you that have arrived clueless in the big smoke. They're usually pretty full but I'll give them a call, put in a word, see if they can squeeze you in. Have a ciggie to calm your nerves. Here, have one of mine.'

'I'll be fine, thank you.'

'No you won't, dear. Not without a nudge in the right direction. Sit there and I'll make the call. Go round and check them out. You'll be glad you did.'

I couldn't figure out what her scam was, but I stayed put. It gave me time to collect my thoughts. My cheque book and cheque card were buried deep in the suitcases back at left luggage, and I still had some money in my bank account. I took out my underground ticket to check it. 'Day Rover,' it read. I presumed that meant I didn't have to pay any more to go back on the tube.

The woman was talking on the phone. 'I know, duckie, but the poor dear's been done over by some scumbag and she's desperate.' Pause. 'No... I don't think she is.'

She leant over to me with her hand over the phone. 'You're not on the game, are you, love?' I shook my head almost apologetically. 'No, a lovely lass, bit out of her depth, that's all,' she said.

I blushed.

'You can? Great, I'll send her straight over.' She turned to me. 'What's your name, dearie?'

'Bob... Bertie. I replied.' Shit, I couldn't even get that right. 'Bertie,' I repeated.

'Her name's Bertie,' she said on the phone. She gave me a wink to acknowledge her collusion in my deception. 'Yeah, I'll tell her to come round straight away.'

'You're in luck, Bob Bertie. They might be able to

squeeze you in. It's 272 Stratford Road, I'll draw you a map.' She sketched out the directions on a scrap of paper. I looked at them, still suspicious, not knowing what to believe. 'Go round and take a look. Call the cops if you like about that lad, but don't hold your breath about them doing anything about it. And remember, love, don't trust a bloody soul down here. Good luck.'

I tried to look grateful. I still wasn't sure I could trust her, but I was a little ashamed at assuming she was in on the scam. I said my thanks and walked out onto the street, wandering aimlessly, in a daze. I looked at the map and realised I'd walked off in the wrong direction.

Sod it, I didn't have any other options. I turned around and headed off to the hostel.

It was a big place. Looked like it used to be an old nurses' home or an army barracks or something. It seemed legit. 'Pankhurst Hostel. Women Only. Budget Accommodation,' read the sign. I went inside.

A small, chubby girl was at reception, peroxide blonde hair, a small silver stud in her nose. I couldn't help but stare at it, I'd never seen anything like that before. 'I'm Bertie,' I said, hesitantly. 'Looking for somewhere to stay. You're expecting me?' I looked around. The posters on the wall were for rape counselling services, battered women hotlines. Welcome to London, I thought.

'Yeah, Nora called. I'm Cynthia, pleased to meet you. Been done over straight off the bus, eh?' I gave a half-hearted smile of acknowledgement. 'Don't worry, we've all been there. In some ways this is your lucky day. What with the summer holidays coming along and some of the girls heading off, there's a bed for you straight away if you want it. Come and have a look around.'

A real mixed bag of people were staying there. Tourists doing London on the cheap, strays and waifs one step away from sleeping on the streets, a few damaged souls averting their eyes as they passed you in the hallway.

Of course I said yes. Got a bed in the dorm, three pound a night, beside the door. Cynthia told me it would be a bit noisy, but when one of the other girls moved out I could take their bed if I wanted. It wasn't too bad, I tried to convince myself. My suitcases would fit under the bed, and there was a locker for my valuables. Could be a lot worse.

I fished out the change in my pockets. £2.47. I was right about the tube ticket so I was able to head back to Victoria without having to use up my last few pennies. The left-luggage guy was still there. He said if I took the suitcases off him and then put them back he was supposed to charge, but he'd make an exception for me. My cheque book was at the bottom of one suitcase and my cheque card at the bottom of the second, so it was twenty minutes before bank closing time when I arrived at Piccadilly Circus, the only English branch of the Clydesdale Bank. Michael would know from my payslips they were my bank and so I was paranoid about going there. But it could only have been a couple of hours since he'd found out I'd gone. If he had the resources to stake out the bank already, I might as well give up now.

I put my head down and darted into the branch. Stop being so silly, I kept telling myself, there was no way he'd have anyone here. That didn't stop the hairs on the back of my neck from standing up as I rushed up the stairs.

I wrote out the cheque, pay 'self' £287, all the money I had left. The teller said she'd have to phone my branch to pay such a large amount. I sat in the corner trying to look invisible, promising myself as soon as I got a permanent London address I was moving to a nice, anonymous English bank.

I got the money and scurried out. 'Haste Ye Back', said the sign above the exit, a little bit of Scottishness in central London. I blinked back the tears and stepped out into the street, my hand stuck in my pocket, grasping the money.

Piccadilly Circus. I'd heard about it all my life but it was just a little roundabout with a Cupid statue on it. Even the neon signs were a let-down, tacky really. But underneath them was a McDonald's, a new American burger chain. I hadn't eaten all day. Putting aside my snobbery about burger bars, I decided to try a Big Mac.

I was surprised you went to a counter to buy your food and then took it yourself to your table. The burger was very different, almost a sweet taste. Served with dill pickle, I'd never had that before either. And the chips, or 'fries' as they called them, weren't like normal chips. Artificial looking, shaped like matchsticks. Perhaps it was because I was starving, but it tasted delicious. My first positive London experience.

I wolfed down the burger with one hand, the other still in my pocket protecting the cash. Then it was off to Victoria to get my bags and the treat of a taxi back to the hostel. It was five o'clock in the afternoon before I lay back on my bed, my cash safely stowed away, a few things unpacked from my suitcase.

I could relax. Surely, the worst was over.

chapter fifteen

I'd noticed a hairdresser's on the way to the hostel from the tube station and the next morning I walked back to it. 'Cut it short,' I said. 'And dye it blonde.' The hairdresser huffed I hadn't made an appointment but I promised her a tip. I wanted it done immediately, so as few people as possible at the hostel would see my old look. I'd tell Cynthia she was my inspiration, she'd like that. As my long, dark, curly hair fell to the floor, a new me was beginning to emerge. When the hairdresser finished I stared into the mirror. A stranger stared back at me.

At the hostel, Cynthia did a double-take when she saw my haircut and gave me a peculiar grin. I wandered into the dorm and looked around. Who to trust, who to believe? Two girls were in the beds across from me. They couldn't have been any older than sixteen and were chattering away excitedly, congratulating themselves on getting this far. They had a rural accent. West Country, if I had to guess, but I'd only heard an accent like that on TV before. They were talking about the same issue that was on my mind, money and how to get it. A skeletally thin woman, dressed head to toe in black, was lying on the bed next to them, skin as pale as a candle, flicking through an Ernest Hemingway novel and dragging heavily on a cigarette. She looked irritated and kept frowning at the girls. They were disturbing her concentration.

'If I might suggest, head off to the hotels in Mayfair and ask if they need chambermaids,' she said. Her voice had a flat tone of resignation, of someone drifting through life. 'Or Fulham. Lots of new restaurants opening. They're always looking for waitresses.' And go off and do it now and give me some peace, said the look on her face.

Taking her words as gospel, the girls bounced off down the hall to live out their adventure.

'I'm not sure kids like that should be on their own in London,' I said to her, to make it clear I was not as much an innocent abroad as they were. 'I'm looking for somewhere to work down here too. Are those my best options?'

'Yes, I was like them once,' she replied. A smile faded and died on her lips. 'Came here looking for the summer of love. Never quite worked out. Yes, waitressing is a good gig to get started. Pay's crap and they'll work you to the bone, but that's why the turnover's so high. I'd get over to Fulham. I hear that's where it's happening at the moment.'

She turned to her book again and I could see she wanted to be left alone. Probably just as well. I needed to think carefully before I let anyone get to know me here.

I headed off to Fulham. And, just like that, I got a job as a waitress at The Golden Egg, day two in London. Saw an ad in the window, walked in and I was hired straight away. I told them I had waitressing experience and I did, sort of, but they didn't check. It was that easy. I was told to start the next day.

There was a hungry look in the manager's eyes when he heard I'd just arrived in London. 'Go and choose your uniform, my dear,' he said. 'You'll want one tight-fitting, that's what the customers like. And if you need any help finding your feet while you're new in town, just let me know.'

I nodded politely and scurried off.

I saw the lady in black when I got back to the hostel. She was in the communal lounge, the only person there. Everyone else had cleared out for the day. I told her I'd got a job, thanks to her good advice.

'Glad to have been of help,' she said. 'At least some good has come out of me being here.'

I gave her a quizzical look, inviting her to say more. Instead, she turned again to her book.

'What are you reading?' I asked.

'Hemingway,' she said, gesturing to the pages. 'I like him. Says all he has to say with as few and simple words as possible.'

'A bit like you then?' I replied.

She looked shocked for a second and then gave a laugh. 'Okay, you got me there. Sorry, I'm going through a rough time at the moment. Not very good company. I'm Rita, pleased to meet you.' She put the book down.

'I'm Bertie,' I said. 'It's me that should apologise. Here's you wanting to be left alone and I'm bugging you. But thanks to you, I got a job today and you don't know what a relief that is. I wanted you to know I appreciate it.'

We circled each other for the rest of the day, a few tentative snatches of conversation every time we met. Rita was treated with wary respect by everyone at the hostel.

She wasn't trying to hustle anyone, it was me that initiated every conversation.

In the lounge that evening, I made a decision.

'Rita,' I said when she put down her book to light a cigarette. 'I've just arrived in London and it's been an eventful couple of days, to say the least.' I paused and took a deep breath. 'I've come down here to get away from somebody. If I buy you a drink, could I pick your brains about how to disappear and survive in London? Given the limited success I've had so far, I've got a lot to learn.'

I could see her weighing it up. It seemed to take forever and I was cringing with embarrassment. I was about to blurt out an apology for being too forward when she spoke.

'Yeah, why not? No point in you making the mistakes I made. We can go to The Coach and Horses round the corner. Just as long as you know my brain is the only part of me that's on offer.'

I blushed. 'Of course. I'm not… you know.'

'Okay. It's just you've got a classic dyke haircut. Not that I mind of course, but don't want to lead you along.'

Mortification. That's why Cynthia was so impressed by my new look. I hoped it wouldn't take too long to grow out. I wanted a new identity, but there was a limit to what I'd change.

We headed round to the pub and Rita ordered a glass of wine. I was amazed; wine in a pub, whatever next? I asked for my usual half pint of heavy. 'It's called bitter down here, duckie,' the landlord said, laughing as he pulled me the drink.

Rita was a bit circumspect about her past, but that

was okay. All I got out of her was that she'd come out of a long-term relationship with some guy that had been abusive. Hit her when he got drunk and cheated on her behind her back. So she'd packed a bag and left and was staying at the hostel until she found somewhere remote to live, on her own, where she could leave the human race behind.

I didn't tell her any more of my story, just said again I'd had to get out of Glasgow in a hurry and that someone was looking for me. She liked I'd changed my name, and didn't ask what my old one was. Laughed when she heard my haircut was only one day old. I didn't tell her about being robbed. Didn't want to come across as a complete idiot.

I leaned forward to confide in her. 'Is it safe for me to stay in the hostel? Isn't it the first place someone would come looking for you?'

She shook her head. 'They don't encourage people with big problems to stay here,' she said. 'Girls find out about it by word of mouth, I doubt if anyone outside London knows about it. If anyone needs real help and support, Cynthia points them in the direction of the women's refuges.'

So that's what all the posters in reception were for. Maybe I shouldn't feel so sorry for myself.

Rita continued to fill me in. 'They had a problem with pimps a few years ago, apparently. Some working girls came to get off the streets, so if that's your game you can't stay. They like you to move out eventually, but I suppose you'd want to anyway. I'm counting the days to when I can start living again. I've tried the fast lane, now I want to find somewhere where no one bothers me, where I can live a simple life, no hassles, no expensive toys, and definitely no men.'

She took a sip of her wine. I could see a real sadness in her eyes. I'd been traumatised by guilt, I've been scared out my wits, but I'd never been hurt or abused so much that I wanted to give up on the world.

'I feel a coward for running away and not facing up to what I left behind,' I said. 'And it's only now dawning on me what it's going to be like.'

'Don't let anyone say you're a coward for running away. Sometimes you have to lose yourself to find yourself. It's taken some shitty stuff to happen for me to find out who I really am. All you're thinking about right now is how to be invisible, but sooner or later you'll have to figure out who you want to be.'

'You're right, the future can wait. Being invisible sounds pretty good right now. How do you manage it?'

'The secret is to create a new identity, without, well, creating a new identity. That draws attention to yourself and if you do something dodgy, it'll catch up with you in the end. What's your second name? Sinclair? Okay, tell everyone it's St. Clare. If anyone notices the discrepancy, blame it on someone mishearing your Scottish accent. And your national insurance number. You've got that for life, but accidentally mix up two of the numbers. Has to be the last four, they're assigned randomly, the rest mean something. If it comes to light with the authorities, you can say again it's an innocent mistake. And if you can't use a P45 from your old job, get a P46 instead. That doesn't involve your old employer. It'll have your correct national insurance number on it, but if you're lucky you can change the number on their files without anyone noticing.'

I'd hit gold dust. I could have never thought of that stuff myself. 'What about my bank account?' I asked. 'I'd like to get a bank account that's got no link to my past.'

'That's smart,' said Rita. 'Open a post office account, they're pretty lax about needing ID. That should deal with your short-term needs. Then open a new bank account, tell them you've been a simple soul using your kiddie TSB account up to now. Have you got enough money to keep the wolves from the door, do you mind me asking?'

'Less than I started with, but yes, enough to keep me going until my first pay. And I've got a flashy necklace a boyfriend gave me. Thought I could try and find someone to buy it if I could.'

'Hatton Garden is the place for that. London's jewellery district. Look it up in the *A to Z*. They'll take it off your hands, no questions asked.'

'Rita, I can't thank you enough. You've shown me how much I need to learn. For the first time since I arrived here, I think I might be able to make this work.'

Rita nodded, but I could see she wasn't convinced. And she was right. I was yet to find out how horrendous London could be.

chapter sixteen

I turned up for work at The Golden Egg the next day feeling good after my talk with Rita and more optimistic about my future. It didn't last. The manager made a point of telling me again how he could help me find my feet in London. All very creepy and I'd only been working there about two hours when I found out what his help entailed. I went into the store cupboard to get a giant-sized baked bean tin as requested and he was straight in behind me, hands everywhere, his body pinning me up against the storage rack.

'No. No!' I said as firmly as I could. I managed to pull myself away from him.

All he did was laugh as I ran out the door. 'Don't worry, my sweet Scottish dyke. We'll have plenty of chances to get to know each other. It's time you found out what a man feels like.' He acted as if his behaviour was the most natural thing in the world.

But it was the other girls who shocked me the most. Bristling with fury, I told the first waitress I saw.

'Welcome to Ollie the Octopus,' she said with a resigned look. 'He tried it on with all of us when we first started working here. Stay out of the store cupboard if you can help it and if he persists, give him a hand job to leave you alone.' She nodded as if to confirm that was the best deal I was going to get.

I was still in shock when I got back to the hostel that evening.

'How was the first day?' asked Rita.

'Shit. Manager's a dirty old man. Tried to grope me and that seems to be the norm, according to the other girls.'

'Comes with the territory of being a waitress, I'm afraid. And don't think the haircut's going to put him off. For most of them screwing a lesbian is a manly duty. Yeah, it's a shit world out there. Just make the best of it.'

The next day Ollie stuck his hand up my skirt when I was behind the till. Then he whipped out his penis when he caught me in the back shop corridor. 'Come on, darling, you know you want it,' he said, leering at me. 'Looks good, doesn't it? Just one time and I'll leave you alone. Talk to the other girls, they all said yes.'

I ran back into the restaurant, closed my eyes and rubbed my forehead to compose myself. A new customer came in. I managed to walk over and take their order and smile as if nothing had happened.

My faith in men was restored when I called Duncan that night. We'd agreed a plan before we left. I'd call the phone box down the road from his flat at exactly 7 pm, so he could let me know what was happening back in Glasgow. It had seemed a good idea at the time, wait a few days for the heat to die down, but it had been driving me mad with worry that he might be in trouble and I'd been tempted to call his flat to check everything was okay. But no, I managed to convince myself that we'd agreed a plan, and although it might be that people only listen in to your phone calls in the movies, it was crazy to take any chances.

It was a huge relief when he answered the phone, his voice full of Duncan energy and buzz. Hearing that familiar voice, his lame little joke, 'Jonesey Chinese Laundry, can I help you?' in a cod-Chinese accent, poleaxed me with emotion.

'Any news from Michael?' I said quickly.

'Have I got a story to tell you, Bobbie.'

Uh oh. I tried to sense his mood from the crackly phone line.

'I decided to take the bull by the horns,' he said. 'Be proactive. That way my story of being left in the lurch without any explanation would have more credibility. So I went into the Avalon Gallery yesterday, said I was a friend of yours and wanted to get in touch, and asked if they have an address I could reach you at. The bloke there looked at me a bit funny and said no, but if I came back at four o'clock, there'd be someone who could help me.'

'Duncan, you idiot,' I cried. 'Why on earth did you do that? I told you to be careful.'

'Michael would find me in the end, Bobbie, and I didn't want to sit about like a turkey waiting for Christmas. I went back at four and there he was. I see what you mean, Bobbie, straight out of central casting. Real villain, he is. But you didn't tell me about his bloody dogs.'

'Lucifer and Satan? He brought them along?'

'Lucifer and Satan, that's their names? Bloody hell, I thought you said this guy was subtle. Anyway, I think they were there to make a statement. They sat very obediently in the corner. He asked if I knew where you were. I said not exactly, London somewhere. Said I was worried you'd left so suddenly and I wanted to check you were okay. And he said, "London, not Edinburgh?" so he'd already got the false trail we left for him. I think he believed me. He made me promise to get in touch if I heard from you, asked me to tell you all is forgiven, that you'd passed the tests to be part of his world and he wanted you back. Very sinister. I'll tell you what, Bobbie, when you suggested calling on call boxes, I thought you were going a bit over the top. But now that I've met him, I can see where you're coming from. Anyway, after he'd finished scaring me witless, he was charm personified. Thanked me for getting in touch. Gave me his business card, all very civilised.'

'Maybe it worked. But just to make sure, I won't call again. I've met someone who's had a similar experience and she's teaching me the ropes. Told me about something called Poste Restante, where you can write to me and I can pick it up at a post office. I can check every couple of days to see if there's any mail. Write to me care of Trafalgar Square Post Office, that's the biggest one in London.' I gave him the address.

'Okay. Very Secret Squirrel. But how are you? Finding your feet down there? Sounds like you've met someone useful. You sure you can trust them? You never see people's dark side, Bobbie, that's why you're in this mess.'

'I've grown up a lot in the last few days, Duncan. You're right, I wasn't on my guard as much as I should have been when I first got here, but I've met a woman who's been through something like what I'm going through. Yes, I'm being careful, but I'm pretty sure she's not out to trick me.'

'Cool. Just be wary. So what's London like?'

'Not bad. A few ups and downs, but I'm surviving. I've had a Big Mac in a McDonald's and I've turned into a lesbian.'

'I'm shocked, Bobbie, deeply shocked. I thought you hated burger bars?'

It was great to laugh again. 'Duncan, I miss you,' I said. 'I know you're being upbeat because you don't want me to worry. But I don't want you pulling any more stunts like getting in touch with Michael again. If there's the slightest whiff of trouble I want you to promise me you'll go straight to the police. Promise me, Duncan.'

'I promise.' I heard a different tone in his voice. 'You're right, these last few days, I've been bloody terrified. I heard a car's exhaust backfire and nearly jumped out of my skin. But I think if you stay out of the way, Michael will give up looking for you eventually. You pissed him off when he thought he'd indoctrinated you into his world. When he sees you're not going to make trouble for him, I'm sure he'll calm down and go away.'

'I'll stay out of your way for a while too, just to be on the safe side. But don't forget to write if you need to get in touch. It's so good to hear your voice, Duncan. I'm missing you already and I'm sorry again for all this mess. And I haven't really turned into a lesbian. I got a haircut by mistake that makes me look like one. You take care, okay? Love you.'

I hung up. Why did I say 'love you'? But I did, I suppose, love him. Goodness knows what he was going through to help me.

I had 60p left, so I called Mum. Kept myself sounding

cheery and excited, play going well, nice people, etc, etc. 'Oh, I'm glad you called,' she said. 'Somebody from the gallery came round today looking for you. Said they needed to get in touch to sort out some paperwork to do with you leaving. I felt silly telling them you were in London but I didn't know where. You must give me a way of getting in touch with you, Bobbie, in case anything happens. None of us are getting any younger you know. Anyway, the chap gave me a telephone number and asked you to call it. Do you have a pen?'

I made a pretence of writing the number down. I never told Michael where my parents lived, and he had tracked them down already. I should have expected that. Look how quickly he got photos of Duncan and me chatting. Duncan. He'd have left the phone box by now. Should I call his flat and tell him? I gripped the phone so hard, my knuckles went white. In the end I decided no. He already knew to be worried.

I headed off to Hatton Garden the next morning before work to sell the necklace Michael gave me. Lots of jewellery shops there, Rita really did know her way around London. I went into the first shop I came to. The guy spent a long time looking at it. 'It's a fine piece,' he said. 'But I'm afraid in today's market conditions I can't give you more than five hundred pounds for it.'

I was stunned. It must be worth a fortune. I was about to say yes, when he gave me a strange look. 'Also, I need to ask how you came by it,' he said. 'Just in case there are any questions. And I'll need ID, something with your name and current address on it. I'm sure you understand.'

'It was a present from a friend. But I'm afraid I don't

have any ID with me,' I replied. 'I've travelled here from... Essex and don't want to have to come all the way back again. Are you sure you can't take it without ID?'

'That's highly irregular. I'll call my partner and see what he has to say. It would be a shame to lose out on such a fine piece. Can you come back in two hours and I'll give you a decision?'

I calculated I would just about have time before I started work. And it would give me a chance to check out other jewellers. 'Thank you,' I said, giving him the benefit of a cheery smile. 'I'll be back at eleven.' He was picking up the phone even before I left the shop.

I walked past the other jewellers until I came to one well out of sight of the first shop. Silly really, I'm sure they were used to people shopping around for the best prices, but I wanted to be discreet. The jeweller there was a jolly, larger than life character, matching braces and bowtie, wearing a blazer with a faded regimental insignia on it.

'I'm trying to sell a piece of jewellery,' I said. 'But I don't have any ID with me. Is that a problem?'

He gave a fruity laugh. 'If we had to ask for ID every time we bought something, our trade would dry up overnight. Discretion, that's what this business is all about.' An exaggerated wink reinforced the point.

I took out the necklace.

He looked at me. 'You're name's not Bobbie something, is it? Bobbie Sinclair?'

I almost fainted. 'Wh-why do you say that?'

'Well if it is, my dear, your boyfriend had someone go around all the jewellers here yesterday. Said you had a big bust up and you might try to sell it in a fit of pique. Told me I'd be on a nice little earner if I got your new address or got you to wait around until he could get here. But I take an old-fashioned view that a gift's a gift, and when you show a young lady a token of your affection, it's hers to do with as she pleases. It's not my place to interfere when the course of true love doesn't run smoothly. But I can see why he doesn't want you to sell it. Beautiful piece.'

I tried to remain calm but I could feel my pulse racing, my skin clammy. 'That's very gracious of you to say that, sir. And you have it right, I'd rather not see him again, or anyone he's got looking for me. I think I'd better skedaddle, so if I were to ask four hundred pounds for it, could you pay me in cash straight away?'

I tried desperately not to let him see how terrified I was. But I couldn't help myself. I glanced anxiously back at the door.

'I don't like to take advantage of someone's impetuousness, young lady. This is worth a lot more than four hundred pounds.'

'Please? I know what I'm doing. And I really do have to go.'

'Sorry, dear. Something's not quite right about this. Suspect provenance, if you get my meaning, so my better instincts say no.'

I rushed off, ran into the street. Tried to get a taxi to stop, but it drove right by. Another one came along and I jumped in front of it. The driver slammed on his brakes, missing me by inches. I ran round to the passenger door and saw someone was inside already.

'You trying to get yourself bleedin' killed?' yelled the taxi driver.

191

I stepped back in defeat, turned and ran, all the way back to the tube station. People stared at me but I didn't care. At the ticket barrier, I couldn't find my ticket. I looked around in wild-eyed panic, searching frantically through my coat pockets until I found it, tucked deep inside for safe keeping. I ran through the barrier, down the escalator, pushing past everyone, until I reached the platform. I stood stock still, back up against the wall, fearful that any moment someone would grab me and shove me onto the tracks.

I heard the sound of the train approaching, felt the wind on my face, saw it light up the entrance to the tunnel as it came round the bend. I glanced around one last time before boarding, but apart from a few old-age pensioners, there was no one on the platform. Breathing hard, I headed back to the hostel, where I stashed the necklace in my locker. I was still shaking by the time I arrived at The Golden Egg.

My mind was in turmoil. Did I tell the first jeweller my new name, or anything about me? I couldn't remember, but I was pretty sure I didn't. But Michael would have a description of me, my new look, and he'd know for sure I was in London.

I felt so drained. When Ollie slipped his hand up my skirt, I couldn't even be bothered to fight him off. I stood frozen, unresponsive, staring out at the diners. Do what you bloody want, I thought, I don't care any more. Two seconds without a reaction was all the encouragement he needed. He pushed himself against my back and his hand slipped round the front, fumbling inside my knickers until he found what he was looking for. I put both hands on the counter and stared at the floor.

'My office,' he said, his voice thick with desire.

I don't remember walking there. The door closed behind me and he zipped down his fly. I started to mechanically jerk him off, staring at him with a blank look of hatred. His hands were under my blouse now and he squeezed my breast so hard it hurt. I went faster.

'Not much to keep me busy there, Bertie. Have to try something else.' He put his hands on my shoulders and pushed me down onto my knees. No point in stopping now. I just wanted to get it over with.

'Tasting a man at last, my little Scottish lezzie,' he moaned. 'You can tell your girlfriends what they're missing. Bring them round here to find out if you like.'

When it was over, he pushed my face into his groin so I couldn't escape. Held me there for a minute. It felt like eternity.

I got up and tried to sort my hair, my clothes. I spat out what was left of him on the floor.

He grimaced. 'That's not very nice,' he said. 'Clean it up before you go back to work.'

I don't think I've ever hated anyone as much as I hated Ollie in that moment. Even Michael paled into insignificance. One of the waitresses saw me coming out of the office and gave me a shrug. I was expressionless, hollow inside.

'Don't worry,' she said. 'He's got a new start tomorrow. Somebody else's turn.'

Somehow I got through the shift and headed back to the hostel. I desperately wanted to call Duncan, but worried it would put him in danger. Rita had heard enough of my problems, and I didn't want to come across as clingy and needy. The silence was broken by the sixteen-year-olds coming back from their day on the town, breathless with excitement they'd been to Madame Tussauds. They'd given up on finding jobs and were blowing the rest of their savings before heading back to Mummy and Daddy. I envied them.

I didn't ever want to go back to The Golden Egg, but I didn't have a choice. Despite Rita's optimistic noises about how easy it was to find a job, it was 1976, the Chancellor had borrowed millions from the IMF to keep the country afloat and jobs didn't grow on trees. I took my precious stash of cash out of my locker and counted it. £243 left. I counted it again. Still £243. I thought I'd more than enough to keep me going for a while but losing two hundred pounds and not being able to sell the necklace meant I couldn't afford to give up my wages just yet.

I had a terrible night's sleep. Nightmares about Ollie, DCI McDonald, the guy who stole my money; they were all there. I dragged myself out of bed in the morning and headed over to Trafalgar Square to check my post box. Nothing. I bought myself a chocolate milkshake in McDonald's to cheer myself up. It was so thick, I had to eat it with a spoon.

I steeled myself to walk into The Golden Egg twenty minutes late. The bastard would probably dock my wages. The new girl looked so young. Donna was her name and only fifteen, the other girls told me. She looked younger. Sleeping rough, ran away from home because her dad beat her up. It's a shitty world out there.

Donna chatted to me in our break. 'Mr Busby has been very good to me,' she said. 'I think he knows I should still be at school, but he said I looked older for my years and so he'd take a chance with me. What do you think, Bertie, do you think I'd pass for sixteen?' She straightened her back and looked to me for encouragement.

'Whatever,' I replied. I wasn't really listening.

'He's going to take me out flat-hunting this evening. Isn't that good of him? I told him I don't have anywhere to stay, so he's offered to take me over to his place, let me get cleaned up and then he's going to introduce me to some landlords he knows in King's Cross.' She gave me a brave smile.

She had my attention now. I felt my heart break.

'Donna, no. Ollie's not a nice man. There's only one reason why he wants to get you on your own.'

King's Cross. I'd heard that was the cheap red light district. That'd be what his 'landlords' would be about, once he'd had his fill of her.

'Oh, Bertie, don't worry. I've had a boyfriend before,' Donna replied. 'I'm grown up for my age. I know what men are like, I know how to say no.'

'Donna, please,' I whispered. 'Don't go with him. There's a place you could stay where I live. It's just for women. It's safe. Please, tell him you've changed your mind, you've heard about somewhere else. Please? Will you do that for me?'

'Oh, well okay. He is gross, isn't he? I'll tell him you're going to help me out.'

'No, don't do that either. Don't give him any details. And don't let him touch you. He'll try that today, once he knows he's not meeting you tonight. Just tell him to get lost.'

Ollie came by and we stopped our conversation.

'Come on, girls, break's over. Customers to serve,' he said with a big grin. He helped Donna on her way with a pat on the bum. I was ignored.

His mood deteriorated when Donna told him the flat-hunting was off. Somehow she managed to keep him at arm's length until she finished work.

I arranged to meet her at The Coach and Horses. Donna arrived first and was waiting outside. They wouldn't let her in, being underage. I walked her back to the hostel and introduced her to Cynthia.

Cynthia was not impressed. 'She can't stay here, Bertie, we're full. You can't invite anyone you meet to come here, you know. We have rules.'

I took her to one side and explained the situation.

'Well, she can have your bed if you like and you can take pot luck on finding a spare one at lights out,' she finally agreed. 'But you can't bed-hop indefinitely. If we don't get a free space in the next couple of days, one of you will have to go. And don't do it again.'

'Thanks, Cynthia, you're an angel. I promise this is a one off. Can I ask you something else?'

Cynthia looked exasperated, 'Now what?'

'I'm changing my hair again. What's the most heterosexual colour? There have been a few... um... misunderstandings with the blonde look.'

She laughed. 'Honey, I'd fancy you whatever colour it was.' Despite everything, she made me smile.

She stepped back and looked at me. 'Why don't you go for a short, light brown perm? Biba Poster Girl look. Suit those gorgeous big brown eyes of yours.'

'Thanks, Cynthia, you're a darling.' I gave her a big hug and headed back to see Donna, who was chatting away to the sixteen-year-olds. I looked at her, pretending to be worldly-wise, but really just a wee lassie blissfully unaware of the horrors out there for the uninitiated. It's easy to get wrapped up so much in your own problems you forget about helping others. I felt good about helping her. For the first time since I'd come to London I hadn't felt overwhelmed and powerless. I had got involved and had felt a sense of optimism and accomplishment knowing I had made one small thing better.

But if I wanted to really feel I had achieved something with Donna I had to do more. 'Donna, you can't go back to The Golden Egg,' I said. 'That guy will end up raping you, or even worse. Stay here until you find another job. I'll take care of your rent and we can share food. I'd feel terrible if something happened to you.'

I couldn't believe I'd just said that. I was tottering on the brink of disaster, and now I wanted to help a complete stranger.

'I can't ask you to do that. You don't even know me. I can look after myself.'

Despite her words I could see an overwhelming sense of relief in Donna's eyes, a cry for help. That settled it.

'No you can't, Donna. It'll be okay. When you find your feet, you can pay me back. I've got plenty of money to keep us both going.'

Of course that wasn't the truth. My pittance of a wage from The Golden Egg meant I was barely breaking even when I took my travel and accommodation costs into account. If it wasn't for my tips I wouldn't be able to eat.

And I had to make sure I kept as much of my savings as possible, I would need them to put down a rent deposit on a flat eventually when I got a job that paid more so I could afford to move out of the hostel. I could just about help Donna, but it was putting my finances on a knife edge. But I couldn't bear the thought of her sleeping on the streets or even worse things happening to her.

For a moment the world felt a more beautiful place, knowing I could help her. But hopefully it wouldn't be long before she found her feet and could support herself without me.

chapter seventeen

I needed to find another job. But where? Carnaby Street, King's Road and Downing Street were the only three addresses I knew in London and there wasn't much chance of a job at that last one. It was my day off, so I asked the sixteen-year-olds if they'd take Donna out with them while I had my Biba perm. Another fifteen pounds gone. I was haemorrhaging money and it had to stop.

I went back to the hostel, changed into a cream Yves St Laurent dress from my Michael wardrobe. I headed out quickly, feeling out of place in that austere environment. There was a bus that went to King's Road from Earl's Court so I headed off there.

Magical. All the shop names I'd read about in magazines. Money everywhere. Recession, what recession? Beautiful people belonging to an exclusive club of fast cars, trendy nightclubs and designer clothes. Summoning all my reserves of poise and composure, I walked into the boutiques in search of a job.

It was awful. A welcoming smile as I walked in, obviously taken for a well-heeled potential customer. But the disdain when I asked about working there. Who did I know, what school did I go to? Mocked my Scottish accent. It wasn't the world for me. I needed to find somewhere

where getting on was not based on class and connections, but on ability, personality, being able to get things done. Chelsea was a world closed to me. It had its own society, its own club, to which outsiders were firmly not invited.

Soho hopefully would be different. That's where Carnaby Street was, so I tried there next. At first I was disappointed again; the mecca of the swinging sixties no more than a little backstreet, selling a load of tacky rubbish. And Soho really had prostitutes. Yes, red lights in the window, 'model available' written on a card next to the doorbell. Strip clubs down dark side streets. I wasn't that desperate. Yet.

I was about to leave when I noticed another world also existed there. Jazz clubs and coffee bars, record studios and guitar shops, bohemian drinking dens. And shiny new offices, all glass and chrome, standing out from the Victorian architecture of their neighbours. I loved the fact that daring entrepreneurs had the nerve to open for business in a neighbourhood like that. They seemed to be advertising agencies and media companies from what I could gather when I sneaked a peek into their reception areas. They struck me as places where they'd be open-minded to taking on people from outside. It was worth a try.

I went back to the hostel and called Tom McGrath at The Third Eye Centre. Luckily he was in and we chatted for a few minutes about how things were going. I was relieved to see there were no hard feelings about me moving on to the Avalon Gallery. He had confounded the sceptics and made The Third Eye Centre a resounding success. His poems were being critically acclaimed and everyone was queuing up to perform his plays. A true Renaissance man.

I told him I'd had to leave Glasgow in a hurry, trouble with a guy, and I was down in London looking for a job. I needed to get a reference and couldn't ask the Avalon Gallery as they were part of the problem. Said if anyone came asking about me he was to say he hadn't got a clue where I was now. I think he'd come from a world where you didn't ask too many questions about people's personal lives, so he didn't pry too much. He promised me a glowing reference, even when I told him it might be for an advertising agency. Gave him some guff about changing the capitalist system from within, which I knew was kidding neither of us.

There was a typewriter at the hostel and I typed up my CV to make it more suitable for an office job. After four years at university, my most marketable skill was the typing and dictation I'd learned in my home economics class at high school. I made some Xeroxes and the next day set about blitzing the studios and agencies for a job. I popped into a photo booth and took a few photos to attach to the CVs. I thought of Duncan's photos, sticking his tongue into Greta's ear. That made me smile. I promised myself I'd stop off at my post box to see if he'd written; it would need to be tomorrow, no time today. I managed to drop CVs off to six agencies before I had to head off to work.

Ollie was waiting for me. 'Quite the guardian angel, aren't you?' he said. 'You should know what a gossip mill this is. I heard two of the girls talking about how you saved that schoolgirl from nasty old me. So you can have your own wicked way with her, you lezzie whore.' He noticed my hair. 'And what's with the haircut? Is that to please your new girlfriend?'

'Piss off, Ollie,' I replied. I'd had just about as much of him as I could take.

'Piss off, eh? Listen, when I have my eye on someone, no one gets in my way. She was a lovely, innocent-looking little girl, was Donna, and I was looking forward to giving her a real education. And your meddling has denied us both that pleasure. So *you* can piss off. Now. Pick up your cards and get out. Here's your last pay envelope. You'll never work in a Golden Egg again.'

Shit. Back at the hostel, I did a quick appraisal of my finance again. It didn't look good, to put it mildly. I wanted to rush over to Soho to see if anything had happened with my job search but managed to convince myself to wait a day, so as not to look too desperate. Instead, I headed off to see if Duncan had written. I wasn't expecting anything, he said he would write every couple of weeks, so I was surprised to find there was a letter from him. I walked across to Trafalgar Square, found a bench and started to read.

There was no joke to start the letter off, just the brutal facts. The day after our phone call, he'd been stopped on the street by two thugs who'd collared him. Big Jockie and Ron, by the sound of Duncan's description. None of the civilised veneer of the conversation he'd had with Michael. They'd wanted to know where I was, and they'd wanted to know right then. Duncan told them the story that I'd disappeared suddenly, only told him I was going to London. He didn't know where. He had no idea how I'd managed to pack up and get my stuff out without anyone noticing.

They'd punched him. I felt sick. It started to rain but I didn't notice. My best friend, beaten up. All because of me.

He said he hadn't seen the punch coming, it had knocked him out cold. When he next opened his eyes, Big Jockie was holding him up, while Ron did the talking. He had a message Duncan was to pass on to me. There was nothing for me to worry about. Michael wasn't angry with me, but I had to call him straight away. Otherwise they would try harder to persuade me.

Duncan said he'd taken himself to the hospital where they'd told him he had a fractured jaw. Kept him overnight because of the concussion, which was why he was only now writing. He was staying at his mum's in Hawick and gave me her telephone number. I sat there and cried. The rain poured down and mixed with my tears.

When I called Duncan that night I knew what I had to do. Go back to Glasgow, face Michael, give in to whatever he wanted me to do. I couldn't believe it when Duncan said no.

'Think about it logically, Bobbie. You've done a better job of disappearing than he was expecting, so he tried a little rough stuff to see if that flushes you out. He obviously believes if I knew where you were, I'd move heaven and earth to get you back to Glasgow to save my skin. If you don't call he'll believe I know nothing.'

'I can't ask you to take that risk, Duncan. I'm coming back and that's all there is to it.'

'Really, Bobbie, I'm not just saying this to make you

feel good. If you stay disappeared, I think it'll be best for both of us.'

'No, Duncan, it's not right.'

'Look, I'll tell you what. Let's see if these two gorillas threaten me again. If they do, I'll be the complete wimp, promise results straight away to get them to back off. Tell them I'll try really hard to track you down, ask them to give me twenty-four hours to get results. Then we'll have the conversation about what to do. Until then, do us both a favour and stay in London.'

I did think about going home anyway, but in the end decided to wait. But I vowed that at the first sign of another threat to Duncan, I would go back, no matter what he said.

Even hearing my CV blitz had got me two interviews didn't lift me from my despair. The first interview was a disaster. Maybe they picked up I was completely demoralised, I don't know. Everything I said seemed to be the wrong answer. Campbell, Peters and Dixon was the second interview and I promised myself I'd try harder.

I walked into the lobby. A huge bunch of exotic flowers sat in a gigantic vase on a glass top table. I breathed in the scent to try to fill me with confidence. I'd done my sums before the interview, I had enough money for another three weeks, four weeks if I broke the news to Donna she'd need to find another way to sort herself out. I tried not to think about the consequences if I didn't get the job.

The impossibly beautiful receptionist gave me a nice smile. Kevin in personnel took me into a room no bigger than a broom cupboard to do typing and dictation tests.

When he closed the door it suddenly felt claustrophobic in there, just the two of us. I waited for the innuendo, the pat on the knee, but nothing. Friendly, but professional. This is ridiculous, I thought, not every man is going to pounce on me the minute he gets me alone in a room. He read out some text for me to take down in shorthand and then tested my typing speed. I managed to scrape through.

Next, I met Hugo, my prospective boss. He bought into my story about being fascinated about advertising and using my initiative to come down to London to find a job on the ground floor. Yesterday I'd bought a copy of *Campaign*, the trade paper for the advertising business, and pored over every story, every photograph. I managed to namedrop Saatchi & Saatchi, Alan Brady and Marsh, and all these other weird company names which were just the surnames of the people that worked there. Hugo looked impressed. I'd chosen the right ones to mention, apparently.

Hugo was very bohemian-looking, wore a cravat, hair a bit too long for a businessman, a patrician lilt in his voice that was charismatic rather than grating, full of effortless charm. We seemed to hit it off as I sat across from him, legs crossed, back straight. I beamed away, looking every inch the eager, enthusiastic, attentive secretary-to-be, while on the inside a gnawing fear tore at my soul. Images of Duncan lying in a hospital bed, the last few pennies in my purse, the groping hands of a middle-aged pervert and Michael's cruel, calculating eyes, all fighting each other to be the one that overwhelmed me.

But I held it together. And I got the job. Personal assistant to Hugo Peters, client services director of CPD.

When I called the next day and heard the news, I allowed myself to think I was actually going to survive.

I told Donna the good news and she told me hers. After hanging around with the sixteen-year-olds, she'd decided to go with them when they headed back to Devon tomorrow. She was going to work on their farm for the summer until she turned sixteen, then find a job down there as a live-in waitress or something.

I gave her my post box address and she promised to write. So that was it. A few night's uncomfortable sleep and a few quid in food to turn somebody's life around. I thought of Joe's suicide letter, of Duncan trying to stay upbeat despite his fractured jaw. If only solving my problems could be that simple.

My parents were pleased, mind. The story of the play finishing early so they couldn't come down to see it, and me staying on in London to make a go of a career down south had gone down surprisingly well. I told them I was working in a prestigious Mayfair art gallery, in case they told someone and it got back to Michael. And they bought into the story that I couldn't give them my telephone number and address just yet as I was moving around so much.

The next day there was another letter from Duncan. I opened it full of trepidation but he said everything was okay. Jaw had healed up perfectly, no lasting damage and no sign of Michael's 'hit squad' as he called them. I wished he wouldn't make jokes like that. He said it proved his theory that after his fit of pique, Michael would now leave me alone. All had gone quiet on DCI McDonald's death and it looked as if Michael had muddied the waters enough to get the investigation put on the back burner. Another reason for him to keep a low profile.

I had turned up for my interview wearing my Yves St Laurent peasant dress I'd brought to London specifically for interviews. Distinctive, glamorous, and without being sluttish. But no more individualism from me. In the couple of days before I started work, I went through the Kays catalogue, bought jersey wrap dresses, sensible blouses and check knee-length skirts on the never-never and had them delivered to the hostel.

I was a refugee from my past, in brown and beige Courtelle. Who I once was didn't exist any more.

chapter eighteen

I had to wait just over a week to start my job. Tom McGrath's job reference came through; it was a corker apparently. I remember Hugo saying afterwards they didn't know whether to write back thanking him for the information or offer him a job as a copywriter. I'd succeeded in becoming Bertie St Clair and got my changed national insurance number in their files. Not bad at creating a new identity.

I came into work bright and early on my first day. My desk was right outside Hugo's corner office on the account management floor. I sat there until ten o'clock before anyone showed up. All his staff were under thirty, and all but one of them were guys. You could smell the testosterone.

I got a nice intro to the account guys from Hugo that made me feel welcome and to my pleasant surprise I made it to the end of the first week without any major incidents. The account guys were always coming on strong, but took it in good spirits when I rebuffed all advances, especially if I could be funny doing it. I was surprised to find myself liking working there. After all my worries about starting a business career, it wasn't that bad. Rita was right, sometimes taking a wrong turn got you to the right place.

I started to get caught up in the passion and excitement of making newer and better ads. The posters were my favourites, especially the cigarette ads. They were not allowed to say anything about the actual cigarette itself, so the ads were very arty, almost self-indulgently brilliant. It did seem ironic the people behind these beautiful, witty, clever ads were a bunch of immature, self-absorbed idiots otherwise known as 'the creatives'. Work-wise I shouldn't have had anything to do with them. They were a different department, located on a different floor, but Hugo was always tearing his hair out about getting timesheets from them, so he knew how much time it was taking to make an ad and whether he was charging the clients enough. But the creative boss thought such administrative tasks were beneath him and so it was left to me to wander up to their floor and get any massively overdue ones so we could work out the account profitability each month.

'You're the new girl from downstairs,' said Spike, the copywriter on the pet foods business as I approached. 'You know, if you were to get a padded bra and wear your skirts a bit shorter, you'd be not half bad. It wouldn't be a sin to see a little more of your legs, you know.'

'I wouldn't want to distract you from your work, Spike,' I replied. 'Now if you can drag yourself away from finding interesting things to say about dog food for a second, is there any chance I could get your timesheets? I'm trying to get the client's account updated for month end and Hugo says yours are the only ones missing.'

'Oh God, Hugo's finally got a secretary that ventures into the lion's den to beat us up about our admin failings. Congratulations, peaches, all your predecessors hightailed it out of here when he asked them to do that. They didn't hire me to fill out forms, love, they hired me to write great ads. You've seen the Benson and Hedges Iguana ad, the Nimble balloon and the Cadbury Smash aliens? Say no more.'

'Wow, you wrote them?' I was supposed to be hassling him for his paperwork but I couldn't help but be impressed.

'No, they are great ads, like the ones they've hired me to write. Look, I tell you what. You promise to dress less like my maiden aunt and I'll get the forms done straight away. A deal?'

I said yes. Hadn't the slightest intention of changing my wardrobe, he knew it and I knew it. But it was what made the world go round and so I went along with it.

At the end of the week, there was another letter from Duncan. He'd been stopped in the street by Ron, on his own this time. Very threatening but no violence. Duncan said Ron glared at him when Duncan said he'd checked again but no one had a clue where I was. He tried to make light of it in his letter but he'd be freaking out. Said he was going to move flat just to be on the safe side, and if a few months went by and Michael left him alone we could try phoning each other again. The first time I could call and say I'd just got his new number and was phoning to say hello from London. If someone was listening, it would fit with his story. Good way to check if the chase was off, he reckoned. I was aching to speak to him, to find out how he was, but that would be stupid right now.

Over the next few weeks I discovered the world of advertising. The only person who rubbed me up the wrong way was Cecil, an account manager in even more of a hurry to make a name for himself than everyone else around there. He was aghast when everyone else treated me as an equal when he believed I was an uncouth Scottish savage. And I made the mistake of letting him see me struggling to collate the timesheet information into Hugo's account planning reports.

'Don't worry, honey, you'll soon get the hang of them,' he said. 'The man who designed these reports deliberately made them easy enough for a woman to be able to fill them in.'

I smiled sweetly and said that was very reassuring.

Helen was the only woman account exec, and she quickly invited me to have lunch with her in the staff canteen. It was nice to see there was no hierarchy regarding managers and secretaries mixing. Her basic advice was that a PA in an agency was expected to also be a waitress, a travel agent and a mistress, but if I was good at my job I'd only have to be two of those.

'As long as I get to choose which two,' I replied.

I had to work long hours to catch up on the administrative mess I'd inherited and I was basically using the hostel as a place to crash out at night, so when I saw the note on my bed asking me report to Cynthia when I got in, I presumed it was the day of reckoning at last. There was an unwritten rule you didn't hang about the hostel forever. What with me having a full-time job now and never being around, I guessed she would be telling me it was time to move on.

Cynthia got straight to the point. 'There's been a guy here looking for you, Bertie.' She saw the look of shock on my face. 'Now don't get alarmed, he only spoke to me, and I'm pretty good at keeping a poker face if we have any unwanted visitors here. Very rare though, for there to be anyone looking for someone from out of town.'

'Who was he, what did he want?' I collapsed on a chair next to her. The jewellers was one thing, but this was too close to home. I'd been too optimistic. Michael was going to get me eventually, I knew he was.

'Private detective. Had a photo of you in a yellow halter outfit at a restaurant. Looked like you were sitting next to someone but that bit had been cut off.' I remembered that photo, Michael had asked the waiter to take it on one of our first dates. I'd thought at the time it was a bit sentimental, a bit out of character.

'Looking for a Bobbie Sinclair, not a Bertie St Clare, so he doesn't know your new name. Asked me to imagine you with short blonde hair like mine so he also knew you'd changed your look since you got here, but doesn't know about your latest haircut. I'm pretty sure it was just part of a random search of places where you'd find new arrivals in London. He had a list of hostels with him, with the ones above us already ticked off, so that means he wasn't specifically targeting here.'

'Cynthia, is he coming back? What did you tell him?'

'Relax, he didn't suspect a thing. Said he was working for your parents, looking to track down a runaway. But that's not true, is it?'

'No, my parents know I'm here and I talk to them all the time. It's a guy I stupidly got mixed up with in Glasgow who doesn't want to let me go. What do you think I should do, Cynthia? I don't want him to find me.' I tried to keep the rising panic out of my voice.

'Look, as I said, I'm pretty sure it was nothing more

than a speculative visit. But just to be on the safe side, you could get your stuff packed up and take an overnight bag over to the Lesbian Collective in Dulwich. It's an invitation-only place so it won't be on the detective's hostel list. I can give them a call and see if you can sleep there temporarily till you find your own place. It was time you were thinking of moving on anyway. And don't worry, I'll tell them you're one hundred per cent hetro, so there won't be any confusion on that score.'

'I don't know. All my problems stem from my choice in men. Going over to the other side might not be a bad idea. Thanks, Cynthia. This is really good of you.'

'Not at all. I know what you did for Donna. There are not enough people like you in the world, Bertie. Whatever's going on between you and this guy, you deserve to have someone looking after you.'

Despite Cynthia's assurances, I felt as if there was a clock ticking before Michael's detective would finally catch me. I tried to figure out what it meant. Was Duncan's theory that Michael would give up on me nothing more than wishful thinking? Maybe Duncan had accidentally said something that had made Michael start looking for me in the Earl's Court hostels. The truth was I didn't know. But Cynthia was right. Anywhere Michael's search had touched was a place I didn't want to be.

I said my goodbyes to Rita when I finished packing. It was quite emotional; she'd been the only person I could call a friend since I'd come to London and I think I'd got as close to her as she let anyone. We didn't make any pretence we'd try to keep in touch. I respected the road she was going down, looking for a way to live a simple, solitary life, to get as far away as possible from the horrors of her past. Although the same was true for me, I didn't want to give up on my future to achieve it. Did that make me a bad person? I'd like to think not, but sometimes I couldn't be sure.

The Lesbian Collective turned out to be a big detached house in the south side of London. I didn't know what to expect, and it was strange to see some of the girls kissing each other, holding hands. A glimpse of another world. I'm sure there must have been lesbian couples in Glasgow, but if there were they must have kept it pretty discreet, nothing like the openness they had in London.

Nobody put any pressure on me to move on, but I felt I was impinging on their set up and was desperate to get a place of my own. Camden Town was the best place to find a flat in a hurry, they told me. I got a copy of the *Evening Standard* as soon as it hit the newsstands and started visiting any bedsit that caught my eye before they got snapped up. I promised Hugo if I was allowed to shoot off in the afternoon to find a place I would come back to work in the evening.

After three attempts of trying to be first, I found a room in a bedsit on Chalk Farm Road. A hundred-pound deposit made a huge dent in the money I had left, but I calculated I could survive until my wages came in. I was sharing with two girls, Linda, who worked in a bank, and Debbie, who was a secretary like me.

I moved in that weekend. Now I had a job, a roof over my head, twenty-three pounds of my escape money left and a place far away from where Michael might find me.

Time to look to the future.

chapter nineteen

London has a fantastic trick of reinventing itself, using what was in the past and turning it into the future. Take Camden Lock for example. It was where the Victorians connected Regent's Canal from the Thames to a big canal from the Midlands and the lock had been pretty much defunct since the 1960s. Then in 1974 it became a great little market, selling all sorts of weird bohemian stuff: jewellery, toys, ornaments, leather bags and belts and the like, vintage and second-hand clothes stalls. And Dingwalls, the old warehouse in the centre, became a super-cool venue where the music was loud because there were no houses nearby.

The whole area was full of character. If this had been Glasgow they'd have bricked up the canal and knocked down all the old buildings and built tower blocks before you could blink. The Camden Market stall holders were a weird-looking bunch; flamboyant clothes, lots of make-up and bizarre hairstyles. And that was just the guys. The more outrageous you looked, the more people would stop at your stall. It was having a big impact on the young people moving into the area and everyone was experimenting with new looks, new ideas. Punk rock had arrived and Camden was its epicentre. I felt staid and boring in comparison.

I thought about trying to sell the necklace to one of the stallholders, but then had a better idea. I went through the *Yellow Pages* in Trafalgar Square Post Office when I was in checking my post box. They had every region in the UK, so I looked up jewellers in Birmingham and the next weekend put on one of my posh outfits and headed off there. If Michael had every jewellers in the UK staked out he deserved to catch me.

I chose the three with the biggest ads and walked in and asked for a valuation. For insurance purposes, I said, but also with a view to selling. Cool, poised and self-assured, like I was bored by the whole thing. £2000 it was valued at, and one jeweller offered me £1500, cash in hand, no questions asked. Gave me his card and asked me to see him first if I'd got anything else to sell. Obviously I looked the part of somebody who had sugar daddies twisted round their little finger. I accepted his offer and walked out grinning from ear to ear, feeling as if I'd just won the pools.

Duncan hadn't heard from Michael again and when he moved flat I was able to start calling him. It was scary at first, and if I was scared, I couldn't imagine how Duncan must have felt, waiting for someone to break the door down any moment. But nothing. I was always careful never to say anything specific on the phone about where I worked or lived, but it looked as if Michael had finally turned his attentions elsewhere.

Duncan was making progress as a journalist. Still working freelance, making good money but it was taking time to build up a steady supply of assignments. But good for Duncan, he'd branched out into creative writing to fill his down time and was writing his first novel, so he told me. Great to see him keeping himself busy.

I called Cynthia at the hostel after I'd been away for a couple of months to check if the detective had come back. I breathed a sigh of relief when she told me no. We chatted on the phone for a while and I caught up on the news from the hostel. Rita had left and gone to live in Scotland, a crofting community in the Highlands. I hoped she'd found the escape she'd been looking for. Her solution to life's problems was to drop out of the rat race. I was throwing myself into it.

Because working in an ad agency was like being in a madhouse. Constant panic the copywriters wouldn't come up with the goods, constant chaos when the account guys agreed to deadlines that were impossible to meet. Half the people went out at lunchtime and staggered back drunk at four o'clock. The other half ran about yelling and throwing temper tantrums at everyone else's incompetence. I'm exaggerating a little, but only a little. Why these big respectable companies gave us so much money to do their advertising never ceased to amaze me.

I tried to stay above it all. It helped I was Hugo's secretary. Everyone wanted two minutes with him and as controller of his diary I was in a position of power way above my status in the organisation. Everyone was sleeping with everyone else and there was a rumour about me and Hugo that I took down more than dictation. I didn't mind. It might help reduce the attention I got from the young bucks in his department but nothing seemed to put them off.

Spike the dog-food guy was the most persistent. East

End boy made good by the sound of him, a bundle of nervous energy with a sex drive to match. Week one he tried the direct approach: 'Hi, I'm Spike, I think we are made for each other,' looking for a quick easy win.

Then he tried the more subtle lines. 'Anyone ever tell you, you look like Julie Christie?' was his opening gambit one day. 'Same hair and eyes. You look just like her in *Don't Look Now*. Great movie, by the way, have you seen it?'

'I'm more of a theatre person,' I replied, as I continued to type up Hugo's morning correspondence. 'Like to see real actors performing in the flesh. More passion.'

'It's always the quiet ones, isn't it? Didn't have you down for someone liking passion in the flesh, Bertie. Don't see you getting a lot of passion after work at the moment. But I'm here to put that right. Like some passion lessons this evening?'

'That's a very tempting offer, Spike, but I'll pass if you don't mind. Life at Campbell, Peters and Dixon is more than enough excitement for a simple Glasgow girl.' Spike got full marks for persistence, but if I was to have carnal activities, they were to be well away from the workplace. There I was Miss Goody Two-Shoes, strictly unavailable to all suitors.

Helen had overheard Spike's latest attempt to entice me out. 'Account men and secretaries, they're like pilots and air hostesses, doctors and nurses,' she said. 'All the girls here have been taken advantage of at one time or another. Good for you in resisting temptation. I wish there were more like you. Would make it easier to get taken seriously around here.'

She was on a mission to get more respect for women

in business and the secretaries lining up to get shagged by the account execs and copywriters didn't help her cause. And she deserved to get to the top, she was one of the few people there who actually seemed to care about others in the agency. For everyone else, it was recognition and promotion at all cost, with a quick stab in the back for anyone who got in the way.

I got into the habit of spending my lunch break walking around the famous historic theatres of the West End. Names that had seemed so magical and remote in Glasgow were now a few minutes' walk from the office. The greatest stages in the world, right on my doorstep. I looked at the names on the billboards: Paul Scofield, John Gielgud, Peggy Ashcroft, Helen Mirren. It didn't seem real these acting gods and goddesses were performing on the stages inside.

But it was a bittersweet experience being so close to theatreland. That was a destiny that was closed to me now. I would never have the courage to try to make it on the stage, knowing any success, any publicity, would give Michael the chance to track me down. But it was not like things were a disaster. Most people would give their eye teeth for a job and a flat in London. I was proud of myself for what I'd achieved. I might not have chosen to go down this road initially, but now I'd done it, I was determined to make the most of it.

★ ★ ★

Early one May evening I was sitting in Maison Bertaux, a great little coffee bar in Greek Street near the office. They served the most amazing cakes and if I was looking for a sugar high to give me a boost to keep going at work late into the evening, I would head over there about six, when most people doing normal jobs were calling it a day. I saw a guy in the corner, handsome in a bookish type of way, reading Edward Albee's script of *Who's Afraid Of Virginia Woolf?* Had it really been a year since I'd stood on stage as Martha and read those great reviews predicting a glittering career on the stage? I shook my head and took an extra-large bite of my millefeuille.

I saw him silently mouthing the words so I went over.

'Rehearsing?' I said. 'I played Martha once. It's a stunning play, isn't it?'

He blinked up at me through his wiry, round John Lennon glasses. 'I'm up for the part of Nick. Audition is next week. If you don't mind me saying, you're not how I imagine Martha at all.'

'Why's that?' I knew only too well, I still remembered the reviews. But it didn't hurt to have a little ego boost from time to time.

He blushed. 'Well, she's old and not… nice, isn't she?'

I laughed. 'How do you know I'm nice?' I put on my best drunk Martha voice. 'I could drink you under any goddam table I want to. If you even existed I'd divorce you.'

'Blimey,' he said. 'Okay, I'm wrong, you are Martha. If I buy you a coffee, can I pick your brains as to how to get the part?'

So that's how I met Henry, budding actor, sensitive soul and my first London lover. Our coffee led to us going to the Donmar together, an experimental theatre in

Covent Garden that had opened a few weeks earlier and was showing *Macbeth* with Ian McKellen and Judi Dench. It was a great evening. The venue was tiny by West End standards, it used to be a banana-ripening depot for the fruit market, but that only added to the intensity of the experience. The new hotshot director, Trevor Nunn, used a stripped-down stage and set, wooden stools and modern costumes, the audience surrounding it on three sides. And what powerful acting. I wouldn't have thought of Ian McKellen and Judi Dench to play Macbeth and his wife. They were a bit young for the roles, but they were amazing, full of darkness, danger and madness. It brought back my love of acting and I ached to be on stage again, feeling the passion and excitement.

I was so enthralled that I couldn't wait to get into bed with Henry after the show. He was a delicate lover. Careful, hesitant, very gentle. I was glad, I needed someone to be patient, to coax back my desires after the horrors of the last few months.

I lay in bed afterwards, the yellow street lamps casting a haunting light over his naked body. He looked so vulnerable without his glasses, I leant over and kissed his forehead. He reminded me a little of Joe as he lay there, the same cute little noises he made as he slept.

Henry was perfect for me, everything I was looking for in a man. That's why I never saw him again.

chapter twenty

What was wrong with Henry? Absolutely nothing. But in the morning I was filled with an irrational desire to flee, to get away as quickly as possible.

I felt haunted. I screwed up my eyes but I couldn't stop seeing the images in my head. The photo of Joe on the coffin, the look in his eyes when I dumped him. And then I imagined Henry's face with that same look in his eyes. A premonition of the future? Or some deep-rooted phobia that had taken over my subconscious, terrifying me as I contemplated the chance of love again? I'd never know. But just as I ran from Duncan's bed that first night he came back after Joe's funeral, I knew once again I couldn't handle the responsibility of loving again.

I told Henry about Joe, how I felt traumatised by the thought of being in love again. I tried to make him understand but my words sounded trite and full of clichés. I think he saw I did feel remorse, that I was screwed up and not plain callous. Maybe that made it better, maybe it didn't. All I knew was I didn't want to risk falling in love.

The pressure at work helped keep me from thinking about what might have been. I'd been there about three months when Hugo started giving me more responsibility, stuff that wasn't really what a secretary should have been doing. It began with him handing me a pile of memos from the morning post and I was expected to write the replies for him to sign. At first he went through them quickly and gave me the gist of what to say. 'Tell Spike this is too expensive, needs to be at least half the cost', for example, or 'Tell him he can go ahead but he needs to come back to me before he shows anything to the client', and so on. Then he started to only go through the tricky or important ones with me, handing me the rest at the end of our meeting, and telling me to 'deal with this lot, whatever you think'.

I had to ask Helen to explain what some of them were about. So much of the business was still new to me, but I was learning all the time. I wrote the replies and sent them out in Hugo's name. He only found out what he was supposed to have written when he saw his copy of the memo the next day. At times I felt I was running half the agency without anyone knowing.

And the business kept coming in. No matter how chaotic it appeared, there was no denying the agency was on the up. Hugo confided in me that there were six big pitches for new business going on and if we secured more than two of them, the troops would stage a mutiny. So when we won the third pitch in a row, he called a big management meeting to work out how we were going to cope. I heard a lot of yelling coming from the meeting room. If they spent less time arguing the workload was impossible and more time doing the work, we'd get more done. And laying off the sauce for a few of them wouldn't have been a bad idea as well.

I got a few funny looks as everyone poured out of the

meeting, though I wasn't sure why. It wasn't my fault we kept getting new business. I'd already rejigged Hugo's schedule for the rest of the day. I'd seen it coming and I was nothing if not organised.

Hugo disappeared off to see the managing director and was back a few minutes later.

'Bertie, got a minute?' he said, with a strange smile on his face.

I went into his office and he closed the door.

'Bertie, I'm sure you realise we've reached the crunch point with resources at the moment with all the business coming in. So I've got a proposal for you. I'd like to promote you to junior account executive. You'll be working with Cecil on his accounts and would move into his team. What do you think?'

What did I think? I was over the moon. Even the thought of having Cecil as a boss couldn't dampen my mood. 'I think it's wonderful,' I replied. 'Thanks, Hugo, for having such faith in me. I won't let you down.'

'I know you won't, Bertie. You've been effectively doing a different job from the one I hired you to do for the last few months anyway. Off you go to see Cecil now and get things worked out. Oh, and there's a twenty per cent salary increase in it for you, but let's keep that between you, me and Cecil. Off you go now.'

And so that was that. I'd walked in the door of the agency not knowing the first thing about advertising, just because I'd wandered around Soho after abandoning my attempt to work in Carnaby Street. And now I was starting out on an advertising career. Is that how life happens? Random events decide everything and nothing you plan for actually materialises? Whatever the answer, it was to be my world now and I was going to make the most of it.

I started making short, low profile trips back to Scotland. Friday night bus up to Glasgow, Saturday spent visiting Granny Campbell and then dinner with Mum and Dad in the evening, hanging out with Duncan for as much of Sunday as he could get away from Kathleen, and then the bus back to London Sunday night. But I was getting deeper and deeper into the mire with my lies about what I was doing in London. My folks still thought I was working in a Mayfair art gallery selling old masters to the English aristocracy and I had a nice polite boyfriend who came from the Home Counties. Even that I was living in a cosy pied-à-terre in South Kensington, although I never gave them an address. Sooner or later I'd have to come clean with what was going on, hopefully by doing a seamless transition from subterfuge to reality. But I wanted to make absolutely sure that Michael was gone before I did that.

And if I thought my career was going well, I couldn't believe how things were progressing for Duncan. He was now well established as a freelance music journalist, and was making a real name for himself as the guy who broke Scottish bands onto the national scene. I kept inviting him down to London, but he always said he was too busy. I think bide-at-home Kathleen wanted to keep him on a short leash.

After the initial heady excitement of my promotion wore off, the reality started to sink in. I was there to do the grunt work, the admin, chasing to get things done. In meetings with clients, I was to say nothing, just take notes and write up the call report so everyone knew what we'd agreed. I wasn't there to make decisions or be assigned any responsibility. Unless, of course, something went wrong. Then it was my job to take the blame so that the big cheeses emerged unscathed.

To make matters worse, Cecil turned out to be even more of an unreconstructed male chauvinist pig and obnoxious English snob once I got to know him. He thought it incredibly funny to go, 'Och aye, the noo' whenever I opened my mouth, and started off every meeting by advising the client that a translator would soon be available to help them understand me.

In his opinion, my role in the agency was to flutter my eyelashes to keep the client distracted, while he persuaded them to part with bigger and bigger budgets. The worst part of the job was that the fat, middle-aged marketing director of our big confectionery client had taken a shine to me, so I was expected to have dinner with him once a week so he could 'go over any client-agency issues in an informal environment', as Cecil put it. What it boiled down to was me having to sit across from the pompous slob in some candlelit restaurant, laugh at his witticisms and have him lean over and squeeze my arm as he told me what a good job I was doing and how much I reminded him of his wife when she was young.

He was harmless enough, I suppose. A bit pathetic, but nothing was ever going to happen and he knew it. It was the young clients who were the worst, always trying to get me in a corner, telling me it would be good for my career if I was 'nice' to them. And it soon became clear that doing more than wining and dining the clients would be appreciated by the agency, all in the line of building good client-agency relationships. Getting Cecil to agree to my expenses was like getting blood out of a stone, but whenever I said I'd been asked out by a client, there was never any problem with me picking up the bill. I ate in great restaurants and became more and more adept at making excuses at the end of the evening while still leaving my client's male ego intact. The look on their faces told me that whoever was the predecessor in my role had been more accommodating.

And the sexual advances at work were constant. Not being a secretary or a frosty ball-breaker the way Helen was regarded, the account execs and creatives were desperate to bed me. Whoever had me first would be the alpha male of the group. Now Spike had serious competition and most of them didn't even have his reasonable level of charm. Sorry guys, I wanted to say, you're all going to stay disappointed. Eventually the interest died down. I think everyone concluded I was either frigid or a lesbian.

The workload was intense and ironically the only way I found to relax was through sex; sex on my terms and with whoever caught my eye. And lots of it. The more I had the more I craved. London was like a smorgasbord of talent and I was in no hurry to exhaust the possibilities. One-night stands became an addiction for me, the only way to cope with the pressure at work.

I started having small successes at the agency. I overhauled the book-keeping system for tracking approvals, sign-offs and spending; not the most exciting of projects but it brought some organisation to what had been a chaotic process before. It showed that much of what we were spending money on had never been officially approved by the clients, so I spent a lot of time over the next few weeks scurrying around securing approval for things we'd already spent money on.

But it was Orange Sunshine, a disgustingly sweet orange drink we were pitching for, that should have rung warning bells about the sort of person I was turning into. Cecil was heading up the pitch team and so I was sent off to the supermarket to get the low-down on what the stuff looked like in-store. We liked to do that for pitches, take a couple of pictures of the supermarket shelves to show we'd done our homework.

I dutifully sneaked a couple of photos. Orange Sunshine looked ghastly next to Robinsons, their big competitor. Robinsons in nice glass bottles, tasteful labels and 'summer days and Wimbledon' imagery. Orange Sunshine, a synthetically lurid syrup in cheap plastic bottles. Disgusting. Why would anyone buy it?

I wandered into another aisle to see the real orange juices on sale. A young woman, a mum judging by the contents of her shopping trolley, was staring at the fruit juices, picking up each one to look at the price. They were all three times the price of Orange Sunshine, but that's because they'd actually seen an orange.

'Looking for something for the kids to drink?' I asked her.

She turned, assuming I worked in the store. 'I like my kids to drink fruit juice, but they're too expensive. Tell your company they need to sell a cheaper version for people on a budget.'

She gave me an idea. I rushed back to the agency.

'Got the pics, Cecil,' I said, brandishing the camera. 'How's the creative work coming on?'

'It's not. You saw that stuff. Looks like something you'd unblock drains with. "Agent Orange", the creatives are calling it. I've had a few challenges in my time, but this one's a corker.'

'Do you mind if I suggest something? There was a young mum shopping when I was in the supermarket, trying to find an orange juice for her kids, committed to doing the right thing for them. But they were too expensive for her. So I was thinking, if the client spent their promotional money on paying the store to stock it in the chiller aisle, instead of on the ambient shelves, it would look much cheaper than the juices it would be next to. Consumers like her would rush to buy it, thinking it must be good for her children.'

'But it doesn't need to be in the chiller aisle. It's so chockfull of chemicals that it would never go off in a month of Sundays.'

'That's not the point. If it were in the chiller aisle, consumers would think it's because it needs to be there and so they would assume it's natural and healthy. Like the rest of the drinks there, only a lot cheaper. As long as the client paid enough, the store would put it there and then they wouldn't need to run price promotions because it would appear so cheap already. All we'd need to do is make ads with lots of sunny, natural, healthy images which would reinforce the point. We'd never actually say it's healthy and natural, so we wouldn't have any problems with the Advertising Standards people, but that's what people would think. By the time Robinsons twig what's going on, sales will have gone through the roof.'

'My God, that's brilliant. We won't be allowed to use a picture of an orange, but everything else will be fair game. Telling the creatives to say nothing at all, but say nothing beautifully? They'll love it. And the shops, they can keep the stuff on pallets in the back of the store. As long as the punters see it in the chiller when they go to buy it they'll think it's like orange juice and we've got them. Well done, Bertie, you've pulled a blinder here.'

These were the first words of praise I'd ever received from Cecil. It was such a thrill seeing everyone get behind the idea, building it up and developing it to win the pitch. It wasn't going to be a campaign developed by some lofty advertising genius. This was me, my idea. I'd proven I could do more than just get the admin right, I could really make a success of things.

It was only when I saw how far the creatives were trying to push it that I started to worry about the morality of the proposal. We were selling a bottle of chemicals to mothers with young kids, pretending it was natural and healthy. The only reason the company got to call it Orange Sunshine was they said it was describing the colour, not the ingredients. The brief was quite explicit that the campaign's target audience was well-meaning but not-too-smart mums on low incomes. It sucked.

'They say no one ever lost money underestimating the intelligence of the British public and this campaign proves that point,' was how Cecil introduced it to Hugo. He didn't say it was my idea, of course, but actually I was glad he didn't. I was feeling ashamed of what I'd done.

The more cynical you were in advertising, the more successful you'd be.

I tried to broach the subject of the morality of the campaign with Cecil, but all I got was a bemused look of incredulity. He was of the never-give-a-sucker-an-even-break school of thought.

Helen was more understanding. 'Don't beat yourself up, about it, Bertie. It's a great idea and we're not conning anyone. Show me anywhere in the ad where it says it's made from oranges, or it'll make kids grow up strong and healthy.'

'That's not the point. We know that's what we're trying to make people think. Look at the photos we're using, families having picnics, going for walks in the country. We're a bunch of snake-oil salesmen.'

Helen looked over her glasses at me and gave me a sympathetic smile. 'Look, if it's really bothering you, think about this. Every TV ad we make has to be approved by the authorities before it goes on air. And the code is based on what has been decided is acceptable or not acceptable to say. It's our job to work within the rules, not say they should be tougher. And yes, there are some dodgy practices out there. But people still buy Nestlé products despite them selling powdered baby milk in Africa, they still bank at Barclays even though they support apartheid. But having said that, Bertie, don't lose that moral compass of yours. We need a few more like you in the business.'

It made sense I suppose. But I could never see an Orange Sunshine ad without feeling queasy.

I didn't have time to dwell on the monster I'd created; we were soon into December and the lead up to Christmas was frenetic. Every client had to have a Christmas lunch and in return we were invited to their office bash. And finally there was our own, client-free, agency Christmas bacchanalia. I must have been the only person to head off home on my own after that one. After weeks of non-stop partying, it was strange to wake up on Christmas Day on my own in an empty flat. Debbie and Linda had headed home for family Christmases and it was just me, with only our bedraggled tinsel Christmas tree for company.

Christmas was, of course, crunch time for Michael. If ever I was going to be at home on a specific day, it would be then and he knew it.

I started to lay the groundwork a few weeks earlier. My fictitious boyfriend Henry was the key player. I'd built a whole world for him by then. He lived in the country, parents were not too well health-wise, he needed to visit them on Christmas Day and I'd said I'd go with him. I promised Mum faithfully I'd be up in the New Year and I'd bring him along, and that cushioned the blow of me missing my first ever family Christmas. Then in January I'd say we'd broken up and it was just me coming.

I made the right decision. I called as early as possible on Christmas Day, the story being that Henry was coming round to pick me up in his car to head down to Surrey for Christmas lunch. I was pleased with that little invention, it meant that I didn't have to deal with Mum wanting to speak to him to wish him a Merry Christmas.

'Is Henry there?' Mum whispered.

'No, Mum, he'll be here in half an hour. Says he's looking forward to meeting you in the new year. Why the whispering? I can hardly hear you.'

Mum giggled. 'I didn't want him to find out an old

232

boyfriend of yours has been round. Dropped off a Christmas present last night and was very disappointed you weren't here so he could give it to you in person. I felt so silly not even knowing the name of the gallery where you work and you've never told me your London address. But he's given me his details if you want to get in touch. Oh, you're a dark horse, Bobbie. You never told me about Michael.'

I knew the name was coming but it still felt like a sickening blow. 'Michael?' I said. 'Michael has been to the house?'

'Yes, indeed. Your father was quite taken by him, although he did say he was a bit old for you. And he owns the art gallery you worked at? Must be doing awfully well for himself. Do you want his number so you can give him a call? I didn't give yours to him. Thought that wasn't quite right, what with Henry and everything.'

'Mum, did you say anything, anything at all, that would help him get in touch with me down here in London? Think, Mum, it's very important.'

'No, nothing. I told him about the acting not working out and you getting the job in the Mayfair gallery, but that's about all. He must have thought I was a terrible mother, knowing so little about my own daughter.'

I needed to tell Mum something, anything, to make sure she didn't talk to Michael again.

'Listen, Mum, there's something I should have told you before. Don't be mad at me, promise?' I took a deep breath. 'Yes, Michael was my boyfriend. But he has a vicious temper. I know you wouldn't think that to look at him, but he does. He used to hit me sometimes and when I threatened to leave him he said he wouldn't let me.

That's part of the reason I'm down here. I should have told you, but I didn't want to worry you. And now I've got a nice life down here, good job, great boyfriend and so everything's worked out for the best.' I leant back against the wall and closed my eyes as I finished my deception.

'But that's terrible, dear. I'm shocked. He seemed like such a nice man. You never can tell these days.' I heard my dad's voice in the background. 'What's that, Nigel?' I heard my mum say to him. 'She says that man used to beat her up. Hang on a minute, Bobbie, your father's coming to the phone.'

Oh no, I thought.

'Bobbie?' I heard his voice, angry as usual. 'What the Dickens is this? That man's been hitting you? He'll pay for it, mark my words.'

'Dad, it's best if I handle things my way. I'm sure it was just one last try to see if he could win me back. It's water under the bridge now. I want to forget about him. He's not worth bothering about.'

'I'll never understand you, Bobbie. But I've learnt once you've made your mind up about something, there's no budging you. But promise me this. If anything like this ever happens again, you let us know, do you hear? I'll not have any daughter of mine being taken advantage of.' He paused and then spoke softly, a tone to his voice I'd never heard before. 'Merry Christmas, Bobbie, hope you have a good day. We'll be missing you.'

Gosh, that was something from him. Never thought I'd hear him say he was missing me. 'Miss you too, Dad. Merry Christmas.' I could feel tears welling up.

Mum huffed and puffed about not calling the police,

but eventually she saw my point and gave up arguing. I asked her to open the present Michael had left. 'Be careful it's not a bomb,' I said, trying to lighten the mood. Maybe a bit tactless. Turned out to be a Capodimonte statue of a beautiful songbird. Was he trying to tell me something?

The phone call ordeal over, I settled down to Christmas lunch. Turkey TV Dinner for one, forty-five minutes in the oven and it was ready. I thought even I couldn't screw that up, but I forgot to prick the foil with a fork. After thirty minutes, there was an almighty explosion. Most of it stayed in the tray though.

It felt so odd, being on my own at Christmas. Not lonely, really, just… isolated, like I was in my own little bubble, cut off from all the family Christmases all around the world. I spread out on the sofa and watched TV all day, pigging out on a box of chocolates. Steve McQueen tried to jump the barbed wire on his motorbike in *The Great Escape*, then Morecambe and Wise had Elton John on their show to do 'Singing in the Rain', while poor Eric had water poured over him.

I finished the last of the chocolates just as the telly closed down for the night. I switched it off halfway through the national anthem. The chocolates had made me feel nauseous, so the next day I decided to take a long walk on Hampstead Heath to clear my head. I persuaded myself everything was okay; keeping Mum in the dark had worked. She knew about Michael now, sort of, and that just left me to unravel the boyfriend story.

But it was funny. I always used to think Christmas Day with my parents was an ordeal. I never thought I'd miss it so much.

1977

chapter twenty-one

Back at work in January and Cecil was in a good mood. Our toilet roll client had won the Gold Pencil, a prestigious advertising industry award, and *Campaign* had turned up to photograph the advertising supremoes behind it. There was Cecil, dressed in a moody black polo shirt, standing on the fire escape with the two creative guys who wrote the ad. They were there for an hour, adopting all number of bizarre poses as the photographer snapped away in an attempt to capture a single picture for next week's edition.

'C'mon, join us,' Cecil said to me. 'The photographer says we need to make the photo a bit more interesting and I told him I had just the thing.'

'No thanks, Cecil, I'm more of a backroom girl,' I replied. It would have been cool, but just too risky.

Cecil decided to treat the client and the whole account team to a night on the town to celebrate, using the agency credit card. 'And of course, you can come too,' Cecil said, with all the sincerity he could muster. 'But just so you know, I've booked a table at Annabelle's so some of the lads might get frisky as the night goes on.'

'Actually, I'd love to come,' I said.

Of course I didn't relish the prospect, but Helen had given me some advice the other day. 'Invite yourself to the boys' nights out with the clients,' she'd told me. 'Otherwise, you'll never build the connections you'll need to get on. Any truly disgusting behaviour happens at the tail end of the night, no pun intended, so you'll have done all your networking by then and can make your excuses and leave. You'll even score extra brownie points for your tact and discretion.'

My response came as a surprise to Cecil. 'Are you sure, Bertie? You don't seem the nightclub type and you'll be the only gal there. Maybe it's best if you duck out of this one.'

'No, honestly, Cecil, I'd enjoy it. I need to be less of a shrinking violet, that's what the guys are always telling me. I promise I won't be offended by anything and if things start to get X-rated and you want me to leave, just give me the nod.'

Gosh, he must have been in a good mood because he said yes. I went back to the flat afterwards and pulled out my disco wardrobe. I slipped on my yellow trouser suit outfit, relieved it still fitted me after all the client lunches. I slapped on the kohl and rouge. It had been a long time since I looked like that.

I wished I'd had a camera to capture the look on everyone's faces when I arrived. Cecil's jaw hit the ground and I thought Spike was going to burst a blood vessel. But ever the consummate ad man, Cecil regained his composure and positioned me next to the client. He obviously considered me an agency asset that could be leveraged.

And I enjoyed the night. The champagne flowed like water, there were celebrities in every corner and you couldn't move for footballers and their pneumatic girlfriends. It was the real thing, not the plastic imitation that was Tiffany's back in Glasgow. The only downside was the client. All he could talk about was work and rugby, and I knew even less about rugby than I did about football.

I tucked into my lobster thermidor. Why shouldn't I enjoy myself in places like this? Okay, I had nothing to do with what we were actually celebrating, but I'd done lots of good stuff at the agency without getting any jollies out of it. You didn't win a Gold Pencil for reorganising the billing system. I was part of a world that said I was worth it now.

I stayed till about midnight. Spike was turning on the charm, much to Cecil's annoyance, as he expected me to do some heavy-duty flirting with the client. Spike didn't know it but he was getting very close to succeeding. The champagne, the atmosphere and the pounding music were a heady mixture and I'd never had more of a test of my resolve to keep my two lives separate. I picked up a book of matches and every time I felt like letting go, I dug a match into the palm of my hand.

When I made my excuses and left it was just at the right time. Cecil had been chatting to a group of girls at the bar. I'll be charitable and call them models and they'd be joining our table shortly. Spike looked gutted when I said I was going, but I gave him an affectionate peck on the lips to let him know how close he'd got.

That night at Annabelle's was the beginning of me getting into the ad agency nightlife. I was making good money and finding plenty of ways to spend it. And the ad guys were fun, full of energy, charisma and self-belief. Okay, they were also the most superficial people on the planet, but once you realised that, you could tag along for the ride. The word got out that I was one of the lads, and it didn't take me long to become a regular feature on the bar and nightclub adland scene. Helen was wary at first, but once she saw there were no stories doing the rounds I'd become the company bike, she became more chilled.

★ ★ ★

I put the partying on hold when Duncan called to say he was coming down to London. Gosh, he sounded excited on the phone. Not because he was seeing me, of course not, but because Bob Dylan was playing concerts in London, his only UK gigs. Duncan had two front row seats for Friday night and he was going to travel down on the Thursday night bus so we could enjoy a full weekend together, just like old times. According to Duncan, Kathleen would rather stab her eyes out with a red-hot needle than spend two long trips on a bus to watch a geriatric folk singer croak his way through a pile of incomprehensible gibberish, so I had Duncan all to myself.

I was there to meet him off the bus. He handed me a bottle of Irn-Bru to remind me of home. His hair had darkened a little, it had an almost carnelian hue, but everything else about him was just the same. I showed him my world, the punk vibe of Camden, the arty streets of Soho, even nipped into the agency to show him my desk by the window and the ads I'd been working on. I told him a few gossipy stories about the crazy things that happened in the advertising business. I wanted him to be proud of me, that against all the odds I'd made it, and I'd got back on track again. But as the day went on, he became more and more subdued. Not like Duncan at all. I suggested we head back to the flat so he could crash out for an hour before the concert and was relieved when he said yes. That must be the reason he was quiet, just shattered after travelling all night on the bus.

We went to the concert that night, the best night out I'd had in London since going to see *Macbeth*. I'd never been much of a Dylan fan until then. His lyrics were amazing, but he had a singing voice that only a mother could love. But to see him standing on stage, bellowing the songs out with such raw emotion, made my hair stand on end. When he finished 'Like a Rolling Stone', I heard a weird rumbling behind us, like a roll of thunder, and realised everyone in the place was roaring and bouncing with excitement. But on the tube back to the flat afterwards there was a distance between us, and Duncan slept on the couch. Neither of us said anything, but it didn't feel the right vibe for one of our old, babes-in-the wood sleep-togethers.

The next day was a Camden day. We walked around the market and took a trip on the *Jenny Wren*, the barge that chugged along the canal as far as Regent's Park Zoo. I realised what I was missing. A real friend who cared for me as much as I did for him, who could listen to my problems and make me laugh. In London, everyone was a little wary of each other, didn't let people get too close.

Duncan was amazed by the punk scene. It hadn't reached the Glasgow streets yet, and in Camden you could see it in all its glory, the multi-coloured Mohican haircuts; bin bag tops; ears, lips and goodness-knows-what-else pierced.

'How are these people able to go into work in the morning?' he asked. 'And I'm covering some of these bands for the music press when they do concerts in Scotland. It's dreadful. They can hardly play, know about three chords and behave on stage like a bunch of yobbos. I know I shouldn't say it, but the music business is going down the drain. Nothing like the musicianship there was when we were kids.'

'Listen to us, Duncan, we're like two old fogeys complaining about the kids of today. How did that happen? The new stuff isn't us any more. Depressing isn't it?'

That afternoon we started to feel close again and it was like I was back in Glasgow. A time when I'd spend the evenings visiting a different student flat every night, lighting joss sticks, smoking dope, listening to Peter Green-era Fleetwood Mac, or all six sides of *Yessongs*. A world where Joe was still alive, I could hang out with Duncan and the only thing I had to worry about was getting my course assignment in on time. I felt a warm glow inside and a calmness I'd not felt in ages.

I was frustrated when I found out Dingwalls had sold out that night. There was a local band called The Catch playing, with a great Scottish singer called Annie Lennox. They'd released a single and had a following through word of mouth around Camden. I saw Annie in the market a lot; she shopped for her clothes there with her boyfriend Dave, who was also in the band. With Dingwalls not

244

possible, I thought it would be good to introduce Duncan to my agency pals. Spike booked a table for anyone who wanted to show up at Annabelle's.

The night was a disaster. A couple of guys from our agency showed up, a couple from Saatchi & Saatchi. First of all, there was the ritual point scoring, everyone trying to do one-upmanship on each other, lots of shop talk. I got caught up in it at first, I guess because that's what I did in that environment, and then I realised Duncan was very quiet, excluded from the conversation. I tried to talk about music, about drama, something I could get him involved in. But when Duncan talked about his music passions, Bowie, Dylan, Pink Floyd and so on, he was made to feel like an idiot.

'Punk's the future, pal,' said one of the Saatchi guys. 'It's going to sweep away all the complacent music-business dinosaurs. It doesn't matter they can't play. The days of twenty-minute drum solos and self-indulgent guitar heroes are over. We're in the middle of a music revolution. Saatchis are breaking down the old order in advertising, the Sex Pistols are doing it in music, and Maggie is going to do it to the unions once that old fart Callaghan gets his marching orders. Money talks, me old sunshine. And the whole world is listening to us now.'

'Money doesn't talk, it swears,' Duncan replied. 'Bob Dylan said that. You're welcome to the world of advertising, but what I do know about is music. And I know that punk will never produce another Beatles, another Bowie. Not if they get a record deal before they know three chords.'

'Beatles? They've split up in case you haven't noticed.

And Bowie? What the fuck is he up to now? Lost the plot completely, off his gourd on cocaine in Berlin, making crap music that nobody listens to any more. Ziggy's dead, mate, and the rest of the old guard died with him.'

'Erm, let's have another drink,' I said.

'No, thanks. This place is too rich for a journalist's salary,' said Duncan. 'I'll stick with water.'

'Relax, mate,' said Spike. At least he was not being an asshole. There was no point playing to win when Duncan was not even trying to come second. 'Let's all be friends, right? No need to worry about the tab. Didn't Bertie tell you we had a business win this week? South African Airways, scooped it out from under the noses of JWT. The bosses said I could pick up a bar tab this weekend to celebrate, so it's everyone's lucky night. Who'd like another cocktail?'

I groaned inwardly. The girl who'd marched to Trafalgar Square a few years ago protesting about apartheid in South Africa was now trying to get people to fly there. Duncan stared at me and his eyes said everything.

'No thanks. I'll get my own drinks, if you don't mind. It's getting late for me anyway. Do you mind if we call it a night?'

Duncan told me what had been on his mind all weekend on the taxi ride back to the flat. 'I don't think you've got real feelings any more, Bobbie, or Bertie, or whatever I'm supposed to call you now. How can you mix with that lot? I've never met a shallower bunch of people in my life.'

I was hurt. 'That's not me, Duncan. It's just the people I work with. Can't you see that?'

'Yes, I loved your tour today. And seeing you again. The old Bobbie is still there, but she's buried pretty deep at the moment. That story you told me about Orange Sunshine? You said you felt ashamed for coming up with an idea to exploit the consumer's naivety, conning people with not much money who are struggling to do the right thing. But it doesn't seem to me you hate the world you work in, Bobbie. You seem to fit right in.'

I tried to explain and went over the arguments Helen had used with me, but Duncan wasn't convinced. Maybe he was right, I didn't have an alarm bell in my head when I got into things too deep. It certainly hadn't gone off when I'd been drawn into Michael's world.

We crashed out when we got back to the flat. Neither of us felt like talking and I needed time to think. I brought him a coffee in the morning. I said I was sorry about last night and I'd think about who I was, that I always wanted to hear what he had to say about me. Sometimes if you play a part long enough it starts to take you over. Maybe that was what was happening to me.

As he left to get the bus back to Glasgow, we said our goodbyes.

'A weekend of highs and lows, Bobbie,' he said. 'I'm sorry if I've been tough on you but I don't want to see the wonderful Bobbie turn into a nasty Bertie. And I loved our tour of London. That showed me the real you is still there.'

'I loved it too, Duncan. And it's great you've given me a prod in the ribs to remind me who I really am. I'll try to behave better from now on. You told me once before I'd turned into someone you didn't recognise with Michael. That time it was too late. This time I'll make sure it's not.'

He got on the bus and I waved him off. There was a homeless man sitting on cardboard outside the bus station. I dropped a pound note into his money jar, like the old Bobbie would have done.

It was the first kind thing I'd done in ages. Duncan had given me a lot to think about.

chapter twenty-two

Duncan was right. I'd drifted away from who I really was. I needed to reconnect with my previous self, rekindle my old passions and values. I saw a flyer for an experimental theatre group looking for volunteers to help put on radical underground plays and decided that it was the antidote I needed. The following Saturday I found myself back with the type of crowd I used to be part of in Glasgow. People who loved theatre, wanted to make a change for good, and who didn't have the scornful attitude to life I saw in the ad world.

I was very clear I only wanted to help out backstage, and something low key at that. I admitted I'd done a little acting, knew my way around a stage, but no, I didn't want to be considered for the part of Natella in *The Caucasian Chalk Circle*. Helping the director, organising the props and costumes, that was what I was signing up for.

The theatre group were a fantastic collection of misfits and oddballs, and could not have been further away from the smooth, slick ad men I spent my days with. I felt I'd come home, that I'd rediscovered the world I wanted to belong to. One of the group, Poppy, was a lot of fun. On the outside, a slightly scary-looking punk, but underneath as playful and innocent as a child. She asked me all sorts of questions about what Glasgow was like and what I got up to in Camden. When she asked what I did, I felt ashamed to admit I worked in advertising, and made vague comments about 'just working somewhere to pay the bills'.

During a break later that day, I saw her skipping merrily away to head outside. We were about to restart the discussion about the play when she came back in, her face flushed with excitement.

'Bertie, can I talk to you for a minute? I think I've got great news for you. Five minutes, is that okay?' she said to the guy leading the group.

He shrugged. 'Okay, but keep it brief.'

I was already worried before we got to the corner of the room. She looked over my shoulder and bounced up and down with excitement.

'You're Bobbie, aren't you? There was a private detective here, about nine months ago. Looking for a Bobbie who used to live in Glasgow, was an actress, last known whereabouts somewhere in London. That's you, isn't it?'

My body tensed as if my stomach had been stabbed with an icy dagger. I couldn't breathe. 'Poppy, what are you saying?' I managed to ask.

In her excitement, she took it as confirmation. 'Guess what? You've got a great-aunt that's died, left you a small fortune and they've been trying to track you down to give you the good news. I wrote the guy's telephone number down in my diary when he spoke to us. I'd never met a private detective before, and thought it was such a great story. Anyway, I popped out to call him. I wanted to be sure it was you before I told you and got you all whacked out of shape, but everything you said about Glasgow fitted. The detective said sooner or later you'd get in touch with one of the drama groups in London and here you are. He's on his way now, so if you wait around afterwards he'll tell you all about it. Isn't that wonderful?'

It was disastrous. And my own stupid, stupid fault for going somewhere where Michael would be looking for me. How could I have been so insane? There was nothing else for it. I needed to get out of there and disappear fast.

'Oh Poppy, this is not good news. This is somebody I don't want to see again. I don't have a great aunt who's died. It's a pack of lies. What did you tell the detective about me? Quick, tell me everything, I need to get away from here fast.'

Poppy gasped and burst into tears. I turned to the drama group. 'I've got a stalker and Poppy's told me he's looking for me,' I shouted over to them, no time to think about her feelings. 'I'm sorry to disrupt everything, but I need to leave.'

Everyone looked at each other in astonishment. I turned back to Poppy. 'Quick, Poppy, tell me! What did you say?'

'I'm always putting my foot in it,' she sobbed. 'That's why I said to myself I was going to be sure of the facts before I blurted something out. Now look what I've done. I'm sorry, Bertie. I've really made a mess of things.'

'No, look, it's all right.' I needed Poppy to tell me exactly what she had said and tell me quick. The clock was ticking. 'You weren't to know. But please, Poppy, what did you tell him? Think.'

'I told him you live in Camden somewhere. That your name is Bertie, not Bobbie. He asked if you had short blonde hair. I said no, short, light brown curly, but he said that was probably a new haircut. That's all, I think.'

'Were you more specific about where I live? About where I work?'

'How could I be? You didn't tell me anything. I'm scared, Bertie. Are you going to be okay?'

'I'll be fine,' I said, trying to smile. 'Probably overreacting, but that's just my way.'

I rushed over to the group. 'I'm sorry,' I said, 'But I'm going to have to leave. There's a guy looking for me and he might come here to find me. If he turns up, say I'm gone and you don't know where.'

'Shit, mate,' said one of the guys. 'This is heavy. Are you sure you don't want to stick around? There's six of us here, we can tell him to bugger off or we'll call the cops.'

'No, really, it's best I go.' I grabbed my things. 'Sorry, everyone, must go now.'

I left behind a shell-shocked group and a distraught Poppy. Once out of the door, I ran on to the main road and got the first taxi I saw. I asked him to take me to Regent's Park. I needed time to think.

I sat on a park bench for an hour or so. It was a disaster. Michael knew my name and where I lived in London. His detective would guess I'd hang out at Dingwalls, Camden Lock Market, all the trendy places around here. It was only a matter of time before he tracked me down. All because I couldn't leave acting alone.

There was only one thing for it. I had to move out of the flat and in the meantime keep as low a profile in

Camden as I could. No supermarkets, no pubs, nothing. At least he didn't have any idea where I worked or what I did, that was something. But it was still an absolute catastrophe.

I went back to the flat and told Linda and Debbie I needed to move out. I'd pay three months' notice to make up for it. I tried to put a brave face on. They asked if they could help but when I said no, they gave me my own space.

I was about to start flat hunting on Monday when Hugo called me into his office.

'We're a victim of our own success at the moment, Bertie. The partners are stretched too thin. Our clients are complaining they never see enough of us. There's a new business pitch just come in and none of us can handle it. Cecil and the other account directors are saying they're maxed out.'

He paused for effect. 'So I'm giving you a shot at heading up a new business team,' he said. 'I've squared it with Cecil and he says as long as you don't let things slip on your existing clients, he's okay to go along with it.'

Heading up a new business pitch. I never dreamt I would get a chance like this so early in my career. Usually it was partners that headed up new business, at a push a senior guy like Cecil. But it was the worst possible timing. How could I move flat while burning the candle at both ends getting a pitch together on top of all my other work?

I smiled enthusiastically. 'Wonderful, Hugo. I won't let you down. Who's the client?'

'Mallard Furnishings. The new furniture store chain that always seems to have a sale.'

I grimaced. 'Well, I love a challenge. Has anyone told them it's the 1970s? Their stuff looks like it comes out of the ark. Don't worry, we'll come up with something that will blow them away.' I tried to look confident.

'Well, they're not Coca-Cola, but everyone's got to start somewhere. Anything we do for them has got to be better than these boring sales ads they have currently. The presentation needs to be ready two weeks from today. Good luck, Bertie.'

I went back to my office and thought. Of course I'd said yes, anything else would have been career suicide. I could look for a flat in the evenings and get up early in the mornings to start packing. That way I could move the minute the pitch was over. Michael's detective was not necessarily still scouring London looking for me, maybe it was just the previous search my foray into the acting world had brought back to life. A two-week delay in moving flat would be fine, I reassured myself. I was going to be so swamped with work I wouldn't be venturing out onto the streets of Camden anyway. And it would probably take me that long to find a flat in another part of London, even if I did want to move sooner.

I was so nervous about my first pitch-planning meeting. I wouldn't be sitting in the corner being invisible any more. Now it would be me telling everyone what to do. I'd been through the previous Mallard campaign the client had sent us and Hugo was right, the ads were uninspiring. The marketing department's job was to take photos of the furniture, trying to make it look as attractive as was humanly possible, and then run newspaper ads cramming in as many photos as possible, with starbursts next to them saying they were fifty, sixty, even seventy per cent off some mythical recommended retail price. There didn't seem to be any market research that found out who the people were who bought their stuff and why.

I spent the next morning visiting their store in Croydon and then headed over to Chelsea to look at Habitat for comparison. It was a depressing experience. Boring, frumpy granny furniture versus Terence Conran's clean lines and simplicity. Habitat had it sussed, whether you wanted a country casual look or urban chic. Not something Mallards would want to hear.

I'd been on a few new business pitches and knew everyone hated them. There was usually some hotshot in charge whose main job was to bully everyone into getting them to give up as much time as possible from their day jobs. Everyone reluctantly wrote their part of the presentation, then it was all changed by the hotshot to make it fit together.

And in this case there was not even a hotshot, just little old me. As I walked into the meeting with my designated creative team and market researcher, I could see the disdain on everyone's face. At least I'd got Spike as my art director; I could use my feminine wiles to get him motivated. Terry, the copywriter, was rarely sober after lunch so I was not expecting much from him. Nancy, the market researcher, was an earnest wee soul, blinking incessantly behind her owlish glasses and clutching the latest Mintel report on the furniture market to her bosom like a comfort blanket.

I brought along the Polaroids I'd taken in the Mallard store to show everyone what they were selling, and one of Habitat's summer catalogues for comparison. It wasn't the most motivational start to the meeting.

'Okay, this is a long-shot pitch for us,' I explained. 'They ship in traditional-looking furniture from a Spanish exporter, and then sell it on as cheaply as possible. So they don't have much money to spend on design, or on advertising for that matter. If someone wants real quality for this sort of furniture, you'd find them shopping in department stores, and they'll be older, middle-aged people with more money to spend. The customers I watched this morning in Mallards were the young marrieds, new homebuyers, so I think Habitat is more the competition than Harrods.'

'Then we're fucked,' said Terry. 'I'm getting a gaff together with me bird at the moment. There's no way I'd buy this crock of shit, no matter what you say to me.'

'Well, thank goodness not everyone has your assertiveness, Terry. From what I could see, the folk in the showroom looked the conventional types. I think they're scared by Habitat, bit risky and trendy for them. Buying furniture is a big decision. Not only financially, but they have to live with the consequences for years. And they're scared of getting it wrong, looking unsophisticated and having bad taste. I think we should play to that.'

'I don't see that in the research,' said Nancy. 'We'd need to check. First thing we'd do after we got the business.'

'I think we should do something different for this pitch,' I said, trying to sound as confident as possible. 'It's a privately owned company, right? That means they can make decisions without having to worry about shareholders. I think we should walk in, bold and assured, and say the answer is the message: "Good Taste Never Goes Out of Fashion". Reassure their customers this stuff will be around for ages, not flavour of the month from a trendy competitor. You write your part of the presentation with that in mind. I won't do any editing because if we all use the same theme, you won't need me to tie it all together. One single unifying idea working across everything, not our usual tactics of everyone doing their own thing and stitching it together at the last minute.'

'Wait a fucking minute,' said Terry, paying attention for a second, 'Last time I looked, I was the bleeding copywriter round here. I'll write the frigging ad if you don't mind. Your job's to get the client to like it, not to bloody write it.'

'It's just a concept, not the copy,' I countered. 'But if you want to do something else, that's great. I think basing this on style will make it a more… visually-led campaign, will put the ball more in Spike's court.'

I saw Spike grinning at that. Anything that gave Terry less work was going to be all right with Terry.

'Suit yourself. I've got a fucking migraine anyway. I'll leave you two to sort it out. Just keep Hugo away from me when he sees the work, so I don't have to pretend I had anything to do with it.'

'Don't you worry, Bertie, I'll save your bacon,' said Spike. 'But if they don't like your idea? We're sort of sunk.'

'Yes, we are. But how else are we going to win it? The other agencies are going to say they can do what Mallards are doing now, but better than the little agency that they're currently using. Mallards only think they need a new agency because they're growing. We're going to tell them they need to do something different as well.'

'Ballsy approach, Bertie,' replied Spike. 'Nice one. I'll give you my best shot. Cost you though, but we can talk about that at the victory celebration.'

'I think you should run this by Hugo and Cecil,' said Nancy, flicking nervously through her papers. 'There's nothing about this in the research, Bertie. And you're putting the cart before the horse, coming up with the answers before we've even been through the briefing process. We're supposed to follow the agency's Six Step Programme for Advertising Excellence.'

'The Six Step Programme is the biggest pile of crap there is, and you know it,' replied Spike. Nancy blanched. 'C'mon guys,' he said. 'This will be the easiest pitch we've done in a long while. Nancy, you can find something in all the bumph you've got in front of you that says this is the answer, can't you, love?'

'Um, I'm not sure. I guess so. But it's a bit unprofessional. The process says we're supposed to start from the research. That's step one. Then we go through the insight gateways. We only get to the execution idea at step five.'

'Let's work together on this, Nancy,' I suggested. 'Don't worry, I'm sure we'll be able to find enough stuff in the research to go through all the gateways. So if no one's got anything else, let's go for it. Great team, guys.'

Meeting over, I went into the ladies' loo, closed the cubicle door and took a few deep breaths. For all my outward bravado I had been, not to put too fine a point on it, a bag of nerves all through the meeting. But I reckoned

I'd pulled it off, just. We were working on a pitch that no one had thought we could win, but now there was a chance we might.

Everything started to come together and I was running myself ragged, checking on the creative work, writing my part of the presentation, while at the same time rushing off to see flats and packing up my stuff in Camden. It was worth it though. By the day of the pitch I'd found a lovely little flat in Battersea; my stuff was packed for the movers coming in a couple of days; and to top it all, we had a great, great presentation. Poppy's indiscretion was like a bad dream.

The final accolade was that agency boss Ben Campbell was going to come to the meeting and do the intro and the glad-handing. Ben never went to the little pitches unless he thought we were going to win them; being involved with inconsequential failure was beneath his dignity.

I'd been in the office since five in the morning, dressing the meeting room with iconic images of taste that would never go out of fashion – Audrey Hepburn, Aston Martin, Coco Chanel fashion and the like. The place looked fantastic. Everyone was psyched. The clients arrived: the marketing director and the brand manager, whom I'd met before. We were just waiting on the Mallards managing director and then we could start the show. I was organising the coffees when he came into the room.

I turned to greet him with my most friendly and professional smile. I even extended my hand for a handshake before I realised. Michael. Still a man very much in control. Only a flicker in his eyes betrayed his feelings. I felt the colour drain from my face, shook his hand awkwardly and collapsed into my seat.

My heart was pounding. How? How could this have happened? Did he find out I was working here? Did his detective track me down? Then everything fell into place. Michael had talked about getting rid of the smurfs and getting new businesses to launder his money. The marketing director had told me the owner was an entrepreneur with deep pockets who was moving into the furniture business, based on his export contacts in southern Spain. I remembered that one of Michael's sleazy business partners lived in Spain. On the Costa del Crime, no doubt.

Ben did the intro, smooth and suave. The same jokes he told at every new business pitch to break the ice. Then I was on.

'And so without further ado, I'd like to hand you over to our agency's fastest rising young star, Bertie, who has a big idea for you. Over to you, Bertie.'

It was catastrophic. I fumbled every page of the presentation, dropped my pile of overhead projector skins, scrambled frantically to pick them up and reorder them. I stuttered and stammered, and when I did get the words out, I woodenly read out what was on the charts, talking like a robot. I looked everywhere in the room, except at the person who would make the decision to appoint us. And gave pathetic answers to even the simplest of questions. It was cringingly, toe-curlingly, embarrassingly awful.

When it came to the summary, Ben stood up and walked over to me. 'I'll just go over the final points if that's okay,' he said.

That wasn't what we'd agreed. For a brief second his back was to the clients and he gave me a glare that left me in no doubt as to what he thought of the presentation. He had never seen the charts he was presenting but, ever the professional, he carried it off with aplomb.

He finished. After an awkward silence, Michael spoke. 'Thank you. I think we've seen enough.' He picked up my business card and pointedly left his hand-out on the table.

Ben escorted them out, leaving me to face the team. I waited for the recriminations and it was even worse when they looked at me in silence.

Finally, Terry spoke. 'Well, their stuff's crap anyway. I've got things to do. See you later.'

Everyone slumped out dejectedly.

Michael phoned me at the office later that day. It was short. 'You don't know me, I don't know you. Today never happened. But don't disappear again in case we need to talk. There are still a few loose ends regarding Glasgow. I know where you are now, so don't run away from me again. Understand?'

He crucified me with Ben. No way was he going to give his business to an agency who chose the office junior to run his account, he said. Going with someone who took him seriously. He made absolutely sure I would suffer, and suffer big time.

Ben didn't know whether to be angrier with me or with himself.

'Hugo over-promoted you, Bertie. Let a pretty face cloud his better judgement. That was the worst presentation I've ever seen in my life. The cleaning lady could have done a better job. If we weren't so short-staffed at the moment you'd be out the door. I've never seen a prospective client so irate about a presentation. But don't worry, you'll never humiliate me or the agency again.'

And, of course, the vultures were circling. Cecil could barely contain his glee at my fall from grace. He didn't say never put a woman in charge, but he didn't have to.

'This is what happens when we don't follow the Six Step Programme for Advertising Excellence,' he complained. Poor old Spike and Nancy got it in the neck for being my partners-in-crime. Spike did offer to take me out and drown my sorrows and it took all my self-control to say no. After all that time of office chastity I didn't want to compound the catastrophe by giving him an apology shag. Helen tried to be sympathetic but I could see she felt betrayed as well. My only supporters were deserting me. But it was Hugo's disappointment that cut me to the quick. He'd obviously received a bollocking from Ben over my screw-up and I felt dreadful I'd let him down.

'I think it's best to keep you away from clients for a while,' he said. 'Scheduling production and trafficking in the back office might be better for you.' He tried not to show how cheesed off he was.

My career was in tatters and Michael had found me. I thought that things couldn't get much worse.

chapter twenty-three

I was on the phone to Duncan that evening. 'I should have taken it as a sign, that silly Poppy girl alerting Michael to where I lived in London,' I said. 'Now after all this time he tracks me down by accident. I still can't believe it.'

'It's incredible,' agreed Duncan. 'You were right not to panic after Poppy called the detective. Moving to another neighbourhood would have been enough to make your trail go cold again, but this is different. Michael knows where you work now. Even if you move to another advertising agency, it would be pretty easy for him to find someone at CPD to let him know where you'd gone. That lot would sell their grandmother for sixpence.'

'I'm scared,' I said. 'Michael talked about loose ends. I think I'm one of them. He won't rest until he silences me for good.'

I could sense Duncan hesitating. 'I don't know,' he said. 'Don't you think you might be overreacting? Look at this rationally. Why would he risk everything to bump you off? He must know if anything happened to you, the finger would point straight at him.'

'You didn't hear his voice on the phone. Ice-cold with menace, it was. Maybe you're right, he's not going to do anything straight away. But who's to know if I am to have an "accident" six months, a year from now? I can't live with that hanging over me.'

'So you're going to quit and join another agency and hope he doesn't track you down?'

'No, as you say, that wouldn't achieve anything. He'd find me and be even angrier if I tried to get away from him again. It's got to be another complete disappearing act.'

'That's a big step, Bobbie. Think about it a little while. You don't need to decide anything this minute.'

Maybe I did need to calm down. Michael told me not to run away, but he also told me to treat today as if it never happened. Maybe he would forget about me and I could try to salvage my career from the ashes of the pitch disaster. At least I could hope.

The next day I'd just about convinced myself it was going to be okay when Michael turned up at the office. The receptionist called to tell me he was waiting for me downstairs and I sat, panicking about what to do. Telling him to go away would be futile. If he wanted to see me, he'd see me. The smart thing would be to play along with him, find out what he wanted and decide what to do from there. I went down to see him, sick with fear.

Michael took me to the nearby outdoor courtyard at St Paul's church in Covent Garden and chose a bench well away from other people. 'So we can talk,' he said. 'Talk frankly.'

He started off all conciliatory. 'I need to apologise for telling Ben you were the reason CPD didn't get our advertising, Roberta. That was a bit harsh. I hope it didn't cause any problems for you.'

'What do you want, Michael?' I was not going to play any games; he needed to realise I'd grown up since we last met.

'Quite direct, aren't you? Well, let me tell you. We've got a little indiscretion in our past, I'm sure you remember what I'm talking about. All the other... indiscretions, shall we say, that I used to commit when you knew me in Glasgow, have been swept away in the last year. The smurfs are gone and my services are now channelled through genuine businesses. Mallards is a legitimate company and I'm its very respectable managing director.'

'I'm sure you are, Michael. Very respectable.'

'Look I know what you're thinking,' Michael replied. 'You think I had something to do with the tragic death of the detective we used in the little game we played. But it was a bizarre coincidence.' He gave a little smile, like he was laughing at a secret joke. 'Oh, I admit it was convenient. I was looking to get out of smurfing and the detective's death did help. Some of the smurfs came to the same fanciful conclusion you did, and kept completely quiet during the investigation. No doubt due to a misguided belief that if I could kill a top cop, I could do the same to them.'

I shook my head, narrowing my eyes to show I was not falling for this in the slightest.

'Coincidences do happen, Roberta,' Michael said. 'I mean, look at us meeting like this. I must admit I was a bit upset you ran out on me. I trusted you with my secrets, just as you trusted me with yours. I thought that bonded us together. So I had some of my people ask around to see if they could find you. Even hired a private detective to look for you in London.'

'I know you did, Michael. I've spent the last fifteen months being chased by him, in case you've forgotten.'

'Don't be angry, Roberta. I had him look for you when you first moved down here. A last attempt at a reconciliation, which is why I stopped by your parents with a Christmas present for you. But after that I said to myself, no more. When my detective called the other day to tell me there'd been a sighting of you in Camden, I told him not to chase it up. I'd given up on ever seeing you again, until our fortuitous encounter yesterday.'

Two men in ill-fitting suits came and sat down on the bench next to us, staring straight ahead in silence. Were these two of Michael's goons making sure I couldn't escape? Surely he wouldn't try anything in broad daylight, with so many people around. I inched away from him, glancing around the courtyard to see where best to run to get away from them. But at that point a third man came up to them, they stood up, shook hands and left.

My relief gave me some inner strength. 'Michael, this is the biggest load of baloney I've ever heard in my life. You want me to believe DCI McDonald's death was a coincidence after Ron chose him as the man you wanted me to sleep with? Give me a break.' I was angry now, angry he would think I was still such a gullible fool, that I would believe this nonsense. Angry he could possibly think being so smarmy and conciliatory could have the slightest impact on my wanting to see him again.

Michael gave a shrug.

For a moment my anger made me forget my fear. 'And

what about Duncan? You had him beaten up so badly he ended up in hospital. And the disgusting room where you had someone photograph me having sex? Do you really expect me to believe you knew nothing about any of that?'

'I didn't authorise any violence. Big Jockie got carried away, and let me assure you I was as shocked as you when I found out. Fired him on the spot. But yes, I knew about the room and the two-way mirror. I was worried a previous girlfriend was being unfaithful and the layout of the flat was convenient for setting up a surveillance operation. You know how I like to keep an eye on people, for their own good. But when she moved out, I had it locked up and had forgotten about it. I was mortified when I was told about the broken mirror and realised you'd found it. I can see how you could've jumped to the wrong conclusion.'

He didn't expect me to believe any of this. He was making up a story so we could both pretend to go along with it. What I couldn't work out was why.

'Our deceased friend is ancient history now,' Michael said. 'Something no one wants to bring up again. I admit it looks unfortunate, our little game coinciding with such a tragic event. But think of how deeply involved you were with me back then, how long you've had these suspicions and haven't said anything. You talk to anyone about this and the police will think you were part of it as well.' He gave me the sinister smile I remembered so well.

'I would never do that, Michael.'

'It's not me you have to worry about, Roberta. I just run a slightly unconventional financial services company. As I've always told you, I'm not into the blood business.

It's my clients who should scare you. My operations would expose them to the authorities and they would take a dim view of anyone who had the potential to make that happen. A very dim view. That's why I wanted to keep you close to me, why I made so much effort to track you down.'

He leant over and took my hand. I didn't pull it away. I needed to go along with the charade until I could get clear in my mind what I needed to do next.

Michael squeezed my hand, a bit too strongly. 'I want to keep you close to me, to protect you from yourself. I don't want you to wake up one morning full of irrational guilt and do something silly you'd come to regret. I saw how obsessed you were about that old boyfriend of yours committing suicide and how silly you were in blaming yourself. Being silly about me would be far, far more dangerous.'

Michael looked around before continuing. 'The best thing is for us to be together, Roberta. I need to make sure nobody develops bothersome conspiracy theories based on your speculation that I was connected to McDonald's death. As I'm sure you can appreciate, that troubles me.'

'Don't threaten me, Michael. I'll make sure if anything happens to me, everything I know about you gets shown to the police.' I tried to keep my voice steady, but I could feel my body trembling.

'Now, Roberta, that's not nice. As I said, I'm not threatening you, just the opposite. I want to help you, especially after my unforgivable behaviour yesterday. In fact, I was very impressed with your ideas, so impressed I've told our new agency they've to find a way to use them for our campaign. That's why I'm here. I want you to come and work for me. To be our advertising manager, to be part of the Mallards success story. Whatever you're being paid at CDP, I'll double it.'

It was too surreal for words. 'Very kind of you, Michael, but I have to say no. I like it just fine where I am at the moment and I think it's best for both of us we don't see each other again.'

The charm dropped. 'I'm sorry, Roberta. I think there's been another misunderstanding. I wasn't asking your permission for you to come and work for me. That's what you are going to do. You are going to come and work for me at our offices in Surrey. You are going to be somewhere where I can keep an eye on you. Now I've found you, I'm going to keep you close. Maybe as close as we were before. You'll find I'm still very generous to those that please me. That wouldn't be so bad now, would it?'

I was dealing with a psycho. An out-and-out madman who thought he could own me, keep me close where I could do him no harm, be his plaything again. No doubt one of many he'd collected over the years. In his twisted world, he really did believe he could convince me that was what I wanted.

'I'm not sure, Michael,' was all I replied. 'Can't you see it will never work, me working for you? Never mind anything else. I think we need to be away from each other. Can't we do that?'

'You know I get what I want, Roberta. In time, you'll come to see it's what you want. Come down to Surrey tomorrow, let me show you around. Let you see I've changed, that you don't need to be scared. That's not too much to ask, is it?'

'I can't do tomorrow, I've got too much on,' I said.

'No, Roberta, tomorrow. Nine o'clock. I'm sure you can manage.'

I knew if I said no, he'd never let me out of his sight. 'Okay,' I said quietly.

'Good. Now tell me your address and telephone number. I'm sure you understand why.'

I made up an address. A street in Camden, well away from my flat.

'We don't have a phone,' I said. 'Arguments about how to split the bill, so we had it disconnected and use the phone box at the end of the street.'

He looked at me suspiciously. 'Very inconvenient, I'm sure. Very inconvenient when people can't trust each other.'

I headed back to work. I'd got an hour, maybe two, before he had the address checked out and found out I didn't live there. I called Duncan. I needed to decide, and decide right then, what to do.

'He thinks you can just forget the last twelve months and the two of you can get back together again?' Duncan was incredulous. 'You're right, Bobbie, he's a nutter. You need to find a way of either saying no that doesn't infuriate him or get the hell out of there before he has you under his control.'

'I don't think saying no is an option.' I took a deep breath. 'Duncan, I've decided. I'm going to run. I'm not worried about packing in a career in advertising. There's are some decent people in the business, but they're few and far between. Ever since that dreadful night at Annabelle's I've realised advertising's not for me. And after yesterday's pitch calamity, there are more than a few people saying I'm not right for advertising. Maybe this means it's time to move on, to reinvent myself again.'

'Have you thought about what you'll do?' I could tell Duncan was agreeing with me.

'I need to do something he's not expecting. He can't know I've got everything packed up in my flat, ready to move as soon as the pitch is over. I'll call around and find removal men who will move my stuff tonight. I'm sure they'll want cash up front, but I can manage that if I head off to the bank now. I'll put my resignation to the agency in the mail tonight and write out a cheque for three months' rent to Linda. Then I'll disappear again. There's no way he'll expect me to move so fast.'

'Where will you go?'

'Head back to Scotland. Not Glasgow, too obvious. Some nice anonymous town.'

Duncan was not convinced. 'Isn't heading back here the first place Michael would look for you?'

'Maybe that's what's so good about it. He's seen I've been smart once, he'll be expecting me to do something clever again. So doing the obvious might fox him. I'm not talking about walking around George Square with a big arrow pointing at me, I'll stay somewhere off the beaten track. And from what I can gather, Mallards is a huge step up in Michael's money-laundering operations and he's pretty much based full-time in Surrey. I think I'd be safer in Scotland than in the south of England.'

'Well all this bluff, double-bluff conniving is a bit too

Machiavellian for me. But if you think it'll work, Bobbie, I'll help you any way I can. When will you get here?'

'If I move quickly, I can make tonight's sleeper train. Meet me at Central Station tomorrow morning?'

Everything happened so fast. I packed as much of my office stuff into my bag as I thought I could get away with without arousing suspicion, then headed out of the office for the last time. I spoke to nobody, felt so bad about not saying goodbye. Maybe one day they'd find out why, but in the meantime everyone at the agency would think I'd dropped out of advertising with my tail between my legs, having failed to meet the grade. I didn't care. I took the tube three stops and jumped in a taxi. I looked behind me to check if there were any other free cabs. There weren't, so if I was being followed I'd got away. My stuff was in the removal van by ten that night and the removal men drove off to Glasgow the next morning. It would remain in storage there until I could figure things out.

I headed off to Euston and bought my ticket with fifteen minutes to spare. The train slipped off into the night. Slipped off to a new life, a new job somewhere, and yet another escape from danger.

Glasgow, April 1977

chapter twenty-four

I'd never been on a sleeper train before. It fitted the drama of my departure, cosseted in a cosy cabin, the hypnotic clacking of the rail tracks like a Buddhist mantra to comfort me as I began the next stage of my life. I didn't remember falling asleep. A knock on the door and my coffee was delivered, half an hour before we arrived in Glasgow.

I stepped out of the train and thought of the world I'd left behind. By now, Michael would know I'd given him a false address and would no doubt be waiting with simmering fury to see if I turned up at his offices. The early birds would be arriving at the agency. It would be eleven o'clock before anyone noticed I wasn't there, probably lunchtime before my resignation letter arrived in the post. I was supposed to be at a client meeting in the afternoon, and I thought about calling Cecil to give him time to organise something, but decided it was best my disappearance was complete and final.

After the isolation of my little cabin, it was odd to step into the bustle of the morning, hearing Glaswegian accents all around. They sounded stronger than I remembered, different but also comfortingly familiar. There was Duncan, waiting for me under the station clock as arranged. We hugged and headed off for a coffee.

'Now what, Bobbie?' he asked. 'Have you any sort of plan for a job, where you'll stay, how you'll vanish again?'

'Not really. Keep it simple, back to being Bobbie Sinclair. Stay away from my old haunts. But other than that, no, I haven't thought of anything.'

'I still can't believe after everything you did to disappear, he walked into your office.' Duncan shook his head. 'Well, we'll know in the next few days. There's no way I can stay invisible. If someone comes knocking on my door, what do you want me to say?'

'If he threatens you again, we have to go to the police. But me giving up everything to get away from him again has got to make him realise he'll never win me back. I want to make it difficult for him to find me, but not go to the same extremes again when I can't even visit my family at Christmas. He's smart. He knows I've left it too late to go to the police. I'm in this too deep.'

'Are you going to tell your parents you're back?'

'I'll not tell them yet. And let's see if anyone gets in touch with you before we see each other again. I've got a bit of money now, so there's no panic financially. I just need to figure out what to do for a living next.'

Duncan reached into his rucksack. 'I've brought something for you. Remember this?'

He produced the job search folder I'd given him, a lifetime ago. The folder I'd decided I would never need again, back when I was full of belief I was on track for wonderful things, that I didn't need to do anything as tacky as look for a job. I took it from him and stared at it, flicked through the pages. First choice employers at the beginning, my notes in the margin about the pros and cons of working for them, my clever questions to ask at the interview written at the end. It was like Duncan had unearthed an archaeological relic from another time.

'You never needed it, did you?' I said, slipping it in my bag. 'I always nagged you to get your act together and sort out your life after leaving university and here we are. Your stuff appearing in magazines every week and me, starting at the bottom once more, running away over and over again. Funny old world.'

'It is indeed. At least head over to my place so you can have a shower and freshen up and make some phone calls to get yourself started. You'll be safe enough doing that today at least.'

Duncan had moved into a second-floor flat in Queen Margaret Drive, looking over the Botanical Gardens. A beautiful red sandstone tenement building, Charles Rennie Mackintosh stained-glass window at the entrance, Edwardian bottle-green ceramic tiles in the staircase. I was impressed. Less so when I stepped inside. Beautiful bay window overlooking the gardens, but no curtains. Not a single poster or painting on the walls. Packing cases in every room.

'It's wonderful,' I said. 'But haven't you been here for about nine months? It looks like you just moved in.'

'Ah, no, you're right. Keep meaning to unpack, never get around to it.'

'And curtains? You've heard of them, haven't you?'

'Advantage of being on the second floor overlooking a park. I should get some though.'

I smiled as I shook my head in exasperation.

After a long shower, I came out to find Duncan typing away at his desk by the window. 'The master at work,' I said. 'Is this the famous novel you've told me about?'

'Sort of. It's time I told you my big news. All happened in the last few days but it didn't seem right to tell you when you were committing career hari-kari and fleeing from your nemesis.'

'Well go on. What's the big news?'

'I'm going to be published. Under a pseudonym in case everyone hates it and it messes up my journalist credentials. I've had an agent touting it around and I heard two days ago one of the Scottish publishing houses wants to go with it. I'm working on the edits they want. It'll be on the shelves in the new year.'

I couldn't believe it. When Duncan first told me he was writing a novel I did my best to sound supportive, but deep down I thought was it was another of his gadfly projects, something to fritter his time on without it becoming anything. I'd no doubt he had the talent, but I couldn't imagine him knuckling down and sticking with it for all the time it needed. A two-page feature for a magazine or a weekly music column seemed to me the limit of his attention span.

'That's really cool,' I told him. 'Not just for coming up with the story, but managing to organise yourself to write it. If you don't mind me saying, Duncan, you're the most disorganised person I know.'

He looked sheepishly at his curtainless windows. 'I've no idea how you could possibly think that,' he said, suppressing a smile.

I laughed. 'You don't need me to give you a kick up the bum any more. Come on, give me the outline of the story.'

'It's called *Scars of Love* and it's the story of a journalist who has it all: beautiful wife, angelic son and high-paying job. His life is just about perfect, until one night he casually sleeps with the wife of his editor and loses his job and his wife in rapid succession. Full of disasters and plot twists. It's about learning to be mature and responsible the hard way.'

'Gosh, sounds impressive. Is it based on someone you know?'

'Yes, someone I used to work with. Someone fascinatingly awful who'd done a lot of stupid and horrible things in his life but turned out all right in the end. Used him as the inspiration for the main character and then built the story around him. *Roman à clef*, they call it.'

'*Roman à clef*? What with you having me "fleeing from my nemesis" and you "romaning your clef", you're getting all literary in your old age. But well done again, Duncan, I'm looking forward to reading it.'

We talked a little more about his book and then I left Duncan to get on with his edits while I flicked through my job search folder. But try as I might, I couldn't get excited about anything I saw there. Starting all over again, on the ground floor, back to where I was two years ago. Depressing. I thought of how I was going to explain my CV. 'Eh, got into bed with a gangster and fronted up his money-laundering business. Had to disappear and got a job in advertising by way of The Golden Egg where I was sacked after giving my boss head. Screwed up my first new business presentation and left the agency in the lurch the next day.' Yes, that CV was going to have the blue-chip multinationals queuing up outside my door.

I listened to the sound of Duncan's typewriter as he bashed away on his novel. That was the answer. I needed to work at something I was passionate about. But that was acting, and there was no worse profession for keeping a low profile.

I got back in touch with my old friends, part of my networking to see what opportunities were out there. My old uni friends added to my gloom. Married, mortgages, careers, kids. Further proof my life was one big spiral of self-destruction. But Deirdre was different. She gave me the first hope that there was something I could do.

'The stage was not for me,' she told me over a coffee. 'I got through *Who's Afraid of Virginia Woolf?* by the skin of my teeth and decided I wasn't going to put myself through that again. There might not be a knight in shining armour to help me pull it off next time.' She gave me a smile of gratitude.

'Nonsense, you were wonderful,' I protested. 'And you love drama, just as much as I do.'

'That's why I got into drama therapy. Have you heard of it? It's really new, took off in the last couple of years or so. Started from experimental theatre, like the stuff we used to do at uni. The theory is people act out something to do with a problem they have, and that's easier to deal with than confronting it head-on. It's got funding from Glasgow social services and there's a group of us who go round schools, rehab centres and community halls and try to help people face up to their problems.'

'Sounds amazing. So is it acting or psychology?'

'Bit of both. For example, I'm doing a workshop tomorrow with a group of girls who keep cutting their wrists like they're trying to commit suicide. But they don't really want to do that, they just hate who they are and want to punish themselves and cry for help at the same time. I'll get them to imagine they're in a castle, trying to escape from an evil witch to help them find out what it is that's eating them up. A make-believe play makes it easier for them to deal with things.'

'Sounds heavy. Fascinating though. But don't you need qualifications for that sort of thing? Surely they don't let anyone do it?'

'Well, you've got to study first. They have a general psychotherapy course at Paisley Tech that's linked to our group. It takes three months and at the same time you're learning the theory, you do vocational training with the drama group to see how you use the techniques in practice.'

'Gosh, it's easy as that? But do you think I'm cut out for it, Deirdre? I've never done anything like this before.'

'You did psychology as part of your arts degree, didn't you? You'd be great at it, Bobbie, with your skills as an actress. And you like helping people. As long as you can cope with dealing with screwed-up people and the heavy stuff that gets talked about, you'd be ideal.'

I thought about it. Something to do that was worthwhile, using drama, the passion I thought I'd have to leave behind forever. And going from advertising to social work. That was reinventing myself, big time.

'I'd love to find out more.'

281

Deirdre looked pleased. 'I'll introduce you to Brad. Moved here from the States, he was part of a drama therapy group that's well-established over there. He works with young people in Castlemilk, dealing with drug problems, crime and deprivation.' She laughed. 'Trendy Soho advertising agency to a housing estate in Castlemilk. That'll be a bit of a culture shock.'

Any doubts were dispelled when I talked to Brad. We met at the community centre after he'd finished running a workshop and went into the main hall, two seats making a little stage, with three rows of seats facing us. We sat on the two seats and it seemed odd but appropriate our chat had the feeling of a play being watched by an invisible audience.

Gosh, he looked very American. Square jaw, perfect teeth.

'So how do you find Scotland?' I asked.

'Turned right at Iceland and there it was,' he replied. 'No seriously, it's awesome to be here. I had an image of castles on every hillside, monsters in every lake, so starting work in Castlemilk was a rude awakening. But I love you guys' sense of humour, the friendliness of strangers in the street, the passion and patriotism of your soccer fans. I just wish someone had told me you speak a different language here.'

I laughed. 'Aye, yer heid's gonna be gowpin if ye dinna ken whit aw thae bampots are blethering on aboot.'

'Stop that right now,' he laughed. 'I've got enough trouble when people do it for real. So let me tell you about drama therapy. In English, if that's okay with you.'

He pulled his seat closer and leant forward. I did the

same. In the cavernous hall, it created a strange intimacy between us.

'It's best described as the intentional use of the healing aspect of play, drama and theatre to help with a person's problems. We try to get people to give things a go, think of new ideas to move on with their life. So many people with problems are in a state of emotional paralysis. The simple goal of learning a few lines and thinking of a solution to a character's dilemma in a play gets them moving again.'

'Does it work? I mean, do people go along with it?'

'It doesn't magically heal people, it's not a silver bullet for life's problems. But if people want to change, it's a tool to help them. I know that because theatre saved me.'

Brad went on to tell me his story. He'd had an alcoholic father who beat him all the time. He played truant from school, got involved with gangs, petty crime, started fights. But a teacher decided to pick him as the lead in the school play, and having something positive to focus on was the turning point.

'I faced up to my problems,' he told me. 'Turned me around, and for five years I was part of the New York off-Broadway acting scene.'

'And you gave it all up to help others?' He seemed too good to be true.

'Oh no, I'm not that much of a saint. I realised I wasn't going to make it big in the business and there wasn't enough work to pay the bills. I was always cast as the handsome dude and there's only one of them for every ten character actors. Unless you're Cary Grant, you can't make a living playing the matinée idol. So when I saw the chance to train to be a drama therapist in Philadelphia, it seemed like a way to keep in with acting and get a regular pay cheque at the same time.'

I liked him. Nice, caring guy, not a starry-eyed do-gooder. Pragmatic. No illusions about how difficult it was for a Yank to turn up and use a poncey thing like drama to change the lives of inner-city Scottish hooligans. His message was that you should face up to your problems, not run away from them, which made me feel a hypocrite agreeing with him. He bought into my story that I'd become jaded by the cynicism and shallowness of the advertising world and wanted to return to my roots, Scotland and my love of theatre. He was looking for someone to join his team, do individual counselling and also be a technical director to oversee the running of the plays. Someone who knew how to put on a performance and could step into it and act if there was a role no one else could fill. And by the end of our chat, he knew he wanted that person to be me.

That was the foundation I needed to get started again. I found a flat in Paisley to be near the college and promised myself I'd stay away from Glasgow city centre and the West End, so there was no way anyone connected to Michael would accidentally bump into me. Duncan had heard nothing from Michael, so I figured it was safe to tell my parents about my return to Glasgow. They were cautiously supportive of my latest career change. I think they suspected something, but as long as I was somewhere they could contact me again, they saw that as a step forward.

'It's best to bide wi' your ain folk,' said Granny Campbell, pleased my regular visits would be starting again. Mum hadn't told her my Michael story so I made London sound like one big adventure.

The three months in college seemed to go by in a flash. I couldn't believe that was all that was needed to become a professional psychotherapist. And the more I saw how drama therapy was being used to help people, the more I became excited about starting it myself. For the first time I was feeling positive about where I was going.

I even managed to convince myself if you'd reinvented yourself once, it would be easier the next time. I couldn't have been more wrong.

chapter twenty-five

I completed my diploma in August and then I was part of the team, trying to make a difference. I wished the course had been longer. I felt woefully under-prepared to tackle some of the situations, but I tried to do my best. I was learning all the time and I loved every minute of it. And I loved working with Brad. He looked like a Disney cartoon prince, handsome in a bland sort of way. But his eyes were like the embers in a fire late at night, smouldering away but occasionally bursting into flames of intensity when he talked about his work.

He was there with me when I did my first group session to help a group of women deal with guilt and shame. Some had worked as prostitutes after dropping out of school, others had stolen money or been caught shoplifting. They wanted to move on, but their memories were holding them back.

One woman told me she had been a petty thief since childhood because her family life had been non-existent and she spent her time in street gangs to find some sense of belonging. I made her pretend a piece of cloth was a baby, who had no one to love her. She had to pretend to mother the child to give her the love she'd never had herself, to soothe and coax it to stay on the straight and narrow.

The woman took the cloth from me. I could see she was feeling awkward. I was too. My heart was in my mouth as I watched to see whether the theory I'd been taught at college could make a difference in the real world.

'There, there,' she said. 'It's okay to be yourself. No one should have to go through what I've gone through.' She looked around the group for encouragement. I could see some of the other women crying. They all looked street-hardened, their faces wizened beyond their years. But inside that shell of cold defiance, they had tortured souls.

'I can hear it's hard for you,' said Brad, his voice filling the room with a calming quiet authority. 'Let's see if you can move yourself to a happier place.'

The woman nodded. The exercise was abstract, metaphorical, yet the woman was connecting to it. 'I love you,' she said to the piece of cloth in her hands. 'I'm sorry I've never said that before. But you'll always have me to love you from now on.'

There was a new sort of silence in the room. I found myself sensing the other women were projecting their own hurt into the scene being acted out in front of them.

'I'd like to hold the baby,' said one of the other women, very quietly. She turned to the woman with the cloth. 'Is that okay?' she asked.

'Please,' said the woman, handing over the cloth. Reverentially, like it was a precious gift being handed on.

The second woman started to stroke the piece of cloth. 'Baby,' she said. 'you need to be held. I know how you feel. You need someone to love you.'

I was still shaking after the session finished. I could see what Deirdre had told me about the work being intense, how it could take over your life if you let it. I thought about my guilt and shame over Joe's death and how it had stopped me from loving again. My guilt and shame for my part in DCI McDonald's death and how it had sentenced me to a life in the shadows of the world I wanted to live in. I wondered if I would ever have the courage to confront my demons like these women had done.

And it was fantastic to be working with people who were passionate about helping others. Because we were working in the most run-down parts of Glasgow, there was a real sense of camaraderie in the drama therapy team. They worked together, socialised together, and, I suspected, slept together.

Straight away I was invited to a weekend get-together. Deirdre, Brad, and two others, Sophie and Karen. It was round at Sophie's flat, the décor a melange of earnest academia, urban bohemia and student paraphernalia. The sort of flat you grow into when you leave university but want to keep the materialistic world at bay. Dinner was three different vegetarian curries and mountains of rice. Dessert was two grapefruit hedgehogs, a valiant attempt at post-prandial sophistication, cheese and pineapple cubes on cocktail sticks to fill up any empty corners after the curry-eating frenzy. It should have been right up my street.

But it wasn't. Dinner was dominated by a tedious discussion on some flaky theory by Karen that we should use the power of gemstones and crystals to soothe the savage ravages of the troubled minds we were trying to help. 'Vibrational medicine', she called it. I'd never heard such a load of old tosh. But rather than pat her gently on the head and talk about something sane, the evening spiralled into endless tedious chattering about one madcap philosophy after another. I wouldn't have minded if they'd known what they were talking about, like when Tom McGrath was explaining his theories on Eastern religions and their relevance to our lives here, but it was uninformed, pretentious clap-trap. I caught Brad's eye at one point and signalled my cynicism. I was relieved he gave me a grin and a skyward glance which suggested he shared my feelings.

He steered the conversation into a new area, talking again about his troubled childhood and how it had influenced his decision to become a therapist. That became the cue for everyone else to go all Jungian and start talking about themselves as 'wounded healers', taking it in turn to reveal a deep-rooted trauma that compelled them to want to treat people because they themselves had been traumatised. That I didn't mind, found it quite moving, actually.

I said nothing and I could see everyone looking expectantly at me to share my story. It was at that point I decided to step back from getting too drawn in. I had so many skeletons rattling in my closet I could run my own ghost train. I'd be a drama therapist, but I wouldn't be one twenty-four hours a day. Once we'd finished work I'd be on my own, be reclusive rather than sociable. That way I wouldn't get my mind filled up with hippy-dippy hogwash and I wouldn't get drawn into making any indiscreet revelations about my past.

They weren't the only reasons. I guess I felt guilty. All the bad things that had happened because of me seemed to lead to me having a better life. I never felt any sense of atonement for Joe's death, or for DCI McDonald's either if it came to that. I'd picked myself up and got on with enjoying life. I felt it was time I had to pay some sort of penance. Helping others, being a bit of a hermit, denying myself access to the delectations of city life, all that might make me feel better about myself. I remembered what Tom McGrath had said to me about Hindu yogis living a life of solitude to be mindful of their sins and to atone for them. It was about time I did some atonement.

After a few weeks of politely turning down invites, the group got the message I wanted to be on my own. Brad was the most difficult to shake off. There had definitely been a spark between us and I wished I could explain to him that my aloofness away from work was nothing personal. Deirdre was tricky too. She never asked why I'd disappeared so suddenly to London and I never explained, but I noticed her concerned looks when she saw me retreating into my own little world.

Eventually they left me alone and I channelled all my energies into my work, providing help to schools, social workers and drug-addiction counsellors. The schools were in some of the toughest neighbourhoods in Glasgow and the job there was to try to get kids who'd gone off the rails to channel their energies into something positive rather than the destructive lifestyles they'd got themselves into. Very scary kids, little thugs in the making and some of them could be completely obnoxious at first. It was obvious they'd come along to the drama therapy classes as a way of staying out of borstal.

One of the first sessions I did on my own was when

I walked into a room with six sullen skinheads. They sat facing me, their arms folded, eyes on the floor.

'Okay,' I said, hands on my hips. 'You've been told to be here, I get paid to be here. We've got an hour to get through together, let's make the most of it.'

'Go fuck yirsel',' the guy in the centre said to me. The group grinned their approval.

'Aye, too fuckin' right,' another said in agreement.

I had to take that negative energy and work with it. 'I could say the same,' I replied. 'But I'm going to do something a wee bit different. Here you, take this, will you?' I threw a small ball at him.

He caught it and deliberately dropped it on the floor.

'You're almost as good as a Scottish goalie,' I said. 'Pick it up and throw it on the floor and make a sound that's like how you're feeling.' The skinhead looked at me in disbelief. 'Go on,' I said. 'We've got an hour until we can all leave, so we might as well do something.'

He picked the ball up. 'Fuuuuck!' he shouted as he bounced the ball. I caught it and threw it to the next skinhead. 'Now you.'

He made a snoring noise as he threw it to the floor.

'Sleepy are you?' I asked.

'Naw. Bored. Bored rigid wi' this game. Bored rigid wi' life.'

'What's so boring about life?'

'This place. Fuck all to dae. You jist work here, you dinnae have to fucking live here.'

'Why don't you move somewhere else?'

'Cos this is where I sign on.'

'So get a job somewhere else.'

'Like what?'

'Kitchen porter in a hotel, for example. You're not telling me you wouldn't be able to do that, are you? I moved to London once and got a shit job as a waitress. But it got me started down there.'

'What's the fucking point?'

'Well, you wouldn't be bored, would you? It could be a way out of this place.'

'Who'd gie me a chance? Naebody escapes frae Castlemilk, hen. That's the way it is.'

'Who says? You don't look like someone who does what people tell them.'

'Aye, yir right. Naebody tells me whit to dae. If I want to be a fuckin' kitchen porter nae cunt's gonna stop me. Maybe I'll dae jist that.'

Slowly I got them interacting and once that started I was able to form a connection with the messages of the exercises. It didn't always happen in the first hour, but it did start to happen eventually.

The social element of the job was heartbreaking. I was working with the detritus of society. Horrifying to see the domestic violence, depression and psychological problems people had to deal with. I tried to give them insights into old problems, strategies for dealing with current ones and metaphors to give meaning to ideas and solutions to get them to a better place.

As I started to gain confidence, I began to play out more elaborate, more involved exercises. My favourite technique was where someone with low self-esteem had to play the part of a saviour of a medieval town or group of explorers. They got lost in a fantasy world where they did something that won respect, and although the acting left a lot to be desired, you could see the first signs of self-belief emerging.

Brad and I were gelling as a team. I would concentrate on the creative side, coming up with different scenes that would get people to explore traumatic events in their past without being re-traumatised in the process. Sometimes the scenes would take a few minutes, sometimes they could last an hour. Brad would concentrate on being supportive to the people we were trying to help. Holding their hand, showing he was listening, saying what he could see from how people were responding to my ideas, all the time trying to move them to a happier, more comfortable space. There was a growing respect between us. And sometimes more than respect. I could see some of the young women we were helping almost fall in love with Brad, and it took all my willpower to stop myself falling under his magical spell.

The real world was slowly revealing itself to me. We were in the middle of the Queen's Silver Jubilee hullaballoo, the papers were full of street parties and Union Jack bunting. You didn't see many street parties in Castlemilk and the only Union Jacks on show belonged to Nazi skinheads hanging out in bus shelters. Britain existed in two parallel universes: the rose-tinted official version peddled by the media, and the real world, where the flotsam and jetsam were washed up on the shores of urban deprivation, ignored and despised by the powers that be. Everyone was closing their eyes to the uncomfortable reality that existed in their own backyard. I thought back to the night when I was sitting in that fancy restaurant with Michael, when he pointed to the anonymous specks of light out the window and asked me if I would do something to help them. I remember feeling ashamed of myself that I didn't speak up and challenge him.

Better late than never. I was doing that now, and it was becoming my life.

1978

chapter twenty-six

The new year saw the launch of Duncan's book. It went well, really well. All of a sudden, Duncan was the flavour of the month amongst all the book reviewers. Interviewed by Melvyn Bragg, shortlisted for the Scottish Book Prize. And most exciting of all, in the bestseller charts, reaching number fourteen one week. Duncan, the great new voice in Scottish literature. Mark Jackson, to be precise, that was his nom de plume. Duncan the author. Who would have thought it?

I was so proud of him. He was doing what he'd always loved, writing his magazine articles and now his book was a success. But he was still the same Duncan, couldn't tie his shoelaces on his own. Lost an important document he was supposed to bring with him for a meeting apparently, thought he might have left it on the train. But he was changing as well, making plans for what he wanted to do next, not just drifting along in a Duncan-like way.

'Got a big decision to make, Bobbie,' he told me. 'The book has given me a bit of a celebrity status in the music press. *NME* want me to come and work for them full-time as a major features editor. I'd be jetting around the world interviewing rock stars. But my publisher wants me to get started on the next book, strike while the iron's hot, keep the momentum going. It's a tough call.'

'Great problem to have,' I replied. 'Can't you do both?'

'Not really. I wrote the first book because I had so much time on my hands when I started working freelance for the big papers and magazines. Even then, it took me eighteen months to finish and that's with having the gist of the story land on my lap because it was based on someone I knew. I need to get the next novel written in a year, I'm told. So decision time.'

'Where are you heading?' I asked, although I could see from the excitement about the launch there could only be one answer.

'Got to be the book, Bobbie. You only get one chance at this. I can keep going on the money from the first novel and there's a big advance from the publisher if I promise it will be ready next year. I can always slink back to the music press if it doesn't work out.'

It was great to see him so happy. I wished the same was true for me. It had been about four months into the job when I noticed the initial wave of exhilaration about drama therapy was beginning to wear off. The sheer misery and deprivation I saw every day was getting to me. Brad had told me I must keep boundaries between my work and my personal life. But I'm not like that. The only people I saw all day were those whose lives had been a catastrophe. Seeing their problems made me more and more believe I was a failure too.

As time went on, my reclusive lifestyle became less to do with penance and atonement, and more to do with depression and lethargy. I spent my evenings in pyjamas in my nondescript flat, watching mindless TV. When Duncan told me he had split up with Kathleen I selfishly hoped I would have more of his boundless energy to cheer me up, but he was struggling to find time for me.

I was losing interest in the things I used to enjoy, like reading a great book or seeking out new experiences. The pounds started to pile on, and as I looked at myself in the mirror I became more and more upset at what I saw. My youth and my beauty were slipping away and there was only a void in their place.

I wasn't so unattractive that I couldn't find some carnal distractions every now and again, but they felt like hollow experiences. I didn't dare venture into the bright lights of Glasgow's city centre, so my hunting grounds were the pubs and bars on Hamilton High Street, with the occasional foray to Hoots, the town's excuse for a nightclub. That was only when I was desperate. It was full of underage drinkers; I felt like a granny there. Although an enthusiastic, lanky young adolescent was always good if I wanted a night of quantity rather than quality.

There was nothing for me out there; there was no answer to life, no certainties about the future. I needed to move on to pastures new, but a voice inside me kept saying I had no chance of that. I lived in an emotional black hole from which there was no escape.

★ ★ ★

At the end of January I met Sharon. I was doing one-on-one counselling with her, helping her deal with a rape three months before. She hung around with some dodgy company and she was blaming herself she had behaved provocatively. The Procurator Fiscal had decided not to proceed with prosecuting the guy, due to lack of corroborating evidence, and Sharon was convinced it meant everyone was saying it was her fault; that she'd been asking for it.

I'd done an exercise with her, to get her to start challenging her inner critic so she could start the process of emotional healing. My role was to stand in front of her, hands on her shoulders, and push her backwards across the room, shouting at her the words of self-reproach she'd earlier used to describe her feelings about herself. Once I'd 'defeated' her by pushing her across the room, she had to find the words and power to push back at me. At first she was paralysed by hearing her own ugly thoughts being shouted at her, so we tried again. That time she did push back.

'No! Fuck you,' she yelled. 'It wasn't my fault!' That was the start of her taking back her self-belief, finding strength from acting out a physical and verbal battle between us.

It was intense and draining for both of us and we found ourselves chatting at the end of the session, as much to bring ourselves down as anything else. Sharon had the same detached attitude to life as I had and so, after an awkward courtship of words rather than any real conviviality between us, we agreed to meet up for a drink.

That was a complete no-no according to Brad, seeing anyone we were helping outside of a professional setting. But I couldn't face another despondent lonely night in front of the TV. As we talked at the pub we surveyed the wreckage of our lives. It wasn't the most fun-filled evening I'd ever had, but it was an evening talking to someone at last who was on the same wavelength as me.

We met up a second time because it was easier than finding a reason not to. It was then Sharon told me her secret for dealing with life. Chasing the dragon.

Red Chicken it was called, the ultimate in a smooth high. Better than weed, better than hash. She got it from Doctor Jimmy, her banker, she said, and he went down to London to get it from the Shah, an Iranian guy who had a source in China.

Red Chicken. Otherwise known as heroin.

'You're a junkie?' I asked in fascinated horror.

'If you're insane and inject, yeah, that's what you'd be called,' she replied. 'But smoking it... that's a completely different bag. You want to find a beautiful world that only you live in? You want to love yourself? You want to keep this alternative universe hermetically sealed from the vile world we live in the rest of the time? If I'd just stayed at home that night I was raped, stayed at home chasing the dragon, I wouldn't be in the shit state I'm in now. It's not the drugs that screw you up, it's the people and lifestyle around them.'

We went back to her place.

It was not the scary experience I expected. After all the Billie Holiday and Velvet Underground songs telling of its danger and horrors, it was, well, mellow really. I shuddered in nervous anticipation as Sharon produced a Disney crayon box, the lovably innocent cartoon characters on the lid incongruous guardians of the evils within. She took out a meticulously folded square of tinfoil, a neon Bic cigarette lighter, a plastic straw and the little chocolate-coloured crystal rocks of heroin, each no bigger than a match head. She unfolded the tinfoil and made a V-shaped crease in the middle.

'Here we go,' she said reverentially. She dropped three little rocks into the crease and began melting them with the lighter to make them stick to the glimmering foil. She put her lips around the straw, eyes blazing with anticipation. The heat was making the rocks hiss and bubble, like a dark satanic witches' brew. A cloud of smoke billowed and boiled up the crease. Sharon sucked it up through the straw, held it in her lungs for twenty, maybe thirty seconds. When she exhaled, her breath was clear and odourless as the heroin stayed inside her and began to weave its spell.

'Now you,' she said.

I could already see a wave of narcotic euphoria sweep across her, a tsunami of pleasure and orgasmic bliss. I took a rock out of the tin, just one to be on the safe side. I flicked on the lighter and watched the heroin writhe and squirm on the foil, like it was alive. My stomach churned with excitement. I sucked up the acrid smoke and pushed it into my lungs.

Like Sharon said, it was just like smoking dope, although more of a beautiful high. It was how I imagined it would be to float on the surface of the Dead Sea, stillness and peace melting away the guilt and grief. I felt the heroin move through me, filling every cell in my body with warmth and comfort. I had no depression, no regrets, as heroin took me into its arms.

'You see?' Sharon said to me.

I decided I loved her.

I didn't wake up the next day wanting more. I thought I'd have cravings but it wasn't as addictive as people said, just a slight afterglow of that nice feeling. It didn't screw me up, like I'd seen cocaine do to some agency guys in London. I could still think clearly. No hangover. No feeling terrible later. It just made me happy and content.

Sharon said she used it most weekends. 'People will tell you Red Chicken's bad,' she told me. 'But if you only take it occasionally, just at the weekend, it's not an addiction. It's like taking medicine if you're ill, or using a survival tool if you're in danger. And if you lead as sick and scary life as mine, you need a little help. I use it, it doesn't use me.'

Yes, I was tempted to try it again but, if I did, it would only be after a long, long time. So I could prove to myself I could keep it under control. I didn't think it was hypocritical to be an anti-drugs crusader during the week and a user at the same time. I was trying to stop people damaging themselves with drugs, getting into the scene without knowing the facts. I was a grown-up, consenting, informed, social-care professional. How I would use it would be completely different.

I waited a fortnight before I took it again. Okay, I know I said I'd wait longer but I didn't see the point. Some people it worked for, some people it didn't. I was one of the lucky ones. I had men during the week and Sharon and I had a nice little serene thing going on at the weekend. We were two creatures of the night, with heroin our cool-fingered handmaiden. It massaged and caressed

303

our troubles away, it tucked us into bed and wished us sweet dreams.

When we were smoking together nothing seemed to exist outside that moment. It made humanity seem beautiful after all the bad stuff I saw during the week. It made my life seem fulfilled, full of purpose, of optimism. It took me into a distant shadowy dream world, where my heart would beat more slowly, my breathing calmer. In the darkness I felt secure at last. Sometimes I took a little more, just to keep the feeling going, but it wasn't a problem. I still had lots of London money left. I could afford it.

Ironically, it was my sex life that proved the danger to my safety, not the drugs. I should have realised something was wrong when I picked up Lou. I should have spotted how screwed up he was. But I didn't. All I saw was a too-tight black T-shirt, showing off a great physique. Boy, did he work out, and boy, did he like to show it.

I wanted a real animal in bed for a change after the last couple of weedy lovers. The lower the IQ, the better the sex, I had discovered. And Lou fitted the bill perfectly. Thick as mince, but with a body to die for.

The trouble was, that was almost what happened. Back to his place, I expected to find a typical working lad's digs. Rangers team photos on the mantelpiece, the Athena poster of the tennis girl scratching her bum, that sort of thing. But Lou's place was, well, a bit gay actually. Lou needed to work something out about himself, but was denying it too much.

And so despite the muscular promise, there was a distinct lack of performance. Only one soft muscle in his body, but it was a rather important one. He threw himself off me in disgust and frustration, flailing the mattress like it was his gym punch bag.

Like a fool, I ventured my theory about his real orientation. Been hanging around too many social workers, I felt I'd got to solve everyone else's problem even when I was off-duty.

'What do you mean, you bitch?' he yelled. 'You think I'm a poofter? I've had more pussy than you've had hot dinners. Don't blame me if you're so fucking hippy you don't do it for me.' And with that, he hit me.

Then hit me again. And again. I blanked out for a second. Opened my eyes, groggy and confused. I needed to get out, and quickly. I grabbed my clothes and ran into the bathroom. Got dressed in seconds, then looked in the mirror. Not good. Blood pouring from my lip, eye swelling up. And pain.

I could hear him punching the mattress and yelling. Yelling at the bed, at me, at himself. I unlocked the bathroom door and ran for it. Glanced around as I reached the outside door. He looked up at me. His eyes had so much pain in them. He didn't make any attempt to stop me. I ran out onto the street. Dizzy, I flopped on the pavement.

I woke up in hospital. I told a policeman it happened in the street, no idea who did it, and gave a generic description of my attacker. I could see he didn't care.

The hospital said they'd let me out in the afternoon. Sharon came and picked me up.

'You need to get something to chill you out, make it go away,' she said. A quick phone call and we were in a taxi to Doctor Jimmy. She'd never taken me to meet him before, but she saw I needed a hit fast.

We went up the staircase of some derelict flats. It smelt of urine and we had to pick our way over piles of rubbish on every step.

'Doctor Jimmy changes where he cooks every week,' she said. 'And they're all shitholes like this. But it'll be worth it.'

She knocked on the door. 'Jimmy, it's Shaz,' she yelled. 'Got that special case for you.'

The door opened and a wiry little guy pulled Sharon inside. He stared at me for a long time. I must have passed the test, as he stepped aside to let me in.

The only furniture in the room was a shiny, black plastic settee and a coffee table. The windows were blacked out by ripped-open bin bags. A skinhead sat huddled in the corner, his face ravaged by raw sores, his eyes rattling in his sockets like dice shaking in a cup. Graffiti on the walls, newspapers strewn on the floor, scattered bits of broken everything all around the room. The foetid smell of vomit hung in the air.

'I need a little more cooked up,' I said as he got ready. 'I'm in so much pain.'

'You want the pain to go away quickly? Best to shoot it up,' Doctor Jimmy replied. 'That's what they would have done to you in hospital, same here. Yeah, just this once, you should do what the doctors do. Let me see your arm.'

'No, I don't think so,' I said, pulling away from him.

Sharon dropped into the shadows.

'Relax.' He was almost whispering. 'There's no need for it not to be cool if you're careful and stick to the rules.

Only shoot up in an emergency, once a week at most. Gives you time to clean up, doesn't let the addiction take hold. That's what I do. The only time I shoot up more often is for an exceptional reason.'

I knew I shouldn't have, but I felt so bad. I needed the pain to go away. Just this once, I thought, because of the pain.

He pushed the needle into a vein, pulled back the plume of blood that confirmed he'd made a clean puncture. I stared in awe and horror. Then he pushed the plunger all the way in. It felt like a sex act, that I was being penetrated by a carnal deity. Even before he removed the needle from my arm I could feel my mind explode. It was the speed that was the surprise, within seconds I was in a dream, floating in a beautiful world. And then the feeling of sex. I could feel myself getting moist, faster and stronger than ever.

I'd stepped over a threshold and the door had slammed shut behind me.

My sex life became non-existent. I think when we got stoned Sharon and I made out, but it was all a bit hazy afterwards, so I wasn't sure if I'd imagined it. And occasionally I had to put out for Doctor Jimmy or one of his friends if I was short financially to score a fix, but that was a purely professional transaction, didn't count.

The only problem was, when you chase the dragon, you need the dragon to live. Being on junk was a twenty-four-hour-a-day obsession; every second was a race against the ticking clock of the build-up of the cravings inside your body. And when the alarm goes off, and you know that if you don't get a hit in the next few minutes your body is going to burn and your mind explode, every remnant of sanity, of reason, goes out of the window. Then I'd disappear into the toilet to shoot up or smoke and life would be good again.

I had a warm protective blanket to wrap around my body. At last I had found a father to love me.

chapter twenty-seven

The more I thought about it, the more I realised drama therapy was a con. We were a bunch of middle-class do-gooders, thinking we could help Glasgow's great unwashed with our arty-farty little games. And Brad was the worst. He could be so up himself with his sanctimonious bullshit. He started picking on me, just because I forgot my lines in one of his precious plays last week. Okay, it was more than forgetting my lines, I forgot what the whole flipping thing was that we were doing. But I was still the best actress in the group. There was no need to get heavy with me.

I couldn't be bothered going to the workshops half the time. Brad always bought my excuses, always believed my little fairy tales about why I couldn't get in to work. But all I did instead was laze around the flat. It was too much effort to get up. There was a photo of myself on the mantelpiece, taken when I was nineteen. I looked beautiful, full of optimism. It was messing with my head so I threw it in the bin.

In the evening I would watch TV with the sound turned down. One time I was watching an inane ITV sitcom, but I could still hear the audience laughter in my head, getting louder and louder until I could feel my ears bleed. I turned the channel knob until all I could see was static, particles from distant stars captured and flickering on the screen. I left it there. I could watch the static for hours, fascinated by these messages from across the universe.

Then I stopped going to work altogether. I'd moved into a smaller flat to have more money for junk, so no one would know where to come looking for me. The initial fake bloom of heroin had long since faded, and my skin was becoming diaphanous, a taut papery membrane stretched across my skull. I was Bob Dylan's 'Visions of Johanna'. The ghost of electricity howled across the bones of my face.

I was becoming a walking cadaver, my voice a listless monotone. The only people worth the time of day were the smackheads I hung out with. But we called ourselves smackheads for a laugh. We could hold our shit together, unlike the junkies and hookers you sometimes saw at Doctor Jimmy's.

But there was nothing worse than rambling dope fiends, so I moved on to hanging out with the alkies in the street. These guys were real hard cases, they could drink straight meths, or hairspray aerosols emptied into a carton of milk. They were the ones who had real problems keeping things under control. I reckoned I was the only person under forty there, but with these guys you couldn't tell. Kids would run up and throw cans and rubble at us, annoying little brats. They found the mattress I used to turn tricks on round the back of the tenement buildings and set fire to it. I ran after them, screaming obscenities. They found it hilarious.

And that bitch Sharon dropped out of my scene, said I scared her too much. Cow. She got me into that world and then she wanted nothing more to do with me. Screw her. Oh, I did already. Screw her anyway.

I don't remember what I said when I phoned Duncan. I must have had a panic attack, calling him up like that, rambling and raving like a lunatic apparently. It must have been scary; he was at my flat an hour later. Must have given him my new address. That saved my life.

I didn't deserve his help. I was defensive at first. Said I must have been drunk when I called him, very sorry he'd rushed over for nothing, no reason to be worried. But he saw the burn marks on the kitchen foil, the straws lying around the place. He'd led a sheltered life, had Duncan, but he managed to put two and two together. He burst into tears when he saw the needle marks on my arms. I think that was when he finally got through to me.

He got moving fast. Drove me to the Southern General Hospital, and I was admitted into the drug ward. I remember the ride on the gurney, the nurse talking calmly to me, checking my blood pressure, taking blood samples, helping me shower.

I was woken in the morning with a light shining in my eye. I blinked in confusion and when I focused there was a guy staring at me, a detached look of concentration on his face. My mouth hurt, my eyes hurt, my ears hurt. Everything hurt. I pulled away, blaming him for the pain. Then I felt it coming, no way to stop it. I vomited. It made me feel worse.

He stepped back, a nurse moved in to tidy me up. 'So, Bobbie, you're awake. That's good,' he said. 'My name is

Dr Carmichael, you're in the drug ward at the Southern General. Do you remember how you got here?'

I shook my head with a groggy embarrassment.

'Your friend Duncan brought you here last night. We gave you Librium and diazepam when you were admitted to get your blood pressure under control. I'm going to come back this afternoon at two and discuss your condition with you. I want you to get yourself together, it's going to be an important conversation.'

'Can I get something to wake me up?' I said. My voice had a husky rasp to it. I coughed and the nurse gave me a glass of water. I gulped it down and stared at him. 'Please?'

'In good time. Sister will be around later. Now get some rest, try to eat something, drink lots of water. The nurse will give you a questionnaire to fill in, I want it completed when I meet you. Any questions?'

I gave a resigned shake of the head and he was gone.

The nurses treated me like a naughty schoolgirl all morning, constantly nagging me to get things done, showing no sympathy for the state I was in. I kept my irritation to myself. Dr Carmichael wasn't back at two, it was nearer four before he turned up. He made me put on a gown and we went to a consulting room.

He read through my answers on the questionnaire. I scrutinised his face for a reaction, but it was expressionless, professional. He put it down and turned to me.

'You need to know the truth, Bobbie. You're a drug addict. I'm a doctor, and for me, heroin addiction is a disease, what we call a chronically relapsing condition. I'm not here to judge you, I'm here to deal with your medical condition. If you want treatment, that is.'

He looked at the questionnaire again. 'You're lucky,' he said. 'You say here you started smoking heroin three months ago and only started injecting recently. If that's true, you can cure yourself, it's still early days. For some people I see, the most realistic hope is to try to stabilise their chaotic lifestyle. You can get yourself better.'

'That's... good,' I replied. I still wasn't thinking straight, but the hospital bed, the nurses, the way I was feeling, it was getting through to me what state I was in. I ran my hands through my hair. I'd showered but could feel it matted with sweat again. 'That's good, doctor,' I repeated with more conviction. 'Can you do that for me?'

He nodded. 'I'm going to put you on an intensive, abstinence-based rehabilitation programme. It's not designed to keep you comfortable, it's designed to cure you. You're young and healthy, in the early stages of addiction and seem to have a good support network of stable friends. I'll prescribe methadone to be taken orally three times a day for three days. It isn't such a strong hit as heroin but the effect lasts longer, so it will bring down the level of opiates in your system in a controlled way. That will be the end of the medication.'

I shuddered at the thought. Three days? Would I be strong enough in three days? It seemed impossible.

'Then what?' I asked in trepidation.

'Then I want you to attend the Glasgow Drug Clinic as an outpatient. They'll give you counselling and support to help you get through recovery. I'll write to your GP and I want you to see him at least once a week. When he thinks you're ready, he'll refer you back to me and we'll see what progress you've made. Do you understand all this?'

I nodded. It seemed so orderly, what he was saying, so matter of fact. I felt like I'd regressed into being a little child, needing a grown-up to tell me what to do. And the little child in me wanted to be good, to make him proud of me. I wanted his paternal love.

Duncan came to see me at visiting time. Brad was with him, their faces a mixture of relief and concern. Brad did most of the talking.

'I blame myself for not spotting this sooner, Bobbie. When you stopped turning up to drama therapy I thought you'd decided to quit your job. When I couldn't find you to talk it over, I thought if you don't want to get in touch, I shouldn't try to track you down, I should let you get on with your life.' He shook his head in anger with himself. 'Here I am, supposed to be trained in helping people with drug dependencies and I don't even see it when it's at my front door. But you don't fit the profile of a hard drug user in Scotland. I'm so sorry.'

'I'll let you off this once, but don't do it again,' I said, trying to smile.

Brad didn't smile back. 'I spoke to the doctor this afternoon. It's good you're Dr Carmichael's patient, he's one of the best. A lot of doctors have little sympathy for self-induced problems and just want to minimise the harm addicts do to themselves and others. All they try to do is control and maintain someone's drug problem. But Dr Carmichael believes junkies can be cured.'

I winced as he said the word 'junkie'.

'You're getting discharged tomorrow and then you're signing on with the drug clinic?'

I nodded in agreement.

'Well, methadone is going to ease your transition from coming off heroin. But when you start coming off drugs completely, you'll still find it tough. You're going to need a lot of support to see you through the next couple of weeks.'

'Dr Carmichael said I hadn't been taking it long enough to be addicted,' I replied. I smiled to convince myself it was true.

'That's good,' Brad replied. 'But don't kid yourself, Bobbie, it's going to be tough. You'll need someone with you. Duncan and I are going to take turns to stay at your flat. And you'll need the help of your parents too. In fact, you'll need all the help you can get.'

'Oh no, don't tell them,' I groaned. I could imagine Dad's reaction, proof that everything he'd said about me was true. 'You know that's a bad idea, Duncan, don't you? They'll freak out.'

Duncan looked at Brad and then at me. 'I think they need to know. You need them, Bobbie, that's what the experts say.'

So Duncan told them. I found out later how it went. They were shocked of course, and predictably, Dad was furious. Looked for someone to blame, wanted to storm off and confront Brad for putting me in danger, wanted to track down Sharon and Doctor Jimmy and get them arrested. But Duncan was amazing. Only let Mum come to see me the next day at visiting time, to let her report back to Dad on what she saw. Duncan left us alone to talk together quietly for about half an hour, although we didn't say anything meaningful. Mum didn't know what to say or to do and I wasn't much help either.

Duncan came back with Brad at the end of the visiting hour. Brad introduced himself to Mum, and said he had been to the drug clinic and had brought along a pamphlet about a one-day course they ran, called The Family Programme. Mum read it hungrily, I could see the look of relief on her face that here at last was someone telling her what to do, the best way she could help her daughter. We hugged and she left to talk to Dad, said she would be back tomorrow. But at visiting hour that evening they both turned up. I'd just had my second hit of methadone so I was as prepared as I could be to have my moment of reckoning.

It was Mum that spoke first. 'Bobbie, you need to let us back into your life again. When you disappeared down to London and were so cagey about what you were up to, we thought it best not to interfere. And when that man turned up at the house on Christmas Eve, your dad and I found your whole story a bit unsettling. And now this. We only want the best for you and for you to be happy. But we can only do that if you allow us to help. Let us into your life. We've been strangers from each other for too long.'

I nodded, more than a little shamefaced. 'Of course, Mum. I don't know how it happened and I'm scared, scared of what I've got myself into, and scared about what's coming as I get myself out of this mess.' As I spoke I could feel the addiction pangs of heroin tearing at my skin. A panic attack was building and the methadone wasn't strong enough to fight it.

Dad spoke. 'Your mum and I met with one of the counsellors at the drug clinic this afternoon and we want to be part of your recovery. They have something called The Family Programme where we find out all about your sickness and help you to deal with it.'

'I'm not sick,' I said, 'I've been taking heroin and now I'm going to stop.'

'Drug addiction is a disease, Bobbie. It says so, right there in the pamphlets they gave us to read. We're your parents. It's what we're here for.'

I hugged him.

I felt Dad stiffen. 'I've never been one for words, Bobbie. But together we can beat this.' He smiled, an anxious smile, but a smile of love nonetheless. I looked up and saw love in his eyes for the first time I could remember.

That day was the darkest moment of my life, but also the most beautiful.

chapter twenty-eight

Dr Carmichael warned me about the endorphins when he was going through my discharge from the hospital. 'They're hormones in your blood that make you feel pleasure and protect your mind from pain,' he explained. 'When you take heroin you stop producing endorphins because the opiates in your body overwhelm your system and your brain shuts down production. But the trouble is, when people come off heroin, it takes a week or so before their body starts making the natural hormones again. You need to be prepared for that.'

'Prepared for what?' I asked. Surely nothing could be worse than the craving I was reeling from.

'Endorphins protect the mind from fears, worries, stress. You'll need to keep thinking about positive things, try and block out any bad memories that come into your head. For a few days you won't have any defences to protect your consciousness, so you're going to have vivid nightmares and paranoia. It can be very scary. But don't forget, it's just a stage. It won't last forever.'

I hadn't been home long before I found out what he meant. I collapsed on the floor, overwhelmed by images and sounds coming from the ceiling, the floor, the door, the windows. Phantasms from the light, wraiths from the shadows. I was smiling with encouragement at Joe as I watched him commit suicide. I saw the fear in DCI McDonald's eyes as I saw him being murdered. There was the young mum in the supermarket, her dead baby in her arms, poisoned by Orange Sunshine. Duncan slammed the door in my face when I ran to him for help. Michael threw me in a dungeon and, as I lay curled up in a foetal position on the floor, he stood over me saying I was his forever, I would never be free. And worst of all, someone was screaming like their very soul was being tortured. Those screams were real.

The first couple of days were terrible. I'd wake drenched in sweat, like I had the worst flu in the world. My bones ached with a frantic itch, as if an army of ants were nipping away inside me. But every time I opened my eyes someone was there for me. Brad wiped the sweat from my hair, the tears from my cheeks. With each spasm of cramp twisting my arms and legs, he massaged away the knots of pain. Mum sat next to me, reading me Gerald Durrell books, full of simple laughter. Dad said little, just held my eyes to his, willing me to succeed. Duncan wrote me poems, describing the pain I was feeling, his hope for my future. His hands were on my brow, mopping my forehead and washing me down with a soft warm cloth, wiping my endless runny nose. Without the four of them I don't think I would have got through it, the vomiting, the diarrhoea, the crushing depression.

Slowly, my body started producing endorphins again and I was able to drag myself forward towards recovery. Every hour, every metaphorical inch forward, I felt a little better, a little stronger. The cramps faded, the nausea passed, the fevers and chills subsided.

Now the problem was I couldn't sleep. I lay there twisting and turning. My head was clear, but everything else throbbed. One minute I was burning hot, the next shivering cold. No matter what position I took, I was uncomfortable. I played David Bowie's *Low* album over and over again, the glacial music of Bowie's own drug-induced calamity resonating in my mind.

After five days, I tried taking a little scrambled egg, a spoonful of yoghurt, but it made me sick. But then, slowly, I started to keep some food down. Porridge for breakfast, a tin of macaroni cheese for lunch, tinned custard for dinner. Brad reckoned once I found something I could cope with, I should keep taking it over and over again until I got my strength back.

At the end of the second week, I reckoned I was strong enough to manage on my own without constant help. I could feel hunger, taste food. Everything was starting to look clear and sharp. But then lethargy took me over. I didn't want to do anything, I didn't want to go anywhere. I was an amoebic blob, unable even to find the motivation to turn over in bed. I didn't even want heroin. The craving was gone, but it had taken my life force with it.

If it hadn't been for Brad I think I would have stayed broken. He knew about a charity that sponsored a place in Ayrshire, 'Maggie's Farm' they nicknamed it, where the farmer agreed to let volunteers mentor people with chaotic lifestyles to work around the farm. Brad made a few calls, persuaded them to take me straight away and drove me down there. I was to stay in a caravan with two other women. Three guys would be in another caravan but we weren't allowed to socialise with them, no matter how innocently. And one of the volunteers would do random drug tests to make sure we were sticking to the recovery programme.

Every day had a set routine, starting at seven thirty sharp, feeding the animals, assisting with other farm duties. It was crop-planting time, so I helped load bags of seeds onto the tractor. My muscles ached from the unfamiliar exercise, but it was good to be feeling physically stronger every day. I was there two weeks, did a lot of jigsaws in the evening, watched a lot of TV. I smoked like a chimney and drank about ten cups of coffee a day, nicotine and caffeine providing the only relief as my body cried out for drugs. I'll cure myself of heroin only to kill myself with lung cancer, I thought. But one step at a time.

The two girls I was sharing the caravan with were Senga and Beverly. Senga was about the same age as me and hooked on barbiturates; Beverly was a middle-aged mother of two, been an alcoholic all her life. I'd been told to use my interactions with them as a chance to grow, to learn from others going through the same challenges, so we had a few sporadic chats in the evening. Beverly took it upon herself to tell us the realities of a life of addiction, not what she considered to be the propaganda by the social workers that we were on a road to recovery.

'Enjoy this wee holiday while it lasts, girls,' she told us as she leaned over to switch off the telly when the programmes came to an end. 'And keep popping them courage pills they give you. Aye, they'll keep the monkey off your back for a bit. But dinnae kid yourself. It's a life sentence we're on, my wee darlings. Next time a hassle comes along in your life, you'll be jist like me and fall off the wagon again.'

'I'm never going through this again,' I said. 'There's been only one thought in my mind since I came down here. What the hell was I doing? I'm going to start living again.'

'Aye, I thought the same at your age. And every time they dried me oot, every time I was pulled out of whatever I'd got myself into, everything was still crap. I'd go along to meetings and people told stories of how messed up their life was. We all said how sorry we were, how brave we were being, telling each other all our shit and everything. But all I was really thinking was, that stramash I was hearing everyone else talking aboot sounded good to me. I wanted to get oot o' there to get paralytic again.'

That struck a chord with Senga. 'I can't face people without my uppers and downers,' she said. Her voice had the prepubescent whine of a spoilt child. 'I'm just naturally anxious, I guess. Everyone goes on about how this is my one and only chance to kick the habit. But you're right, Beverly. I just want to get my strength back so I can start getting high again.'

I looked at the two of them. Beverly would have been attractive once, but the ravages of alcohol had not been kind to her, to put it mildly. She said she was forty-two, but she looked sixty. And Senga had that dead-eyed look I'd seen in so many of the dropouts hanging around Doctor Jimmy's. They were not me, but if I didn't do something about it, they were who I would become. That moment of clarity convinced me. I had to find the strength never to go back to the hellish world I'd left behind.

When it was time to go back to Glasgow, Brad and Duncan came to pick me up.

'I don't think it's a good idea to come back to drama therapy, Bobbie,' Brad said. 'It's too dangerous at the moment for you to be close to temptation, too easy a route back into the drug world. I don't trust myself to spot the warning signals.'

'Can't I do the psychology and crime sessions, stay away from the drug stuff?' I said. I wanted my life back, to function again.

'I don't think that will work. Things aren't that clear-cut,' replied Brad. 'Don't get me wrong, Bobbie, I want you back. Not just as a professional member of the team but also because of you.'

Before I could say anything, Duncan spoke. 'I've just finished my Scottish book tour,' he told me. 'The last signing session was in Fort William yesterday as part of a loop through the Highlands. Nice store, caters for tourists and walkers and the like. They do a roaring trade on people coming in to look for a good read when the weather outside is atrocious. Which is all the time, apparently. They're looking to take on more staff for the holiday season. What do you think?'

It sounded perfect. Was it? I stared out of the window before I spoke.

'Not a bad idea,' I replied. 'All that scenery to look at and spending my day nudging people in the direction of a good read. Bit cheerier than what I was doing with you, Brad. No offence.'

'None taken,' he said. 'You guys have got some beautiful mountains up there. Not up to the standards of the Rockies, but pretty. Yeah, real pretty.'

'Where would I stay?' I asked Duncan.

'No problem. There are lots of places where you can rent short term. You can see if you like it, and if there's a job over the winter, take it from there.'

So that was that. I took the train up to Fort William, met with Pete, the manager. Easiest job interview in the world; he was delighted to have the best friend of a famous author working in his shop. Found a lovely cottage to rent in Spean Bridge, a village a few miles out of the town, where I'd wake up in the morning to the sight of the Grey Corries from my living room window. Duncan gave me a loan to put down the deposit. My London savings had long since disappeared.

I went to see my doctor. He took my blood pressure, did all sorts of blood and urine tests and sent me off to see Dr Carmichael. I agreed to come down to Glasgow on my day off every week for follow-up treatment at the drug clinic, for counselling on how to spot risky behaviour and resist temptation. I agreed to give up alcohol, put my sex life on hold, stop all the things that could lead me into wanting to take heroin again. I even managed to cut back my smoking.

Each time I came down to Glasgow, I checked in with my parents. There was never any criticism now, only support, and Dad and I were starting to have the sort of relationship I'd always wanted. All that distance, all that time wasted, but it was behind us now. And of course, I visited Granny Campbell. She was getting quite frail and had moved into a care home. It was difficult sometimes talking to her, she repeated the same stories over and over again. She was very happy I'd given up the drama therapy, didn't like me mixing with the wrong sort of people, as she put it. I talked to her about missing out on life's dreams, whether she felt like that when she was my age. It was very different in her day of course, people didn't expect so much.

One day at a time, I was taking my first tentative steps towards normality.

Fort William, May 1978

chapter twenty-nine

Working in a bookshop kept me busy; the nice polite conversations about what I'd recommend to the Lochaber bookish middle-classes and the tourists were a lovely way to spend the day. I got caught up in books for the first time since my English literature days, rediscovering how they could spirit me off into other worlds and other times, where I could explore my fragile dreams. I spent the long summer evenings with my latest find from the bookshop, curled up on my sofa with Jasper the cat, my new companion. Firing up my imagination once more, letting light come back into my life.

And, believe it or not, I actually got interested in football. It would have been impossible not to really. Scotland had qualified for the World Cup in Argentina and for a few heady weeks the whole country was 'On the March with Ally's Army', as our World Cup song promised. Ally McLeod, the Scottish manager, convinced a gullible nation we were going to win the tournament. It was just the atmosphere of daft optimism I needed to keep my spirits high; even our humiliating performances against Iran and Peru didn't bring me down. Heroic failure, that's what we're good at. And I still remember Archie Gemmill's brilliant goal against Holland in our final match, when for one brief moment it looked, against all the odds, that we might still qualify for the next round. I whooped for joy and danced around my wee twelve-inch black-and-white TV. I hadn't felt that good since I took my bows at the end of *Who's Afraid of Virginia Woolf?* in 1975.

Brad was totally bemused by the football madness that swept the country. 'Mass psychosis', he called it. I was seeing more and more of him now. After his sniffy comments about our pint-sized Scottish hills, I regarded it as my patriotic duty to get him into a pair of hiking boots and give him an education on Scotland's scenic magnificence. We would meet in Glencoe, him driving up from Glasgow and me coming down from Fort William and, after a day bashing about in the mountains, we'd have a celebratory pint at the Clachaig Inn before he headed home. I never invited him to stay. There was only one bed and I knew what that would lead to. But we were both happy with the boundaries of our relationship and we were growing closer the more time we were spent together.

Duncan would also come climbing with me. The old Duncan would have turned up at the start of the walk and realise he'd left his climbing boots behind, but the new Duncan had his mind fixed on climbing all the Munros, the name for a Scottish mountain over 3000 feet, and was methodically ticking them off. I couldn't work out why it meant we were never allowed to climb any hill that didn't make this magic threshold, but I didn't complain. It's a guy thing, I suppose.

He had been struggling to get started on his next book,

so it was great when he said he'd begun writing at last. Another thriller, was all he would tell me. I kept asking to have a read, but I got a firm no.

'You don't want to see how the sausage is made,' Duncan said. 'Wait till it's finished. When it's ready, you'll be the first to read it.'

Conversations with Brad always came back to drama therapy, the work he was so passionate about. The group was going well; they'd introduced new safeguards for people working on drug projects; my little legacy. The drugs problem was growing now, lots of cheap heroin coming in from Pakistan. I made a lame comment about being a trendsetter, but Brad didn't find it funny.

'I still miss drama therapy, you know,' I said during one of our post-climb drinks. 'I felt for the first time I was doing something worthwhile, with real meaning. Don't get me wrong, I love the job I'm doing now. But changing someone's life, giving them help to get out of whatever dark place they'd found themselves in, that was special.'

'Are you thinking about coming back?'

I hesitated. 'I don't know. What do you think?'

Brad thought for a few seconds. 'I'd say no.'

I tried not to look disappointed. 'Why?' I asked. 'I've been clean for six months now. And I'm never going back to drugs, I can promise you that.'

'I'm so proud of how strong you've been, Bobbie. The number of people who can make a clean break from heroin is depressingly small. That's why I don't think you should put yourself in jeopardy again. Being face-to-face every day with the sheer hell of people's lives can be overwhelming. Was overwhelming in your case. No, as much as I'd love to work with you again, you owe it to yourself not to put yourself at risk.'

'Maybe you're right,' I reluctantly agreed. 'But I wish there was something I could do to support people who are going through what I went through. I couldn't have made it without help.'

'Have you thought about volunteering for the Samaritans?' Brad asked. 'You only deal with people on the phone, for a few hours a week. It would give you the distance you need to be safe, but you could still help people out.'

'Samaritans? Aren't they just a bunch of women in twinsets and pearls doling out platitudes over the phone?'

'That's a pretty outdated stereotype, actually. I've seen them in action and what they do is very important. All sorts of people do the volunteering. The point of being a Samaritan is what they call 'active listening', coaxing people in distress to explore their feelings. You don't have to come up with the answers, you just try to help the person calling to come up with them themselves.'

'You reckon I could do it? And not get screwed up again?'

'I think so. You could maybe volunteer for a couple of hours a week and stay aware of how you're feeling. Would you like me to put you in touch with them?'

So that's how I got my life back in balance. Pete made me part of the skeleton staff he kept on at the bookshop during the winter, and for four hours a week I answered the phones at the Samaritans in Glasgow. Sometimes I did the night shift on my day off, from one o'clock in the morning to seven. I talked to people about loneliness and broken relationships, people who had committed a shameful crime, people contemplating suicide. That was how I should have dealt with my guilt for all these years. It wasn't a hobby or something to fill my time, it was a way to get stability and fulfilment back into my own life.

And then another great thing happened. I was working in the shop, restocking the shelves from a delivery that had just come in, when I noticed a woman browsing our second-hand book section, her bony frame rattling around inside a well-worn Barbour jacket and hand-knitted sweater. She looked familiar: her jet-black hair and pallid complexion stirred a hazy recollection inside me. Then I realised. It was Rita, the refugee from life who I'd met way back when I first arrived in London.

'Rita? Good God, it's you isn't it?'

She turned and looked at me, her face an embarrassed confusion.

'It's me, Bobbie,' I said.

'I'm... sorry,' she said slowly. 'I know you... how?'

'In London. At the women's hostel. You were reading an Ernest Hemingway book. Gave me tips on how to disappear.'

'Bertie! Of course. You've changed a lot.'

I blushed with embarrassment. 'Oh sorry. That's right, I was Bertie when I met you. What on earth are you doing in Fort William?'

'I moved to Scotland. Living in Scoraig, an alternative community in the far north. We live on the shores of Loch Broom, there's no road to us. Cut off from the outside world, and that's how I like it. I'm married to a crofter now, Danny. He's restored my faith in men.' She smiled.

'I'm doing our monthly run down to Fort William for supplies for the community. But what are you doing here?'

I told her bits and pieces, how the guy looking for me had made me uproot again, and after a spell working in Glasgow I was settling into life in the Highlands. We arranged to go for a coffee when the shop closed, so we could have a proper catch-up.

It turned out Rita had managed to work out the philosophy that I had been striving to identify for myself. 'Life is simple,' she told me, 'but we insist on making it complicated. Confucius said that 2,500 years ago, and it's even truer today. If your heart lifts when you see a rainbow, if the sight of the first green shoots of the new season's crop fills you with joy, then you can be happy with small things around you. That's the life I lead now. Everyone in the twentieth century feels so pressurised to keep on buying the latest stuff, to live up to other people's expectations of what you should do, who you should be. We end up frustrated and miserable.'

'I wish you'd told me that when we first met,' I joked. 'I've spent the last three years trying to be someone I'm not, trying to forgive myself for things I've done wrong. Maybe you're right. Maybe I shouldn't set myself impossible-to-achieve goals. I'm happier now than I've ever been, and my life couldn't be more basic.'

I saw Rita every time she came into town and our chats became the final part of my discovery about how I wanted to live. Climbing in the hills made me relaxed and healthy, taking pleasure from the simple joys of nature. My work at the Samaritans gave me a sense of self-worth, making a difference to people's lives. Rita helped me discover my true values again, made me aware of my tendency to get sucked into morally dubious lifestyles.

Finally, I was comfortable in my own skin. Finally, I'd got some stability.

That was to last about another four months.

★ ★ ★

Late October Duncan called, told me he was ready to let me read his book. Invited me down to Glasgow to celebrate. He was looking decidedly shifty when he arrived at the restaurant, obviously not confident the book was going to be as good as his first one. But he'd chosen the Ubiquitous Chip to tell me about it, Glasgow's newest and best restaurant, so it couldn't be that bad. I thought it would be churlish of me to question the extravagance so I went along, promising to enjoy myself. And of course, to give him encouragement about his book, no matter what.

We ordered our nouvelle-Scottish fare and when the waiter left, Duncan pulled out a big wodge of paper, the grand unveiling. He rubbed the back of his neck, pulled his chair back slightly. His hand caught the edge of his fork and it fell off the table. He bent down to pick it up.

'Sorry,' he mumbled. I smiled reassuringly. I'd never seen him so nervous.

He gave a little cough. 'Let me tell you the story, Bobbie. A young woman gets caught up in a plot with a notorious gangster to eliminate one of his rivals as part of a wild lifestyle of sex and drugs.'

I couldn't believe it. 'Oh no, Duncan, tell me you're

joking. Are you serious? I've given up everything, all my dreams, to disappear from you-know-who. And then you write a fucking book about it?' I saw a few of the other diners glance over. There was some serious tut-tutting going on.

He stared down at his feet, unable to look me in the eye. 'That's just the start. Ninety-nine per cent of the book is completely made up, there's nothing that links the story to you. He dropped his voice to a whisper. 'Even if Michael read the book, he'd never recognise any part of it. But I needed a nugget of a story to get me started. *Roman à clef*, remember?'

'Fuck your *roman à clef*.'

The maître d' came over. 'I'm going to have to ask you to tone down your language, madam,' he said.

I gave him a grim nod of acknowledgement and turned back to Duncan.

'Just how do you expect me to take it?' I hissed. 'And the secrecy, the "I-don't-want-to-show-you-it-because-it's-not-ready" excuses? Lies. You've behaved like a complete shit. Why the hell did you do it?'

His face contorted into a grimace. I could see his ears go red.

'I needed a plot idea. Just the essence of something to get started. The publisher was pushing me like crazy and nothing was working. What happened to you seemed like a good starting point and once I got writing, the story took off in another direction completely. There's no way I would do anything that would endanger you, Bobbie. Don't be angry with me.' His hands fluttered over the manuscript, like he was expecting me to snatch it off him at any second.

I sighed. 'I'm not angry with you, Duncan. I never could be, you know that. But I think it's reckless and stupid to use something as dangerous as this for a book idea. Could you really not have come up with something else?'

'Honest, I think there's no problem. I'll make you a deal. Read the book. If you think there's any chance, any chance at all that it will lead to you, I won't send it to my publisher. I don't care what pressure I'm under, if you say no, that's it.'

I looked at him sceptically. 'You'd throw away a finished novel after all the work you've done on it?'

'I'm serious, Bobbie. I knew if I told you before, you'd get me to stop writing it. I'm convinced I've made it so different from what really happened it will never lead to you, and I'm happy to take the risk you'll be okay when you read it. And don't forget, it will be published under my pen name. Michael will have no clue I've written it. But I mean it. If you say no, it goes up in smoke.'

So I read it. And it was good. It was not me at all, the clever sod was right. I would need to be completely paranoid to think Michael would link me to it. If he still even bothers about me; there'd not been any sign of him looking for me since I left London. The main character, Anna, lived a double life of a social worker by day, cruising bars for men at night. Her gangster boyfriend used her to smuggle drugs into the country by flying her in and out of Bermuda for wild sex parties. The gangster was completely different from Michael and the honey trap had been changed to a drug bust set-up. In the second half of the book Anna kept re-inventing her life to escape from the gangster, he almost caught up with her on every other page. Thank goodness life's not like that. Duncan had behaved appallingly, but he was not a bad person. But definitely cowardly in putting off the confrontation until the last moment.

I thought of the danger he'd been in when he helped me with Michael, smuggling my belongings out of the flat, getting beaten up for keeping quiet. How he nursed me through my addiction. I said once I owed him one.

Time to honour that.

1979

chapter thirty

Duncan's second book, *Escape from Danger,* was launched in November 1979. The front cover was an artist's interpretation of a young girl with a Jekyll and Hyde persona and it took all my self-control to avoid making waspish comments whenever I sold a copy. 'It's me, you know,' my inner rogue wanted to whisper.

I remember one customer looking at a woman walking off with Duncan's book. He turned to me and said, 'Great novel. Finished it last night, couldn't put it down. Mark Jackson's got another winner there.'

I would tell Duncan that. How it was not only selling but was getting spontaneous acts of praise from complete strangers.

That was before...

'It's Bobbie Sinclair, isn't it? My name's Ian Stevenson. I'm the Crime and Investigations reporter from the *Daily Mail.* If you don't mind, I'd like to talk to you about Mark Jackson's new book.'

'What? Sorry, I can't help you.' I pulled the book I was holding tight against my chest. 'You need to talk to the author. Not to me, I just work in a bookshop.' Nothing had prepared me for that moment.

'No, it's you I want to talk to. Our book critic did an

interview with Mark and asked him a question if his novel was based on real people and events, since his first book was based on Nick Warren, the music journalist. Mark got all shifty when he denied it, so she passed it on to me as a tip. I did some rooting around and found out his real name is Duncan Jones. And then I discovered you.'

He smiled as if it was a compliment. 'On the face of it, you don't seem to be like the girl in the book at all. But people who knew you at university told me how you suddenly and mysteriously disappeared to London and nobody heard from you for months. Can you tell me, Bobbie, are you Anna in the book?'

'What? Sorry, no comment. Jane, can you serve this customer?' I ran off. Not exactly the actions of an innocent.

He came after me, swung in front and stopped me in my tracks. I stood stock-still as he scrutinised my face. 'I'm sorry to be insistent, Bobbie, but I need your answer. I'll get to the bottom of it eventually. It'll be a big scoop to announce the true story behind a book that's supposed to be fiction. If you co-operate, we can make sure we tell your side of the story.'

'Sorry, no. I have nothing to say. Please leave me alone.'

I went into the back office and phoned Duncan. Luckily he was at home.

'Duncan, did you say anything to a reporter from the *Daily Mail* that could have made them think your book is based on me? I've just had a reporter confront me in the shop asking me if I'm Anna.'

There was a long pause. 'Oh shit, Bobbie. Yes, a critic

did ask me, but it was a question out of the blue, they didn't know anything. And I denied it of course. She tried probing but when she saw she wasn't getting anywhere she moved on. I thought I'd convinced her there was no truth in the story. That's why I didn't mention it to you. Didn't want to worry you.'

'Shit, shit, shit, Duncan. They've found me. How did they do that? Duncan, what have you done? Do you know what this means?'

'There's no way they'll run a story like this without proof. I've no idea how they found you in your bookshop up in Fort William. Honest, I didn't tell them. I'll see if anyone's been in touch with my publisher. Don't worry, I'll be discreet. Bobbie, I'm so sorry, I don't know how this could have happened.'

No point in beating him up, the damage was done. 'We'll talk later,' was all I said. I put the phone down and thought about what to do next. For a moment I considered heading out the back door and running. Running and running and never stopping, becoming an endless gypsy, my world in a suitcase.

Instead, I headed back into the bookshop like I was sleepwalking. I found myself standing behind the till, the shock replaced by disbelief. I'd finally got free of Michael. There had not been any sign of him trying to find me since I left London. Because he'd decided there was no point in still chasing after me, because I'd stayed silent or because I'd been successful at shaking him off, it didn't matter. Now a newspaper reporter had succeeded in doing what he'd not been able to do again, track me down to where I worked. How the hell had he done that?

The horror began to sink in. My picture would be in the paper, Mark Jackson would be named as Duncan Jones. There would be all this speculation that I was the girl in the book who got mixed up with a gangster and ran away from him when she got mixed up in his shady deals. Ended up working in a bookshop in Fort William. Michael would see it, and not only would he know where I was, he'd realise the story behind the book would be investigated. Once again I was a danger to him.

Searing pain shot through my body. An overwhelming, insatiable desire for heroin. To make the horror go away. I pushed the thought away, but it came back even stronger. How could I get junk? Who did I know?

Pete called out to me from his office. 'Phone call for you, Bobbie.'

Heroin. What I needed was Red Chicken, a voice inside me kept repeating. Red Chicken, Red Chicken.

I went back and picked up the phone. It was Duncan.

'When I put the phone down my publisher called. The *Daily Mail* has been on to them too and they spoke to someone who'd met you at the book launch and knew you worked in a bookshop in Fort William. And that crime reporter Ian Stevenson has been on the phone, wanting to do an interview with me. I've said no, of course, but it sounds like he definitely thinks there's a story here.'

'What are we going to do, Duncan, what are we going to do?'

'I don't know. What do you think?'

'Look,' I said, 'I can't stay on the phone. Let me think about this and I'll call you. Don't say another word to anyone. Okay?'

'Of course. I'm sorry, Bobbie, really I am.'

I hung up the phone.

I needed to discuss it with someone. Who? Not Duncan. He was as traumatised as me, no good trying to get any sense out of him. And his guilt was off the scale.

I tested Pete's patience by making one more quick phone call to Brad and asked to see him down in Glasgow when I finished work. He asked what it was about, I said something important, but I couldn't talk on the phone. A demon in my head whispered with sinister charm I'd have time to head out to Hamilton to find some nice, soothing, calming heroin, just one tiny little hit to get me through this. Just one. A siren song of seduction was luring me to return to my nightmare.

I met Brad just off Great Western Road. We went to a nearby hotel lobby to talk. The drama group was still doing well, he told me. There was a tension in the air as we went through the motions of a few seconds of anodyne chat. Brad could sense there was something momentous coming.

I told him everything. My lifestyle, Michael, the two deaths I'd been responsible for, everything. What Michael had photographed, how he threatened me. I told him about the reporter turning up at the bookshop. That I was convinced they'd run the story eventually and I would go to jail. Either that or be found floating down the River Clyde when Michael tracked me down.

Brad gave a deep sigh. He looked thoughtful. 'Duncan could never have imagined this would happen. He would never have published the book if he thought it could harm you. He cares for you, Bobbie.'

'I know, I know,' I replied, managing a thin smile. 'Bloody Duncan. He's ruined everything.'

'Try and forgive him, Bobbie,' Brad replied.

'We'll see,' I said. 'At the end of the day, my life is about to be destroyed, because he couldn't think up an original idea for a book. It'll take me a long time to get over that.'

'That's one way of looking at it,' Brad replied. 'Another way is you can be responsible for your own actions at last. What do we teach people at drama therapy? Avoiding conflict only postpones the inevitable. I think you've proven that point here, Bobbie.'

'Don't be hard on me, Brad, I don't need that right now,' I replied.

'You need to speak to a lawyer, and straight away,' he said. 'I don't know much about the law in Scotland, but in America we have a thing called plea bargaining, that's what would happen in a situation like this.'

'This isn't America, Brad. I'm going to jail. Perverting the course of justice, accessory to murder, blackmail. Accomplice to Michael's money-laundering racket.' I picked up a sugar cube and crushed it in my hand. 'I'm scared. What's going to happen to me?'

'I don't know. You don't know. That's why you need to speak to a lawyer straight away. Look, I've got the number of a firm that handles the legal side of any social problems we come across. Why don't I call them now and make you an appointment? You have to do it, Bobbie. I'm sure they have attorney-client privilege in Scotland, so nothing you say can be used in court. I'll check all that first. If I find it's okay to talk to someone, will you do it?'

Brad thought about things in a different way to

Duncan, I realised. Duncan would take my decision and support it, try to make it work. Brad was much more challenging.

'Are you sure?' I said. 'Maybe they won't run the story if we keep denying it?'

'I think you should talk to a lawyer anyway,' Brad insisted. 'You don't know what the consequences will be yet, neither does Duncan. But you need to do something. You can't spend the rest of your life with this hanging over you.'

He was right. The next morning I called Pete and said there was a family emergency that meant I had to rush down to Glasgow. At two, I was sitting in the offices of Johnson and McGregor, the solicitors, meeting with Steven Bovey, one of the partners. I shook Mr Bovey's hand. I don't think I'd ever seen someone so overweight, but he was very smartly dressed, obviously had a bespoke tailor make his pinstripe suits. The overall effect was of substance, gravitas. The sort of person you'd want on your side.

He listened attentively as I went through the story of Michael and DCI McDonald. He occasionally leant forward, joining his fingers together to make a triangle as he pondered on what I told him.

When I'd finished, he leant back in his chair, his eyes narrowing in concentration. 'So, Miss Sinclair, let me tell you what I think. Firstly, the *Daily Mail* will not run this story, or risk naming you as someone who's lived a double life or consorted with gangsters. They certainly won't run anything to do with Michael Mitchell, or DCI McDonald, because it looks like they know nothing about that. Unless your friend Duncan, or,' he glanced down at his notes, 'Brad were to say anything further that is indiscreet.'

'So you think I'm okay?'

'It depends what you mean by okay, Miss Sinclair. I'm saying at this moment in time, based on what you've told me, no paper will publish this story. Oh, there might be a coy diary piece, speculating on where the author got his inspiration, but nothing worse than that. No, that's not the real issue here. The real issue is how you want to proceed with what you know about DCI McDonald's murder. You played a material part in it and you have listened to what I would consider to be a full confession from the main perpetrator about his involvement in money laundering. You should consider going to the police with this, and straight away.'

'I don't want to go to jail. And that's what will happen if I tell them everything.'

'Let me deal with that in three parts. You've got to ask yourself if you can sleep easily at night, knowing you have information that could bring the perpetrators of a terrible crime to justice. That part is what I'd call your moral dilemma. Secondly, you need to consider whether you want to spend the rest of your life looking over your shoulder waiting for this Mitchell character to catch up with you. That part is your personal welfare dilemma. Only you can decide how you feel about these two issues. But on the third part, the legal consequences of going to the police, I can provide some input and assistance. If you tell me to do so, I will put in a call to the authorities and make an appointment for you to be interviewed, under caution, by the detectives assigned to the case. If they decide to proceed with an investigation into your allegations, I would put in a further call to the Procurator Fiscal, saying I will advise you to co-operate fully with the investigation, even if it means incriminating yourself, on condition they grant you immunity to appear as a Crown Prosecution witness. Of course, it's up to the Procurator, but it's not you they are after. It's Michael Mitchell and this Big Jockie hitman of his and their criminal enterprise. In my judgement, such an application on my part would be successful.'

It dawned on me he was telling me I wouldn't go to jail if I went to the police. A flood of relief surged through my body. But it was such a huge step. I tried not to think of what I'd be asked at the trial. I tried not to think of Michael, what he'd do to stop me testifying.

'Can I think about it?' I finally said.

'Of course. Take as long as you like. Nothing you've said here today can be used in any way and I'll do nothing without instructions from you. But if I could just venture one observation on the first two dilemmas I've outlined. A terrible crime has been committed. You need to weigh up the importance of justice versus the short-term personal safety issue and long-term embarrassment that would result from you bringing this man to justice. That's a value judgement only you can make.'

I went back to Fort William and thought about it all night. I didn't discuss it with Duncan, or with Brad. It had to be my decision. First thing the next morning I called Mr Bovey's office. It was time to be a fighter, not a runner.

'I'll do it,' I said.

chapter thirty-one

I went straight back down to Glasgow in the morning and was at Mr Bovey's office at twelve. He wasted no time in setting up my police interview. As we set off in a taxi to Partick Police Station, he ran through a few final points with me.

'You discuss this with no one from now on, not even Brad and Duncan,' he said. 'Do you understand that?'

I nodded.

'Answer every question as fully and honestly as you can. Don't worry, I'll be there to make sure you don't do anything wrong. Do you have any questions?'

It occurred to me I'd no idea how much it was costing me, but it seemed inappropriate to ask. Other than that, my mind was a blank. I should have had a thousand questions, but all I could think about was the ordeal ahead.

We arrived at the police station and I waited till he paid the driver. As we walked up the steps, he said, 'Oh, and on a personal level, I'm proud of you, Miss Sinclair. I know this can't be easy.'

I tried to keep that thought, that I was doing the right thing at last, as I was introduced to DCI Chalmers. A brooding hulk of a man, there were no social niceties about him. It was straight to the interview room without any further preliminaries.

Chalmers filled out a form with my personal details. Also noted down Duncan and Brad's names and addresses. He sat down and read the statement I'd written. Not a flicker of expression. Nothing to give away what he was thinking.

The questions started. Slow, methodical and deliberate.

'You met Mitchell at Tiffany's disco. Who was there with you?'

'No one. I was looking to meet someone for the night. He invited me over.'

'And you were in a habit of going out on your own to have sex with strangers?'

I felt my cheeks flush. 'Yes, my boyfriend had just committed suicide. I wasn't ready for another serious relationship.'

'But you had one with Mitchell? And you went to work for him?'

'Yes, because he said he could... open doors for me, get me started as an actress.' When I heard myself say these things it seemed like someone else I was describing.

'Just to open doors? That's why you slept with him? And you took a job at an art gallery even though you suspected, no, sorry, even because you knew, because he told you, your job was a front for his criminal activities?'

I saw him shake his head. Disbelief? Disapproval? I couldn't tell.

'Yes. I slept with him and I worked for him. But I slept

with him because I enjoyed it. No other reason. And all I did at the gallery was sell paintings. That's not illegal.'

'And part of being in a serious relationship and sleeping with him because you… "enjoyed it", was that he would choose strangers for you to sleep with, as a sex game that he got kicks out of?'

'It was just once,' I replied.

'Oh, so that makes it okay, does it?' He raised his eyebrows and looked at me. A glassy stare that gave nothing away.

I kept silent.

'And when DCI McDonald is found dead, and you read it in the papers, you decide the right course of action is not to go to the police. Instead you hop on a bus for the bright lights of London. That was the right thing to do, was it?'

'No, of course not. I see that now, but I was terrified. You don't understand how scary Michael is.'

Mr Bovey jumped in. I'd almost forgotten he was there. 'Did he threaten you? Say he would harm you if you went to the police?'

'Yes. Well, no, not in so many words. But he made it clear that he would.'

Chalmers gave Mr Bovey a silent look and continued his interrogation. 'Yes, he did, or no, he didn't? Or maybe you imagined it?' He gave an exaggerated sigh.

'He had someone look for me all over London. Had my friend Duncan beaten up to find out where I was. Even twice tried to trick my parents into telling him how to find me.'

'The actions of a spurned lover, perhaps. And then

you meet, completely by accident after all this effort on his part, and you slip through his fingers again. Quite an achievement, if I might say so.'

'I'd packed because he found out what part of London I was living in. I was able to disappear fast. You've got to believe me.'

'Oh, I believe there's something going on between you and Michael Mitchell. I'm just not sure what it is. DCI McDonald was a colleague of mine all through our time together in the force. And a friend too, for what it's worth. If this Michael Mitchell was responsible for his death, believe me, I'll get him. But Mitchell's come up clean. None of our contacts in the gangs have heard of him. From what we can find out, he seems to be nothing more than a respectable businessman. More than that, he's well connected with good causes and the arts world. His responsibility for DCI McDonald's death is speculation on your part. That's not good enough.'

I had been so worried about what was going to happen to me, I'd not even considered that I wouldn't be believed. 'But why would I make it up?' I protested. 'Why would I run away to London to get away from him, give up the chance to be in a movie? Why would he have people try to track me down, destroy my career when he finds me, and make me run again?'

'A good lawyer will find answers to all that,' said Chalmers. 'And Mitchell would definitely have the best. An overactive imagination on your part perhaps? Maybe you had a lovers' tiff and he wanted you back. Maybe he thought criticising you to your advertising bosses would get you back working for him and back in his bed.'

We took a break from the questioning. Chalmers sent someone round to my old flat, to check there really was a door to a hidden room in the stairwell. By the time we met again in the afternoon, he'd confirmed there was and the flat was owned by one of Michael's companies. And he'd no doubt checked the photos of DCI McDonald and me. When we started the next round of questions I could see he thought my story was beginning to sound credible.

We went over the whole thing again, this time in painstaking detail. 'Let's deal with some of the other characters in your story,' said Chalmers. 'What can you tell us about Big Jockie?'

'I don't know his second name. He's a big man, with puffy cheeks. Looked like an overgrown hamster. Scary. He was Michael's enforcer with the guys he used to place money into bank accounts, the "smurfs", he called them. Whenever one of the smurfs got out of line, Big Jockie would be sent along to have a "quiet word" as Michael called it. I remember Michael said when he stopped using smurfs, Big Jockie wasn't needed any more. He said he fired him because he beat up Duncan but I don't believe that. So Big Jockie's not part of his set up now.'

Chalmers looked at Mr Bovey. 'Big Jockie McPherson,' he said. Mr Bovey nodded. 'And when did Michael stop using smurfs?'

'I guess sometime in 1976. You know this guy?'

'Oh yes. Came to our attention about that time. He set up a protection racket in the East End. Obviously decided on another line of business when Mitchell no longer needed his services. But sadly for Mr McPherson, he's got the muscle but not the brainpower to run his own racket. He's in custody, awaiting trial.'

Big Jockie being behind bars was reassuring. I wasn't sure how many enemies I was making during my confession, but having Big Jockie out to get me was something I'd rather not think about.

'I'm not sure Mr McPherson will be minded to co-operate with the enquiry,' said Chalmers. 'We still need to find some other corroborating evidence. Was there anyone else who knew about the blackmail and murder? Think carefully, it's very important.'

'No, they were the only two involved, I'm sure of it.' I could see the look of disappointment on Chalmers' face. He said nothing, he wanted me to think some more.

'Wait a minute,' I said. 'There were rumours at the time that DCI McDonald was thought to be receiving money from organised crime. That's true, isn't it?'

Chalmers' face gave nothing away.

'Well, if it is, if Michael planted information that money had been paid to him as part of the plan to discredit him, I bet it involved Mr Jenkins, Michael's accountant. I don't know where he is now, but if he's still around he must be pretty key to Michael's operation if they're using businesses to launder money now, instead of smurfs. Not only would he know about the money laundering, he would also know about the plot with DCI McDonald if he arranged for that payment.'

Chalmers was writing furiously. 'I think that's all for the moment, Miss Sinclair,' he said after a while. 'I'm sure your lawyer has told you to say nothing about this interview to anyone.'

I nodded.

'Good. Well, we have the element of surprise on our side. Mitchell is not going to expect you to go to the police after keeping quiet so long.'

I listened for a note of censure in his voice, but he continued to talk in the same measured, downbeat tone.

'We may find, after all this time, he's let his guard down. Maybe we can find something to tie him and McPherson to the murder. At the moment we don't have enough to convict him, even with your statement.'

He ignored the look of disappointment on my face. 'Now, he's going to find out very shortly we're investigating him and he'll be able to work out you're responsible. I need you to lay low for a while. You'll need to tell your parents, and anyone else he could use to track you down, to be extra vigilant. We can provide support if necessary.' He stood up, the interview was at an end. 'Thank you for coming in, Miss Sinclair. One of my colleagues will discuss personal safety options with you. So unless you've got any questions, that will be all for now.'

That brought home to me the nightmare that I'd got myself into. I had to tell my parents the whole story. And months of waiting to find out if Michael was going to be arrested, all the time him knowing I was testifying against him. That was an even worse thought. But deep within me I felt relieved I was finally doing the right thing, taking the first step on making amends for my silence.

I told my parents the next day. There was a long silence once I'd finished the story. The cups of tea had remained untouched all through my long, stumbling monologue.

It was Dad who spoke first. 'What you have to know,

Bobbie, is your mother and I will support what you're doing. I know you and I haven't always seen eye to eye, and I'm sorry about that. I'm sorry you didn't feel you could come to us when you were going through all this.'

Mum nodded in agreement, gulping back her tears, trying to get some words out but failing miserably. But it was all right. I knew what she wanted to say.

I told them the about the telephone number the police gave me, a fast response number in case there were attempts from Michael to use them to track me down. They tried not to look scared. I explained I was going to be sequestered while the investigation was going on. I was not allowed to tell them where I was living, but I would call every week.

I called every day.

1980

chapter thirty-two

It was early evening in late January and I'd just arrived back at the air force barracks where I was staying, RAF Leuchars in Fife. It was certainly what you could call a safe house; lots of reassuring security to get into the officers' quarters where I had a little flat. Duncan had also been made to disappear. He would be a witness to corroborate his part in the story, what I'd said to him, seeing the hidden room, getting beaten up by Big Jockie. I wasn't allowed to know where he'd gone, wasn't allowed to talk to him. The wait had been agony. When I heard Mr Bovey's voice on the phone, I knew this was it, the moment of reckoning.

'Bobbie,' he said. 'There have been developments.' He'd started calling me Bobbie after the police interview but I still felt more comfortable thinking of him as Mr Bovey.

He didn't wait for me to respond. 'The police managed to get search warrants. Raided Mitchell's house, Mallard Furnishings in Surrey, the estate agents, art gallery and travel agency simultaneously. And they've got something. One of their forensic accountants has been through the books with Jenkins, who was having kittens during the whole investigation. They got enough to convince him he's going down, for aiding and abetting grand larceny if he's lucky, conspiracy to murder if he's not. Jenkins buckled and took the same deal as you. Because of his heavier involvement in Mitchell's activities, it had to go all the way to the Lord Advocate, but he's going to testify against Mitchell in return for immunity. Michael Mitchell was arrested this morning. He's in custody now and McPherson has also been told he's being charged with murder.'

I tried not to think of Michael in his cell. In fact, I couldn't think of anything.

'Things are pretty hot at the moment. The police will be calling later today, but in the meantime you're not to leave the air base until the trial, unless it's a real emergency. I'll come up to see you tomorrow. It looks like we're going to get our day in court after all.'

★ ★ ★

The months dragged by until the trial. The night before I was due to appear I called Granny Campbell. That was the worst thing about being stuck in Leuchars, not being able to visit her. Mum and Dad said it would be too stressful for her to travel to see me, and it was difficult to keep a conversation going on the phone most times. But it was one of her good days.

'Oh, Bobbie dear,' she said. 'They're saying terrible things in the papers about you. I'm going to call them up to give them a piece of my mind, confusing you with someone else. And the *Glasgow Herald* too. Such a respectable paper, fancy them making all this up.'

'Don't worry, Granny, I've spoken to them. It's a mistake, it's going to get sorted out. Don't worry about it.'

'Oh, I'm pleased to hear that. They shouldn't mess with my Bobbie. You don't need propping up, that's for sure. That's what comes of living in London. You should come back to Scotland you know. Bide amongst your ain folk.'

'But I am back in Scotland now, Granny. You said that to me before, when I came back from London. Remember I told you I work in a bookshop now? I brought you a book of old Glasgow photographs you liked so much.'

'Did you, dear? Can't remember, I'm afraid. Now why did I call you, Bobbie? What was it to tell you?'

'Just to tell me I don't need propping up, Granny. That I've got the strength to stand up for myself.'

'Oh dear, I sound such a nag. Nice talking to you, Bobbie. Visit soon.'

I didn't call anyone else that night, it would have been too intense. Mr Bovey was confident that the police would have enough to get a conviction. Michael's payment into the fictitious DCI McDonald bank account was the 'smoking gun', as they called it. But it was by no means certain. The coroner had recorded an open verdict at the inquest; Michael had done a good job of making it difficult for the forensics to tell whether or not McDonald shot himself. And the police were singularly unimpressed when they found out I'd done time in rehab; it didn't exactly add to my credibility as a witness. But they felt they'd got enough to suggest it was an aberration which happened well after the events with Michael. Hope so.

The trial was the first time I'd seen Michael since we met in London. Chatting to his lawyer before proceedings started, relaxed and smiling, with all the insouciant complacency of a homeless cat. He looked the same, wearing his usual expensive, conservatively tailored suit, starched white shirt. Cufflinks matched the pattern of his tie. Shoes polished to an immaculate sheen. He looked invincible.

The strangest thing about that day, waiting to take the stand, was the peculiar sort of respect everyone showed Michael and me. I was always addressed as Miss Sinclair, Michael as Mr Mitchell. I was asked if I wanted a glass of water, fussed over. It felt in a perverse way that I was the lead actress in a play again. I was due to be called straight after the lunch break. The two legal teams gossiped away as we waited for the judge, sometimes about a legal detail, sometimes about a personal matter that seemed almost out of place in a setting of such formality and solemnity.

The chatting ended when the judge walked in. 'All rise,' said the clerk and it became a scene totally familiar from countless TV dramas. The judge walked in, slowly and majestically in his robes and wig.

I took the stand and gazed around me. The jury, who would decide Michael's fate. Only two women, I didn't know if that was good or bad. The judge, a small, unassuming sort of chap when you looked past the accoutrements of his office. Stern to the barristers, kind to the jury, scrupulously polite to Michael and me. A nice old man, really.

I looked up at the public gallery. Brad was there, giving me a smile of encouragement when I caught his eye. No Duncan of course, he was the witness after me. But lots of other people I knew. Maybe some of them were there out of ghoulish fascination, but I'd like to think most came because they cared about me, wanted me to know I had their support. Brad, Deirdre, a few old uni friends, Jason from The People's Theatre, Tom McGrath from The Third Eye Centre. It was like finding out who would turn up at your funeral.

But the thing that made it difficult to keep myself together was the presence of my mum and dad in the public gallery. There they were, in the centre. They'd walked to court with me, past the photographers, showing their solidarity. I was so proud of them.

I tried to prepare myself for the humiliation ahead. It was going to be hell. But what kept me strong was the thought that I was doing the right thing, facing up to my actions rather than running and hiding. Rightly or wrongly, I'd helped kill DCI McDonald and I was preparing myself to answer for it.

I felt an eerie calm as I stood in the witness box, almost a sense of liberation. The courtroom was packed. The trial attracted a lot of publicity, particularly in the tabloids. There had only been the forensic evidence so far, and the coroner's report. Now Jezebel was on the stand. It promised to be a lurid testimony.

I took the oath and declined the offer of a seat. I wanted to stand, to keep my concentration, to speak with as much authority as possible. The prosecuting lawyer started the questioning, asking about me, to show the jury what sort of person I was and then moving on to my relationship with Michael. I could feel everyone's eyes boring into me as I spoke. I looked straight at the lawyer, locking my eyes on his as I told my story. I could hear the click-clack of the stenographer typing away in the background, bestowing weight and significance on every word, every half-formed sentence. Creating a record forever of the stupidity of my actions, how gullible I'd been. I glanced up at the public gallery, caught my dad's eye and he smiled at me. I struggled to regain my composure. I didn't make that mistake again.

Several times I was tempted to gloss over a minor point, to save myself more embarrassment. But I resisted the temptation and pushed myself to say more, to fill in the extra details that lay behind the question. I spotted DCI McDonald's wife in the public gallery, stoical, composed, not looking at me. She deserved justice, no matter what I had to go through for her to get it.

When the prosecution lawyer was finished I felt naked and drained. Michael's defence lawyer rose to his feet. I felt a shiver of anticipation go around the courtroom. I felt like the stag at Glensporret House, with the lawyer looking down the barrel of the rifle.

He spoke in a monotone, almost disinterested voice, like the questioning was beneath his dignity. Lots of questions about the places where I'd lived, the jobs I'd done, my time at university. None of it was relevant. The prosecution lawyer objected to the questions about Joe's suicide but Michael's lawyer said it was a key part in the build up to me starting a relationship with Michael, so the judge let him go ahead. Faux sympathy as I recounted the story, just to show he wasn't a complete bastard.

Boy, they had done their homework. The men I'd been with, the drugs. On and on he went, raking over the minutiae of my life. His voice changed. Slow, sinuous and seductive as he delved into my sex life. Every salacious revelation paused over, revelled in. Sometimes he would turn to the jury and raise his eyebrows in oh-deary-me shock. The questions about my heroin addiction. Systematically painting a picture of someone without morals. Someone who shouldn't be believed when they accused a respectable businessman of blackmail and murder.

I was not going to let him humiliate me. I had to keep my mind clear for the questions about DCI McDonald. They were the ones that were important, all the rest were collateral damage. He was trying to wear me down so he could destroy me at that part of the interrogation.

Finally the time came, and his voice changed again. Deeper and lower now, like Vincent Price in a horror movie. He started by going over the sex dare game, tiny notes of incredulity in his voice that I didn't know what was going on.

'So, Miss Sinclair. What you're asking the court to believe is you are an innocent abroad in all this, a young and virtuous girl who had no inkling of Mr Mitchell's dark side, but who nonetheless went along with a degenerate and depraved sex game to please him. Is that right?'

I picked up on the danger signals in his question. 'I never said I was virtuous. I'm not on trial for my morals. And yes, I knew Michael had a shady side. But he kept it hidden from me. I never suspected an ulterior motive for the game.'

The questioning continued. Unreal, like a bad dream. The jury was drinking in every detail, absorbed and focused, fired up by their own importance. I kept shaking my head, not in denial of the events I was describing, but because I was thinking of my own stupidity. I couldn't believe I'd ever been part of this.

I went over the attempts Michael made to find me. Talked about how meeting up with him had been a ghastly coincidence. And how that had convinced me to flee again.

'Very dramatic,' the lawyer said. 'And very convenient you had your bags already packed just in case this unlikely meeting was to happen.'

I started to protest but he raised his hand. Cowed by his authority, I fell silent.

There was an even stronger conviction in his voice. 'Indeed, Miss Sinclair, all Mr Mitchell did that day in London was invite you for a talk on a park bench in full view of every passer-by. After you met, as you admit, completely by chance. He wished to see if he could rekindle the relationship between the two of you and apologise for his perhaps heavy-handed criticism of your advertising presentation. And furthermore, I put it to you that when you were not indulging in one-night stands with complete strangers, or injecting yourself with heroin, you were living in a fantasy world, imagining demons lurking in every shadow. That day you were despondent because you'd messed up an important meeting in front of your bosses. You took it upon yourself to take flight from London in a moment of impetuousness, displaying the same reckless behaviour that led you into hard drugs, promiscuity and goodness knows what else. And when you told this to your long-suffering friend, Duncan Jones, he thought it such a fantastical story that it was just the thing for his latest work of fiction.'

His voice rose as he became more passionate. I desperately wanted to interrupt, to tell him, to tell the jury, that believable as his argument sounded, it wasn't the truth. But I couldn't. His speech had an unstoppable momentum, an unassailable conviction. I started to sob. A wave of despair flowed through me as I realised how it would look. That I was broken, because he'd forced me to confront the truth.

I summoned all my resolve to stop.

It was too late. He'd taken my crying as the cue to shift gears. His voice dropped, like an actor wrapping up a soliloquy. Soft and intense because there was no need to persuade the jury. That job was done. He just needed to get my capitulation.

'Fiction,' he repeated. 'Because that's all your story is. Fiction, pure and simple. And when a reporter confronts you with it, you are so embarrassed by your Walter Mitty behaviour you try to make the world believe it's true. Even if it means damaging the reputation of a perfectly respectable businessman, whose only crime was to fall in love with you.'

I couldn't believe it was possible to twist the truth so much. I had to defend myself.

'I'd packed because I was moving flat as a result of Michael tracking me down to Camden,' I blurted out. I turned to the prosecuting lawyer for support. He was scribbling furiously and didn't look up. I swallowed hard, thinking what to say next.

In that moment's pause the lawyer jumped in with

a final comment. 'Of course,' he said, flapping his hand to contemptuously dismiss what I'd said. 'Yet another uncanny coincidence for the jury to consider. That will be all, Miss Sinclair. I have no further questions.'

I didn't want it to stop there. I'd made a fool of myself. He had made it look as if I had made the whole thing up. The prosecution lawyer got up and made me reiterate the key facts again. The blood pulsed through my head, I couldn't even put any conviction into my answers.

The judge ordered a short break and I went out into the hall to recover my composure. Mum, Dad, my friends, they came and joined me. Everyone said well done, that I was very impressive. They were just saying that. I felt terrible I'd let everyone down. So terrible I hadn't started feeling the fear of Michael's reprisals when he got off and came after me.

I needed to be in court to hear the rest of the case. Duncan was great, answered every question with quiet authority. I came back the next day to listen to Mr Jenkins' testimony. The guy looked scared out of his wits, but just about managed to explain how the money-laundering scheme worked. There were lots of documents shown to the jury to support what he said, but it was difficult to know how much they followed; it was pretty technical stuff. Michael's lawyer tried to make out that Mr Jenkins was the mastermind behind the money-laundering scheme and Michael was unaware that his businesses were being used in that way. It was a real stretch and I could see the jury wasn't buying it.

Mr Jenkins described making the payment to a false DCI McDonald bank account, but of course there was nothing that showed Michael authorised it. Michael's lawyer argued that Mr Jenkins had made everything up, after being caught bang to rights money laundering, in an attempt to avoid going to jail. That would have required creativity and imagination, not two personal qualities that Mr Jenkins had in abundance.

Finally, there were the manageresses of Michael's estate agents and the travel agents, and that artist whose painting Michael had asked me to sell. She had gone on to sell over twenty paintings, according to the Avalon Gallery books. They each swore blind they knew nothing of the businesses being used for money laundering, but admitted to being Michael's girlfriend at one time, and still being his occasional lover. The life he had planned out for me. All his little finches, trapped in his cage.

When Michael's defence started, I listened to his lawyer paint him as a paragon of virtue, a successful businessman, sponsor of the arts, and donator to good causes. Rumours of his other activities were just that, rumours.

My stomach lurched as Michael took the stand. His lawyer had obviously advised him to deny everything, concede nothing. His answers were composed, measured and succinct. He said as little as possible, gave the prosecution nothing much to latch on to. The best strategy: damage limitation.

It was Big Jockie McPherson's testimony that was the most chilling. He stood in the witness box, gripping the sides of the lectern in front of him. It looked like he could crush it like a matchbox at any second. He answered the prosecution's questions like a monosyllabic robot.

It looked so incongruous, that brute of a man trying to defend himself using the language of the courtroom. All through his testimony, I kept thinking that Michael would have told him to get rid of me. I looked at his gargantuan, impassive face. Would that have been the last face I would have ever seen?

Even Michael's lawyer was overawed. His questioning was almost reverential, none of the scepticism and sarcasm he demonstrated with me. Big Jockie came across as a killer, an unstoppable force of nature. And with the proof they had that he was on Michael's payroll, hopefully it was obvious to everyone that could only have been for one reason.

The jury was out for just over two days. I wondered if it was good or bad it was taking so long. Surely there wasn't so much to consider? I kept asking what it meant. 'These things take however long they take,' was all Mr Bovey would say. I feared for the worst.

Then it was time for the verdict. High tension. The preamble played out like all the clichés of a hackneyed courtroom drama. The jury filing in, some averting their gaze, others making darting glances at Michael as he stood in the dock. Michael guilty on all counts, so was Big Jockie. Gasps and muted cheers. I struggled to fight back my tears.

The judge thanked the jury and turned to Michael. Gone was the avuncular, courteous manner I had seen all through the trial. Now his voice was stern and castigating as he described to Michael the people he had ruined with his life of crime. How he caused the death of a committed public servant, a loving husband and father, by his ruthless attempts to evade justice. Big Jockie he described as a cruel, calculating killer, willing to do the most unspeakable things if the price was right.

A life sentence for Michael. The same for Big Jockie. Louder cheers that time, as the public gallery grew more assured of their right to express their feelings.

That night I heard what Mrs McDonald said in her statement, that she was pleased with the life sentences but nothing could bring back her husband. No mention of me. Deep down she must have blamed me and hated me. That was what I deserved.

It was over. Michael was gone. I could begin again.

chapter thirty-three

With the verdicts announced, the papers went wild. The *Daily Mail* gave themselves full credit for everything, saying it was their investigative reporting that started the chain of events that led to the conviction. *The News of the World* had the most coverage; four pages dedicated to the gangs Michael was linked to, the rackets he'd been involved in. 'Justice at Last' was their headline. Two pages on me, a couple of old one-night stands came out of the woodwork, painting me as a sexual predator who devoured a different man every night. Pathetic, especially with all the coy innuendo they used to protect their readers' sensibility while making it absolutely clear what I was supposed to have been up to.

The other papers took me by surprise. 'Tart with a Heart', said the *Daily Record*. 'Atonement' was the one-word headline in the *Glasgow Herald*. It seemed I'd struck a chord with my candour and honesty. I was a journalist's dream, generating huge amounts of salacious column inches and at the same time giving them an excuse for a national debate about what were acceptable morals for young women in the 1980s. I thought it would never end.

Duncan's publishers were of course over the moon about all the publicity the book was getting, and Duncan was trying his best not to look too pleased and excited that sales had rocketed. But he couldn't keep his feelings hidden when he called me about the movie rights deal.

Yes, that's right, Paragon Productions took out an option on the book, which meant they'd reserved the rights for a limited period in order to make it into a film. His agent told him not to get too excited, apparently loads of books get optioned and very few film deals ever materialise. Try convincing Duncan of that though. His appalling lack of judgement in writing the book had made him a best-selling author knocking on the door of Hollywood, had put one of Scotland's biggest gangster behind bars, and had removed the menace in my life and turned me into Britain's best known fallen woman. Ironic really.

But that was just the beginning. With everything going on I'd become almost immune to what the next day's papers would bring in terms of new revelations, what unexpected twists and turns would happen next in the never-ending soap opera that was my life.

The phone call came at the first quiet reflective moment I'd had for months. I was ploughing through *Zen and the Art of Motorcycle Maintenance*, Robert Pirsig – very good book. Ideas were playing around in my mind, things like religion, travel, what might be my next incarnation. Take the Magic Bus to India, head off backpacking across America, go to Australia, join Rita in Scoraig. I was at a crossroads and as I slowly got my energy back after the draining experience of the trial, I was searching for what to do next.

I was annoyed at the interruption but answered the

phone anyway. There was a pause after I said hello, more cheerful than was necessary, in case it was friends or family checking to see if I was okay.

'Ah, Bobbie. Great to have reached you.' The voice sounded familiar but I couldn't place it. The tone was formal. Formal but nervous.

'Who's this?

'Peter Dawson. You might not remember me. Joe's father.'

Oh no. Surely not another nightmare about to happen. Joe's suicide had featured in the trial but only to provide the background to my lifestyle. I had said nothing bad about him. In fact I said he was my first true boyfriend, that it was my feelings for him and the guilt I felt about his death that had set me on the path to ruin. Had the shitty *News of the World* decided that this was to be the next chapter in the saga of licentious Bobbie, to rake over old miseries and drag two grieving parents into this sorry debacle? The bastards.

'Mr Dawson. I thought I recognised your voice.' I steeled myself for what was to come. Whatever he wanted me to do to fend off the papers, I would agree to.

'Bobbie, there's something I'd like to talk to you about.' Pause. 'My wife and I discussed this, and she thinks, we both think, we need to talk to you about Joe. If it's a good time to talk. We're not disturbing you, are we?'

What a question.

'No, it's a good time to talk. How are you both?'

'I'm fine, we both are. More to the point, how are you? That trial must have been awful. But you played such an important part in bringing those gangsters to justice.'

Get to the point, I kept thinking. Please. I heard a woman's voice in the background. She was telling him to get on with it too.

'Ah, yes. The thing is, Bobbie, there's something we think you don't know about Joe. It was mentioned at his inquest but you'd moved away by then and there didn't seem any point in getting in touch. And anyway, no one knew where you'd gone. We thought you were getting on with your life, putting the whole sad business behind you. We didn't want to bring back bad memories.'

Please say what you're calling about, I kept thinking. My heart felt like it was about to explode. I said nothing. My last question had let him go rambling off on a tangent, and I wanted to hear whatever he had to say as soon as possible.

'Joe. He was a troubled boy. Sensitive. Bullied a lot at school. We were so pleased when you two started dating. He seemed happy at last.'

There was another pause. Only a second but it felt much longer.

'That wasn't the first time Joe tried to kill himself, Bobbie. He tried to commit suicide at least once before. Before he met you he'd been very depressed and swallowed a lot of pills from our medicine cabinet. He'd been seeing a counsellor for about a year, but once he met you, he stopped. We thought it had been a phase, an adolescence thing. I've spoken to a counsellor myself since. He said Joe could always relapse when things were bad and there was always a danger he'd try to take his life again.

I burst into tears. 'Mr Dawson, why didn't you tell me?'

'I know, Bobbie. My wife said at the time we should, but I said no. It was the shame. Our son killed himself and we weren't able to help him, to stop him. We didn't want anyone to know he was ill, we wanted to protect his memory. The inquest was very low key, what with it being during the miners' strike and everything. We kept it secret all this time. Now we've realised how wrong it was we didn't tell you.'

I didn't know what to think. I couldn't be angry at a man who had lost his son and was now telling me a painful, dark secret after all these years. He had the right to hate me, to have nothing more to do with me after Joe died. And yet he had found the courage to tell me something that, though he couldn't have known it at the time, had sent me on the wrong road. It was dawning on me that everything I had based my life on, the trauma that stopped me having another serious relationship, stopped me from falling in love, was based on not knowing the truth.

'Oh, Mr Dawson.' My voice felt strangled in my throat, my mouth was dry. 'Mr Dawson. This is such a shock, I can't take it in. Do you mind if I call you back? I'm sorry. It's too much to comprehend. Can I call you back, please?'

He gave me his number. I sat in silence for I don't know how long. I couldn't structure my thoughts. But I called him back. There was one thing I had to know.

'Hello, Mr Dawson. Bobbie here. Can I ask you one question?'

'Of course, Bobbie,' he replied. 'What is it?'

'Do you think I was responsible for Joe's death?'

He sighed. 'That's the same question I've asked myself

378

many times over the last five years. But about me, whether I'm responsible, not you. No, of course you weren't, Bobbie. Joe was a fragile, troubled young man who couldn't handle life. You're not responsible for what happened. I'm sorry, I should have told you at the time, and I've always felt guilty I didn't. And when I found out the mess your life had got into, I was horrified. I can only hope you'll forgive me.'

A weight lifted. It would take a while for the impact to sink in, but I knew I'd get back my ability to love and be loved again.

★ ★ ★

I woke up the next morning to a world without fear, without guilt. It was a world where I no longer had to look over my shoulder, worrying that my past was going to catch up with me. A world where I didn't have to fear the devastating consequences of a failed relationship. I would still have to carry the stigma and responsibility for DCI McDonald's death, but I'm sure Michael would have found another way to ensure his silence. I was just the most convenient pawn at his disposal at the time.

Duncan phoned me. Stupid, daft, brilliant Duncan, who'd put my demons to rest without even realising it. 'We need to meet,' he said, the excitement in his voice crackling down the phone line. 'We need to meet now, and I mean now. Whatever you're doing put it on hold. You're never going to hear news that's going to top this.'

Want to bet, I thought. And what was it about Duncan he couldn't give you news over the phone? I didn't want to spoil his big moment, but I knew what it was about.

Things had been moving fast about agreeing the movie deal for the book; there had even been rumours in the papers. I was happy for him.

But what he had to tell me was way past my expectations.

'The movie deal is done. And we're getting a Scottish director who I think understands the story, not a Hollywood hack who'll turn it into a piece of formulaic rubbish. And not Frank Fontane, you'll be pleased to hear.'

'That's wonderful,' I said. Duncan looked like he was in full flow with his excitement and it was probably the last word I'd get in edgeways for a while.

'Whatever,' Duncan said dismissively. 'But that's not the big news, Bobbie.'

He could see my surprise. What could be bigger than that?

'I've been thinking over and over about how I can make amends for putting you through hell these last few months.' He was looking awfully pleased with himself. 'I managed to get my agent to put a clause in the movie deal, a "rider" they call it, that says they have to audition you for the lead role of Anna. The producers have heard what a good actress you are. If it works out it will be an amazing coup for the movie.'

To say I was astonished was an understatement. I'd always dreamt of being in a movie and now an audition for a lead role. Handed to me on a plate.

'Oh gosh, Duncan. I can't believe it.' Then doubt and fear came over me. 'But I haven't acted for years, unless you count the drama therapy. I'll be criticised for cashing in on the trial, profiting from DCI McDonald's death. I don't know, it feels tacky to me.'

'Calm down, you haven't got the part yet. I'm sure that will be part of the considerations. But what do you think, Bobbie, are you up for it?'

Of course I said yes. It would send tongues wagging again about how much of Duncan's book was based on me, but for a chance to become an actress again I could cope with that. I was sure in my heart of hearts I'd never get the part, that the movie people were just playing along with Duncan's delusion. But I wanted to see if I could get into acting again, and it was a chance to get me back on the radar.

I hardly saw Duncan over the next few weeks. His world was a constant flurry of media appearances, book events and business decisions. The book was being launched in America next; he headed off there to meet a whole new level of movers and shakers.

The days went by until my audition. The gateway to my dreams.

I flew down to London for the screen test, expenses paid by the production company. I arrived the day before and had a nostalgic wander around my old haunts. Camden Market had grown out of all recognition. It was open on weekdays now, not just the weekend. Some of the edginess had gone out of it; there were a lot of stalls selling mass-produced stuff masquerading as craft fare, but it still had the old magic. I didn't look up any of the old agency people. It was a big day tomorrow and I needed to be focused. I snuggled up in my hotel bed with a copy of the script. An early night, very sensible.

The next day I smiled inwardly at the wardrobe and make-up beforehand to make me look like the character I'd be playing in the film. Which of course was me. During the screen test, the camera was in the corner, the one-eyed monster that was silently recording my performance, the few moments of film that would determine my destiny.

It went well. They were taking it seriously, and the director turned out to have seen me acting in *Who's Afraid of Virginia Woolf?*

I dared to dream.

My mind was full of what-ifs, worries, hopes. The wait was endless, but when the call came it wasn't the director, but the casting supervisor. I knew instantly I hadn't got the part.

'Hi, Bobbie, Jenny from the movie here. I'll cut straight to the chase, we're not going to cast you as the lead character. Your screen test was great, but the producers think the risk of bad publicity is too high. But we'd like to offer you the part of Anna's Glasgow friend. It's a meaty part and I'm sure you'll do it justice. What do you think?'

It was my stepping stone to getting started in the movie business. Of course my performance would be heavily scrutinised, given the circumstances, and I would have to brace myself for criticism, but an aspiring actress couldn't complain about the publicity.

Then Duncan came back from America and introduced me to Patti. Stylish, slightly androgynous, looking like an alabaster ambassador from outer space who'd won first prize in a glamorous vampire competition. Patti, the photographer from *Rolling Stone* magazine who he met during the first book launch and who had photographed him for the big article they were running on him in the autumn. Patti, Duncan's fiancée.

★ ★ ★

Sometimes I think fate has a hand in everything. If it hadn't, then I'd never have married Brad. We started dating just after the movie shoot. Things were tentative at first, but with no more trauma about the responsibilities of love, my feelings for him grew stronger and stronger. Our love was a world of excitement and quiet times; passion and conversation; laughter and pathos. We supported and challenged each other. I'd never shy away from problems again.

We moved to America, as much to get away from any repercussions from the past as anything else. I carved out a niche in the American film industry; in the independent movie scene I'm the go-to actress for parts needing a Scottish lass. That's when I was not with Brad in Philadelphia, committed to making a difference with drama therapy. I've got my freedom, my safety and my heart back again. Even a bit of an acting career. And on the other side of the pond, the best friend anyone could have. Duncan: my biggest supporter and my biggest fan.

Should you be at someone's funeral, if they died because of you?

Of course you should. Just as you should never avoid any of the difficult things in life because it seems easier in the short term. Yes, you can run away; staying around is so much harder.

But it's the only way to reach the end. The end of love's long road.

Thank You!

Thanks for reading *Love's Long Road*. I hope you enjoyed it. If you did, I would very much appreciate it if you posted a review. Every review, no matter how short, helps readers find new authors.

You might be interested in reading my other novels featuring the main characters in this book. *Silent Money* is the prequel to *Love's Long Road*, and tells Michael's story and how he became a crime lord in 1970s Britain. *A Friend in Deed* is the sequel, and is set over forty years later. It tells the story of Duncan, who is now a sixty-something journalist and blogger.

Best wishes
GD Harper

Acknowledgements

My thanks go to the following for their assistance in helping me write this book: Debi Alper, Janice Hardy, Agnes Harper, Elena Kravchenko and Helen Prosser.

My thanks also go to Edward Albee, David Bowie, Bob Dylan, Graham Greene and Mario Puzo for the way they inspired me with their creativity.

Many thanks to the authors of my source material.

For information on the 1970s: *Camden Lock and the Market*, Caitlin Davies; *Cosmopolitan's Survival Guide*, Hazel Meyrick; *Crisis? What Crisis?: Britain in the 1970s*, Alwyn W. Turner; *Get Smashed*, Sam Delaney; *Groupie*, Jenny Fabian and Johnny Byrne; *Looking For Mr Goodbar*, Judith Rossner; *Mad Men*, Mathew Weiner; *Student's Own, The 1977 Glasgow University Student Handbook*, ed. Stuart Dobbin and John McAleer.

For information and insights into heroin addiction and rehab: *The Heroin Chronicles*, ed. Jerry Stahl; *Heroin: The Treatment of Addiction in Twentieth-century Britain*, Alex Mold; *Heroin Addiction and the British System: Volume 1. Origin and Evolution*, ed. John Strang and Michael Gossop; *Junky*, William S. Burroughs; *A Million Little Pieces*, James Frey; *Shantaram*, Gregory David Roberts; *Trainspotting*, Irvine Welsh.

For information on organised crime, money laundering and the Scottish legal system: About Business Crime Solutions Inc.; John Lea, Professor of Criminology, Middlesex University; Sheriff Seith Ireland.

For advice on psychology and drama therapy: Pippa Ford, Dr Mairi Harper; Emma Rasalingam.

Many thanks also to the numerous bloggers and websites who provided me with snippets of information here and there, and especially to Wikipedia.

Any errors or omissions are mine alone. The Bob Dylan concert at Earl's Court was, in fact, in 1978.

The dialogue from *Who's Afraid of Virginia Woolf?* and the quotes from the Bob Dylan songs 'It's All Right Ma, I'm Only Bleeding' and 'Visions of Johanna' are copyright. The description of *Who's Afraid of Virginia Woolf?* in chapter three is by the movie critic, Walter Chaw.

Tom McGrath was director of The Third Eye Centre from 1974 to 1977, and the facts about him are true. However, the personality and words attributed to him in this book, apart from his own words describing his work at the *International Times*, are purely my own invention. He died in 2009. And of course, any similarities between anyone working at The Third Eye Centre and Bobbie, or any similarities between real people and places and the fictional ones in the book, are complete coincidence.

Printed in Great Britain
by Amazon

42534613R00223